CROWNED CROWS
I

Crowned Crows of Thorne Point

CROWNED CROWS BOOK I

VERONICA EDEN

CROWNED CROWS OF THORNE POINT

Copyright © 2021 Veronica Eden

All rights reserved.

No parts of this publication may be reproduced, stored in a retrieval system, or transmitted in any form or by any means, electronic, mechanical, photocopying, recording, or otherwise, without the prior written permission of the copyright owner, except in the case of brief quotations embodied in reviews and certain other noncommercial uses permitted by copyright law. For permission requests, write to the author at this website:

WWW.VERONICAEDENDAUTHOR.COM

This is a work of fiction. Names, characters, places, businesses, companies, organizations, locales, events and incidents either are the product of the author's imagination or used fictitiously. Any resemblances to actual persons, living or dead, is unintentional and co-incidental. The author does not have any control over and does not assume any responsibility for author or third-party websites or their content.

AUTHOR'S NOTE

Crowned Crows of Thorne Point is the first book in the Crowned Crows series following a gritty brotherhood of antihero bad boys and the feisty heroines that capture their hearts. Each book in the series should be read in order to understand the continuing plot. If you're not a fan of morally bankrupt book boyfriends, steer clear.

This dark new adult romance contains dubious situations, crude language, and intense sexual/violent content that some readers might find triggering or offensive. **Content warning** for themes and brief mentions of off-page suicide and mentions of predatory grooming. Please proceed with caution.

Crowned Crows series:
   #1 Crowned Crows of Thorne Point

Sign up for Veronica's newsletter to receive exclusive content and news about upcoming releases: bit.ly/veronicaedenmail

Follow Veronica on BookBub for new release alerts: bookbub.com/authors/veronica-eden

ABOUT THE BOOK

TO GET AN AUDIENCE, YOU HAVE TO GIVE UP SOMETHING. A SECRET, A FAVOR... SOMETHING THAT HURTS. WELCOME TO THORNE POINT, WHERE DARKNESS RULES.

ROWAN

I enrolled at Thorne Point University to be closer to my brother.

Now my world is falling apart.

Ethan is missing.

Every day I can't find him it plays on repeat.

The search for answers turns up nothing and I'm running out of options.

But there's a rumor on campus.

And I'm desperate enough to seek out the Crows as my last resort.

Wren Thorne's reputation precedes him, but I won't take no for an answer.

WREN

The night belongs to us.

We run this town.

Wear the rumors like crowns.

But after losing the most important thing to me, my brothers are all I have left.

Our bond runs deeper than blood.

When Rowan comes looking for our help, I do one thing I shouldn't:

break all my rules.

She asked for monsters? I'll show her one.

PLAYLIST

Obey—Bring Me The Horizon, YUNGBLUD
Teardrops—Bring Me The Horizon
Broken Pieces—Apocalyptica, Lacey
Unperson—Nothing But Thieves
How Does It Feel?—Tonight Alive
Animals—Architects
Nightmare—UNDREAM, Neoni
Yes Offense—Unlike Pluto
Monster—Willyecho
Closer—Nine Inch Nails
STFD—TeZATalks
Cravin'—Stileto, Kendyle Paige
Legends Never Die—League of Legends, Against The Current
Dancing With The Devil—Demi Lovato
la di die—Nessa Barrett, jxdn
I Hate Everything About You—Three Days Grace

The Legacy—Black Veil Brides
Can You Feel My Heart—Bring Me The Horizon
FEED THE FIRE—coldrain
Throne—Bring Me The Horizon
The Violence—Asking Alexandria
Ready Set Let's Go—Sam Tinnesz
Nightmare—Scarlet City, Anxxiety
Darkside—grandson
Fallout—UNSECRET, Neoni
Painkiller—Three Days Grace
I Am the Fire—Ghost Monroe
DARKSIDE—Neoni
Kerosene—Rachel Lorin
Can't Stop the Fire—Leslie Powell
Give 'Em Hell, Kid—My Chemical Romance
RISE—League of Legends, The Glitch Mob, Mako
Snake—Halflives
Misery Business—Machine Gun Kelly, Travis Barker
Stay And Decay—Unlike Pluto
Sound off the Sirens—Sam Tinnesz
Madness—Ruelle

"Some people fear the darkness of night when they should fear the darkness of the human heart."

P.W. Imel

CHAPTER ONE
ROWAN

Foggy smoke curls through the red stage lights filling the decrepit estate ballroom. It creates a haze, highlighting the hedonistic abandon of the bodies grinding on each other to a heavy beat of music. Hands reach into the air above the crowd and drunken laughter mingles with the telltale sounds of some casual public fondling. It's an odd mix, people partying amidst cracked molding and peeling wallpaper.

The Crow's Nest Hotel is the place to be for Thorne Point University students. It's not where I like to be. This is my first—and last—time in this creepy, run down estate-turned-nightclub. Let the ivy finish swallowing it and return it to the earth.

I scuff my Vans on the ancient floor and tuck my denim jacket tighter around me as I move through the crowd. A guy from my Media Theories ass dances up on a girl in a black leather miniskirt and a sheer mesh top. It shows off her fancy bra, one that's meant to be seen as Mom would say.

All around me it's the same—people decked out like this is a legit nightclub instead of an abandoned turn of the century hotel half reclaimed by nature and time. I feel out of place, but I can't go back now. Not when I've come this far looking for answers.

If it wasn't for Ethan, I wouldn't have applied to college in Thorne Point, Maine. But I've always idolized my brother and chasing in his footsteps is what I've been best at for twenty-one years. From the time I could walk, I followed him everywhere. College was no different, same degree focus in journalism and everything. So here I am, on the rocky coast of Maine at the start of my senior year, wading through sweaty drunk people because I have no other choice.

Thinking of Ethan makes it hard to breathe for a moment, anxiety climbing up my throat to choke me. I can't picture the worst. It keeps happening anyway. That's what a true crime Netflix binge will do.

"Rowan!" The guy from my class waves me over without missing a beat, drink held high while he nearly bends his dance partner over. "Come dance!"

"I'm good." I raise my voice to be heard over the music.

"Come on! Don't be like that." Mesh top chick arches against him, looping her arms back around his neck. "Come have fun with us!"

"You study too much." The guy from class winks. "Semester's just getting started. Live a little."

They both hold out their hands to me this time, the girl giving me a heated once over. *Oh. Oh.*

Well, I'm not really down for a threesome tonight, but thanks for the compliment. When I point to the shadowed area at the back of the ballroom, their expressions shift to seriousness.

"Not here to party," I say.

"Good luck," the girl in the mesh top replies grimly.

Yeah. I'm gonna need it.

Nodding, I move on, weaving through the people writhing to the DJ's mix. It's difficult to tell if my heart beats faster because of the pumping music the DJ spins on stage or if it's nerves. The few things I've heard about the guys I'm heading for aren't pleasant. Discomfort twists my stomach.

Whatever happens, I have to get them to agree to help me. Finding Ethan depends on it.

The word is that these guys own this nightclub. Most of the students at Thorne Point University have trust funds. As a grant student, I'm one of the few odd ones out. Dad's life insurance helped, but without the grants me and my brother never would've been able to enroll here.

I slam down hard on the thought of Dad and the gnawing guilt that always comes with thinking of the accident.

My lip throbs from how hard I dig my teeth into it. By the time I wrestle the memories of my dead father behind a mental fortress, I've nearly bitten through the skin. Sidestepping two drunk dudes carrying bottles of top shelf champagne, I prod at the tender pulse in my lip.

Ay yo, I'm surrounded by rich people check, I think scornfully in the tone of a trending TikTok sound bite.

It never bothered Ethan that everyone in this city seems loaded, but as I pass a trio of girls rocking diamonds with their designer dresses I have to wonder what made college students buy this property other than the fact they could.

The place looks straight up haunted from outside. Its crumbling structure sits on a hill overlooking a jagged cliffside drop to the ocean. In its heyday it was probably beautiful and regal, but now the eerie stone and brick building gives off big gothic mansion aesthetic vibes complete with an old shrubbery maze that's half dead.

It took me a solid fifteen minutes of white-knuckling my steering wheel before I coached myself to get out and take the winding stone path to the club's entrance. The whole time I was trying not to jump out of my skin, wondering why the fuck anyone would voluntarily treat themselves to Thorne Point's own house of horrors. I would've happily avoided this weird excuse for a party spot all the way to graduation, but I have to be here.

The Crow's Nest Hotel holds my last resort to find my missing brother. They watch from the shadows at the back of the room.

CHAPTER TWO
ROWAN

The rumors around campus are what brought me here. People say these guys will do favors. For the right price, they'll do anything.

A thick wad of cash burns a hole in my pocket as I weave through the dancing college students. It's everything I have saved up. I emptied my bank account, except for the five bucks I put in my gas tank to get up here from the campus in the heart of the city.

Not sure how I'll manage rent on the apartment, but that's a problem for Future Rowan.

For Ethan, I'll give up anything. Even the apartment we've shared since I started my freshman year. Whatever it takes to find my brother.

The red DJ lights don't flicker at the back of the room. A pit forms in my stomach as I force my feet to move.

Did the temperature just drop? Or is that draft because there's a broken window, or maybe a missing chunk of wall somewhere nearby? I shudder through the chill and come to a stop in front of a group of guys enjoying the wild show from their seats on a dais.

The Crowned Crows. Thorne Point's own version of the mafia according to the rumors.

There are four of them sprawled like kings in threadbare vintage furniture as their makeshift thrones. A few girls are with them, seated on laps and giggling when two of the guys whisper to them.

"Colton," one of the girls squeals as he sets down a cigar, slips his long fingers between her thighs, and teases beneath the hem of her short mini dress.

My teeth grind. They seem more absorbed in doing body shots with champagne—which is really just spilling champagne down cleavage and licking it up because they can afford to. The girl's protest from before dies off in a moan as Colton sucks on her throat.

"What, baby?" His wicked chuckle is contagious amongst his friends. "Can't waste any."

"Hey!" I finally bite out when they act like I'm invisible.

I have their attention now. The full intensity of it has the base of my spine tingling with the urge to flee from danger, but I won't back down.

Their gazes range from bored, to carnal, to indifferent, to angry and cold once they realize I'm here to crash their private party. My nose wrinkles. It stinks of the smoke curling from their cigars.

The blond with ruthless blue eyes is in the middle in a wingback chair. There's something about the way he carries himself—not just with confidence, but absolute power—that makes me guess he's the infamous Wren Thorne.

The suit he's wearing looks as if it was made specifically for him. Like his friends, he has a girl seated on his thigh, her manicured nails trailing over his muscular chest through his half undone shirt. The outline of a nipple piercing is visible. He seems bored, head propped against his thumb and forefinger. Bored but brutal looking.

My heart gives a shocked flutter at the sight of him at the center of the group. The way people whisper about him, I pictured something out of my nightmares. But he's handsome with a strong jawline and broad shoulders. His blond hair is slicked back, the sides trimmed short.

Wren's sharp gaze locks with mine—then I understand. They might be a group, but everything about him declares him the king.

"I need help." I inject steel into my voice.

The corner of Wren's mouth twitches. He doesn't answer. Rolling my shoulders back, I climb the steps of the raised platform. One of his friends—Colton—blows cigar smoke in my face. I cough, waving away the acrid smoke.

"What the fuck, dude?" I snap, glaring.

Colton would be irresistibly attractive if it wasn't for that cocky edge to his dimpled grin. He shrugs, flicking disheveled dark brown hair out of his eyes. With the motion, my attention drops to the crow inked into his neck that dips into the open collar of his black shirt.

The guy next to him is decked out head to toe in tight dark clothes that don't hide how ripped he is. A lip ring sits at the corner of his mouth. He's eerily still other than the flick of his wrist when he plays with a switchblade, no girl in his lap. I don't blame them—dude's creep factor is dialed up to a hundred.

Balling my fists, I direct my next attempt at the last guy in their group this time, the one with striking golden brown eyes and bronze skin.

"I said I need help. Rumor has it you're the guys to come to."

He gives me a hungry once over that makes the tip of my ears burn. Those golden eyes draw me in. Instead of responding, he chokes the neck of a champagne bottle and brings it to his lips for a swig.

Pursing my lips, I swing my attention back to the man at the center of the group.

The drag of Wren's blue gaze over me isn't a seductive caress. It's the opposite—mercilessly cold and calculating. He's sizing me up and I get the sense I've been found wanting.

Frustration singes my nerve endings while I search for an angle to work as if this is one of my story snags. I need their help, no matter how much he annoys me.

With the smallest dismissive gesture, the girl perched on Wren's knee hurries off demurely, eyes cast down. He barely moved his fingers, not bothering to lift his hand from the armrest of his chair. The others follow after her.

My eyes narrow. Wren might be hot, but more importantly he seems like an asshole that expects everything to be done at his command.

Colton releases a lamenting groan before he settles, putting his cigar between his teeth, studying me. "Speak now or forever hold your peace."

He's in one of my classes I realize. When he cares to show up. He was there for Thursday's lecture nursing a hangover in the back of the dimly lit room. It's such a weird departure to think of any of these guys as college students when they're spending their nights like this.

Shaking my head, I shove aside my incessant thoughts before my curiosity gets me in trouble. "My brother is missing. I want you to help me find him."

Wren tips his head to the side. "That's not something we do. Go to the police."

"You think I haven't tried that?" A haggard noise gusts out of me. "I've been hounding them, but they're not giving me anything. Not their jurisdiction, not their problem. They don't care."

It takes everything to keep my shoulders from slumping. I've been at this for weeks after Ethan didn't come home.

Silent mirth shakes Wren's shoulders and Colton snorts. They're both laughing at me. The terrifying guy remains silent, continuously messing with his knife and the one with the panty-dropping smirk sticks his tongue in his cheek while he shakes his head. My chest rises and falls with my irritated breaths.

"I have money." Licking my lips, I gather the courage to dig out the wad of cash in my pocket. I thrust every penny I have to my name toward them, ignoring the tremble in my arm. "I'll pay you. I have to find my brother."

"Do I seem like I need your money?" Wren sneers, the humor blinking away in a flash. He indicates his suit—custom tailored maybe from how well it fits—and his wrist where an expensive watch interrupts the tattoos creeping across his hands.

My head jerks back. I can't—*won't*—take no for an answer. I'll make them help me one way or another. It's just...if they don't want money, then how?

Wren's sneer turns into a cruel smirk at the pinch of my brows. He leans back in the chair like a king to be worshipped. "You don't know how we work. You're out of your league, little girl. Run along."

This fucking jerk.

"No." I set my jaw and flip my messy braid over my shoulder. It's the same reddish brown shade as Ethan's, a daily reminder of what's missing from my life when I look in the mirror. "What do I have to do to get your help?"

Wren gives me another once over. Colton traces his lower lip with his tongue, exchanging a look with the golden-eyed guy.

"There's always the fun way," Colton says lewdly with a wink. "Happy endings all around."

They snicker amongst themselves when I tense. There's a heated flash of interest in Wren's cool gaze, there and gone in a second.

"A secret," he finally answers after leaving me dangling at the mercy of his friends. "You can pay us with a secret." He leans forward. "Make it a good one. If we don't like it, well..."

The grin he gives me is deadly.

I stiffen, working hard to keep my face perfectly blank. Cracks form in the mental fortress I built around the memories of my dad and the accident.

"Well? What have you got for us?" The guy with the hypnotic eyes demands, raking his fingers through thick shiny black hair that falls over his forehead in a swoop.

"How do I know you won't turn around and use whatever I say against me?" I ask warily.

Wren gives me a smirk and his gaze flashes with that hint of interest once more. "You don't."

I wait, but he doesn't say more. He continues leveling me with that unwavering, powerful look. He knows he has me. I need him, but he doesn't need me. I exhale forcefully.

It probably doesn't matter to Wren if I don't follow through. I either give him what he wants, or I'm out of options.

This secret... I shake my head and drop my gaze to the floor as I think. There's nothing I want more than to find my brother, but I can't. Not this.

"I have nothing to hide."

It's a miracle my voice doesn't break.

Wren stares at me for a beat. My palms tingle with the need to shove them in my pockets. It's like he can see right through me with those devious icy eyes and know the worst parts I hide away.

He peruses me as if he has all the time in the world, gaze sliding over me from head to toe in a way that makes a hot and cold sensation rush across my body. This is a man who takes everything he wants without resistance and something in me responds to it. I fight the urge to squirm for an entirely different reason so I don't give myself away.

"A favor, then." Wren's friends shoot him quick glances, but his focus stays on me. "You'll owe us in exchange for our help."

Throat burning, I nod. A favor. It could be anything, but I'll do it.

Whatever he wants, it's better than serving up the one painful secret I'll never give up.

CHAPTER THREE
WREN

Do what we do long enough and reading people becomes second-nature. To know when they're lying. When they're hiding something that could destroy them.

It's part of the thrill. I'm fascinated by the lengths people are willing to go and revel in ripping their darkest secrets from them.

Even in the shadows me and my brothers shroud ourselves in, I can tell she's hiding something. She has no idea who we are, who she came to beg for help.

I'll cut it from her if I have to. Normally, I'd already have done it. I can feel the questioning glances the guys direct at me for hesitating and letting her owe us a favor instead.

We grant few exceptions. If we need it, we'll take it. I'll temporarily allow her to keep the secret she doesn't want to pay us with.

For too long I've been coasting in a vast chasm of emptiness. Day in and day out, completely numb save for the bursts of anger, the sole emotion that can still touch me. But there's something about this pretty little thing with the stubborn tilt to her full lips. She strolled up to monsters and put on a brave face instead of running. Her fire is the first thing to intrigue me in years.

It's made me do something I don't do: break all my rules. Maybe I need to take that as a warning. Nothing makes me stray from control.

Except when my boys and I finally tracked down my little sister's teacher two years ago. Harold Coleman, the predator who manipulated her, poisoned her mind, drove her to suicide.

Shoving a hand in my pocket, I grip her heart-shaped locket. Bastard thought he could hide from me, but we found him thanks to his need to groom another girl out in Ridgeview, Colorado. It didn't matter how far he ran, we dragged him back to Thorne Point. I still hear his screams, his pathetic begging before I ended him.

It didn't bring my sister back. Without Charlotte, my world is a dark place of static noise.

"Colt." I don't have to say more, sinking back into the emptiness that drowns me. Sometimes I welcome it instead of enduring the ache of missing my little sister.

Colton sits forward, elbows propped on his knees. "Name?"

"Ethan Hannigan," she answers, green eyes wide because she thinks I let her get away with keeping a secret from me.

All in good time, curious little kitten.

Colt sucks in a quiet breath at her brother's name. He recognizes it. I glance his way, but he shakes his head. He'll tell us later.

Jude huffs in amusement. "He means yours, sweetheart."

"Oh." A hint of color fills her cheeks and the static clears for a moment, drawing my attention. "Rowan. Also Hannigan, obviously."

"We'll be in touch." Colton's thumbs fly over his phone screen. Within an hour the genius hacker of our group will have a full workup on her. He glances up when she hasn't moved. "That's it, babe."

Rowan's lip curls and I swipe my tongue over my own in anticipation of how she might mouth off. The need for control rears up in me, eager to tame. The urge to take her long braid and wrap it around my fist to see how much she can handle before she cries out fills my head, pulling heat into my groin.

She passes her gaze over the four of us, lingering on me, then disappears into the crowd, swallowed up like a riptide in the ocean. I search for her auburn braid amidst the red lights and curls of smoke long after she's gone, drawn by the flare of interest she stirred. It's futile, but still I scan the crowd, leaning my head against my fist.

Frowning, I push her pretty features from my mind.

The music, dancing, and scent of sweat mixed with alcohol doesn't fill me with the same thrill it used to. The old ballroom is brimming with energy I love, but I'm done for the night.

"Let's go."

My command is followed without argument. We're a brotherhood without a leader, but more often than not Levi, Colton, and Jude look to me before we make a decision. It's been like that since we were kids in high school. Loyalty—something we believe in so deeply we inked them into our skin. It's how we operate, with utmost trust in each other.

Our bond runs deeper than blood. They're all I have left. My parents haven't been the same since Charlotte died and neither have I.

After we leave the Crow's Nest, we end up at one of our exclusive fight rings. This one is near the docks in the shipping district, the air thick and tangy with the ocean only a few blocks away. The chaotic energy here is just as much of a rush as the hedonism that goes down at our club. I live for it, the way people lose control. It feeds the twisted thing inside me.

At least it used to, before I stopped feeling anything but murderous anger.

I leave Jude and Colt to handle pick ups from the bookies we employ to drive our revenue while I go to the back room for a drink. They're both better at dealing with people, while Levi and I prefer to use physical force. After the first swig of vodka, my phone vibrates. It's a text from my father. I ignore it with a grunt.

The old man only cares about work, and since I technically graduated in the spring his hounding is growing relentless to take up the family mantle. It's one long ass line of sons following in their father's footsteps in my family. The Thornes. Fingers in every pie in Thorne Point dating back hundreds of years to the founding members of this city.

I have no interest in doing as I'm told. I've built my own legacy with my friends. One I'm proud of that we're building into more.

When I head back out into the main room of the warehouse with the bottle of vodka choked in my grip, Levi is in the ring. He's shirtless and beating the shit out of his opponent, lip ring removed but he kept the barbell in his nipple. He doesn't have to worry about the danger of leaving metal on his body when he's the deadliest thing in there.

I track the lethal movements of his tattooed body, impressed by his ability to mask his intent. There's no way to tell what he'll do next, an expert at avoiding telegraphing his hits until it's too late. His lips twist in a contemptuous frown that usually puts people off. Rightly so; my friend is more monster than man.

If he's up there, it means we're doubling our profit tonight. There's no match for Levi Astor.

A smirk crosses my face as I weave through the rowdy throng screaming at the fight. One look at me and they quickly get out of my way, either because of my name or because of my reputation.

We have a few of these set up around town. One near campus draws in dumb rich frat boys to make easy cash off them. This location attracts a more elite patron—businessmen, socialites, and politicians. These people want to watch down and dirty fights with no fluff or glam. The only rule for the fighters who step in the ring here is that there are no rules. The crowd wants to see a bloodbath and we provide.

Levi proves it by dealing a vicious roundhouse kick that catches his opponent across the mouth. Blood and spit go flying, along with a tooth. The fighter sways on his feet, likely struggling against blacking out. The wild atmosphere is palpable as people cheer and wave their money in the air, hungry for the violence.

I find Jude and Colt, dismissing the woman in Colt's lap playing with her pearls. She shoots me a haughty look. He whispers something to her that makes her giggle before she slips away.

"One of your mother's friends, isn't she?" I bring the bottle of liquor to my lips. "Into undergrads?"

Jude and I may have officially graduated, but Colton and Levi are still in their senior year of college, both of them younger than us.

"It'll make the next event on her social calendar more interesting if I can get that chick to suck my dick while my mom praises the canapés." Colton shrugs with a devious grin, taking out his phone. He's always got a device or two in his hands. "My dick doesn't discriminate. Pussy is pussy and she's a hot cougar. Where's the downside in that?"

"Put that on your wedding announcement." Jude snorts and elbows him. "Your mom will love it."

A sharp bark of laughter leaves me. The DuPonts are part of the socialite crowd. New money compared to mine and Levi's families, but Colton's parents made a name for themselves. Out of the four of us, Jude Morales is the only one that wasn't born with a silver spoon.

We met him at Thorne Point Academy and recognized the same illicit thing in him that lives in the rest of us—the instinct for survival and the drive to be in control of mayhem.

On his first day as a scholarship student Jude tried to con us. He was damn good, too. The smooth-talking fucker almost swindled me out of the five hundred bucks in my wallet.

The easy smile drops from Jude's face as two cops enter the warehouse. He nudges Colton and jerks his chin. His demeanor changes once the first one pushes her way through our shouting patrons while Levi exits the ring.

Pippa Bassett. Youngest detective on the force. Instead of joining us at Thorne Point University, she was recruited into the police academy. Every time I see her betrayal flares hot and vicious in my gut.

She speaks to the fresh-faced rookie with her, pointing at Levi with a frown. Fucking perfect. Ever since the driven brunette defied odds to make detective she's pushed the rookies to follow academy training instead of falling in line like every other pig on the city's force. The rest are bought and paid for with bribes and generous donations, mostly from the senators pushing for reelection. It's how things work around here, but she's nursed her righteous vendetta against us for years.

"Look alive, it's our favorite pain in the ass," I say mildly. "Jude, handle that."

"I'm on it." His jaw clenches. "She knows better."

I hold back a scoff. She used to. His ex-girlfriend was one of us once, a long time ago. Before Jude's stint in a juvenile detention center. After that, we learned we can't trust her. It's the reason we bound ourselves together with a tattoo of a crowned crow perched on a skull surrounded by words we'd never fail to remember again: *loyalty above all else.*

It's only because we respect Jude that we haven't punished her.

"You're in my prayers," Colt says solemnly, then his face splits into a wide grin. "Can I have your Ducati?"

Jude flips him off as he stalks up to the woman who still owns his decayed heart. We watch him herd Pippa against a column, bracing his palm as he flirts with that signature tilt to his mouth, tugging on her blazer. His shoulders remain set with a tense edge as she glares at him. Jude quickly drops the act while they argue. He gestures sharply with his hands and she crosses her arms.

"Oh great," I snarl when the stubborn bitch shoves Jude out of the way.

"Think our boy is losing his charm?" Colt mutters while Pippa stalks closer, Jude following.

"Pippa," I greet in a flat tone, adjusting my cuffs. "Never a pleasure."

"Don't 'Pippa' me, Thorne." She scowls, thick dark brows pulled tight over gray eyes. "You're done. I'm calling this in."

I offer her a sinister smile. "Are you? Adorable. I love how you just keep going."

Over her shoulder, Jude's got his phone pressed to his ear. A muscle in his jaw jumps when he rakes his gaze over his ex.

"Sergeant Warner, hey," Jude speaks into his phone, keeping his eyes pinned on Detective Bassett when she whirls to face him. "Yeah, it's Jude Morales. How's your wife?" The corner of his mouth kicks up in a triumphant smirk. "Good, good."

Pippa's spine is rigid while Jude talks to her direct supervisor, one we know very well is partial to bribes. When the phone is held out to her, she blinks. Jude wiggles it and she relents, flashing Colt and I a fierce look.

She steels herself before answering. "Hello?" Warner's shout is loud and she flinches. "Sir—But sir, I—"

Colton snickers at my side. Jaw set, Pippa turns her mutinous fury on Jude while her boss reams her out over the phone.

"Yes," she mutters. "I understand. Here."

Pippa throws Jude's phone hard enough to hit him in the chest. He grunts, catching it with nimble reflexes. Levi walks up just in time, mopping sweat from his body with a towel. There's no hiding what we do here and it only makes Pippa more furious.

"Until next time," I say.

"I will catch you when you've run out of favors to cash in, so you assholes better watch your backs," she promises.

Pippa can try, but it's an empty threat. She can't prove anything.

My brothers chuckle darkly and I join in, tucking my hands in my pockets. "We won't hold our breaths."

Colton wiggles his fingers in a cheeky wave. Releasing a rough sound, she leaves, pausing long enough to wrangle the rookie still gaping at the recognizable faces of the patrons. Jude watches her ass sway the entire time on her way out.

"Let's get drunk." Colt tucks Jude and I under his arms as he steers us around. "Levi's buying."

"Why me?" Levi's growl is nothing but shadows.

"Because you won your fight," Colt tosses over his shoulder. "And because I'm pretty sure the mayor's niece and her friend are about to give you a nice tip as thanks for leaving your shirt off. Her friend's hot, you down to share?"

Levi rumbles, cutting a look in the direction Colt nods. Jude and I snort. Sure enough, the women follow us where Colton leads. Neither of them entice me the way Rowan did.

The emptiness has its claws in me, but with my brothers by my side it can't drag me under as easily as it does when I'm alone.

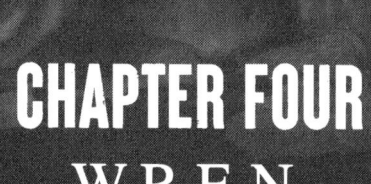

CHAPTER FOUR
WREN

"Are we taking the missing person thing?" Levi asks a few nights later, gruff and all business while he examines a knife before strapping it to his boot. The reverence he reserves for his knife collection is this side of psychotic. Weapons are important to him, but we're among the few who know the reason why.

The darkness we all harbor brings us closer together as brothers. Binds us by our demons, the shadowy nightmares like living entities. Each of us have learned how many shades of gray paint this world, and those murky shades are where we've made our home.

Tonight we're in the sublevel beneath the Crow's Nest donning black hoodies, baseball caps, and half face masks that will leave us unidentifiable to security for tonight's agenda. We wouldn't need the extra protection with Colt's skills, but we're nothing if not efficient. Jude checks a length of climbing rope and hands it to me while Colton syncs his signal scrambler. Our target won't see us coming and won't be able to call for help.

Most of the rumors people whisper about us are true—the Crowned Crows never fuck around.

"We've never done it." Jude pushes his sleek hair back to fit the hat.

"Doesn't matter. We agreed to the payment." I snap my fingers in Colt's direction, slinging the coil of rope across my body. "We're taking it. Did you finish the background check on the girl?"

He crosses to his computers. The state of the art set up he built takes up most of one wall.

After I bought the property, we had the basement level renovated to suit our needs. The walls are covered in dark soundproofing material. The large training gym is Levi's domain. Several other rooms connect to the main area with Colton's computer system and a lounge.

"This is what came up with the doxx I ran on her, plus what I pulled from campus files." Colt moves the window of his online poker game to a different monitor and leans back in his gamer chair, hands folded behind his head. "Rowan Hannigan, twenty-one, a grant student at the university, originally from a little beach town in Maryland. Lives off campus in an apartment building—kind of a shithole if you ask me, but whatever. She's a senior majoring in communication with a focus on journalism. I'm in one of her classes. It's my nap lecture when I need to be seen on campus."

Two monitors show photos of Rowan and her life on campus pulled from social media profiles along with personal information and her transcripts. In several she's with a guy who looks like her, the same reddish brown hair, same almond-shaped eyes behind his thick black plastic framed glasses. His are more of a gray with hints of green, while her shade of mossy green is hypnotic. Where she's all soft curves and long legs, he's taller and gangly. They have an identical lopsided grin when they laugh, but on her it's gorgeous. There's no doubt he's her brother.

Colt sobers from his usual impish disposition, rubbing the back of his tattooed neck. That's never a good sign coming from him.

"What is it?" I demand.

"Her brother. Ethan." Colt taps a few keys on a wireless keyboard and the information shuffles on the screen. "I think I know him. Sort of."

"I don't recognize him." Jude's head tilts as he studies Ethan's photo. "Does he owe us or something?"

"He's a journalist that showed up in Ridgeview last year while Fox was there. This guy caught our boy and his flower girl snooping around at a warehouse. It was all part of a shell company's front to cover up the drug ring."

Ridgeview. It's not the first time our problems have been tangled up with the wealthy Colorado town. It's where we traced Coleman two years ago after he ran from Thorne Point.

Colt's screen displays files from Nexus Lab. His foster brother returned to his hometown for revenge after spending a few years running with us. The punk of a kid ended up falling for his childhood best friend he was holding a grudge against.

"Fox and Maisy were given everything on a drive Ethan had compiled while he was investigating undercover," Colt says. "Want me to call Fox?"

"Not yet." I squint at the screen and fold my arms. "Who owns the shell company?"

"Stalenko Corp. It's a holdings company with Russian bratva ties. Hard to pin them down, there hasn't been a peep of web chatter since their front was busted." Colt tugs on his ear and ruffles his dark hair so it's even more of a mess. "Their thugs kidnapped Maisy for digging too deep. If Ethan was still looking into them and he's gone missing, the dude's probably dead."

I make a rough noise in agreement. These types of businesses are cutthroat. We all know how much they're willing to get their hands dirty, especially Levi.

"This complicates things," I mutter.

"So," Jude drawls, lifting a brow in question. "Tell her he's probably sleeping with the fish in the cove for digging too deep?"

It's highly likely.

Normally we'd consider it the obvious outcome and be done with it. If something isn't worth our full effort, we won't waste our time. The guys all look to me to make the final decision, expecting me to write this off. I should, but something stops me.

If he wasn't her brother, I wouldn't have ignored my rules for Rowan. A broken part of me understands her desperation. Slipping a hand in my pocket, I smooth my thumb over Charlotte's locket. I always carry it with me, ever since I retrieved it from that sick fuck Coleman. The metal is cool and unforgiving, as empty as the hole she carved out of my chest when she took her life.

"No. We'll still look into it," I decide. "Colt and Levi, you both watch Rowan while I put feelers out with our guys."

She's hiding something and I like to know all angles I'm working with.

"Shouldn't be a hard job," Levi says.

Colton kicks himself into a spin in his chair. "I'll put it to my subjects."

Jude snorts and shoves the back of Colt's head, stopping the endless twirling. "You and your nerd army."

Colton has a network of hackers that we utilize. He calls himself their king. To become part of his brood of computer geniuses, he tests them, leaving traps with his trojan methods. If they can code their way out of it, he recruits them. If not, he laughs about their digital demise, considering it a form of natural selection.

"Didn't your sweet nana teach you not to call anyone names, asshole?" Colton flips Jude off. "Don't make me spam all your devices with obscure fetish porn and genital enhancement ads to prove a point."

"Leave my abuelita out of this, dick," Jude shoots back. "Or I'll tell her not to make you extra budín de pan anymore."

Colton utters a pained sound and launches from his chair. "You wouldn't! You know how much I love that woman and her desserts."

"Enough," I bark. "Let's go. We're behind schedule."

After last checks, we leave and climb into a blacked out SUV at the end of a row of cars and bikes. We pull away from the Crow's Nest, weaving down the moonlit tree-lined drive to head toward campus. The only sounds in the car are the muted song playing on the radio and the methodic flick of Levi's switchblade opening and closing.

Colton taps my shoulder with the back of his hand from the driver's seat, the corner of his mouth tugged up in a crooked grin. "What sort of favor will you call in?" His tone lilts with suggestiveness. "That chick is hot. We could have so much fun with it compared to our usual song and dance."

My muscles tense at the implication of *we* and what it entails. There will be no *we*.

I shake my head to clear the irrational need to own her when I know she has secrets to hide. "Focus. We'll deal with Rowan Hannigan later."

"Blessed with that big brain, and all you do is think with your cock," Jude snarks from the back. "This is why you keep falling into bed with sorority chicks."

Colt grins at the rearview mirror. "You know which big part of me I prefer to think with. He makes all the best decisions. And don't even fight me, you all have eyes."

The guys mutter their agreements from the back and I clench my jaw as jealousy slips over me like oil, drawing out a feral, possessive part of me that wants to fight my own brothers to lay claim to a girl. Another rule of mine I can't break. Nothing will come between us. I won't allow anything to destroy us.

Colt studies me from the corner of his eye. I know that look. He thinks he's uncovered a new point to prod at, too perceptive and far too clever for his own good sometimes. Idle hands and all that.

"How far do you think you could push her if she thought it was payment? I'm envisioning her in a maid uniform waiting to take orders around the Nest." His voice thickens and his gaze grows distant. "Or better yet, nothing. Keep her waiting by a bed to use that mouth. Shit, yeah. She could be our personal little doll. Let's do that."

A deep growl rumbles in my throat. Hot arousal washes over me at the images he paints of Rowan.

Picturing the messy braid and those full lips that caught my interest the other night, I imagine her on her knees before my wingback seat at the Crow's Nest, hair wound around my fist while I drive my cock into her mouth at a controlling and punishing pace. The idea of how those green eyes would spark with fire makes my hand flex against my thigh. I hold my body in tight discipline, refusing to let Colt know he got to me by shifting to relieve the pressure of my fly against my swelling dick.

"I don't need favors and coercion to get a woman naked at my mercy. It would be pointless to waste a favor for that." Some of my restraint slips, the hint of an ultimatum bleeding into my rough tone. "And I wouldn't be sharing."

"You're no fun, big guy." Dropping the joking, Colton taps the screen of his phone mounted to the dash, then returns his hand to rest over the wheel. "Ten minutes before the security patrol changes shifts."

The drive to campus isn't long. It sits near the heart of the city. Thorne

Point University is a prestigious college housing elite students from all over the country—the best in their fields of study from wealthy families who have a long line of alumni. Much like everything else in this city, legacy is all that matters.

During the day it's beautiful with its historic stone buildings from a bygone era, wrought iron gates, and cobblestone walkways. Ivy climbs over many of the castle-like buildings, but unlike the state of the Crow's Nest, it's purely for aesthetic purposes, well maintained by the groundskeepers.

At night, however, it feels like a liminal space, a pocket of time that makes peoples' hearts race when they walk alone down the shadowed paths, unable to escape the tense unease that pervades the air. I live for the campus at night like it's our own personal playground.

The SUV slows to a stop on a circular drive at the end of Greek row and my heartbeat calms to a steady cadence. This moment right before we unleash our chaos is a sacred ritual for me. I breathe it in, basking in the anticipation of what's to come.

"Let mayhem reign," Levi murmurs in the darkness.

I flash an unhinged grin at my best friends. "Go."

With the order, we're off, moving as one. We've done enough crazy shit like this and more to understand how we operate together. Levi pulls ahead to the campus patrol station near the dorms while Colton engages the scrambler to block anything in the radius from connecting to the nearby cell towers. A choked off noise slips away under the cover of night before Levi slinks out of the guard kiosk, the guy on shift passed out on the desk.

Pi Kappa Alpha house looms before us. The fraternity is home to prestigious society legacies and heirs of families with names that carry weight. My father expected me to pledge. I wouldn't, not when I had all the brothers I needed by my side.

Jude and Levi follow me while Colton circles around the side of the building to wait for our signal. A small drone hovers above his head, only noticeable because I'm looking for it. He'll keep our cover while we work.

The door is unlocked thanks to an owed favor. No one is awake. The beginning of semester ragers have these guys by the balls. My mouth tilts up at the side. There was some help to make sure no 3 a.m. night owls would interrupt us.

With a nod from me, we move up the staircase and take a left. The last door is where our target waits. Any one of these douchebags could be another serial rapist, but we're here for this one.

Jude props himself against the paneled wall, smirking while Levi carefully turns the doorknob. Heavy snoring greets us as we file inside like harbingers of death. Jude closes the door silently and we each take a position around the bed.

Our frat boy is tangled in his sheets, sprawled on his back, one muscled arm flung over his head. The anticipation that's been thrumming in my veins since we left the car reaches a snapping point and a ruthless thrill floods my system.

"Now," I command.

Levi flashes a humorless smile and slaps his hand over the guy's mouth while Jude leans close to his ear.

"Boo," Jude snaps.

The guy jolts out of his sleep, fight-or-flight instinct kicking in hard the minute he spots three shadowy figures towering over his bed. He goes to yell, but Levi has a good hold on him. A pitiful muffled shriek is all that makes it out.

"I love it when they scream." Jude snorts and flicks the frat boy on the nose.

He flinches, doing his best to force out another protest. It won't save him. The rest of this house was dosed with enough tranquilizer to put them down through their afternoon classes tomorrow. Same with the neighboring houses on either side, all courtesy of a catering delivery to the Greek row block party yesterday.

Bracing my hands on the foot of the bed, I level him with a cool stare. "You've been naughty. We've come to collect retribution."

Panicked, his beady eyes swing back and forth between the three of us. He attempts to shake his head, the motion more of a stuttered twitch when Levi's grip tightens, digging into his jaw.

I hand Jude the rope and cross my arms as the guys hogtie the frat boy while he blubbers. Bending down, I swipe a rank smelling sock from the floor and circle to Jude's side. He cinches the knot and steps aside.

The idiot in the bed turns away from Levi tying his ankles. "Please, whatever you want—I'll get my dad to pay you, just, just don't—"

"Search the room." I plant a hand on the pillow and lean over, letting him squirm. "Cry all you want. No one's coming to bail you out. They can't even hear you." A light laugh slips out. "Tranqs work wonders."

The frat boy's watery eyes bulge. He renews his struggle. I grab his jaw and pry it open wide enough to shove his sock inside. He gags, body curling in on itself.

"Let's go before he shits himself," Levi growls. "I'm not dealing with that."

Jude snickers as he rifles through the desk for anything we can use. "It was one time, man. Once."

"Once is one time too many, asshole," Levi complains as he drags the guy from his bed.

He makes a pained sound when his head thumps on the floor. Levi nudges him with the tip of his heavy boot.

"Fair." Jude leaves the desk to open the window. "I've got nothing."

"Give Colt the signal," I say.

We rig the rope using furniture to support the weight. Jude leaves to join

Colt outside beneath the window as we lower the frat boy down. He's given up on squirming, quick to stop fighting the inevitable. Definitely on the flight side of things. Pathetic. I snort when Jude purposefully lets him drop to the ground.

"Call Penn. Time for that deranged hermit to drag himself out of his cabin in the woods," I say to Levi on our way out. We don't trust many of our underlings, preferring to handle things ourselves, but Penn is like Fox Wilder, near enough to being one of us. "Have him clean up the dorm and take care of this guy's car so no one looks for him."

"Got it."

We meet up with Colt and Jude, helping them hoist our trussed up target. The four of us carry him to the car. When Jude opens the trunk, the frantic wriggling starts up again. Levi grumbles and hauls him into the back, clamping a pressure point in the guy's neck to knock him out.

"What a crybaby." Colt's attention is on his tablet. He nods, confirming his sweep is good. "I took care of his status. Officially withdrawn, already filed with his transcripts."

"Good," I say.

He does an impression of Optimus Prime. "Roll out."

"You're a fucking nerd," Levi says.

"You love it," he shoots back as we climb in the SUV. "Without me, who would provide you with free entertainment?"

"I can afford Netflix. So can you."

"It's the principle, man." Colton shakes his head and starts the car.

We drive away as if we were never here.

CHAPTER FIVE
ROWAN

Every normal minute of my day feels like a betrayal to Ethan. I can't focus on my Ethics professor's dull voice at the bottom of the lecture hall. This is the last place I want to be right now. I'd rather be out looking for my brother. Unfortunately, none of my professors give a damn about excuses for missed assignments, and I can't let my grades drop or I could put my grant status in jeopardy.

If I lost it, there's no way I could afford even half a semester here. I rely on the financial aid I get from my grants. Insurance money from Dad only covers so much of my tuition. It would mean going home to face Mom and I can't. It's better with distance between us.

So I drag myself to classes and spend half my lectures neurotically checking my phone to see if Ethan's answered any of my texts or calls, or posted something new to his social media accounts. I don't know what hurts more, the disappointment when there's never a change, or the dwindling flame of hope that seems smaller and smaller every passing day.

Without him I'm a complete disaster. I keep making enough coffee for two in the morning in the hope he'll be there, like always. But he's not. Instead, it's just me and the growing pile of laundry cluttering our apartment. It's a blunt reminder of how alone I am without my brother in my life.

Two months. He's been missing for two months.

When he left, Ethan said he'd be back in a week, maybe two. The story he's been chasing for years as a freelancer finally caught a new break that had him obsessed and in his head. He can be hard to reach when he's working, but by the end of July I grew uneasy.

When the semester started, I knew I couldn't ignore the gut feeling I had any longer. My efforts ended in dead ends—I had no choice but to go to the Crows last week.

Something was different about Ethan.

Instead of his normal goofy smile while he ruffled my hair, he'd been stiff. Jumpy. It didn't help that we had a big fight the night before he left. I thought it was time to finally tell him the truth about what happened to Dad. He didn't take it well.

"That'll be all for today. See you next week," the professor announces.

Thank god. I shove my laptop and notebooks into my canvas messenger bag and dart down the steps to reach the door. The itchy sensation of someone watching me tickles the back of my neck, but I don't turn.

Isla is in the hall when I get out, leaning against a polished wooden archway. She looks right at home against the fine architecture in her sheer loose white blouse and sleek pencil skirt—all designer, I'm sure.

Three and a half years in, and I'm still not used to how sophisticated this place is with its rich wood paneled interiors and delicate paned glass windows. It seems more like a gothic castle than a college.

"Hey babe." She tucks a strand of brown hair behind her ear, offering a wide grin. "You need to get over this guy already. We don't waste our energy on dick for brains boys who think they're too good for us when we're awesome."

She pointedly eyes my ripped jeans that probably could use a wash and the oversized long sleeve t-shirt I stole from Ethan with the regal TPU crest emblazoned on the chest. I might not be as fashionable and feminine as my friend, but she's not wrong about the jeans. There's my relaxed grunge style, and then there's the grief and anxiety soaked *who cares about clothes my brother is missing* state I've been existing in. I make a mental note to do laundry this week.

A reluctant smirk tugs at my mouth. I haven't told her why I've been so uptight and frazzled yet. She's been working every angle trying to get it out of me and this week I'm heartbroken over some douche who had a secret arranged marriage with a hotelier heiress. Like I'd see anything in one of the rich yuppies in this city.

Isla lives for dramatics. She's ridiculous, but it does work to get me smiling again.

"There's my girl." Her striking light blue eyes are warm with affection. She hooks her arm through mine. "Student union or the cafe with those little bistro sandwiches you inhale like they're on a buffet line?"

Heat colors my cheeks and I elbow her. "Student union."

"Are you sure?" She gives me a playful look of sympathy, manicured brows drawn together. "I hate to separate you from your one true love. I wish you'd let me take you to the club more. The ones at that cafe are nothing compared to the spread there."

My nose wrinkles. "I'm sure."

I let Isla drag me to the country club her family belongs to one time sophomore year, not long after we met in a class we shared. With a career politician for a father, currently a prominent senator, and a mother related to the Vanderbilt family, she grew up used to that lifestyle. Most students here are from families like hers. My family wasn't hard up, but going to college surrounded by people dripping in wealth was an adjustment. It's a different world in Thorne Point.

We stroll through the double doors of Withermore Hall and follow the path lined with sycamore trees to get to the student union building. Isla tells me about a dance class she's thinking of enrolling in before the deadline closes for changing schedules as we pass through a wrought iron gate.

The campus is beautiful in the early fall, the old trees swaying, occasionally dropping their leaves onto the cobblestone pathways cutting through the sprawling grounds. The historic stone buildings seem right out of a fairytale—I really did believe it was a castle when I first visited Ethan and fell in love with it here.

"What do you think?" Isla asks, biting her lip.

The hesitation in her tone makes me snap back to attention. "Go for it. You keep saying you want to try out the dance classes and it's our last year before we graduate."

"Yeah," she says slowly, a crease forming on her forehead. "I want to, it's just... My dad would be annoyed. It's not part of my core curriculum for poli-sci."

"Screw him. If you want it, then you should do it."

The encouragement helps her perk up and she gestures excitedly with her hands while talking about the dance courses TPU offers. My heart aches sharply for a second, more than the constant dull pain I've been dealing with, because the passionate look on Isla's face is the one Ethan gets when his stories capture him.

I rub my chest and offer her a weak smile when she pauses. Whatever she sees makes her switch back to coaching me about getting over this fake guy. I should tell her the truth. I never planned to keep it from her, but talking about Ethan being missing makes it feel more real, like he's further out of reach.

The sense of being watched doesn't go away. It's trailed us the whole way from my class. Playing it off like I'm listening to Isla chat my ear off to get me over my nonexistent break up, I angle my head to peek out of my peripheral vision. My lips press into a line.

We're being followed.

It's become a pattern in the last few days and it's getting on my last nerve. Instead of their help, this feels more like they're toying with me.

With a quick movement I snatch Isla's arm and whirl around. "You might as well eat with us if you're going to keep stalking me, you creeps."

Colton and his edgy friend with the dark hair whose one personality trait seems to be playing with knives slow to a stop. Colton's mouth curves and he tucks his hands in the pockets of his jeans, playing it casual. His friend flicks his intense brooding scowl from me to Isla, lingering.

"You owe me twenty bucks," Colton says to him.

The scary guy grumbles and digs into his wallet. As he hands over the cash he glares at me. "Be more aware of your surroundings."

My brows fly up. "Don't stalk people."

He scoffs, shaking his head. When he makes to leave, Colton grabs him by the shoulders.

"Aight, come on, Levi. Can't let the big guy down. It's chill, we'll have lunch." He lowers his voice, but I hang back to hear as we head for the campus food court. "You know how he gets. I'm not dealing with his control issues today."

"I'm sick of babysitting," Levi growls, low and dangerous.

Isla is rolling with this like a champ, ignoring the way people stare at Colton and Levi joining us. "Do we want to do the seafood place or the Italian one? I'm kinda feeling Italian, plus they have the best espresso on campus."

I release an embarrassing sound at the promise of the thing that keeps me going—coffee. "Yes. Coffee."

"Mhm, that's what I thought, you junkie." Isla squeezes my arm tighter and whispers in my ear, "You are so telling me what the hell is going on later."

I nod and throw a glance over my shoulder at my stalkers, two of the Crowned Crows I begged for help almost a week ago. I never expected it would come with them following me everywhere.

At their mention of babysitting and who ordered it, resentment clashes against a rush of heat pooling in my stomach. Damn Wren and damn the way he makes me react to his control. Five minutes in his presence and he's dominated my thoughts, leaving me wondering what sort of favor he'll want. There's one direction my mind goes, but I shut that thirsty bitch down hard.

Once we get lunch from one of the upscale dining options—which I make Colton pay for as penance for shadowing me; Levi finds it amusing judging by the twitchiness at the corners of his perma-frown—the four of us find a table.

Well, no.

Colton sends Levi ahead and his surly expression and reputation do the rest, the occupied table clearing out. The guys who were sitting there are big beefy dudes in backwards caps who look like they could easily bench press Isla and I together, but they fall all over themselves to offer Colton and Levi the table.

"Allow me, sweetheart." Colton pulls out the seat for Isla and drops into the one next to her before I can take it, draping his arm over the back of her chair. "I'm Colt and it's an absolute travesty we haven't met before."

She holds out for a minute, darting a glance my way. I shrug and she answers. "Isla."

"Vonn?" Colton's tone is light, but the way the corner of his mouth tips up in lazy triumph when she nods tugs at my suspicion. These guys are said to be connected enough to know anything about anyone. It's not a lucky guess on his part that he knows who she is. "My dad has a slip at the same marina your dad uses."

"Colton DuPont." Isla purses her lips in consideration when his grin stretches. "That makes a lot of sense actually."

"Glad my rep is doing all the legwork for me," he says.

Rolling my eyes, I take the seat next to Levi and spend a few minutes ignoring the guys while I inhale the decadent aroma of my coffee. When I take a sip, I can't help the content hum. It snags Colton's attention and he traces his lip with his thumb, fixated on my mouth.

"If that's how you sound drinking this sad excuse for coffee, you should let me take you to this little place I know. It's in Florence, but we can make a weekend of it." Colton slouches, his knee bumping mine under the table. He does nothing to hide the interest in his flirtatious tone. "Then after you can make that sound again." He drags his teeth over his lip. "Some other sounds, too."

The laugh that escapes me takes me by surprise. Colton's got game, but he knows it. Smirking, I lower my lashes and tilt my head coyly.

"Is that how you get all the girls?" I ask. "International jet setting and those boyish dimples?"

The curve of his mouth is smug and unrepentant. "Nothing beats the Mile High Club to melt panties."

"Sorry, what was it you told me on the way over here?" I speak to Isla without taking my eyes off his cocky half grin. "Don't waste my energy on dick for brains boys? Yeah—" I give him a once over "—pretty sure that applies to guys full of themselves, too."

An amused sound puffs out of him and he lays a palm over his chest, rubbing like I've wounded him with my assessment. "Okay, I see you."

Dropping the harmless flirting, he sits up, digging into his food while playing on his phone. Isla watches the guys with open curiosity while we eat.

The urge to ask them if anything has happened yet pushes at my throat, but I hold it back since she's here. Instead, I sip my coffee and stuff pasta in my mouth every time I want to ask.

Isla has no problem talking to them, carrying the conversation with ease. She tells us about how the new driver her dad assigned to her looks like one of the city's founders and how eerie it is. She has a theory he's a time traveler or a ghost.

"Shit, really?" Colton chuckles, shaking his head.

She pulls out her phone to show him. Colton elbows Levi, but he just grunts and pretends we don't exist while he eats his food. Isla takes her phone back and makes a distressed sound.

"What is it?" I ask.

"There's another update about that rumored serial killer case in the news. 'The notorious Leviathan strikes again' it says." She frowns. "No other concrete details in the article though, just more rumors and criticism for the detectives. What's the point of reporting on a new development then?"

"Clickbait. So they can get the views." Colton's easygoing demeanor takes on an edge.

"What do you think the connection is between the killer and mythological sea creatures? I mean, yeah, we're by the ocean, but why that specifically?"

While she speculates, Levi glares at her and Colton tenses. He forcibly relaxes himself, but I caught the flash of stiffness in his posture and the quick glance at his friend. The curious need to know more has me watching them closely.

"What's more badass than a creepy as fuck sea monster?" Colton jokes. His gaze slides back to Levi, mischief dancing with the artificial humor in his eyes. "Bet he's got a big dick."

Levi's knife scrapes hard against his plate as he cuts his food with vicious movements. It's the only indication he's listening intently.

"First of all, why is the killer a man?" Isla shoots back. "And would he though, if he's using a giant sea creature as his moniker?"

Levi goes still beside me. It's eerie, like he's not even breathing.

"Giant fantasy sea creature, powerful as shit?" Colton pokes his tongue in his cheek. "Yeah, my dick's a leviathan, too, baby."

I lean forward. "So it's a mythological sea snake that doesn't really exist? What a shame."

Pride shines in Isla's eyes and I roll my lips between my teeth at Colton's startled expression. People must not challenge him enough for him to look at me like I just opened a door of possibilities. Maybe everyone else is too afraid, but I'm not. I stare him down for another beat before Isla's laughter bubbles out of her. Colton joins in while Levi rolls his eyes.

It's weirdly not that bad eating lunch with them once the tension eases. There's still the underlying irritation that they keep following me, but Colton has a disarming charm that makes him fun to be around.

He talks a lot about his friends, telling me that the fourth member of their crew is Jude Morales and that they've all been causing mayhem with each other for years. No matter how I word my questions, he remains tight-lipped about Wren Thorne other than the few vague stories he spins for us to recount their greatest hits. Part of me thinks he makes it up on the spot to fit the wild rumors, but the smug way his mouth crooks has me second guessing myself.

For twenty minutes, I'm not stressing myself out over finding Ethan as soon as possible. The guilt of taking my mind off him catches up to me later.

* * *

After my last class ends in the early evening, I hop in my car and head for the apartment I share with Ethan. It's not too far from campus, closer to the side of Thorne Point that's less manicured lawns and ornate stone statues and more normal to me. Things around the neighborhood are a little run down, unlike the wealthy areas of the city.

My phone buzzes when I reach the second floor. It's a FaceTime call from Mom. As usual, an unpleasant lurch twists my stomach before I shove it down and answer.

"Hey, what's up?"

"Did you eat yet? It's Wednesday." She puts her face too close to the phone, but I can still make out her excited smile. She loves this plan she worked out when I moved away where we have dinner together and video chat. "I'm having grilled chicken."

"Not yet." I offer her a tight smile and flip my phone to show her the front door with our crooked unit number while I fumble with my keys. Without my brother, going inside to an empty apartment is a punch to the gut. "Just got in from my last class. I'm thinking frozen pizza."

"Rowan," Mom chides. "Real food."

"What?"

I elbow the door closed and drop my things on the overstuffed armchair I love curling up in, flipping the phone camera before she can see the state of the place. Ethan's the clean one; I tend to amass clutter. I write better in chaos.

"Fruit, protein, carbs—totally balanced." I kick the disastrous pile of laundry behind the couch so it's hidden. My heart pangs with longing for Ethan's steadfast, supportive presence. I'm spiraling without my big brother to keep me together. "Pizza is the ultimate meal. I stand by that."

She makes a dismayed sound while I put a frozen pizza in the small oven. "At least eat a vegetable with it."

"I think the lettuce I bought went bad," I hedge to cover for the fact I didn't buy any lettuce. The fridge is mostly empty except for my stash of coffee grounds. Groceries have been low on my list of priorities. Ethan usually handles buying them. "I'm fine, I promise."

"Coffee isn't a food group, sweetie."

She tilts her head, taking me in through the small video connection. Her auburn hair is styled in soft curls, highlighted by the stylish tunic shirt she's wearing. It matches her shade of lipstick. Like Isla, Mom is my opposite—chic and bubbly.

A niggling of guilt spears through me at the smile she gives me. It's only because of grief counseling that she was able to find peace and smile like that after we took Dad off life support the summer before my freshman year.

It's my fault he's gone.

After he passed, I vowed I would never take away Mom's hard earned peace. Not when I've already taken everything from her. Instead I live with the truth of what I've done on my own.

"Look, it's got chicken on top." I hold up the box and clear my throat to get rid of the roughness in my voice.

"Okay. As long as you're taking care of yourself."

Swallowing past the lump in my throat, I nod. "How was your pottery class?"

Mom brightens and holds up the piece she was able to bring home.

The abstract vase shape is brightly colored and goes with the collection she's amassed on the shelves behind her. She's chased life hard despite losing her husband. Her motto these days is all about following her heart to whatever makes her happy.

"Very pretty," I compliment while taking my dinner out of the oven. Half of the cheese shifted to one side. It's a sad looking pizza. "What's this one mean?"

"New beginnings," she says after considering her creation for a minute. "I was inspired by the sunrise over the beach when I was walking Teddy. He says hello, by the way."

Ethan encouraged her to get a dog a few months after I came to Thorne Point so she wouldn't be so lonely. The rescue dog adores her as much as she loves him.

Breathing becomes hard for a minute and I put the phone down, pretending I need my hands free to slice my pizza. I don't deserve her for a mom. Not someone like me, capable of something terrible. It's my fault she went through hell, but she came out on the other side of it choosing joy over her grief.

"Is Ethan home?"

Her question drags me out of my head and I force out an uneven breath. "What?"

"I was trying to get a hold of your brother, but he hasn't called back. I just wanted to say hello. I missed his voice since he checks in less lately. Have you heard from him?"

"I, um." Shaking my head, I get myself under control, believing the partial lie I'm about to give her. "He's been traveling for a story, so he's not home. I'll tell him to call you when I hear from him."

She accepts it easily enough. We both know how hard it is to reach Ethan when he's buried in his work.

I hate lying to her. If she knew everything, she wouldn't love her horrible daughter.

We talk while we eat and somehow I manage to keep it together, putting on my mask of hard-working college student. When I hang up I sink into the couch, rubbing my throbbing temples. It's not until I realize I'm sitting in Ethan's spot that I scramble up.

"Fuck," I hiss, shifting to the opposite end.

Peering around the small apartment I share with Ethan, my chest burns. I've left his stuff alone, the little mementos of his presence gathering dust. I'm afraid if I do anything with it that it'll make it real, that he won't come back.

I miss my brother.

Reaching out, I touch his chipped mug on the coffee table. He favors it because he thinks it's lucky. When I first moved in for school three years ago, I tried to throw it out, but he wouldn't let me. The memory washes over me as I trace the scuffed lions that bracket the Thorne Point University crest.

"You can't throw it out, dude." Ethan cradled the mug closer to his chest.

"Why not? It's chipped. You'll cut your lip, dork. I totally know how you get when you're sucked into your work." When I reached for it again, he angled away, shoving his glasses up the bridge of his nose. *"Ethan. Come on. Just buy a new one."*

"Nope. My apartment, my rules. You should move into a dorm on campus if you're going to diss my favorite mug."

My muscles seized and my eyes grew wide. He insisted I move in with him instead of living on campus.

"Hey." He put his hand on my shoulder and squeezed. *"Sorry. I didn't mean it. I wasn't thinking."*

I pushed out a brittle laugh and brushed him off. "It's stupid."

"It's not. It's okay to not be okay yet, or ever. Grief takes time."

Ethan scrubbed at his brow, looking older than twenty-three, tired and sad. My throat closed over. He'd been hiding it from me how much Dad's death affected him. I thought it was bad when he was in the hospital on life support, but pulling the plug was so much worse. Fresh guilt twisted my stomach.

"Look, no one expects you to just be good overnight." Ethan sighed. "It's only been a couple of months, and on top of that you're away from home to start your freshman year."

I shrugged, the movement jerky and wooden. "It's better than being at home."

At the muttered admission, Ethan's expression softened. Once he ensured his mug was safe from me, he nudged me over to the overstuffed armchair by the window in the one brick wall.

"Let's write." He grabbed the leather satchel to pull out his laptop.

This was why I followed in his footsteps. I sat there, tracing the edge of my computer for a few minutes, covertly watching him get absorbed in the story he was working on. Once I started, I couldn't stop. I wasn't writing about anything in particular, allowing the thoughts to flow from my head. The sound of our typing calmed me down.

My gaze locks on the armchair. It's mine. Ethan always preferred the couch. Scraping my fingers over my face, I release a heavy sigh.

I have to find him.

CHAPTER SIX
WREN

THE metallic scent of blood hangs heavy in the air. It mixes with the sour tang of piss and the pathetic whimpering grunts our captive frat boy makes when Levi drags the sharp tip of a knife over his restrained forearms threateningly.

"A name. You can't be that stupid. The choice is more of this, or making it all stop." I spit at his feet when all he does is attempt to cower further into a hunched position. Whatever. He won't hide from any of us. "Just give me the name of whoever the fuck helped you cover up your mess."

Instead of answering, a fresh trickle of liquid pools beneath the chair he's strapped to, mixing with the sticky dried stain of urine from when we started two days ago.

Goddamn it. He keeps pissing himself. How does he have anything left in the tank?

Levi exchanges a terse look with me, tongue prodding at his lip piercing. My nostrils flare as I push out an annoyed exhale. At this point, I'd kill the idiot just to get rid of him.

That's not what we've agreed to do with this rapist piece of shit, though. It would've been the easy way out.

"P-please," the captive frat boy begs hoarsely. His face is swollen, bruised, and bloody. "Please, I—I have money. I've told you, my dad will pay whatever you ask. Just let me go."

The force of my snort jerks my head. My patience has run out for the night. "Lev."

"Yeah," he says as I turn to leave. Lowering his voice, he whispers a nightmare into reality, "Have you heard of the Leviathan?"

"No! No, god, I don't—no, please!"

Frantic cries and the unmistakable sound of Levi's fists hitting the guy we kidnapped follow me out of the room, barely audible once the heavy door slams shut, leaving me in the empty hall with my thoughts.

I pinch the bridge of my nose but it doesn't dull the ache in my temples. Partially dried blood stains my knuckles. I survey the back of my hands before striding down the hall to the main area of the secret level beneath the Crow's Nest to clean up. The restless energy I can't shake skitters beneath my skin. I'll need to hit the gym for a workout to burn it off.

Colton leans back in front of his computers, feet kicked up on the desk, absorbed in an online poker match on one monitor while he plays a battle royale game on another. A third window in the bottom corner runs a scrolling code he initiated to search for Ethan Hannigan.

"Go! Go, go, now!" He smashes buttons on the controller, splitting his attention to make his play and call the bet his opponent makes in the card game. He groans when the river card is revealed. "My queen, someday I'll get you."

"Stop flirting with the AI," Jude mumbles from his sprawl on the couch. "No matter what your perverted brain thinks, it can't consent."

He's shirtless, drowsily rubbing at his smooth bronze stomach. He's like a cat, capable of napping anywhere. His Crow tattoo sits over his heart, the only thing he'll allow to touch it after the number Pippa did on him. I flick the top of his head on my way to wash my hands in the open layout kitchen next to the gym. He grunts and flips me off, not bothering to waste his effort on swiping back at me.

"Queen_Q isn't AI. She lured me in with that bluff. Again." Colton tugs on a lock of dark hair hanging over his eyes, reverence seeping into his tone. "No programming is capable of beating me at poker. But her?" With a dopey grin, he folds his arms behind his head. "A worthy adversary."

I leave them to their bickering and strip out of my hoodie as I step into the gym to work out the aggression strangling me. It's always there, an inescapable weight that sits on me, waiting for the smallest instigation to trigger my rage. Anger is the only thing I can feel in the vast emptiness.

After I pull on a loose pair of shorts, I go for the punching bag, needing to hit something while I shut out the world. Not bothering with music, I run through a quick warm up and throw myself into it. The *thump* of my fists hitting the bag is satisfying, but still my body feels tight and twitchy. My breathing grows ragged the more I move.

A growl tears from my throat as I dig harder, muscle memory and instinct kicking in. Coleman's face is the one I picture slamming my fists into, but he's gone now. He only lives on in my head.

My lungs burn as I think of the night I killed him. Body broken beyond repair, and still it wasn't enough. It didn't bring my sister back.

I catch the swinging bag, resting my forehead against it. A tingle of awareness pricks at the back of my neck. With a slight shift, I see a silhouette at the edge of the gym.

Levi's stare presses into my back. I hate it when he sneaks up on me.

"We have a rule," I grunt.

He's too good at becoming one with the shadows and blind spots. Colt decided he has to make some fucking noise or he'll put a bell on him.

Instead of answering, he circles around the bag to brace his shoulder into it, the silent permission to start my set over implicit. With a sigh, I begin a punishing jab sequence that makes my muscles bunch and burn.

Levi watches my form, muttering corrections. He trained us all, even Colt's foster brother who was desperate for an outlet for the fury he carried. But out of our group, Levi Astor is the only one who has put deathly focus into turning his body into a weapon.

It takes longer than I expected with the intense look he levels me with, but finally he says something twenty minutes later when sweat drips from my body.

"What's up with you?" Levi catches my fist before it collides violently with the punching bag again with an unimpressed look. "You haven't been the same since we caught Coleman."

Damn it. I huff and step back, rolling my shoulders. He knows me too well. We all do—it's easy to read each other when we understand the dark secrets that shaped us into who we are.

For a brief moment I consider punching him. He'd take the bait into sparring, but he's as stubborn as I am once he decides to worry about something.

I open my mouth to answer, but nothing comes out. Empty guilt scrapes me from the inside and I hate it. Coleman fucking deserved what I did to him for the torment he put my sister through by preying on her. The only reason I can come up with is that I didn't do it sooner to maybe save Charlotte. I scrub a hand over my face and drag my hair out of my eyes.

"I'm fine." It's all I get out before I clench my jaw hard enough to hurt.

"Bullshit," he scoffs. "You haven't been fine for a long ass while. It's been almost two years."

I can tell by the way Levi side-eyes me that even the darkest monster among us thinks I went too far.

"I know." My jaw works.

My life was never idyllic, but I had Charlotte. She was my light. Since it's been snuffed out, nothing's been the same.

Revenge. It's what I went after. Didn't help. Not a damn bit. The anger hasn't dulled or faded in the slightest, still raging as fiercely as it has for years.

My younger sister is still dead. Mom's still checked out on a daily cocktail of pills and whatever bottle she can reach. My father is…

"Yo." Colt leans against the door to the gym, waving one of his tablets. "We've got a visitor."

"What do you mean?" I stalk over.

He hands over his device. The live security feed of the grounds is pulled up, a girl with a familiar messy braid poking around. The sight of her pushes at my already loose control.

I tighten my grip on the tablet and Colt eyes me like he's worried I'll snap the fucking thing in half.

"Easy, big guy," he says mildly, reaching for it.

"How long has she been here?"

He shrugs. "Ten minutes or so."

I push past him and stride into the main room. Levi and Colt follow. Jude's no longer napping lazily, gaze sharpened and alert.

"Put it up on the monitor," I demand.

Colton taps out a command on the screen. The feed enlarges on his wall of monitors and a low snarl vibrates in my throat as she sneaks around near our cars. This digs at my boundaries and I'm close to a breaking point. If she tests me, she won't like the consequences. The secret she kept is only safe because I let her get away with it, but with this, cutthroat greed rises alongside my menace.

Dark fantasies mix with the thin hold on my control. She walked into a den of beasts, her willfulness an enticing challenge in itself. I want to see how brave she is when I capture her, strip her bare, and tie her to my goddamn bed.

"Let's show her what happens to people who trespass uninvited." Jude's suggestion is edged with danger.

A sick grin splits my face and I crack my neck from side to side. Hunting her is going to be fun. I was right before, she's out of her league and has no idea what we're capable of. My wickedness is mirrored in my brothers' expressions.

"Spread out. But she's mine to catch."

CHAPTER SEVEN
ROWAN

This was a great idea in my head, but as most of those go, it works out better in theory than in practice. I curse as my foot catches on another overgrown vine in the path I'm sneaking along. The ocean air is chilly and I'm regretting the denim jacket I threw on over a flannel. I tug the jacket tighter as my boots scrape on the weed-choked gravel.

Mom's always been on my case about how impatience and curiosity would likely be the death of me. I can't shut either off, so it's probably true.

Ethan understood. He used to assure me curiosity was something that made someone a good journalist. Pausing for a moment, I listen to the distant crash of waves at the base of the cliff while I weather the burning ache in my chest.

Heart in my throat, I edge around an eerie statue of an angel to reach a terrace at the side of the Crow's Nest Hotel. I can't believe I'm back here within a week, but the Crows weren't doing anything to help find my brother and I'm sick of waiting.

It's early enough that dusk hasn't set in yet, the sky awash with fading streaks of deep reds, oranges, and purples. This place is even creepier without the thrumming base beat and the club crowd. A row of nice cars and motorcycles line one side of the terrace by an ivy-covered wall. Beyond them, a wide stone staircase leads up to an entrance that's seen better days, the bay windows on either side of the door cracked or missing glass.

An unpleasant scraping sound has me freezing. I look around and decide it was a tree branch. One was hanging low over the angel statue I passed. Just as I'm about to accept it, the noise comes again, closer this time. It's distinct, like the blade of something sharp dragging on stone. My stomach bottoms out and I feel my pulse in my palms as I dart through the hedge maze that spans the front of the hotel grounds.

Deep, haunting laughter echoes behind me as I whip around the bushes.

"Shit," I hiss when an unruly branch catches on my shirt.

I fight with it and wince at the scrape against my skin. The sound of footsteps on the other side of the hedge wall makes my heart thump. I free myself and release a relieved sigh before taking off. Another laugh sounds, trailing me on the other side of the bushes. This time it's more playful, but no less threatening. Wide-eyed, I search for an opening to dart through.

There. I almost miss the opening that blends with the rest of the hedge wall.

"Better hurry," the voice on the other side of the maze taunts. Mischief drips from his tone.

"Mother fu—" I break off and grit my teeth.

Colton. I know it's him. He's enjoying this.

"What's gonna happen when you're caught, hmm?" He breaks off in a chuckle.

Narrowing my eyes, I grab a stick and hurl it further down the path. I hold my breath and wait, willing him to take the bait. There's nothing but silence for a second, then the sound of retreating footsteps. Something buzzes overhead, but I ignore it and slip through the hidden opening when Colton is far enough away.

Just as I think I'm fine, the hedge in front of me shakes vigorously and a pair of hands shoot through the gnarled dead branches. There's nothing I can do to hold my scream in. Is he going to give up on the maze and force his way through to get me? I'm not taking that chance.

Spinning on my heel, I dart off, losing track of the amount of turns I take through the maze. It's getting darker now. The faint buzzing doesn't go away and cruel laughter punctuates the rapid beat of my heart.

With a sickening thought, I realize I'm being hunted. No. Not just hunted, *herded*.

These bastards are trying to scare me, leading me where they want me to go. For all I know, they're aiming to get me so turned around I accidentally plummet to my death off the cliff edge to the ocean below.

Hell no. With a rough frustrated noise, I change directions and double back the way I came. There's no way I'm letting them scare or intimidate me.

I hesitate at an intersection to listen. It sounds like they're far off now. Did I come this way, though? I can't remember and in the fading light it's difficult to tell. A twig snapping nearby has me running blindly again.

As I collide with a wall of muscle around the next turn, I let out a startled *oof*. Big hands grab my arms, trapping me. I struggle on instinct, stomping on a foot. It doesn't have the desired effect. All I get for my trouble is a rumble of laughter. I snap my head up and glare at my captor.

Wren grins at me, arrogant and sadistic. "Enjoying an evening stroll on my property?"

He doesn't have a shirt on, granting me a view of his perfect, sweaty body with muscles cut from marble. The tattoos I caught a glimpse of before wrap around his neck from his back and paint his forearms in a twisted depiction of roses. In the dim light I can just make out feathers and royal motifs inked around his neck. He likes crowns. My gaze drags back up his abs. A shiny black barbell pierces his nipple and his blond hair is damp at the roots. Without the product he used to slick it back it hangs in his cool blue eyes.

Holy fuck.

Wren was powerful in a suit Friday night, but like this, in nothing but workout shorts clinging to his hips? His domineering broad frame nearly blocks the path between the hedges and my heart beats faster for an entirely different reason.

"Fuck you." The bitten off words leave me before I can think, my teeth bared.

A deep, amused sound rolls through him. Unlike Colton, it's not playful. On Wren it sounds dangerous like a live wire dancing too close to a body of water. It pierces through me, setting my blood on fire. I lick my lips and swallow at the rush of heat and want that bowls me over.

"Mouthy, are we?" The humor drops away as the hint of a sinister growl edges into his tone. "That won't do."

He herds me with ease, using his massive body to his advantage. I have no choice but to stumble until the hedges poke into my back. He follows, keeping me caged with his grip on my arms, bringing his hard chest close so he can feel each rapid heave of mine.

The scent of him encompasses me—a crisp aftershave and the musk of his sweat. The alluring combination is heady and leaves me lightheaded. Or maybe that's the rush of adrenaline from being chased and caught. My pulse flutters in my neck as we stare each other down.

"Why are you trespassing?" Wren demands, warm breath fanning over my cheek.

"Trespassing? Come on, you have half the damn campus here every weekend." I shudder when he pins me to the hedge, feeling his growl at my backtalk. "Back off."

"No." His clipped response orders me to obey.

I struggle against his grip just to prove I'm not like the obedient woman who sat on his lap last weekend. The curve of his mouth brushes against the side of my face and he nips my skin. I startle and fight against the throb of desire in my clit. Why does he make me feel like this?

"Answer the question," he grits out.

"And if I don't?"

When I tip my chin up defiantly he takes it as invitation to graze his nose down my throat, inhaling. My swallow is thick and the exhale I push out is shaky from the feel of his lips teasing my skin. The chill in the air has been chased away.

Towering over me again, Wren grasps my jaw firm enough to let me know he's the one in control right now. "Just answer the goddamn question, Rowan."

Another burst of heat races down my spine to coil low in my stomach. His icy eyes are hard and expectant. I'm not getting out of this without doing what he wants first.

"You said you'd help. It's almost been a week." I hate how wobbly my voice becomes. His expression doesn't change and I sigh. "I came to make sure you were looking for Ethan."

His sharp jaw shifts. "Curious little kitten. You're not the only person who has our favor. Others actually pay the price we require."

My head jerks, the branches behind me catching on my braid. His hand goes to the back of my head to untangle my hair from the hedge.

"It's already been two months since he left and I have no idea where he is. Can't you—" I shake my head. "Just drop the other stuff if it's not life and death."

"On the contrary. I'm very good at multitasking."

I frown at his arrogance, giving him a disbelieving once over. How is this pompous asshole my last shot at finding my brother?

My attention lingers for too long on the barbell in his nipple. A smoky chuckle from him snaps me out of it, but the look on his face says *caught you*. Heat flushes my cheeks and he speaks against my ear.

"You think you could handle me, kitten?" He pulls back, looking me up and down with a feral smirk. "I'd break you in half."

The words should piss me off but they don't. God, they don't. Instead they steal my breath and make my knees weaken with the desire to fall to them before him.

Wren knows it, too. Those blue eyes burn into me as he traces his lower lip with his tongue.

My breath hitches when his weight presses me into the hedge. This time it's a sweet sort of pain when the branches poke me because his lips hover just over mine. He drags his big palms down my sides, grasping my waist. Those gym shorts do nothing to hide the hard length digging into my stomach.

A strained gasp escapes me. Jesus. Maybe he would break me.

There's barely an inch of space between his mouth and mine. I want him to close it. My tongue darts out to swipe my lip in anticipation.

The faint buzzing from before returns somewhere overhead, then drifts away. It makes him stiffen.

Cool air runs across my overheated body when he takes a step back. Confusion clouds me and I almost reach out to pull his warm, firm muscles against me once more. I stop myself at the last second, thank god. There's hope to salvage my tattered self respect. Because the next words out of his mouth snuff out the last of the fire simmering beneath my skin, leaving me cold.

"Time for you to go."

"I—are you serious?" I fold my arms and his brow arches slightly.

"Deadly."

My brows pinch. "You're a complete dick."

"I am. Let's go."

Wren takes my elbow and steers me out of the maze. He knows the way, like he's walked the overgrown pathways a hundred times.

I can't believe I was ready to kiss him.

"Are you going to press charges for trespassing?" I sass, giving in to the urge to be bratty.

His profile is an immovable statue, but there's a faint twitch at the corner of his mouth. "No." He rakes his teeth over his lip. "But don't think I'll let it slide if I catch you a second time, kitten."

The itch to challenge him more rises up, but I shove it down for now.

Outside of the hedge maze, his friends wait for us. Jude and Levi seem bored, but I think it's an act because their attention remains locked on Wren's controlling grip on my arm. Colton has his phone out and a small drone hovers above his head.

I gasp. It emits the same buzz I heard. That was how they were able to track and herd me.

Colton winks and gives me the lopsided smile I'm beginning to recognize as his signature flirty one. "You give good chase, babe. That was clever with the stick, but..." He waves his phone at me. "Well, let's just say next time we play, we're doing it for real."

"Shame we couldn't catch you." Jude tilts his head so his sleek hair swoops over his forehead. His hands are the ones that shot through the hedge to spook me. "Bet it would've been fun."

The fingers above my elbow tighten. It's an almost possessive hold on me.

"Take her home." Wren releases me with a shove that sends me stumbling before I catch my balance.

"Hey! You can't just order me around," I shout at his stupid sexy retreating back. I can barely make out the tattoos, but I see black bird wings and a skull. It spans his shoulder blades and wraps around his neck. "What about my brother? What are you going to do?"

"Nothing," Wren says curtly without turning. His hand flexes into a fist at his side, veins prominent in his forearm. "Not until you learn to do as you're told. Otherwise, I'll demand more payment than you're willing to give. I'll start with every secret you have, and that'll just be the beginning."

I stiffen as a wave of indignation crashes over me. Fighting the way he wants to control me—against the danger he exudes gives me a rush, but it can't happen. I won't let it.

Almost kissing him earlier was a mistake. I need him to find my brother and that's it.

The heavy implication of his words hit me. He has to be bluffing to see if I'll fall into his trap. It didn't seem like he knew I was lying about my secrets.

An arm drops over my shoulders, drawing me out of my fuming thoughts. Levi has left and only the other two remain.

"Come on." Colton squeezes me in a half-hug that calms me down. He sweeps his arm grandly toward the row of expensive cars in the terrace. "I'll let you pick which ride we take."

I perk up at the thought of the motorcycles zipping through the streets. "Can I drive?"

Jude barks out a laugh. "Not a chance. Levi would carve you up for touching them."

"Seriously?" I purse my lips and drag my feet as they lead me over. "You guys suck. I hate you all. But especially *him*."

"Nobody really likes him, so it's cool." Humor laces Colton's tone. "I don't even think he likes himself most days."

The pang that hits me in the chest takes me by surprise. I smother any sympathy. Wren Thorne is just a jerk on a power trip.

Once the Crows help me find Ethan, I don't have to see him ever again.

CHAPTER EIGHT
WREN

AFTER a shower, I still feel the phantom shape of Rowan's soft curves against my body. I scrub my skin with a towel until it's raw, getting an unrelenting rule over the attraction to her. Nothing breaks my control, but she tempted me tonight.

She's business. Nothing more. I won't forget it again.

When I rejoin the guys in the main lounge, I ignore the pointed stares from Levi and Jude and an unsubtle cough from Colt.

"Ask for his," Jude says with a smirk.

I know that look can't mean anything good. Whatever's about to come out of Colt's mouth is either going to get my fist to his stomach or get him thrown out of here for the night. I understand how their minds work from knowing them all so long.

"Ask for my what?" I drop onto the couch at the opposite end from Levi.

"Your go to softener." Colt spreads his knees wide, slouching on the cushions. His hand rests on his crotch, gripping suggestively as his voice lilts. "Y'know, you're all hot and ready but the timing's not right. Gotta pull it back with something. What's your softener?" He appears thoughtful for a beat. "Mine's thinking of my mom's tiny pomeranian taking a shit. For such a small butthole, it produces so much."

I roll my eyes and throw the pillow beneath my arm without answering. It catches him in the face and a low chuckle rolls through me.

Levi snorts. "Told you. That's what you get. I swear, you've got a death wish."

"Not as much as you do, you angst ridden knife boy," Colt shoots back with an unrepentant crooked smile, squeezing the pillow between his hands.

Levi grins wide and menacing, producing one of the blades he always keeps on him with a lightning quick flick of his wrist. The corner of my mouth kicks up and I shake my head. Only when I'm with them can I catch these fractions of normalcy where I forget for a minute that the darkness is waiting to drag me back under.

They're all I have left. These three are the ones who keep me from completely succumbing to the empty shell of myself.

"No permanent marks, Lev." I glance between him and Colton with a sly smirk. "What would he have to lure the girls in if you carve up his pretty face?"

"My charm, obviously." Colt remains cocky, unfazed by the threat of bodily harm by his best friends. He's used to the way we bust each other's balls. "Plus, my tongue will still work and they always scream when I use it, so."

To drive his point home, he wags his tongue at us, playing with the silver ball piercing. Jude laughs at Colt's smug expression.

"Guess I'll have to start with that." Levi cocks his head, tracing the tip of his blade over his lip. "I'll pin it to my wall for a souvenir."

Colt claps a hand over his mouth, then over his dick for good measure. Levi chuckles, darting his tongue out to taste the knife. Colt flattens his brows and flips Levi off as best as he can while protecting his favorite parts of himself. A rare genuine laugh punches out of me.

"I know you love those more than you love anything, but that can't be sanitary," Jude says.

A muted notification bell from the corner of the room snags my attention. The code has stopped scrolling on the monitor.

My amusement fades. "Did your search finish?"

"Yeah, looks like it." Colt bumps his fist against Jude's shoulder and goes to his chair, throwing himself into it so he spins around. What he finds snuffs out his cocky mood. Squinting at the screen, he rubs his jaw and hums. "I can't find him in the usual network as Dolos."

Colton is our eyes and ears when it comes to all things tech. The internet is his domain, so he chose an alias of the Greek god of trickery and cunning deception.

I rise from the couch to watch over Colt's shoulder with my arms crossed. The programming language means nothing to me, but it helps me feel ready in the face of the unknown.

"What does that mean?" Jude asks.

"That either Ethan Hannigan is very good at covering his tracks—" Colton pauses to toss a skeptical look over his shoulder. "—highly unlikely, the dude is a journalist not Jason Bourne. Or, someone else has wiped his digital footprint. And if that's the case, they're good. Like, as good as me good, because these search parameters should've pulled him no problem. There aren't any recent credit card hits, no ATM withdrawals. It's damn near impossible to operate one hundred percent on cash alone and avoid detection on some camera or another these days. I can't even find when he left Ridgeview, but Fox told me he split last year."

An undercover freelance journalist digging into secrets has just as much at stake as an undercover cop. People kill for less.

A troubled feeling settles in my chest. "Try a different strategy. I want to exhaust our available resources before we need to pull strings on this."

"Got it."

"That just leaves the sister," Jude murmurs thoughtfully.

I go still, cutting my gaze to Jude. My first instinct is to keep Rowan out of this, but she's willful and challenging. She's like a curious cat. Twice as stubborn, too. It stirs my need to control, to dominate. The temptation creeps in again, stroking alongside my attraction to tease it back to the surface.

My fist closes around the phantom feeling of gripping her waist. Part of me wishes I didn't send her away and gave into the desire to taste those plush lips, swallow her gasps. The way her body responded tonight... Maybe she could handle me. Breaking her would be a sinful pleasure.

Christ, she needs to get out of my head so I can think straight.

"We need more eyes on her to know more." At my command, all of their heads snap up. I point at Colton. "Rearrange yours and Levi's schedules. Take her classes."

Colt's brows lift, but he doesn't argue, pulling up a new window on the computer to do my bidding. Levi levels me with the same inquisitive stare he had in the gym earlier tonight. He can look at me until his pitch black eyes burn holes through my skin.

This is for her own good. She's lucky we felt generous tonight. If it had been anyone else trespassing, there would be very different consequences. We open the Crow's Nest on weekends, but every other night it's ours and ours alone.

"And what about our guest?" Jude nods to the hall that leads to the room the frat boy is in.

"That," Colt says enthusiastically, "turned up a ton of results. You'll love who his dad is golf buddies with."

Jude folds his hands behind his head. "Who?"

"William Barlow," Colt supplies with a waggle of his brows.

Levi scoffs, scrubbing a hand over his jaw. "The dean of Castlebrook College. Figures."

I exchange a glance with him and stroke my chin. It's not a huge surprise that our delinquent captive is family friends with another man whose family dates back to the founders of Thorne Point. Connections get people everywhere in this city. William Barlow is well versed in mutual back scratching when problems arise for the young heirs.

"What do we know?"

"I'm so glad you asked, big guy." Colt cracks his knuckles and taps his keys to pull up several windows of information, one a profile on the dean. "I did some mining and it turns out, Castlebrook has had some of its own heat lately. It's against their chapter of Pi Kappa Alpha. Investigation's still in progress and the fraternity was put on probation. There was a hazing incident—the guys chased chicks dressed like bunnies across campus and—"

I lean over and smack the back of his head when I sense his attention shifting. "Focus."

"Right." Colt clears his throat and adjusts himself. "Softener thoughts."

"Pi Kappa Alpha. That's the fraternity most of the school's star rugby team belong to," I say.

"Same chapter as our friend." The way Levi says *friend* is chilling. "What a coincidence."

"There's no such thing," Jude says.

The two of them argue about whether or not coincidences are ever real for a minute while Colt motions me closer.

"You know I like patterns," he says.

"Yes?"

He points to a list on the left of the screen, mouth set in a disappointed frown. "If I trace transfer students between Castlebrook and here, the influx of female students is enough to make me wonder."

"Never a good thing."

He flashes me a brief smirk before it falls. His expression grows serious as he enters a keyboard shortcut. "A new girl transferred here in the last few weeks, accepted right before the probation. When I reversed the pattern there was only one female student who left Thorne Point."

It speaks volumes. People from all over the country do everything they can to scrape their way into Thorne Point University, but to leave is nearly unheard of. Especially to transfer to the rival school.

With my gaze narrowed, I take in what Colt's screens show us. "So what's the dean doing about all of it?"

"Hosting a dinner, apparently." Colt hums as he hacks through the dean's email through some backdoor he left the last time we needed to use him. Colt explained it to us once, but we don't get how hacking works. "Highlighting outstanding members of the chapter. Looks like a networking thing. It's this Friday at his residence on campus."

He's already opening Photoshop to create an invitation for us to use without me having to say anything. When he isn't dicking around, Colt's mind is more intelligent than the rest of ours combined.

With one of us at Castlebrook College for this dinner, we'll be able to kill two birds with one stone. We'll take care of our previous task so the frat boy isn't left to rot in his own piss for another week and still have time left over to find out how else the dean's connections could help us.

"Add a plus one to the invite," I say. "Rowan's going."

"Which name am I putting on this?" Colt's tongue sticks out of the corner of his mouth while he copies the invitation.

"Mine." Jude stretches his arms overhead and springs to his feet in a fluid motion, as smooth as he is with his silver tongue. He swaggers over, slinging an arm over my shoulders. "Parties are my forte. It'll be a night she'll never forget."

"Nah, you're all talk," Colt says. "Rowan's going with me."

"No," I growl, not liking the idea of Rowan with either of them. "I'll be the one going."

There's a beat of silence, then Jude and Colton snicker, leaning heavily on each other. Those fuckers—they did it on purpose to bait me. With a low grumble, I move away.

"Don't forget to check in on the guy overseeing the card game there," Colt calls. "He missed the last drop off."

I wave a hand in acknowledgement. Turning my back, I press my phone to my ear after dialing. A slow satisfied grin stretches when she answers without knowing it's me on the other end of the line. I wonder if she's heard what's said about curiosity's effect on mortality.

"Time to repay the favor you owe, kitten."

CHAPTER NINE
ROWAN

THE minute I open my door on Friday night, I find Wren waiting in the hall like an expensively dressed sentry. The charcoal suit is tailor-made for his muscular frame and makes his blue eyes stand out in stark relief against the dark fabric. His blond hair is slicked back, not a strand out of place. Stepping toward me, his cunning gaze slides down my body, sending an acute spark of warmth racing over my skin.

When I'm around him, he commands my attention whether I want to give it to him or not. He's the only person who has been able to bring me to the surface of the fog I've been living in since my brother left.

"No." It's decisive and final.

My head jerks back. "No?"

"No." Wren gives me another once over. "Change."

I press my lips into a thin line and prop my hands on my hips. When he told me what he wanted on the phone, I thought he was kidding. Except I don't think someone like Wren Thorne knows how to joke.

It doesn't matter that he looks fucking fantastic in the suit or smells like his intoxicating spicy and clean aftershave that does funny things to my insides. Underneath all that, he's a dick who expects everyone to fall in line. And something in me doesn't want to follow his ridiculous orders without a fight.

"Have you ever killed anyone with all that big dick energy you throw around?"

Wren doesn't answer, but there's the faintest shift in his dominant expression that seems entertained by my sass. It's the same look he had the other night in the hedge maze outside the hotel. He expects me to do as he says, but I don't think he's above fighting me to ensure I obey.

That thought shouldn't make my heartbeat pick up and my stomach tighten with excited anticipation.

Needing to cool my head, I change tactics, crossing my arms over the simple black button down I paired with the black dress pants Mom made me buy for interviews. "Why do I have to help you when you've done nothing for me yet?" My brows furrow. "What could be more important than finding a missing person?"

A dark shadow falls over Wren's face. When he takes another step forward, I stubbornly stand my ground to show him I'm not afraid of his intimidation tactics. His lips twitch and he crowds me until I'm forced to shuffle back a step. An unwanted ripple of warmth pools between my legs. Still, I refuse to give him an inch.

He braces a hand against the wall behind me. "Because you owe me and I've come to collect. If you don't, then we won't help find your precious brother."

I swallow down the panic that surges at his ultimatum. I hate that I need him.

"We're not going to a dinner with the dean of Castlebrook College with you dressed like that. You look like hired staff, not someone who would be believable on my arm as a date." The cold sneer on his face as he takes in my outfit grates on my irritation. "Now go back inside and dress yourself accordingly. Or do I have to dress you myself?"

I suck in a breath so quickly at the threatening suggestion that I can't do anything to hide the way I react to the idea of him making the choice for me. A hot blush tingles in my cheeks. He waits for an answer, eyes burning with intensity as they catalogue every inch of me.

"Fine," I push out in a rush. My tongue feels sluggish. "I'll see what else I have. Don't expect me to look like all the other society darlings that strut their stuff around campus, though." I level him with a hard stare, jaw set. "I'm not like that."

Wren holds my gaze and grasps my jaw in his large hand. "No, I imagine you're quite far from it. You have ten minutes to change or we'll be late. Don't keep me waiting, or I'll decide what you wear for the rest of the damn year."

* * *

"Castlebrook College isn't in Thorne Point," I say when we get out of Wren's gunmetal gray Aston Martin.

I drag in a deep inhale of cool autumn air. The drive from the city wasn't long, but every second I felt choked by his ego.

This college is in a neighboring town. When Isla heard I was coming here she tried to bribe me to take a picture of some hotshot rugby player, something Wolfe. Castlebrook is the official rival school of Thorne Point University, but I don't have any interest in covering stories on the athletic teams.

"Astute observation." Wren settles his hand on my lower back to guide me.

An odd thrill races down my spine. Despite not kissing me the other night, he has no problem touching me whenever he wants. The feeling of his hands on me, casually broadcasting that they belong on my body puts a slew of thoughts in my head that make my mouth dry.

"It used to be, before Thorne Point redrew its city limits several decades ago," he says. "They were sister schools when they were first established."

We walk along a wide path through a campus that closely resembles the regal stone buildings of Thorne Point. It's easy to see the identical history in the architecture.

Wren's touch grazes over the smooth material of the sheer cream blouse I found buried in my closet. I forgot I borrowed it from Isla. On her it's perfect, but my breasts are bigger than hers for a snugger fit. If I was worried Wren would veto keeping the same pair of pants on when I left my apartment a second time, I had nothing to fear—he took one look at my tits straining against Isla's expensive blouse and gave me a wolfish grin.

"So it's outside of your little turf or whatever, isn't it? You're not the King Crow here."

He smirks. "I don't need turf. My name alone is enough. People kneel before me when and where I want them to."

I pull an unimpressed face at his arrogance. "Then why do you need me to pose as your date for a cover, oh great and powerful one? I doubt I'm as important as you believe you are. Am I just supposed to be an ornament?"

Wren's hand slides from my back to my waist, massaging it as he brings me close against his side. He bends his head to press his lips against my temple. My stomach dips with a burst of arousal.

"Because you wanted my help." To an onlooker it might appear like he's being a doting boyfriend, but his voice is gritty with the promise of consequences for disobeying him. "Pay your favor, or you won't get what you need. I'm not reminding you again."

Not trusting myself to hold my tongue from a smart remark, I nod, pursing my lips into a tight line. Thankfully the conversation drops until we reach the dean's residence.

The historic estate house is at the edge of campus. A sculpture of two crossed keys in the stone framing the door catches my eye while we wait to be let in. It's on the door, too. The knocker Wren used is a key. When the old oak door opens, the muted din of chatter rolls onto the porch.

A woman in all black shows us in. Wren shoots me a pointed look and I roll my eyes. Her clothes are an exact match of what I was wearing when he picked me up before I changed.

"The dean has invited guests to join him in the parlor," she says. "It's down the hall and—"

"I know," Wren interrupts. I elbow the prick for his rude attitude and he squeezes my hip in a brutal grip in retribution. "I'm familiar with the home. Thanks."

It's barely audible and tacked on as an afterthought, but I feel less like decking him for being an ass to the woman for doing her job. Wren directs us down a narrow hall lined with gilded framed paintings and old black and white photos. Most show groups of men and I scoff. The keys repeat as much inside the house as they seem to outside. I wonder if it's like how some people are obsessed with collecting baskets.

I can't keep a question from tumbling past my lips before we have to play happy couple. "Why is it so hard?"

"What?" Wren mutters.

"Not being a total dick all the time."

He pauses outside the room where the chatter is louder, mouth tilted up at the side. One hand braces on the wall. There isn't much room to maneuver in the hallway, so he effectively traps me once again. He seems to love trapping people at his mercy.

This close, his aftershave makes my knees weak and my breath stutters through the desire coiling low in my stomach. *Don't go there*, I remind myself.

"Because, Rowan," he murmurs, stepping near enough for his charcoal suit to brush against my chest. Erasing the distance between us, he speaks against my lips, the graze of his skin on mine intimate. "It's my default setting. Never expect anything less from me. I'm the furthest thing you'll find from kind."

I scowl at him and feel his broad chest vibrate with an amused rumble. He drives me crazy. I look forward to the day I can get far away from his power high. Until then, I need him.

Wren takes my wrist and tugs so I follow him into the parlor. It's full of students in blazers with frat letters pinned to their lapels and an older crowd they're schmoozing with. Wren didn't tell me much about tonight's dinner except that the students needed some positive publicity and something about networking opportunities.

An older man I recognize from the photos in the hall is at the center of the room talking to a couple. The guy is around my age, but his girlfriend is younger and eyes the dean suspiciously. Her purple hair seems out of place in this stuffy traditional parlor. I immediately admire her boldness.

The dean spots us when we enter and color drains from his wrinkled face. He mutters something to the young couple and hurries to us. Even I have to be mildly impressed by Wren's power move to walk in the room and have the dean of the college rushing to him.

"Mr. Thorne," the dean says in surprise. "I don't remember having my secretary extend an invitation to tonight's gathering."

"And yet there my name is." Wren's confidence doesn't waver as he presents a crisp white invitation.

"Yes, I see." The distinguished man stares at the card in Wren's hand for a beat before clearing his throat. "Well. Do enjoy yourself. And give my regards to your father."

"Undoubtedly." Wren tucks the invitation into his suit jacket. His hand finds the small of my back again, fingertips pressing through the material of the sheer blouse with commanding force. "Let me introduce my date for the evening. This is Rowan Hannigan. Rowan, William Barlow, dean of Castlebrook."

Mr. Barlow's gaze passes over me, lingering at my rack without even hiding it. I shoot Wren a glare, beginning to understand why he'd drag me here. I'm the flashy distraction. My ornament comment from earlier wasn't too far off base.

Wren kisses my cheek, arm wrapping possessively around my waist. "Say hello, sweetheart."

Bastard. My cheek feels warm where his lips touched, heart fluttering at the endearment. We're only pretending to be together. I need to remember that this isn't real.

"Thank you for inviting us into your home. You and your wife have impeccable taste," I say as sweetly as I can manage while being openly objectified by a man old enough to be my grandfather. It's an unfortunate skill most women perfect by the time they're in their teens thanks to lecherous men like him. The dean gets control over himself, snapping his eyes up to meet mine. "Are the keys in the decor a personal interest or do they mean something?"

Wren's palm sweeps down my spine. I'm not sure whether it's silent praise or a warning. I can't keep my curious mind from being interested in the answer.

"They're a...family motif of sorts," Dean Barlow stammers. "Please excuse me."

He slips away, tossing one more glance at Wren before practically racing from the room. I arch a brow. The retreat looked a lot like running away in fear.

"I guess you weren't kidding about your name's effect on people." I snag a flute of champagne from a tray. "The rumors about you are pretty juicy."

Wren's hard gaze doesn't stray from the door the dean left through. "I'll be right back. The dinner should start soon. Talk to some of the students. They should have some interesting stories of their own about the rumors on this campus."

Before I can get more detail out of him, he's striding away. Part of me wants to ignore his directions and sneak after him to find out what he's up to. It's got to be more interesting than frat boys.

"Now's the perfect time, Linc. Come on, we have to find out why those girls transferred. I know it's connected to the bunny hunt."

I turn around and find the girl with purple hair talking to her boyfriend. He's tall and built enough to be a football player with the muscles his blazer can barely contain. Their bodies naturally angle toward each other as if they've known each other a long time, but when he takes her hand it has a sense of newness to it in the way he hesitates and looks around before threading their fingers together.

"Not yet." She pulls a face and he cups her cheek like he can't help himself. "We'll talk to him, I promise. We're already on thin ice and I don't want to piss him off before he decides the rugby team is suspended for the season."

"Lincoln," someone calls from across the room.

He looks between the person calling him and his girlfriend with a conflicted expression. He leans in and cradles her face in his hands, kissing her forehead tenderly. "Hang on. I'll see what Nate wants."

"I can't believe I still have to compete with my brother for your attention," she murmurs jokingly.

The sarcastic jibe makes Lincoln grin. When he goes to talk to a guy that looks just like his girlfriend, I sidle up to her.

"Pro tip," I offer with a friendly smirk. "During the dinner, excuse yourself to use the bathroom. It gives you time to look around without being missed."

Her face lights up. "That's a great idea. Thanks."

"No problem." A pang hits me in my chest. "My brother is the one to thank for it. He's crafty like that."

I learned all my best tricks from him.

"He sounds cooler than mine. I'm Briar." She offers her hand and I take it. "I'm a sophomore here."

"Rowan. I'm in my last year at Thorne Point University, actually. I'm here with someone who knows the dean."

Briar whistles. "That hot guy you walked in with?"

I open my mouth to deny it, but nothing comes out. Instead I offer a stiff shrug, remembering my role. "I think he's talking to Dean Barlow. What did you want to speak to him about? It sounded important."

Briar tucks a curl of purple hair behind her ear, darting her gaze around the room. "A girl here got…drugged without knowing." The heavy implication in her tone has me standing straighter on alert. "There wasn't a report about it. She's transferring, but the fraternity my brother and boyfriend are in is on probation because it happened the night they set up this stupid game. I'm here to help her get the guy who did it to her."

"One of their frat brothers did it?" I cast a hard look around the room at the students with pins on their lapels. "Do you know who?"

"No." Briar bites her lip. "She wouldn't tell me. He wore a mask. She might not know."

"Probably paid off," I mutter more to myself than her, my mind working through how it likely shook out.

"Thorne Point is pretty much impossible to get into without connections, so yeah." Briar sighs.

Before she says more, we're called into the dining room for dinner. Wren appears at my side as the party moves between rooms looking satisfied with himself. I stick close to Briar and snag a seat beside her. Wren is on my other side and Dean Barlow takes a seat at the head of the table to his left shakily, eyes bouncing between Wren and one of the frat brothers further down the table.

Wren is the one in charge here, not the dean deferring to him. He doesn't have to sit at the head of the table because whichever chair he picks is his throne.

My gaze falls to the place settings and I experience a mild rush of panic. Who needs that many forks for a meal? Briar and the others don't seem to share my dilemma and I remind myself how many people from this area come from money and have gone through every etiquette lesson imaginable from a young age. I'm not part of that world. In my head I repeat a mantra I heard once—start from the outside and work my way in.

The dean lifts a crystal wine glass. "We honor your pledge to integrity and high moral character tonight, gentlemen." Briar scoffs quietly and Lincoln soothes her. "Your future is ahead of you and you build the legacy you'll leave behind during your time at Castlebrook." He gulps audibly when Wren does nothing more than cock his head slightly. "Don't forget that."

It seems like an odd way to end a toast. My need to know everything pricks at my senses and I have to force a bite of the salad course into my mouth to keep from asking Wren what he said to Mr. Barlow. Maybe he threatened him. The dean is frail in comparison to Wren's broad muscled frame. My overactive imagination supplies an image of Wren callously dangling the old man outside a second floor window to get what he wants.

Not two minutes into the first course, Briar excuses herself like I instructed. Lincoln rests his arm across the back of her empty chair, staring after her with a concerned expression. I cover a laugh with a sip of wine.

Wren doesn't miss my reaction, raising a brow. "Did you make a friend?"

"Yup." I tilt my head in his direction and feed him a deadpan response. "Thanks for dropping me off to my first day of preschool, dad."

The joke flies out of my mouth without my control. Before I can feel weird about my own dead father, it backfires when heat flares in Wren's cool eyes. They dip to my mouth, down the column of my throat at the open neck of my blouse. My cheeks feel hot and I take a deeper drink of the wine. The corner of Wren's mouth curls and he returns to eating, smug like he's learned a new tool to use against me and has filed it away in his arsenal.

"Do you by chance have a brother, Miss Hannigan?" Mr. Barlow asks.

"I do. Ethan, my older brother," I say, surprised. "Do you know him?"

He nods. "I thought so. You look so alike."

I lick my lips, trying not to get overexcited. "How do you know him?"

"He interviewed me once, years ago when he was still in college for a hundred year legacy piece. Every generation in my family has attended Castlebrook. I was a student myself and eventually became the dean." A thoughtful expression crosses his face. "He asked me about the significance of the keys when he first came here, too. You must share his inquisitive nature."

"Oh. Yeah." I swallow and grip my knife hard enough for my knuckles to turn white. "He has a really sharp mind."

The urge to follow Briar to snoop around is strong, but I hold out until dinner ends. Almost everyone joins the dean in a cigar lounge, including Wren. I know it's crazy to think there'd be anything here. The dean himself said it was an interview from years ago, but I can't ignore the connection. If there's a chance there could be a lead on Ethan here, I'm looking for it.

I slip upstairs and pull my phone out, taking photos of anything that catches my eye. There's less than I hoped, the upstairs hall resembling the one downstairs—photos and paintings of old dead guys who have their name on every building in Maine. I don't find anything interesting about the dean except for a heavy dose of narcissism. Moving to an office, I hope I'll find something that could connect to my brother.

The room is dim, lit only by uplighting on the bookcases taking up the wall. It's a study with twin leather armchairs and a desk. I picture Ethan sitting in one of the chairs while interviewing Dean Barlow for a mind-numbing story about his family history at Castlebrook. Ethan would've hated it, I bet. He always liked the stories about secret corruption and money laundering best.

"You're predictable," I mumble when a framed article on the bookshelf snags my attention.

It's the one the dean mentioned about his enduring hundred year legacy. I take a photo of it before turning the frame around. My heart falls when there's nothing.

"Damn it."

Putting it back, I release a heavy sigh. It was wishful thinking to believe I might find clues here. Ethan has been obsessed with the story he's been working on for over a year. He wouldn't have had contact with someone like the dean for a while.

Before I leave, the lacquered wood molding of the bookcase makes me pause. It has the same crossed keys symbol in the design. I narrow my eyes. It sort of reminds me of the one in the TPU crest. I hold up my phone and capture a closeup on the symbol to sate the feeling nagging me.

The door opens. For a second my heart stops, thinking I'm busted. An excuse springs to the tip of my tongue. It dies when I realize it's Briar. She looks over her shoulder and I hear what must have sent her scurrying in here—low voices.

She halts when she notices me. I shrug.

"Need me to distract them?" I offer, nodding to the door.

"Yeah. No one can know I was up here." Breathless, she backs up to the window and undoes the latch. "Thanks."

When the voices sound closer, I abandon what I was looking at and move to the door. Briar has slipped out the window. Pressing my ear to the wood, I strain to listen.

"—worrying about your problems rather than causing more. You don't want to disappoint me." The voice is deep and threatening.

I wait until it sounds like they've left before I open the door. Big mistake.

A huge shadowy figure fills the frame, then pushes me back into the study. Fear steals the air from my lungs and a scream climbs my throat, until Wren's aftershave hits my nose.

"Was that you in the hall?" I breathe. If he's angry at me for going rogue, I'm not backing down. "How did you know I was up here?"

"Pointless questions," he rumbles.

My back hits the bookcase I was snooping through. He dips his head, nose tracing the shape of my cheek bone. *Oh.*

It feels good when he handles me like this, a corner of my brain whispering to let go. It fills my head with a fantasy of kneeling in front of him. Air gusts from my lungs.

He pins me to the shelves with his firm body and I feel his erection. I drag in a heaving gasp, choked by the rush of arousal. When his big hands grip my hips, I clench my thighs together.

"Stop being so impulsive, you curious little kitten."

My heart skips a beat and a strangled sound escapes me. His voice is a dark and sensual caress against my throat. I shouldn't want this...but I do.

"Or what?" I push out, gripping the fine material of his jacket.

I feel the curve of his mouth against my skin. His hands flex on my hips.

"Or I'll have to punish you."

CHAPTER TEN
WREN

I'VE never been so on edge doing work for the Crows. A simple task like tonight should be a walk in the park—shake down a man in power for information and oversee one of the revenue streams that lines our pockets independently of our families. Simple. Yet I'm off-kilter because Rowan is a distraction.

She hasn't spoken a word to me since I peeled my body away from hers in Barlow's study without continuing what I started. It put her in a pissy little mood and the sway of her plump ass in those tight pants was designed specifically to punish me as much as I want to punish and control her. Instead of reaching out to wring her neck or grab her ass, I shove my fists into the pocket of my slacks as I stalk across the campus toward the student residences.

I crave giving orders and having them obeyed, but it turned me on tonight when she followed her impetuous heart and hunted around for William Barlow's secrets.

Rowan huffs for the thousandth fucking time and I stretch my neck, closing my eyes at the satisfying pops. If she doesn't stop testing me with her attitude, I'm going to snap. And when I do, I won't stop until she's a ruinous mess begging for mercy that isn't coming until I'm good and ready to let her go.

"One more stop." I put steel into my voice so she'll understand I'm not fucking around. "Behave this time."

"Yeah, yeah. Or you'll spank me," Rowan sasses. "Big bad King Crow with his big dick in charge. I get it."

I grit my teeth. I want to do so much more than drive my palm against her stubborn ass until it's red. I nearly fell to the lure she has on me, ready to bend her over Barlow's desk and fuck her.

Focusing on anything but the way those mental images make my cock swell, I remain silent until we reach the dorm building where one of our grunts runs the game. On the way, I send the recording on my phone of the conversation I had with Barlow to the guys. The dean confirmed what we already knew—someone in power was cleaning up our captive frat boy's mess. Now we can deal with it.

By the time I slip my phone back in the inside pocket of my jacket, we arrive at the stone steps descending to the basement apartments of one of the freshman dorms. A bird feeder hangs from a low tree branch, signaling the game is on.

"It's here."

"You've gotta be kidding me." Rowan stands at the top of the steps, hands on her hips. "It's a literal underground card game. Cliché much?"

I said as much to Colton, but he assured me that it was the most strategic location on campus in part because he could hide his gadgets that kept the players from cheating and the poker game from being discovered by security.

"I don't have all night." With my hand at her back, we go down the stairs. Before she walks in the entrance to the illicit card game, I grab her arm and make her meet my eyes. "I mean it. Keep that pretty mouth shut in here."

"Yessir," she snaps, green eyes glittering.

I force the groan that wants to claw its way out of me back down and trace her lower lip with my thumb. "Don't play this game with me, kitten. You will lose."

No matter how much I'd enjoy nothing more than that. We're here on business.

Inside it looks like any other dorm building. The long hall stretches and branches off at the end. I stalk to the left without waiting for Rowan. The guy guarding entry to the game stands, then falls back in his seat once he recognizes me.

"Are there students in these other dorms?"

Does her nosiness have no end? "No."

"That's a lot of open housing."

Clenching my teeth, I elaborate so she'll leave it. "Colton. He had this floor removed from the school's housing system. It shows up as a filled in basement."

"Seriously?" The fact she sounds impressed both irritates and stirs pride in me. It's a confusing mix. I'm struck by the urge to punch Colt over it. "How do the students not wander down here or say anything?"

I pause outside the door and turn a smug look on her. "Because they're too busy trying to win back the money they lost to notice."

When I swing the door open, Rowan's eyes widen and her lips part. Thanks to Levi, we got the soundproofing right, the energetic din in the room barely audible until we enter. Two tables fill the room, but her insatiable curiosity leads her to the renovations we did a few years ago, connecting all the rooms in the basement to host more games at once. Each table is full of players with one thing in common—the drive to gamble.

"This isn't just a poker game," she whispers more to herself than me. "This is a whole ass casino operation."

I can't drag my eyes from her as a warm, unfamiliar ember unfurls in my chest. What is it about her that lures me under her spell? Instead of seeking out Tyler, I find myself tracing her steps as she explores. We garner a few glances, but most of the players are wrapped up in their games.

"Why here?" she asks.

"We have one at every campus within an hour radius."

The fact I'm telling her anything about how we run things should be a warning flag, but she has this way of getting me to ignore my rules.

She whirls to me, mouth hanging open. "That's like six schools."

"It is."

She weaves through the tables, watching a clever looking young black girl in a leather jacket over a purple fishnet shirt punch the air when she wins the pot.

"That's how it's done, boys," she crows at the groaning players at her table while she collects her winnings. Fingering her braids, she winks. "Can't beat a queen."

Tyler is in the third room I follow Rowan through, scurrying over. He's a gangly guy who favors oversized t-shirts and baggy jeans. "Boss. You're here."

"I am." My gaze doesn't leave her back. She continues on, chasing her hunger for knowledge. I turn my focus to Tyler, a scowl taking over my face. "You know why."

His throat bobs with a swallow. He rips the beanie from his head and fiddles with it. I lift a brow at the nervous dance of his fingers.

"It's just—I forgot what day it was, you see, and—"

Tyler flinches when I take a silver lighter from inside my jacket. I flick the ignition methodically and a slow, feral grin stretches my mouth. He can't look away from the powerful flame of my custom butane lighter.

"Let's go talk outside." I wave a hand. "Don't want to mess with the energy in here. Nervous people don't bet as much."

Pinching the back of Tyler's neck, I lead him into the quiet hall and wait for him to explain why he missed our deadline. The schedule keeps everything else running and if one falls out of balance, they all will. Me and my brothers didn't spend years building this system to have it fall apart because of a sniveling shit like Tyler.

He doesn't speak. The panicked expression tells me what I already know—the money is gone. I sigh and flick the lighter.

"Tyler, Tyler, Tyler. You're disappointing me and I hate when my expectations aren't met." I keep my voice light, but the dangerous edge in my tone is clear. "I can't let that slide."

"I, please, I didn't—"

"Shut up." I drop the understanding act, tolerance growing thin. "You're going to confess your mistake. And it was a mistake, wasn't it? You wouldn't be stupid enough to think it was a good idea to cross us. If you're lucky, I won't kill you for it."

"Oh god," Tyler chokes. "I don't want to die, man."

He tries to fight me when I grab his wrist. I glare at him, digging my fingers into his flesh. He's no match for my strength when I have my thumb jabbing the tendons in his wrist. With a mangled sound, he stops struggling, whimpering when I hold the lighter under his palm and flick the trigger without letting the flame catch.

"Tell me," I demand. "I'm not a patient man, Tyler. Don't keep me waiting."

He holds out longer than I expect for someone who seems ready to wet himself at the sight of me. I ignite the lighter and wave it beneath his palm. For every pass, I hold the flame under his hand a little longer so he can feel the heat building. His whole body shakes and his eyes bounce between the fire and me.

I work my jaw. "You're starting to piss me off."

"It wasn't that much," he finally says in a rush. "It was—it was only a little here and there. I was gonna be short, and I knew it."

Here and there. This wasn't a one time occurrence. He was skimming off the top.

At my irritated growl, Tyler shudders. His beady eyes fly around the hall for a rescue that isn't coming.

"So you skipped payment," I spell out. "And thought you got away with it when no one said anything."

He nods miserably. "I needed the money."

To feed a drug habit if his disgusting nails and the sallow bags beneath his eyes are anything to go by. Fucking junkie stole from me and blew it all on a chemical binge. My lip curls and I twist my grip on his wrist, wanting to break it. But that wouldn't be enough pain for this transgression.

Rowan steps into the hall, looking around with a puzzled crease in her brow like she's searching for me until she takes in the scene. She freezes. I can't exactly dispose of a body with her around. I'll have to have Penn come down from his hermit cabin in the woods to take care of this later. Her presence doesn't deter me from doling out a punishment now, though.

I tip my head to the side and study Tyler. "Do you know what they say about crows?"

"What?" His glassy eyes blink slowly.

"They always remember the faces of those who crossed them. Bad fucking idea," I snarl.

He screams in agony and terror when I break his wrist anyway, then force his hand down on the flame from the lighter, holding it there until his skin cooks. I release him and he slouches against the wall, pale and panting heavily.

"W-why," Tyler moans, hand trembling as he cradles it protectively.

The smell of his burnt skin is foul, stinking up the hallway.

"So everyone knows not to steal from the Crows," I grit out. After a beat, I smile unpleasantly. "Be thankful. You get to live another day."

More like live a few more hours until Penn hunts him down. We have no remorse for those that think they can dupe us at our own game.

Rowan releases a small sound of horror, hand covering her mouth. I glance her way, not sorry she saw. Her whole body is like a bow strung too tight that's about to snap, ready to spring into action.

"Keep what I said in mind." I put the lighter away and smooth the lines of my lapels. "Crows don't forget our enemies."

Tyler nods frantically and scurries away when I jerk my chin in permission. Rowan watches him go. When his wheezing and quick shuffling steps are no longer audible, she strides up to me, green eyes spitting a fire as potent as the one burning in me.

"That was..."

She trails off, at a loss for words. I've finally found out how to stop her constantly running mouth.

"Necessary," I finish.

"No, it was brutal," she corrects, leaning against the wall to drop her head back. Her throat works and I want to lean in to mark it up with my teeth. "Barbaric. You didn't have to go that far."

The constant anger simmering in my blood threatens to boil over. She's judging me and a savage part of me wants to go toe to toe with her and show her she'll never win with me. I've been playing nice, but she's just like every other person that crawls to us begging for our favor. She lied to our faces, hid the secret she's keeping. And she thinks she has a right to judge me?

Those in power have to act to stay in control. It's a truth as old as humanity itself.

"So I should've let the punk continue to steal from me? To undermine my businesses? No, Rowan. This is what we do. This is who we fucking are." I slam my hands on the wall on either side of her and get in her face, growling my last warning. "This is what you came to us for. If you didn't want monsters, you shouldn't have come looking in the darkness for help."

She sets her jaw and furrows her brows, remaining still. "You're sick."

A humorless laugh rumbles in my chest. I'm miles past that. "You have no idea, baby."

Rowan shoves at my chest, exerting a lot of effort to move me. I don't budge. Her smaller hands on my pecs make me want to crush her against the wall and crash my mouth over hers to tame her wildness. It's only when I decide to give in that she gets what she wants. I head for the exit with long strides. She rushes after me.

"Okay, I helped you," she says halfway across campus. "Now you're going to find my brother, right?"

A sigh hisses out of me at the hope in her voice. I had that same hope once. Charlotte's locket sits inside my jacket pocket, resting against my heart.

We agreed to take Rowan's problem on, but the most obvious answer is usually the correct one. Ethan Hannigan probably isn't alive. We'll do what we can to find him, but that makes me the person stealing a sibling away from someone.

When we reach the car, I slip out of the jacket and roll the sleeves of my shirt up. Rowan's gaze lingers on my forearms once we get in.

"Give me the weekend to take care of another matter," I finally answer.

"Then I'll see what I can do."

* * *

The night isn't over yet. After I drop Rowan off at her apartment, a summons I can't ignore pings my phone. My father, calling me home for a meeting.

I drop my head against the headrest and pinch the bridge of my nose, massaging the dull ache away. Before I pull away from the curb, I rake my fingers through my styled hair, messing it up so strands fall across my forehead.

My father hates it when I leave it unkempt. Says it's the mark of a boy instead of a man. I haven't been a boy in a long fucking time.

Gripping the wheel, I steel myself to reinforce the barbed cage around my heart in preparation to go home to a house as empty as me.

On the way, I call Jude and put him on speakerphone while I weave through the shadowy streets of the city.

"What's up?" The background noise of his grandmother's laugh and the soulful vocals of Ana Gabriel mute as he moves away to talk.

"I'll be back late. I sent what we needed from Barlow, but my dad called me over."

"Ah, shit, man." The sympathy in his tone earns a grunt from me. He knows how much I hate going home. "I'm going back to the Nest later. I'm with abue tonight."

Jude loves his grandmother more than anything in the world. She raised him. Everything he does is to give that care back to her, like the new house he bought her with our first big take in college.

"Give her my love."

When he became our brother she adopted Colton, Levi, and myself as her own.

He chuckles. "She's going to ask why you haven't come to see her lately."

I sigh and change the subject. "Call Penn for me. Tyler is no longer in our employment."

"Little shit," he growls. "What did he say?"

My lip curls. "That he needed the money and thought he was getting away with it. He blew it on drugs is my bet."

Jude barks a cruel laugh. "Yeah, right. I'll tell Penn. He'll have to drag his cock out of his girlfriend's magic pussy for five minutes to do it."

I shake my head. Penn's obsession with the girl he stalked until she became his is unparalleled. "He'll do it. I've gotta go."

"*Later.*"

Minutes later, the Thorne estate looms ahead of me and dread settles in my chest. It's a sprawling turn of the century monstrosity of tradition with tall windows. The house always feels like it will swallow someone and never give them back. It's my least favorite place in the world. Charlotte was the only brightness in it and she's gone.

Pulling in beneath the arched iron gate, I park in the circular drive by the fountain, not planning to stay long. I leave my jacket off and sleeves rolled up to further annoy my father. Before I head in, I take the locket.

The door swings open before I reach it, the butler offering a solemn nod. I sigh and lope past him, taking the grand staircase up to my mother's rooms first. Dad can wait a little longer.

Upstairs, the wings are lined in a plush carpet running the length of the antique wood floors. This estate has been in the Thorne family for generations.

Mom's and Charlotte's old room are both in this wing. She moved her private rooms because it was the only way she could cling to feeling closer to her dead daughter. When she's not lost to the fog she self medicates with.

I rap my knuckles on her door before entering. The sitting area is empty, a tray of tea left untouched. One of her maids will come in soon to retrieve it. I move further into the dark, sour smelling suite, pressing my lips together.

A lump sits in the middle of the bed beneath the covers. I stop at the side of it, glancing at the numerous prescription pill bottles on the nightstand. Reaching out, I stroke greasy blonde hair back from Mom's clammy forehead. She emits a faint moan and rolls over, lost to the haze.

She was beautiful and charming once. She laughed a lot and enjoyed hosting parties. The perfect society wife.

Some days I'm angry at her for choosing to numb herself, but I understand the desire, wishing I could disappear far enough down a bottle to forget the pain for a while. The difference between us is I come up for air. She doesn't, barely leaving her rooms.

I leave her alone and go back to the hall. I don't mean to, but my feet freeze in front of my sister's door. I haven't come here in a while and I need to touch it. Laying my palm over the cool wood, I gasp roughly. The misery of missing her is impossible to bear when I'm here, straining to remember the sound of her voice.

It echoes in my head as a memory rises up.

Levi ran ahead of me and I followed down the hall. Charlotte was sprawled on the floor outside her room, always dropping down anywhere with her books from the time she could read. Levi made it around without trouble, but her stack of books tripped me when I jumped to chase him. My aim was to avoid her gangly legs, failing to account for how many books she needed around her to read one.

"Watch it!" I huffed with all the importance I could muster at thirteen. "One of these days you're going to take someone out with these."

"I can read where I want. I'm learning."

She didn't bother looking up, too engrossed in her latest fascination—last week Ancient Egypt, this week Greece. My lips pulled to the side, a weird bubble of pride growing in my chest. Eight going on eighteen like every other well-bred young lady, except unlike them she didn't care if the others her age were obsessed with some boy band or what to wear to upcoming charity soirees. She was who she was and owned it.

"Whatever, nerd." I ruffled her hair fondly.

"Nerds rule the world." Without glancing away from her book, she held up a peace sign. "Knowledge is power."

"Wren!" Levi called.

"Yeah, coming." I flicked Charlotte gently on the head. "Later. Don't forget to ask the cook for lunch."

Charlotte gave me a beaming smile. It felt good to watch out for her, even when she annoyed me.

Each year that passes makes it harder to hold on to, like pieces of her are fading away beyond my grasp.

My chest aches fiercely, stabbed by the acute pain of grief. It's as sharp as Levi's deadly knife collection, gutting me over and over with fresh agony every time the wound scabs over. I curl my hand into a fist, swallowing back the urge to punch the door. I blow out a ragged breath and step back.

There's no more stalling. Might as well get this over with before I end up extending this little visit out longer than necessary.

My feet drag with each step as I head to the ground floor. I slip a hand into my pocket to hold the locket.

The study is the only room my father spends the majority of his time in. I doubt he's visiting Mom in her rooms. If he could, he'd sleep in the study or his office. Since Charlotte's death he's thrown himself into work harder than ever. As children he was a stern but mostly absent father unless there was an event.

His work has become the only thing he truly cares about.

I reach the double oak doors and push them open.

"Hugo," Dad says from his seat by the fireplace. "You came this time."

A wave of revolt washes over me. "Don't call me that."

He grants me an impatient look for having to have this conversation again. We'll have it until it sinks in. "It's your name. The one your mother and I gave you."

"So is Wren." I go to his decanted spirits on the bar cart without invitation and pour three fingers of Scotch into a cut crystal tumbler. "Which is the name I use."

"Your middle name." Dad scoffs. "It's a dishonor to your grandfather to snub his name the way you do."

My shoulder hitches unapologetically. Dad's old man is rotting in his grave. I doubt he cares that I never liked his name.

"I'm busy." I swallow a healthy mouthful of smooth aged Scotch. "Say what you need so badly so I can go."

Dad stands to lean against the ornate marble mantel. "We're family, son. You can't run forever from your responsibilities. Everything passes to you." He angles his head to look at me. "I expect you to uphold our family traditions. I've given you extra time after graduating because of Charlotte, but you can't shirk these obligations forever."

I clench my teeth hard. A muscle in my jaw twitches while he spins the gilded ring he wears on his smallest finger, the one he always fiddles with when he's thinking. He's had it for as long as I can remember. The flat top has two keys crossed and the date of the city's founding in Roman numerals.

Tossing back the last of my drink, I slam the glass down on his desk. "You'll have to wait longer, Dad."

With that, I spin on my heel and stalk out, ignoring his strained shout.

The last thing I want is to have my parents' life. It's why the four of us banded together in high school. Colton and Levi feel the same. Jude's the lucky one of the group with a stable home life and family that loves him. His goal has always been providing a comfortable life for his grandmother.

Dad and his associates built their empires to rule over Thorne Point. I have no intention of joining their ranks to have a replica of his life. My father didn't raise me to be one of his pawns. He can keep his keys to his kingdom.

I want to rule Thorne Point alongside my brothers from the dark of night. The underworld we've built for ourselves is our domain.

CHAPTER ELEVEN
ROWAN

Campus is dead as usual on Sunday morning. At this hour most people are still sleeping off their partying from the night before. I'm sure many of them were at the Crow's Nest.

My shift at the library starts in twenty minutes. First, I'm taking a detour. It won't matter if I'm late. No students show up before noon. Even the freshman slack after the first few weeks of the semester, all their plans and promises to tackle college swirl down the drain once they realize no one's keeping track of them.

I took Isla's hints and did laundry yesterday. It led to an impromptu cleaning session to clear the cluttered chaos of my mind. I wish I'd done it sooner.

The first time I looked around the apartment for clues on what Ethan was investigating, I found nothing, but this time I turned up a scrap of paper with his hastily scribbled handwriting on it next to the desk we both use for ignoring our clean laundry that needs to be folded instead of a workspace. It's become my lifeline.

The note is folded and tucked inside my bra so I don't risk losing it. I'm surprised he wrote something down, preferring to keep his notes and his calendar digital so he always has access. He used to tell me it was too easy for a notebook to be lost or stolen, so it's best to get with the times and encrypt all my writing projects. I thought he was being a paranoid nerd.

My mind keeps circling back to his favorite piece of advice, wondering why he would write something down. Did he know he was going to go missing, so he left it for me specifically?

I wipe a clammy palm off on the flannel shirt tied around my hips. I can't think like this is one of my true crime documentaries to piece together. I swallow thickly. Those always end with a body.

The thought is unimaginable. I shudder and take a gulp of cooling coffee from my cardboard cup to settle my stomach.

Withermore's tall doors loom before me. It's where I have most of my core classes for my major. Where Ethan spent most of his time on campus when he was a student here. A pang hits me hard. I'm always going to be following in his shadow.

Except now I have to stand on my own two feet without him there to catch me when I stumble. I'm adrift without him.

I enter and find the TA offices. In Ethan's college days he was a teacher's assistant, and a student he made friends with has the same office while working on his doctorate.

The door is locked, but it doesn't stop me from rifling through the mailbox on the wall. I don't know what I'm hoping to find, but my gut tells me to look anyway. Maybe Ethan sent something.

One of the envelopes has the school crest printed on it and I pause, studying it. My thumb smooths over the lions on their hind legs bracketing the shield with a fleur-de-lis and the crossed keys. I lift my gaze to peer down the hall. The same crossed keys image is in a small metal circle that repeats a few times until the hall ends at an intersection. A crease forms between my eyebrows.

How many times a day have I walked these halls in the last four years? This is the first time I'm noticing it since the key overload at the dean of Castlebrook's house Friday night attuned me to it. Seeing it in an unexpected place draws on my curiosity, making me wonder where else it might be. I want to research the history of the school to find out why the crossed keys are part of the TPU crest in the first place.

"Rowan?" Brian's voice makes me jump.

I press a hand to my chest and clutch my coffee cup tighter. "Oh—shit, you scared me. I didn't think you were here on the weekends."

Brian groans. "I'm not usually. I set my office hours for times when I'm least likely to see students. I needed to get some work done. Midterm prep is starting early."

"Already?"

"Don't get me started." He unlocks the door and lets me in first. "What did you come by for?"

"Um, here. Your mail." I hand over the stack I was holding, attempting to exude confidence instead of guilt. "Have you heard anything from Ethan lately?"

He shakes his head and dumps the stack of mail and his briefcase on the crowded desk he shares with two other TAs. "No, not in a while. I don't think I've seen him since we grabbed drinks when the summer session ended. Actually, when you see him, tell him he still owes me twenty bucks."

I hold back a sigh. That was close to the last time I saw him before he left for work. "Thanks anyway."

Brian reads the defeated slump in my shoulders I can't hide. "He's absorbed in a story again?"

"I think so." I toss my cardboard cup in his trash and offer the note I found at the apartment. "Does this address and time mean anything to you?"

He takes it and reads it aloud. "'1201 *South Cove Road, 11pm.*' Nope. Other than recognizing Ethan's handwriting, I don't know what it's for. I think that's near the industrial shipyard. Maybe a meeting with a source?"

I step forward, twisting my fingers together. "He didn't tell you anything about the story he's been working on?"

"Not in any concrete detail other than to say it was the story of a lifetime. He's superstitious about his stories before he breaks them." He shrugs. "Always been like that, from what I can tell."

It's not something I can argue. Ethan gets downright cagey when it comes to his assignments. Rubbing my forehead, I take the note back when he offers it. As I tuck it away, Brian clears his throat awkwardly.

"What?" I look down at the fitted camisole I have on under my favorite denim jacket, thinking he's uncomfortable watching a woman tuck something into her universal secret pocket—her bra.

He rubs at his neck. "I happened to grab coffee in the student union last week."

"And?" I prompt in a slow drawl.

"I saw who you were eating with." He glances around as if Colton or Levi will spring into existence. They'd probably like people to believe they could. "Are you okay? The things said about those guys are dangerous. People say they're a gang, that they kill as a game and make people disappear. Some even think they're the ones behind the Leviathan thing. It's insane. This is a college campus. I don't even know why they're allowed to attend classes here, other than the obvious that they're all loaded."

"I'm fine." I snort, waving a hand dismissively. They're not as scary as the rumors say. Wren burning that guy's hand jumps into my head. Violent, yes, but I'm not afraid of them. "I bet half of that shit isn't true."

In fact, I bet they started them just to make themselves seem more intimidating. Colton probably gets a huge kick out of it.

"You're sure?" he presses earnestly. "You're not in any trouble?"

I shake my head. "Thanks Brian."

"Anytime."

I leave his office behind and mutter to myself. "What did you get yourself mixed up in, Ethan?"

The question won't leave my head as I settle in for my usual routine in the silent library. I normally enjoy the quiet morning shift surrounded by the scent of old texts. It's when I get my best writing done on the secret fiction projects I've been working on for myself, but today it's like an echo chamber that has me picking at my nail beds. To ease my anxiety and keep my overactive imagination from coming up with a thousand and one horrible scenarios, I plan to search the history of the key symbol.

Pulling out my laptop, I set it on the counter and type *crossed keys symbol meaning* into the search engine.

The results populate and I skim through them. Many links and a Wikipedia page talk about the keys symbolizing keys to the kingdom, most often meaning Heaven. An article on academia talks about the keys signifying unlocking a brighter future and broadening perspective.

I don't get far into reading before I'm interrupted. Colton leans an elbow on the desk and grins at me when I look up to find him there and Levi standing behind him.

"'Sup, Ro."

"Ugh," I groan. "No. It's too early, too *Sunday* to deal with you. Don't you fuckers sleep?"

Colton chuckles, drumming a rhythmic beat on the counter. He leans in like he's divulging a secret. "No one's sleeping on you, baby. Especially not in this badass grunge chick look." He nods sagely, checking me out. "Hot, very hot."

Levi smacks the back of his head. I duck to hide a pleased smirk while Colton rubs at his skull. He rakes his fingers through his messy brown hair and plops a coffee on the counter. The decadent aroma makes my mouth water.

"Bribery?" I ask, just to be a brat.

"Chivalry," Colton corrects. "I've noticed how much of a caffeine addict you are. All yours, have at it."

I take the cup, wrapping my palms around it to soak up the warmth. I hum when I inhale the divine scent of the roast again. This isn't just coffee, this is *good* coffee from the upscale shop off campus. The first sip almost makes me moan. Fuck, that's good.

"Whatever, you can stay. I can't stop you." I shift my gaze between the two of them and bite my lip around a smug smile. "Apparently I hear I'm in grave danger by even speaking to you, because rumor has it you make people disappear and kill them for sport. You could be preying on me in my emotionally compromised state to recruit me for your cult." I hold up the coffee. "Brainwashing me."

Colton lifts himself onto the counter beside my laptop with little effort. I catch a flash of abs before his graphic t-shirt falls back into place.

He flexes a bicep. "The only cult I have is the Colton DuPont is a Sex God cult."

Levi rolls his eyes and shoves him. "Fucking idiot."

Colton nearly topples, but maintains his perch. He spins my laptop around and clicks through my search results without asking.

My brows jump up. "Nosy much?"

"You have no idea," Levi mutters, toying with his lip ring.

"What are you doing? I'm bored. God, the library is dull. Oh, hey." Colton types as fast as he talks, constantly in motion in one way or another. "Your security sucks. Gotta do something about these firewalls or the big guy will have my balls. I'm very close with them."

I stare at him. "Dude."

"Just let him do it or he'll steal it and do it anyway." Levi sighs and leans against a pillar next to the counter.

"If you're bored, you can both leave," I say mildly. "I'm not sure if you're aware, but you're in the library. You know, the place students come to study? And neither of you seem to care about classes, just following me to mine."

Levi's lips twitch and he makes a show of glancing around. "Don't see anyone else here."

"Besides, babe," Colton says without looking up from the screen. "You're stuck with us. Get used to it." He flashes his charming grin at me. "We're awesome. You should feel lucky."

Propping my chin in my hand, I watch him have his way with my laptop with a narrowed gaze and grumble, "Like I won the damn asshole lottery."

A puff of laughter leaves Levi as he plays with a knife he pulled from his boot as if it's a normal thing to do. He makes an odd picture braced against a marble pillar in a leather jacket, black hair hanging in his face, surrounded by books, and deftly flipping a knife blade to pommel in his long tattooed fingers.

"Boom," Colton says a few minutes later, presenting my laptop back to me. "Good to go. Now no one will be able to access your Hub search history, among other things."

"You say outrageous and invasive things because you like the attention and the sound of your own voice, right? Someone not get enough love as a kid, so you act out?" I smirk when his cocky expression falters. "Yeah, that's what I thought."

He traces his lip with a slow swipe of his tongue, tilting his head. "This isn't high school. You don't have to blush at the mention of masturbation and porn. It's natural, baby."

I match his head tilt, allowing my voice to go smoky and suggestive. He's the type who has to be beaten at his own game. "Who said I was? We're talking about you and your projection problems, not what gets me hot when I touch myself."

Colton releases a petulant grumble under his breath, cheeks flushed. Over his shoulder, Levi is openly grinning. It's kinda scary, but maybe it's because I'm so used to his brooding frowns. His eyes meet mine and he nods. I think his respect for me has grown by challenging his friend and calling him out.

I pull my laptop closer and return to reading about the symbolic interpretations of keys while Colton continues to sulk. Eventually he gets over it and disappears for twenty minutes, returning with a towering stack of books in his arms. He deposits them on the counter, hopping onto it again before picking up a book at random.

"These are all about symbolism." Surprise colors my tone as I sift through what he brought. He hums in acknowledgement, paging through his selection. He saw what I was researching and decided to help. A faint smile tugs at my lips. "Apology accepted."

Colton perks up and winks at me. He holds up his book in one hand. "This says keys are considered lucky talismans and represent access, knowledge, and success. Superstitious people hung them over their beds in Europe for good dreams. Cool. Why are you interested in this?"

I shrug, not ready to explain myself until I have a better idea about the reason why this nags me. Until then, I'm going to follow my gut and find what I can about the crossed keys.

While we research during my slow shift, Levi moves to the arched stone windows lining the wall, perching on the windowsill like a dark guard, an arm casually resting on his bent knee. It's my new normal to have them around and I'm beginning to get used to it, even find some comfort in their presence.

* * *

On Monday my warm and fuzzy feelings are nowhere to be seen. I was trapped so deep in a nightmare about finding more clues Ethan hid around the apartment that by the time I woke up I was late as hell. The dream was uncomfortably vivid and I can't shake the sense that time is running out. I've taken to carrying the note I discovered with me.

By some stroke of luck, I make it to my 8 a.m. class on time, but at what cost? I didn't have a minute to spare to get coffee, not even the cheap vending machine kind. My entire body groans at me for going without my caffeine fix, and I blame that travesty for missing a very important change as I jog up the steps to my usual seat in the third row on autopilot.

A pair of legs stop me in my tracks. They belong to Colton. He's sitting in my spot, ankles crossed and resting on the empty seat in front of him. I've grown used to his more frequent attendance in the one class we share and being followed by him and Levi, but he's not in this one.

"What the hell are you doing?" I grumble.

All he does is grin and wave to the open seat beside him. Not in the mood for his antics without coffee while still shaking off the webs of the nightmare, I turn to go. Levi is there. His tall, imposing frame blocks the way. My nostrils flare and I choke the strap of my bag.

I briefly contemplate jumping down a row to escape them. I think I could weather the weird looks it might garner. Writers are eccentric creatures.

The idea must be written all over my face because Levi huffs and silently holds out one of the three coffees he brought with him. I squint at it, waiting for the ulterior motive to jump out. It's from the same place as the one they brought me yesterday. Free coffee is free coffee. I take it before he revokes the offer and resign myself to an hour of sitting between them.

At first I ignore them, sipping coffee while the professor begins the lecture on ethics. If I didn't need this class to graduate, I wouldn't have subjected myself to it first thing Monday morning. The professor is a hard ass that only offers this time slot for the fall semester.

"You should come back to the Nest this Friday," Colton whispers. When I don't acknowledge him, he shifts closer. "Sometimes we do theme nights."

On my other side, Levi has stolen the armrest for himself. His knee bumps into mine and I have to rein in the urge to slam my leg against his in retaliation for his rude manspreading.

I flash Colton an irritated glance. "And I care because?"

His playful deep green eyes are bright. "Because I'll be there, obviously."

"Obviously." I sigh, shaking my head. "I wish you guys wouldn't party when you're supposed to be helping me."

"We're working on it. Promise, babe."

I don't answer, sinking my teeth into the meat of my cheek. I haven't told them about the note I discovered at the apartment. I'm afraid if I give it up, I'll lose one of my last connections to Ethan. Irrational as it may be, I feel like the note could help bring me the answers I'm desperate to find.

The class continues like that. Colton whispers to me like he doesn't realize or care that there's a room full of students trying to absorb information while he's gossiping with me. Levi remains quiet at least, but if his elbow digs into my side one more time I'm not liable for my actions.

I don't retain a single thing the professor says on today's topic.

When the class finally ends, I mouth a silent prayer and make a hasty escape. They follow, trailing behind me. Glancing back, I spot Colton pausing to flirt. Levi has disappeared. I don't know why they both sat in on my class, but I hope to never repeat the experience.

Except Levi beats me to my next class, waiting for me. And Colton is at the one after.

Tuesday is the same. They're glued to my side in every course on my schedule, sometimes only one of them, and other times they're together to torment me. My efforts to lose them in crowds are fruitless, as if they know where I am at all times. They're either psychic or psycho.

I have no idea what they're up to, but for now I'll wait them out. The only thing I know for certain is that Wren has to be behind this.

CHAPTER TWELVE
WREN

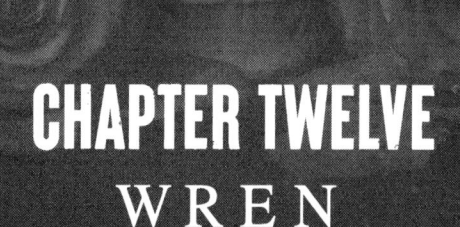

Briny ocean air mixes with the stench of death at the shipyard. The methodic slap of seawater hitting the dock cuts through the furious haze overtaking my mind. The body of one of our best informants lays at my feet in the misty midday sun, a bullet hole in his forehead and throat slit after the fact just to make a disgusting mess.

It's a clear message: *back the fuck off*.

The problem is the unknown sender. My hand flexes into a fist at my side. They know who we are, dumping the body in the shipyard near one of the fight rings we run in the shipping district.

There was no effort to conceal or dispose of him, which says that whoever did this either doesn't care or isn't afraid if we find out who did it. Neither bode well.

I glance from the remains to Penn, our jack of all tasks who called us here, to the guys. Each of their expressions match mine, grim and pissed off. It's not our first time seeing a dead body and it won't be the last.

"This is sloppy," Penn says.

He would know as our go to guy for clean up. Brooding and antisocial, he could pass as Levi's brother. His dark hair is long enough to curl over his forehead and his tall body is lean but strong. He's one of the few people we trust enough to keep close—we even paid his tuition to Thorne Point University. We came across him when his grandfather died because of us. It worked out in our favor since he turned out to be skilled at going unnoticed.

Penn is known around the city as the Reaper.

"On purpose, though," he adds. "They knew what they were doing."

Jude nods in agreement. "Shit's fucked up. As far as I know, he'd barely started putting feelers out about Hannigan like we asked."

"And someone knew it," Levi says.

"You don't think it was a crazy coincidence or that he was caught up in something we didn't know about?" Colton splits his attention between us and his tablet while he accesses the CCTV feed for the docks. "Stranger things have happened. Maybe it was a drug deal gone wrong."

Levi studies the body in a cold, detached sweep. "No. If a drug deal went south it would be multiple gunshot wounds, maybe dumping the body in the water. Rushed and frantic. Cutting someone's throat and shooting them in the head is a pointed move."

I agree with him, this is personal. It stirs my anger to the brink of snapping.

No one moves against us, but this is an open challenge to our power in this city over a missing journalist.

"I want to know what the fuck Ethan found that would create this kind of pushback for looking into it." My glare finds Colt. "Time to call Fox. We need people we can trust if bodies are going to start turning up in the goddamn street."

"Got it." He spares the body one last look before walking off.

Levi's haunting eyes meet mine. I don't need him to say it—I'm thinking it, too. I truly suspect Ethan Hannigan is dead since we haven't been able to find him.

The infuriated growl I've been holding back tears free. I stride away from Jude, Levi, and Penn. My thoughts cycle between a manic tumble of rage and a calculating assessment of the enemies we've made over the years building our thrones as the kings in this city.

We have no problem with the corruption in Thorne Point—we just want to be the ones in control of it. It's why I won't work for my father. The night belongs to us. No one is fucking taking it from me and my brothers.

If they expect a rash reaction, whoever is behind this hasn't been paying close enough attention. The person who pulled the trigger on the informant is unimportant. Someone hired for the hit, or private security with a military background who doesn't mind getting their hands dirty—it doesn't matter. What does is that now we're aware someone wants to go against us. We won't move until we can cut the head of the snake off.

The real problem is Rowan. My body goes rigid while my thoughts turn. If there's someone picking off people connected to the Crows and it's related to her brother, I can't ignore the possibility whoever this is will go after her, too. Or worse, she could stumble into this on her own. I don't trust Rowan not to get impatient and land her sexy ass in trouble.

Another feral sound rips past my lips at picturing what would happen to her if that happened.

I might not trust her, but the instinct to protect her is genuine.

Every inch of my body ripples with dangerous energy. It rattles through me, turning my breathing shallow and ragged. My knuckles crack as I slowly form a fist again. I need to let off steam.

I'm nodding before I've fully reached a decision. Colton ends his call with his foster brother and I return to the group.

"Fox got the encrypted message I sent. He'll be here in a few days," Colt says. "I got the CCTV footage and sent it to my cloud server. If they're sloppy on purpose, they want us to see the action."

"Good," I reply. "Penn, find out whatever you can about this before taking care of it. Send everything to Colton."

He nods and goes to a bag nearby. Pulling out a camera, he returns and begins documenting the scene.

Jude slings an arm over Levi's shoulders. "We'll make sure the shipyard security is seen to before they get the idea to call it in to report it." His tone turns bitter and his hazel eyes harden. "Can't have Pippa sniffing around this. She'd only add it to her case against us if she makes the connections."

"Don't worry about that. There's no evidence." Colt wiggles his fingers like he's performed a magic trick. "I wiped the footage and looped it after I sent what we need back to my system."

With that handled, we're done here. There's only one more thing to deal with.

I swipe a hand over my mouth and watch the sunlight glint off the water lapping against the rocky coastline on either side of the docks. "Pick Rowan up from the campus today."

She's involved in this now. There's no flying under the radar from whatever is coming.

Part of me has the desire to go out and find her myself, bring her to my side and keep her within my sight. I could lock her away in the penthouse I have downtown, the one I only use for the seldom business meetings I accept.

"And take her home to her apartment?" Colt clarifies. "I just checked in with my stand-in, and she's fine. Still in class for another hour." He mimes holding a gun to his head and makes a dramatic show of blowing his brains out. "Boring as fuck. That's why it was my nap lecture before Rowan detail. Then according to her texts, she's meeting up with this chick Isla after to study. She's chill."

Ignoring the roar in my blood that desires her tempting mouth, I shake my head. This isn't about that. It's for her safety, not because I'm battling how much I want to make her fucking mine. "I want eyes on her at all times, not just on campus. Bring her with you to the fight tonight."

"First she's a trespassing pest, now you want to bring her in?" Jude smirks, crossing his arms. "This girl has you in knots, man."

"Fuck off," I growl. "Just get it done. And don't let her out of your sight."

With the final authoritative word, I leave to blow off steam until tonight. I need to get close to my baseline if I have any hope of keeping my opponents alive. In my current state, I'm likely to kill them with my bare hands.

CHAPTER THIRTEEN
ROWAN

I gave Wren the weekend, but by Wednesday my annoyance returns with a vengeance. The only Crows I've seen are my permanent stalkers—Colton and Levi are everywhere, more than before. On top of making a point of eating lunch with me no matter when I end up grabbing it, they're in all of my classes and follow me all over campus. I gave up arguing with them to leave me alone after Colton proved they were on the roster for the classes. They better not be watching my apartment, too.

The one Crow bastard I want to hear from has gone radio silent and I have no way of contacting him.

Colton swears they're looking for Ethan, but he's been tight-lipped about the details. I asked him for Wren's real number, figuring he'd be the easy one to ply since he's so flirtatious and friendly, but he's harder to crack than Levi.

I touch the cheek Wren kissed, imagining the phantom warmth of his lips. For a man so hard in every other aspect, his lips are smooth. It's his tongue that's sharp enough to cut. Heat pricks the back of my neck when I picture what a tongue that lethal could do to other parts of my body. Dropping my hand, I shake my head, disappointed in myself for wishing I knew what kissing him was like.

I've stewed through the two long classes on my schedule. Now that they're done for the day, I'm meeting up with Isla on the quad. She texted five minutes ago to let me know she's waiting in our usual spot.

The late afternoon sun filters through the trees on my way there, painting the cobblestone path in dappled light. It's still early in September, but the leaves are turning shades of red, yellow, and orange. This is my favorite time of year in Maine, but my enjoyment of anything has dwindled while I worry about Ethan. Almost two more weeks have passed since I petitioned the Crows for help, creeping closer to the three month mark since I've seen or heard from him.

My phone buzzes with an incoming call in the pocket of my leather jacket. Releasing a groan, I dig it out and squeeze my eyes shut when I see it's Mom.

I hover my thumb over the accept and decline options indecisively, finally pressing answer at the last second. "Hey. Sorry, I just got out of class."

"It's okay, sweetheart. How was your day? Wednesday schedule, right—just the two classes?"

I bite the tip of my tongue. She's so great about remembering little things. Dad was forgetful, but she always had his back up to the day we terminated his life support.

My voice comes out thin when I answer. "Yup."

"I just wanted to check in. The ladies at the support group have organized a Paint and Sip party."

I gulp hard and hug an arm across my waist. It's good that she has her widows support group to lean on. I just fucking hate myself for creating that reality for her.

"Sounds great. Send me a picture of what you make."

My throat burns when she laughs, light and unburdened. If only she knew...

"It'll probably come out abstract. You know how wine goes to my head. But it sounds fun." There's a faint sound of her bracelets clinking. I can easily picture the way she always twirls her wrist when she's brushing something off. "Anyway, I just wanted to see if you heard anything from your brother yet. He still hasn't returned my calls. Is this another long work trip?"

Hot pain stings my eyes and my vision goes blurry. I clear my throat and get myself under control, reaching for a white lie like I always do with her. "Not yet. I'll tell him his days are numbered if he doesn't call you soon." The attempt at humor falls flat to my ears, the unsettling nightmare from Sunday night filling my head. "Listen, I've got to go. I'm on my way to meet up with a friend to study. Have fun painting tonight."

Mom hums. It has a bittersweet edge to it instead of her bubbly positivity. "Your dad would be so proud of you, Rowan. You know that, right? I know things were hard after the accident and all that pain resurfaced when we let him go, but look how hard you've worked to finish your degree."

The breath that rattles out of me almost knocks me to my knees. My gaze flies around to the other students on the path with me. Self-loathing slithers over me from head to toe, oily and slick.

God, I hate myself. Between seeking out help from the Crows, getting sucked into their orbit, and worrying about Ethan, I haven't thought about Dad in days.

Guilt is different when you forget about it, coming back with renewed force when it crosses your mind again.

A dark corner of my brain questions why I should think about the dead. It's the same part that whispers that I'm a monster for what I did.

"Yeah, Mom." Hopefully she doesn't hear the strain in my voice. "I know. Bye."

Because I'm a coward, I end the call before she can respond, hastily shoving my phone back into the pocket of my jacket. My knees wobble, but I keep my head on without breaking down in the middle of campus.

Thankfully the universe serves me a much needed distraction in the form of my friend waving at me from the long strip of grass in the center of the square. Other students dot the lawn, enjoying the warm afternoon. I surreptitiously swipe beneath my eyes, hoping my eyeliner and mascara haven't smeared from the tears that escaped while I was pulling myself together at the seams.

"No shadows today?" Isla asks when I reach her on the quad. I shrug, not caring. She glances around as if they're lurking behind a tree or some other edgy emo boy shit Levi would be likely to pull. "Girls' study date, then. This is nice, it's been days since I've had you to myself. Come on."

We reach the sun-warmed grass and I collapse on it before she sets up the blanket. The urge to curl into a ball and shut out the world is almost unbearable.

"I know you live in black jeans, but you can still get grass stains. Get your ass on this blanket." Isla prods me with the pointed toe of her stiletto.

I do as she says with a faint groan and sit for a moment before unpacking my notes. The words run together while I listen to her chatter.

"I love the class so much," she huffs, flipping a mass of thick chocolate wavy hair over her shoulder. "I wouldn't have to study as hard as I do now. My body knows how to move. The professor assumed I had some training, but my parents never let me do ballet. I want to switch majors and take more dance classes, but when I brought it up at the club, Dad shut me down hard. He said

I'm close to finishing undergrad, so I'm not changing the path I'm on."

"Screw your dad." I tap a pen against my notebook. "This isn't an era where men get to dictate what women do."

"He'll hold my trust fund hostage if I don't listen to him. It's his favorite way of controlling my willful whims as he likes to call them." Isla worries her plump lower lip, bright blue eyes solemn. "He said he doesn't care if I feel like I was born to dance."

"Seriously, fuck that." I reach over to squeeze her wrist. "Follow your heart, girl. Money isn't everything. Come crash on my shitty couch if it comes down to it. We'll find you a job, it'll be fine."

The sadness clears from her face, overtaken by determination. "You're right. You're so right! I love you."

She leans over to plant a kiss on my cheek and flips off a group of guys throwing a football nearby who ask if they can have one too. Settling on the blanket with a textbook, she kicks off her heels. I roll onto my stomach to keep from picking at the loose threads at the holes in my skinny jeans instead of going over my assignments.

Focusing on studying is impossible. I get through a page of planning a research paper before my mind drifts. The sense of dread from my dream keeps getting its claws in my thoughts. The lack of action on the Crows' part is only adding to my frustration. I kept up my end of our deal.

If they don't do anything, I'm taking matters into my own hands with my new lead. The note I found has to mean something.

A shadow falls over me in the late afternoon light. It doesn't move. I contemplate burrowing in the crook of my arms, but Isla nudges me.

Heaving a sigh, I look up. Colton and Levi stand over me. People on the quad are staring.

"Haven't you seen enough of me?" I snark.

"I wouldn't say no to seeing more," Colton teases. He quickly grows serious, which is enough to have me sitting up. "Unfortunately, this isn't a social call. He wants to see you."

The corners of my mouth pinch. "Wren?"

Levi flicks his dark eyes to Isla, then nods. I scrape my fingers through my tangled hair.

"You're coming with us."

Levi isn't asking. This is a summons from the asshole King Crow himself. I brush myself off as I climb to my feet. "Raincheck on studying?"

"Of course," Isla says. "I'm a little put out I'm not invited, boys. I thought we were bonding during lunch."

Levi's gaze snaps back to her.

Colton chuckles and pats him on the shoulder. "Next time, gorgeous."

I swear I hear Levi growl before he strides ahead.

"Ready?" Colton bumps his shoulder into mine.

"For what?"

"First, food. I'm starving. Then when it's time..." His crooked grin stretches in satisfaction. "A night you'll never forget."

CHAPTER FOURTEEN
WREN

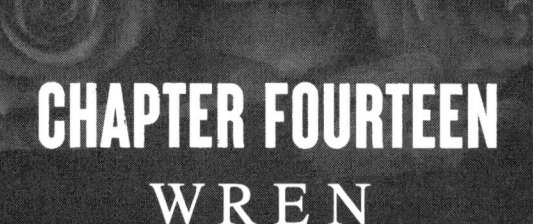

IT took hours to get myself under control. I'm still nowhere near calm, but I'm not in danger of killing whoever I fight tonight.

By the time I make it to the location, the guys are walking up with Rowan. She laughs at Colton while Jude smirks and tucks his motorcycle helmet beneath his arm. Levi shakes his head at whatever they're saying, but from a distance I can see the upward hitch at the corner of his mouth. My steps falter and I'm struck by how much Rowan looks like she fits right in with my brothers. Like she belongs amidst a group of monsters.

She's wearing tight black jeans with a wide rip in one knee, a leather jacket, and a low-cut top that matches her eyes and rides up to show off a tantalizing strip of her stomach. Her hair isn't braided today, the thick russet locks framing her face. She looks like everything I crave right now.

More than one asshole looks her way, including Colton. I nearly lose the control I worked hard to regain, overcome with the urge to show everyone admiring her who she belongs to.

I pause near the entrance to the old brick firehouse to wait for them. Word for tonight's fight only went out an hour ago, but people already stream in. Jude jerks his chin up when he spots me, leading the others over.

"You look like shit." Rowan's greeting carries a sarcastic bite that makes my blood pump faster as she rakes her eyes over me.

She can bitch at me with that attitude all she wants. I see the way her gaze lingers on the stretch of my v-neck shirt over my biceps and chest. She can't deny it.

"You don't," I counter, lifting a brow and taking her in with a slow drag of my eyes over every inch of her. "These are the rules: what you see inside doesn't leave here, don't wander off, and don't talk to anyone who isn't one of us. Understand?"

A sour expression settles on Rowan's face and she folds her arms. I want to grin because all it does is give me a better view of her cleavage. Instead, I keep her locked in my stern gaze. She should be grateful I want to protect her by keeping her close.

"You're such an uptight asshole," she mutters.

One of the guys snorts. I swipe at my lip with my thumb and entertain the idea of dragging her ass into the ring to face off with me to see how long her feistiness would hold out before I tame her. The fantasy ends with her hair in my fist and my cock plunging into her pouty mouth. Fucking tempting.

"Yes I am. Do you understand the rules?"

She throws her arms up. "Doesn't seem like I get much of a choice. You had your boys basically kidnap me and drag me all over the city."

This time I can't stop a callous grin from breaking free. "Good. You're learning."

"If I kidnapped you, you'd know it," Levi cuts in. "You came willingly."

"Can't stop the kitten when she's curious," I taunt, watching the flash of irritation flicker over her beautiful features. "Admit it."

Rowan almost lasts a full minute before grumbling under her breath. "Fine. I'm...interested to know what all the secrecy is about."

I chuckle as we head for the door. My own curiosity tugs at me, wondering if what she sees tonight will be what she imagined or if she came up with wilder theories about us.

The inside of the firehouse is converted to accommodate our needs with a platform in the center for the fight, providing the perfect view from anywhere in the room. It's filled with hazy cigarette smoke and the smell of sweat. Unlike the upper class audience we draw at the warehouse in the shipping district, tonight's attendees are mostly men, bloodthirsty and ready for all out violence.

There are no rules to regulate the fight to appease the harder audience. Survival cut down to its very core.

It was supposed to be Levi in the ring again, but I'm swapping places with him. I need it to kill the restless beast rampaging inside me for retribution before it overtakes me.

We slip through the crowd and take her to a corner of the room where she isn't likely to get in trouble. The lustful appraisals she attracts quickly become averted eyes once the men we pass meet my eyes. Levi sweeps our surroundings, always on alert for potential threat and seeking exit points.

"People are staring at us," Rowan says.

"They always do," I say.

It's what power does, draws people in like a beacon. We each command that kind of attention on our own, but when the four of us are together it's palpable in the room.

Rowan studies me like she finally sees why people fall in line around me. Coming from her, it awakens a long-dead part of myself that I haven't felt in so long, not since before my sister died.

"Isn't it awesome?" Pride colors Colton's tone. He spreads his arms. "I worked out the system. The location rotates along with the kind of attendance we draw at each one. Frat boys get your typical beer-fueled slugfest, then we've got something more traditional for those who want the thrill of walking on the dark side while they clutch their pearls. Only we know where the next match is and who it's for."

Rowan covers an amused sound with her hand over her mouth. "Honestly? After all the juicy rumors, I was expecting a cult initiation meeting. Maybe a kinky sex dungeon. A fight club is kind of a let down."

Colt's easygoing smile falls. He looks put out that she's not impressed. "It's not a fight club, it's business."

"People have been beating the shit out of each other since the dawn of time," Levi says in a gruff undertone, crossing his arms as he surveys the crowd. They're growing restless, hungry for the action to start. "It's human nature. Violence is a universal language."

"No point in going against instinct and baser urges." I do nothing to wrangle my smirk. People stir up the rumors about us and we let them run rampant because it serves a purpose for our reputations. "We work smarter, not harder than we have to."

"I was expecting something more, I don't know." She flaps a hand. "Elaborate. Like your nightclub."

"Nah, extravagance is so much work." Jude scoffs and draws her close, tucking her under his arm.

She allows it. His attention flicks to me for a moment, dropping to the fist I didn't realize I'd curled when he touched her. The curve of his mouth is the kind of devious that puts me on edge.

"This seems simple, yeah? But the most beautiful things are simple," he continues while he lights a joint. He offers her the first drag, but she shakes her head. "And simple means controlling this is easy. We can do it in our sleep and it still keeps us flush. That way we're free to get creative on the side."

Not to mention feared for the secrets we strip from our guests eager to watch a bloodbath. Some nights we charge a cover fee for entry, others they pay a secret or a favor. Just like those that want an audience with us at the Crow's Nest.

Jude and Colton keep it all vague, skirting the legality of how we operate—namely the lack thereof. In addition to the price patrons pay to play with our chaos, it's what goes on inside under the radar that's more interesting than the fight we use to distract from Jude's silver-tongued conning and Colton's hacking of any device that walks through the door. Levi and I just provide the misdirection with our fists while the real tricks go down.

"Why do this if you're all loaded?" When her question draws all four of our gazes she shrugs. "Come on, I've seen your car collection. You said as much the night I first came to you. That you don't need money. You can't tell me you're not wiping your asses with hundreds just because you can."

My explanation is bitten off. "I come from old money, but I don't touch it. Everything we have has been built for ourselves as a group."

"Wow, did I snub your ego there, big guy?" she sasses, picking up the nickname Colt likes to goad me with. A glint fills her eyes and she offers me a smile that's all teeth. "Yeah, sorry not sorry."

I don't give her the reaction she wants, but my fingers twitch with the need to wrap around her throat and squeeze for every time she challenges me.

Jude chuckles and tugs her closer beneath his arm so her side is plastered against his, shoulder to hip. "Don't be, sweetheart. It proves you can hold your own. Every guy wants that in his woman." He traces the tip of his tongue over his lip and tilts his head to look my way. It's how I know he's doing this on purpose to mess with me. "It makes things more interesting between the sheets."

Jealousy and possessiveness war for dominance, rocketing through me in a dizzying rush. My mind sears with one thing: *Rowan is fucking mine.*

It doesn't matter that I know Jude's all talk because his heart has only ever beat for Pippa since they were in high school. My mind becomes a singular force, focused only on getting him away from her.

"That's enough." Nostrils flaring, I bat his arm off Rowan's shoulder and step into her until there's no space between our bodies.

Jude slips away, but neither of us acknowledge him, too busy staring at each other. Her tits rise and fall against my chest. I want to feel them without anything between us while I fuck her until she screams.

Rowan's chin lifts in defiance, but something inviting in her eyes hooks into my chest. "Is that what you like, big guy?" Her tone turns softer, lilting with suggestion as she rests her hands on my shoulders and presses closer. "Does it make your dick hard when you picture fighting with me?"

My hands find her hips and my head dips. The room bleeds away until all I can concentrate on is her. That enticing strip of skin between the bottom of her shirt and her jeans is warm under my thumbs.

"See," Jude interjects slyly. "Gets him all riled up."

"New venture idea," Colton adds in a bright tone. "Let's open an OnlyFans and film them hate fucking. We'll make bank. I'm chubbing up just from watching this."

"Shut up," I growl at them without tearing my focus from her. "This isn't why I brought you here."

The playful glimmer in her eyes fades and hardens. "Technically, they brought me here." She darts a look at my friends before leaning in, rising on tiptoes to murmur in my ear. "And I think you're afraid. You pull back every time. All that big dick energy, and for what?"

My lip curls back from my teeth and my fingers dig into her. It would be so easy to shred my control and claim her as mine.

A seductive, amused sound bubbles out of her and she grips the material of my shirt, tugging in retaliation. She fucking likes this. There's nothing demure about her. If we came together it would be a turbulent crash of lust.

"It's time." Levi's interruption brings me back from the brink of snapping.

I'm dangerously close to the line as I do exactly what she accused me of—pulling away. At first I thought I could remain indifferent around her. She doesn't matter. *Shouldn't* matter to me. But she infuriates me and turns me on every time she parts those lush goddamn lips.

I don't only want to fight and tame Rowan. I want to fucking consume her. Own every fucking inch of her, body and soul until the truth is burned into her.

Her eyes bore into mine as I step back, the triumph of being right written all over her face. She thinks she won. I blow out a breath and rake my fingers through my hair.

"Don't let her wander." I meet each of my brothers' gazes. Before I walk away, I issue one last command for Rowan. "And you? Don't take your eyes off me."

"Go get 'em, killer," Jude calls.

I flip him off without turning back. The crowd parts for me automatically. When I reach the raised platform at the center of the room, I rip off my t-shirt. Tossing it aside, I leave the barbell piercing in my nipple. My boots come off next while my opponent—a big burly fuck covered in tattoos—climbs onto the platform.

A chorus of shouts and cheers sound from the rowdy spectators. They press in on all sides to get as close as possible to the promise of violence.

There are no rules here. Only bloodshed.

My mouth stretches into a sick grin and I crack my neck. The guy I'm fighting squares off, sizing me up. I can feel Rowan's gaze on me from across the room and anticipation buzzes along my skin.

There's no starting signal. We lunge for each other at the same time. I shift my stance and avoid the punch he throws. My elbow drives into his lower back, jabbing his kidney. The guy grunts and grabs my hair. Shouts fill the room as I get my leg around his knee and knock his balance off. While he's distracted, I sink a fist into his gut and shove hard when he releases his grip on me.

Standing over him, I swipe the back of my hand over my mouth. I plan to stomp on him, but he rolls and springs to his feet with a surprising amount of spryness for a man of his size. The pattern repeats—circle, look for openings, collide with fists. We're evenly matched, trading blows while the audience shouts their wild commentary.

The release I was seeking is heady. I filter all my rage at someone messing with us and all my frustrated desire for Rowan into the fight. In a quick move, I grab his arm and twist, using my leverage against him.

The snap of bone makes me laugh. He chokes on his cry of pain, bringing his broken wrist in close to guard it. His eyes are wild as he evades me. I'm toying with him because I thrive on this. The desperation. I love to see how someone breaks. What pushes them when they're closed in.

Knowing Rowan is watching makes me much more heartless than usual. I'm actually invested in the outcome. I want to win tonight.

Grinning, I wave my opponent, baiting him. "Come on. Let's go."

She asked for monsters? I'll show her one.

CHAPTER FIFTEEN
ROWAN

The energy in the building is violent and chaotic. My heart pounds in my chest, skin tingling with rising adrenaline. Blood sprays in the makeshift ring when Wren throws a punch that catches the other fighter across the cheek. Watching his vicious attack against the other guy is turning me on.

Taking my eyes off Wren is impossible. I follow every flex of his muscles with a growing hunger. My nipples have tightened to hard buds and I'm unable to stop myself from shifting to rub my thighs together to alleviate the ache of want. Fuck, my imagination runs wild with desire. If he jumped from the ring and kissed me, I wouldn't stop him, no matter how much I hate his controlling nature—I'd welcome it.

Wren is merciless against his opponent. Lethal. Hot as fuck with that pierced nipple.

Between the tense moment with me before he stepped in the ring and the depravity of his ruthless grace, my panties are so soaked I feel it when I move.

The tattoos I've only glimpsed before are on full display, rippling with each powerful movement of his body. The crow wearing a crown covers his shoulder blades, wings spread wide while it perches on a skull. A scroll with gothic lettering I can't read from here wraps around the design. Thorny roses twisted with crowns and feathers creep down his forearms and onto the backs of his hands. On one arm, the black roses are engulfed in fire. On the other, white ones are spattered with blood.

My breath hitches when our eyes meet while he brutalizes his opponent. I clench my thighs together and lick my lips at the savage way he grins at me before hitting the guy again.

"Ooh, damn." Colton winces. "He didn't come to play tonight."

"Is it always like this?" I ask. "He's not going to kill him is he?"

Levi's brooding voice answers from behind me where he leans against the wall. "He's drawing it out. Playing with his food."

"When he's in a bad mood, it's like this," Colton says.

That still leaves my question unanswered. Do I want to know? Does it change anything if he's capable of killing someone?

Who am I to judge when I'm capable of the same thing?

Feeling short of breath, I rip a hair tie from my wrist and scrape my hair into a ponytail. The cool air on the back of my neck doesn't help the flush spreading across my whole body. God, I'm practically panting after the asshole in the ring who has been nothing but a dick to me.

Yet I can't stop myself from baiting him. Something about his dark callousness calls to a part of me I keep locked deep inside. There's no denying anymore that I want to ride his big dick despite how much he pisses me off.

"Here. You look like you might be thirsty." Jude interrupts my horny on main mental spiral, returning from wherever he disappeared to and offers me a cool beer.

My face prickles at the teasing innuendo. I'm not just thirsty watching Wren, I'm parched in the middle of a desert. "Thanks."

The corner of his mouth tugs up. I thumb the label, appreciating that he gave me an unopened one. He takes out a set of keys and pops the cap for me. I study him as he takes a pull from his own drink.

Colton and Levi I'm beginning to understand from spending so much time around them, but I don't really know what his deal is. This is the longest I've been with him since the night I snuck around outside the Crow's Nest when they all hunted me in the maze. Jude doesn't carry himself like the others. It's in the way he watches people, as if he's looking for his best in.

"What's your deal?"

"My deal?" Jude picks at the label on his bottle and smirks. "Trying to figure me out?"

"I guess. Wren's clearly the take charge or else guy. Levi's the edgy one. Colton's the jokester. But you I can't really figure out."

The curve of his mouth is enigmatic. "That's the way I like it."

"You're the same age as Wren?" I guess since I haven't seen him around campus at all.

Jude nods, glancing at Colton and Levi. "Lev and I are a little closer. We're both twenty-two. Wren's twenty-three. We were a year ahead of them in high school at Thorne Point Academy."

"Private school." My nose wrinkles. "Typical."

"For them, maybe." An unreadable look clouds his handsome golden brown eyes for a moment.

"But you went there with them."

"Scholarship student." His piercing gaze finds mine. "It's a little different for us, isn't it?"

I roll my lips between my teeth, understanding what he means. If I didn't have my grants, I wouldn't be at Thorne Point University.

"So you all know each other from when you were teenagers."

"Yeah. They've known each other longer since their families run in the same social circles, but when we became friends in high school we stuck together."

Jude is friendly as we continue to talk. He manages to effortlessly get more details about my life out of me than I learn about him. All he tells me about his family is his grandmother. His down to earth nature reminds me of Colton, but he allows flashes of the darkness lurking behind his charming smiles to creep through.

A feral yell from Wren snaps my attention back to the ring in time to see him deal the final blow. The huge guy he's been fighting staggers, then collapses in a heap. The entire room erupts with a cacophony of cheers and yelling. Some look enraged that the guy they bet on lost while others have a contact high from being surrounded by the intense violence.

"And that's our cue." Colton takes my hand and nods to a door nearby. "The back way's easier to get out."

"We're leaving? What about—?" I gesture to Wren standing victorious on the platform over his knocked out opponent, body glistening with sweat and blood that isn't his, shoulders heaving with his ragged panting.

"He won't be far behind. After a fight he needs a minute to himself." He waggles his eyebrows. "Come on, I get to show you our own personal Bat Cave. It fucking rules. I'd move there permanently if I could get away with it."

"What the hell?" I laugh and allow Colton to lead me through the back exit into the chilly night.

After being inside the humid room surrounded by sweaty people, a shiver runs down my spine. Levi and Jude are right behind us. We head for the blacked out Escalade Levi drove and Jude swings a leg over his bike.

As we pull away, I twist to peer at the firehouse, wondering about Wren's headspace after a fight. The curious part of me that's drawn to dangerous things wishes I could get up close and personal with him like that.

* * *

Colton wasn't joking about the cave thing. Beneath the Crow's Nest, they have a basement that's badass and screams vigilante justice. I feel as if I've pulled back the top layer of the mysterious front they put on to get a look inside, but all I have are more questions about who the hell these guys are.

"So is this where you take all your kidnapping victims to lock them away and have your wicked way with them?" I ask as I explore the main room, skimming my fingertips over the black leather couches.

Levi grunts from the couch and flicks his lip ring with his tongue. "Again, you came willingly. Eagerly, even."

Jude collapses next to him, combing his fingers through his shiny dark hair, offering me a sinister promise. "And now we'll never let you leave."

I spin to face him, ready to give him a piece of my mind. The expression on his face makes me relax. He's only teasing me. It's hard to tell what he means when he speaks so confidently that I'm baited into believing whatever comes out of his mouth.

Without the body heat from the crowd at the firehouse, I'm cold again. I pull my ponytail out and let my hair cascade around my shoulders.

"Let me show you my setup." Colton almost bounces on his feet with excitement like a kid, leading me to the wall of computer monitors. He taps a few keys and pulls up security feeds showing different parts of the desolate hotel. He points to a view of the terrace outside where they chased me the night I snuck around. "Good times, right?"

I eye him skeptically. "Yeah, sure. Fan-fucking-tastic."

"I've got the feed from that night recorded. Want to see?"

"Do I want to watch a bunch of cocky assholes herd me through their creepy hedge maze? Pass, dude."

"Fair." He takes me by the shoulders and shuffles me over, standing behind me. His fingers move quickly across his wireless keyboard. Encrypted computer code fills the screen. "And this is my baby."

"What am I looking at?"

"My own network. They're hackers like me. Well, beneath me. No one's as good as I am. That's why I'm their wicked king." His laughter puffs over my cheek. "This is how we're going to find your brother. I swear to you, we will."

"Really?" I bite my lip as an unexpected wave of emotion hits me. "It seemed like you guys didn't really care about me or Ethan."

"Maybe not at first, but now? You're in with us, baby." He gives my shoulders an affectionate one-armed hug from behind.

"Does that mean I get a matching BFF tattoo?" Smirking, I turn to flick his neck where his crow is inked.

Wren has one on his back. Colton's is an exact match. I'm betting Levi and Jude have the same art as well.

"Matching ink is sexy." His mischievous green eyes become hooded as he cups my face, thumb brushing my cheek. "I like having you here. You're really fun to be around."

"You're not so bad either. Still could do without the stalking."

Colton is handsome, but I'm not attracted to him. Not in the same way being around Wren tugs at something deep and molten in my belly.

Still, I don't pull away when he leans in, curiosity keeping me in place. If Jude or Levi pulled this, I'd shut it down immediately, but I don't feel like he wants to pressure me, moving slowly as if he's waiting for something. He likes testing limits. I've learned that much about him and feel like we have that in common.

Colton's lips barely ghost against mine before he's ripped away from me. A massive frame of muscle stands between us and I smell Wren's crisp aftershave. I touch my mouth, amused by this whole thing.

"The fuck is going on?" Wren snaps. He's freshly showered, the heat of it still clinging to his body. "I tell you to bring her back here and find you about to make out with her?"

"We didn't even fully kiss before you shoved yourself into this like he stole your toy. It was hardly making out. More like an affectionate thing between friends." I lean around Wren to meet Colton's eyes. "That's all we are—friends. And not the kind with benefits."

He laughs wryly and ducks his head. "Yeah, babe. Got it. Won't happen again."

Wren releases a rough sound and whirls to me. He pins me to the wall next to the computer screens and my heartbeat skips with a flutter of excitement. This feeling is what was missing with Colton. The veins in Wren's forearms are prominent and his jaw tics from how tight it's clenched. I feel every hard inch of him when he presses into me from his pierced nipple to his cock.

Pulse speeding up, I lick my lips and squint at him. "You got something to say?"

"Leave, Colt. Everyone get the fuck out," he barks, blue eyes locked on mine. "Now!"

I'm vaguely aware of Colton backing away with his hands raised in surrender, smothering his amusement. "Relax. Jude said you needed a push was all. If you're ever open to some fun together, hit me up though.

I'm definitely down for that party."

At Wren's possessive growl, he leaves. The room is empty except for us and Wren's giant ego.

My teeth rake over my lip. "What's wrong, don't play well with others?" I must have a death wish to keep taunting him, but I can't stop the words from spilling free. "It must suck to want what you won't let yourself have."

He takes my wrists and presses them to the wall on either side of me. "If it's something I want, I'll take it."

"Yeah? I'm not stopping you." There's no space between us and the air is thick with tension. "Like I said, you're all fucking talk. We've been here before. Is it going to be the same song and dance this time? I'm getting sick of the melody."

His grip flexes, sending a thrill down my spine. Heat pulses between my legs, but if I squirm he'll win this unspoken thing between us. Releasing one of my wrists, his large hand grasps my jaw to tip my head up, focus zeroed in on my mouth.

Fuck it, I'm doing what I want.

"Kiss me," I order.

Wren groans and his mouth crashes over mine, hot and demanding as he devours me. The kiss is an all consuming tempest. It makes my heart race as we claw at each other.

He rips my leather jacket off, discarding it without care as he greedily roams his hands over my tight camisole, squeezing my breasts through the thin bra beneath. I shudder from the rush of cool air over my flushed skin. One strong arm winds around my waist to tug me closer against his firm body so there's no escape from his seductive kiss. I wouldn't want to—it's too good.

When it ends, I'm already craving tasting his mouth a second time. My entire body is burning up and we're both panting.

"Let me make one thing crystal clear to you," he rasps in a gritty tone against my swollen lips. "You're mine. This mouth?" The pad of his thumb traces my bottom lip. "Mine. You kiss no one else but me. Your body? Also mine. Every inch of you." He leans back in, his words a fiery growl across my skin. "Fucking *mine*."

I swallow thickly. I've never been so turned on in my life. My head is dizzy with the fog of lust, but I can't let him win that easily.

"If I'm yours, then prove it," I whisper before biting his lip. "Or is a kiss all you're good for?"

A dangerous, predatory rumble leaves him and he plunges his hand into the waistband of my jeans, yanking. My stomach bottoms out at the rough feel of his fingers mere inches from where my pussy is aching for him to touch me. I'm so close to the edge he could send me over with barely any pressure.

"A kiss is only the beginning, kitten. I would've taken it from you whether you wanted me to or not. Just like I'll take everything else. I've staked my claim on you now, and I'm a greedy bastard." He grazes my cheek with his teeth. "There's no turning back."

With that promise, he pops the button on my jeans and shoves them down to mid-thigh. His mouth curves and he snaps the bikini strap of my thong before bending to toss me over his shoulder. I yelp, gripping the material of his shirt. His palm comes down on my ass, the clap of his skin on mine ringing out. I squirm at the excited arousal that rushes through me as he grabs a handful of one cheek.

"I'm going to enjoy this," he says in a smoky tone that gets me hot.

"What are you—?" I don't finish my question before my back hits the leather couch cushions where he deposits me.

Wren admires me spread out for a moment before he braces over me, stealing another swift kiss. It's over before I want it to be, but his lips feel so good dragging down my neck, over the tops of my breasts. He pauses to bite my nipple through my top and thin bra and I cry out, wrapping my arms around his head.

A quick smack to my throbbing pussy through my panties almost makes me sit upright, startling me and ripping a moan from me.

"Fuck!"

He pinches my clit and I hiss, back arching. His voice is deep and sinful. "Better be quiet. Or don't. Let them hear me ruin you."

When he rubs my pussy firmly with the entire heel of his hand, I scrape my nails against the leather and whisper, "Oh my god."

"So responsive," he mutters while he plays with my folds and teases my clit through my underwear. I bite my lip to muffle my cries while I rock against his fingers for more, wishing he'd rip off my thong already. "I like you like this. My needy little kitten. Fuck, you're sexy."

The sharpness of his teeth high on my thigh near where I'm growing desperate from him is a shock of pain that makes me moan again. I'm so close to coming and he's barely touched me.

"Like it like that?" Wren chuckles and sucks at the sting his teeth left behind while petting my pussy through the thong. "Your panties are drenched. Yeah, I'm going to take great pleasure in marking your body as mine."

I slam my eyes shut as the arousal intensifies and a relieved noise flies free when he finally peels my panties down. He doesn't touch me right away and I squirm in the hope he'll give me what I want. When I open my eyes, I find him staring at me with the hungry look of a predator.

"All fucking mine," he growls.

The possessiveness twists my insides up.

Wren maneuvers my legs so they're spread as far as they can be while trapped by my jeans, but he's too impatient to take them off. He buries his face between my legs and the first stroke of his tongue on my clit tears my breath from me.

"Oh shit, shit," I whimper. "I'm going to come. Use your fingers, I want to feel them in me."

The vibration of his laughter against my swollen folds is almost too much stimulation. A couple of tears leak from the corners of my eyes. His mouth is perfect, tormenting my pussy with his skilled tongue. He obliges my pleading request, gliding two fingers through my slick folds and sinking them in me with little resistance from how wet I am.

Jesus. He doesn't wait for me to adjust, pumping his thick fingers insistently. If that's the size of his fingers, my brain goes hazy with want at the thought of how big his cock will feel. The heat builds with intensity, my stomach tightening when he sucks hard on my clit.

"You taste so goddamn divine."

The sensation of him speaking against me has my hips bucking up. He curls his fingers deep inside me and I grab his head for something to hold on to as I tip over the edge into ecstasy.

Wren groans against my pussy. He keeps devouring me with his tongue and fingers, allowing me to grind on his face while I ride out the shocks of my orgasm. I'm trembling all over by the time I nudge him away from my oversensitive body.

"Holy shit," I mumble deliriously.

The clink of a belt and a grunt from him draws me out of the haze settling over me from coming so hard. His cock is out and my eyes widen.

Okay. The big dick energy is warranted.

I lick my lips and his eyes gleam as he looms over me stroking himself. Reaching down, he thumbs my lip.

"Open up for me, Rowan." He watches intently when I open my mouth and lick his thumb. "Fuck, little kitten. *Fuck.*"

His cock bumps against my lips and I suck on the tip while his fist pumps. A tortured sound punches out of him and his come fills my mouth. He pushes deeper into my mouth, grasping my face. I hold his hooded gaze and swallow.

"Take it," Wren rasps. "Take it all, baby."

Warmth spreads over my chest and up my neck. I suck his dick until he nearly tips over the couch, catching himself at the last minute by bracing a hand on the armrest above my head. After he catches his breath, he straightens and tucks himself back in his pants.

Sitting up, I wriggle my panties and jeans back on and run my fingers through the tangles in my hair. It's probably a hot mess after he had me writhing around. My limbs are languid, relaxed in a way I haven't been in months. Part of me can't believe that just happened. Another part of me is blissed out on the catharsis of submitting to him.

"Come here," he demands, tugging me to him.

Wren sinks his fingers into my hair and his lips collide with mine. I hold on to his strong arms and press closer. The taste of both of us mingles together on our tongues. It's sensual and slow, but no less ravenous than the first time.

He kisses as he approaches everything else—with power and control, expecting no resistance.

When we part, my eyes flutter open and find myself pinned by his arctic blue eyes. The slow, devilish smile he gives me promises to drive me wild. A thrill shoots through me at the thought.

For the first time since the car accident that sealed my dad's fate, I don't shove away the darkest part of my heart. With Wren, I feel like I could embrace it.

CHAPTER SIXTEEN
WREN

Taking Rowan to her apartment after I made her mine was an irritating necessity so I didn't drown myself in her distracting body. And so I didn't take her home. Not to the penthouse, but where I actually live. Only three other people know where my place is—my best friends. I might covet Rowan's body and want to keep her safe, but I still don't trust her.

I haven't wanted a woman in my bed more than once ever in my life, but with her all I can think of is the next time. We almost made it to round two parked in front of her shithole apartment building with her grinding on my lap and my hand buried down the back of her jeans to grab her divine ass as we kissed. The thought of it alone makes my dick hard.

It's been two days. I've forced myself to stay away, unsettled by how many rules I'm willing to break for her. How much I might let her in if I'm not careful. In that time at least one person has kept watch over her round the clock. We're protecting her, though she doesn't know it yet.

While I've managed to keep away, I haven't been out of contact with her. My knees spread wider as I sink deeper into the cushions of the couch at the Nest, scrolling through our message history. She texts like she talks—a million individual messages for each thought as they occur to her instead of taking the time to type it all out at once. Three more messages come through back to back and the corner of my mouth tugs up as my heart does a funny little squeeze.

It's strange that she can cause this reaction. The damn thing's been dead in the water since my sister died. There's something about her my heart recognizes, something that makes her impossible to ignore.

"Son of a bitch—got me again, you elusive temptress," Colt grumbles at his computer. Another online poker game is up on one of the monitors. "Someday I'll get you, my queen."

We're sitting around waiting for Fox to arrive. Doing nothing is making me restless, but Levi barred me from hitting the gym again today so I don't injure myself.

"That Q chick kick your ass again?" Jude smirks from the couch across from me. "How much money did she swindle you out of this time? You're off your game if you can't distract her from winning by flirting. It's like I've taught you nothing."

Colton groans and slumps over the desk. "Queen_Q doesn't accept DMs, ever. Trust me, bro, I've tried everything. I can't trace her IP, either—she masks it." He glares at the screen. "I can't believe she evades me. I can't recruit her to my network and I can't get the message to her that I'm ready to lock it down and Wifey her ass because I'm half in love with her."

"Only half?" I mutter wryly.

"Shut up." Colt sighs, stroking the bank of screens mounted on the wall lovingly. "Someday I'll find you, sweetness. Then it's game over because I'm making you mine."

Levi's head jerks with his snort. "You're a twisted little fuck, you know that?"

Colt spins around in his gamer chair to grant us with a psychotic grin. "Coming from the notorious and terrifying *Leviathan*, that's saying a lot."

Levi growls. "I told you not to call me that."

"Why not?" Colt's mouth stretches wider as he tips forward. "It's your real name. That's why it's hilarious you picked it as your nightmare fuel alias. Man, I wish I could've told Ro and Isla that day they were talking about sea creatures. The truth is so much funnier."

"Fuck you," Levi seethes. "My name is Levi, not that shit my parents decided."

"Enough," I bark.

Colt's expression shifts from deviant to downright unhinged as he turns to me. "What's wrong, big guy, not getting your dick wet yet? You're so uptight."

The growl I release doesn't warn him off. I explode to my feet, swiping the knife in Levi's hands, and grab Colt by the collar of his Henley shirt as I pin him to the same wall where I first kissed Rowan two nights ago. The blade presses into the column of his throat just shy of nicking the skin.

"You want to repeat that?" My words come out low and threatening.

We might all be brothers, but sometimes we butt heads when the joking crosses a line. It's what happens when a bunch of insane bastards who feel everything so intensely spend all our time together. We'd die for each other, but we're also willing to fight each other.

If you can't hold your friends at knifepoint from time to time when they piss you off, are you even friends?

Unrepentant mischief flashes in Colton's green eyes and he holds his hands up. "Easy, man. I'm just messing around."

My jaw clenches. "When aren't you?"

Blowing out a breath, I pull away, tossing Levi the knife. He catches it deftly, arching a brow at me.

The pissing contest ends when a sensor pings on Colton's computer. Unbothered by my actions, he plants a hand on the desk and presses a sequence of keys to bring up the security feed. A chuckle rolls through him.

"Foxy's home."

Fox Wilder and the girl with him take the entrance from the terrace that leads to our secret doorway. Minutes later, they arrive in the main room. Fox cuts an imposing figure in a leather jacket, rugged and brawny with scars on his knuckles. He swipes tousled brown hair out of stormy blue eyes that soften when he meets Maisy's kind hazel ones. She's his opposite in every way—light brown hair pulled into a ponytail, bundled in a bright multicolored knit poncho over workout leggings, and exuding a languidness like she's found a secret zen in life.

Colton drags Fox into a hug first, then Maisy. Out of all of us, he's closest with his foster brother and his girl, keeping in regular contact after Fox left. The rest of us have only met Maisy a handful of times over the phone. When Colt allows her room to breathe, he snatches her left hand and examines the ring on her finger from all angles. Twisted pieces of gold and silver metal are shaped like a daisy holding a purple crystal and polished sea glass.

"Look at you, Foxy, being all perfect for your flower girl making this," Colt says warmly. "Has my mom seen this yet? She'll die and think it's your best creation yet."

Fox grunts, peeling out of his leather jacket. He bumps his fist against Levi's and nods to Jude. It's the first time he's been back in Thorne Point since he left to enact his revenge plan two years ago. Maisy and Fox went to live in

California last year to make a new home rather than returning to the darkness of Thorne Point. He's grown up in that time, his savage anger easing.

"I think it is, too." Maisy holds up the ring and wiggles her fingers. "By the way, thanks for interrupting the moment, dick." She fake punches Colt's arm. "You owe me big time. And I'm not doing any yoga sessions with you."

Colton pouts. "But I'm still trying to get my crow pose down. What kind of hot yoga instructor refuses to teach her student? Porn has lied to me." A clever look crosses his face. "Make me your Man of Honor, I'll make it up to you."

"Quit flirting, asshole," Fox grumbles, wrapping an arm around Maisy's waist and tugging her back against his chest.

"Can you guys believe the baby of the family is getting married first before all his big brothers?" Colton acts like he's wiping a tear. "He's all grown up and leaving the nest."

Laughing, Maisy absently strokes Fox's wrist. "You can't anyway. You know Thea's my Maid of Honor. We decided in seventh grade."

Colt hums, eyes hooding. "Bishop's little cutie. The redhead."

When we were hunting for my sister's predator and found him in Colorado, Colt tracked his movements through a cocky computer genius with a penchant for blackmail who was suspicious his teacher wasn't who he said he was. He was right. With his help, we were able to get the bastard. Colton has stayed in touch with the guy and his group of friends.

"Connor's *wife*," Maisy corrects with a sly smirk, pulling out her phone. "I'm totally telling him you said that. Devlin, Lucas, and I had a bet. Thanks for the fifty bucks you just won me. Expect a cyber attack in the near future."

"Tell him he can bring it, but he'll never beat me." Colton laces his fingers together and cracks them as he stretches his arms overhead. "I love pissing that guy off with clickjacking attacks when he least expects it. Especially since he keeps refusing my offers of recruitment."

I clear my throat and everyone grows serious, remembering the real reason we called Fox here.

Without missing a beat, Colt pats Fox on the shoulder on his way back to the computer. "You're both staying with me while you're here—no arguments. We'll get drunk later to celebrate the good news." He collapses into his chair and pulls up feeds from the CCTV at the shipyard. "Nelson rolled up after the morning rush at the docks died down, just like usual. See how he looks around and puts his hat on that hook? It's like he thought he was meeting one of us. Someone could have spoofed my encrypted signature or masked it so it seemed it was coming from one of the numbers we use to contact him."

"Shit," I grit out, blood running cold. We've met Nelson at that exact spot before. "They've been watching close. Too closely to know how to call him there and make him believe it was to see someone for Crow business."

"Right?" Colt grimaces and waves at the screen. "And they'd have to be really fucking good to do it. I think he figured that out about the time this dude rolls up and gets in his face."

The man is bulky, stomping across the frame in heavy boots. He flicks a cigarette butt aside and grabs Nelson by the front of his hoodie. The aggression increases when Nelson shakes his head, keeping his mouth shut.

"Why don't you go check out the gym?" Fox runs a hand down Maisy's arm. "You can call everyone and let them know we got in okay."

She squints at him. "What did I say? Together, or not at all. You're not hiding this part of yourself from me."

He sighs and kisses her temple. It's a marked difference in the angry punk who first arrived in Thorne Point when he was fifteen.

"I don't want you to trigger any bad memories about when you were taken," he murmurs to her.

She smiles and cups the back of his head, tugging him to lean down for a tender kiss. "Me and you."

"Yeah," he says gruffly.

We all watch the rest of the CCTV feed play out, ending with our informant's demise. Emptiness expands in my chest as we watch the man shove Nelson away. He draws a gun and shoots him point blank, then carves up his throat. He hardly waits for our guy to take his last breath before he strides off. Colt switches up the footage, showing another angle where the bulky man gets in an SUV with a phone pressed to his ear and drives off.

Fox goes closer to Colton to watch the footage loop from the beginning. "Traceable?"

"Yeah, after some tricky traffic camera hopping on my part."

"Pippa will love that if she finds out," Jude says.

Colt waves him off. "I covered my tracks." He clicks to another window. "This is where it led to."

A dilapidated warehouse on the other side of the city fills the screen. We never go to that area because the prime real estate that's useful to us is closer to the docks rather than up by the cliffs.

"Holy shit, seriously?" Maisy nudges Fox aside, eyes wide. "It's the same. I'll never forget that logo."

On the side of the building the man enters, SynCom is painted in bold black letters. The corners of my mouth turn down. Who the fuck has come to our city and why don't we know about it?

"The shell company Stalenko Corp used to buy out Nexus Lab," Fox says. "The one they use to pull all the strings on their drug ring."

"The chatter in hacker circles on the web about Stalenko's rumored Russian bratva ties died down after what went down in Ridgeview when you blew the whistle on the whole thing." Colt pulls an unhappy face.

"Question is—what have they been doing since then? My guess is they're employing someone as good as I am to keep a low profile so there's no repeat from before."

"Or someone helped them lick their wounds," Jude says. "If they couldn't keep their cash flow going without supply to sell to buyers, someone had to step in."

"How long have their operations been active here?" Levi asks.

"At least a year," Maisy says. "That's how long it's been since the Nexus Lab CEO—my mom—was sent to jail."

"Could be as long as a decade, though." Fox scrubs a hand over his face. "We know they were staging their takeover of the pharmaceutical company back when we were kids and both our parents worked in research. Her mom was willing to take the bribe and accepted the position they wanted to give her." A conflicted look crosses his face. "Mine..."

Maisy takes his hand. "These people are criminals and killers."

I almost bark out a cynical laugh because so are we on a good day. "So they thought they could just pick up the pieces and establish the supply for their drug ring here? I don't think so."

"Did you bring that flash drive Ethan gave you?" Colt asks.

Fox hands it over. "When we saw him last before all the shit went down he said he was heading back east to follow this trail he first found working undercover in the internal records department to continue his investigation on the corruption. I think he was going after the shell company next to build the story he was working on about others tied to it all—politicians and other businesses. He called it a network."

"That fits the description of almost every prominent person in this city," I say.

Jude rubs the back of his neck. "Discovering the twisted secrets of a company owned by a shell as a front for a mafia organization is one thing, but digging deeper to expose them is even more dangerous. The risk doesn't seem worth whatever national renown he could garner for breaking the story."

"When we met him he said this was just one piece of his story. He wanted the whole thing." Maisy casts her worried gaze at the floor. "Is he... Do you think they—?"

"We don't know," Levi says. "But it's likely."

Despite knowing it's the most probable outcome, thinking of Rowan finding that truth out sends a slimy lurch through my gut.

It's the same thing I felt when I discovered what Charlotte had done to herself. I was coming home from campus to surprise her for the weekend. I'm the one that found her. If I can keep Rowan from experiencing that, I'll do everything in my power to protect her from it.

"Let's scope this place out tonight," I say. "We'll find out who we're dealing with and find Ethan."

"Damn, I left all my good stakeout outfits at home since we left on such short notice," Maisy says.

"You're not coming," I say archly.

She gives me a once over and smirks. "Yeah, I am."

Great. Another one just like Rowan.

I fold my arms. "Then you stay in the car. If I think you're going to sneak off, I'll handcuff you so you stay put."

"Kinky." Maisy shrugs. "Fox gets final say on whether we invite people to play with us."

Jude releases a startled laugh and elbows Fox. "I can see why your revenge plan ended up with her stealing your heart instead."

"Nah." Maisy wraps her arms around Fox. "He's my best friend. Our hearts never forgot it."

Ignoring them while they joke around, I study the information on the screen. "Meet back here by nine."

I will not have a mob dealing drugs in this city without it going through us first. Drug running is messy and rife with screw ups. It threatens the careful status quo my brothers and I have established. If this Russian bratva group was crippled by what happened in Colorado, they must have friends in high places here. I want to know who is involved.

* * *

Later that night, we arrive at the warehouse in two separate blacked out SUVs, parking in a discreet spot. The cliffs at this side of the city curve to follow the coastline, providing a view of Thorne Point's downtown lit up at night. Sea air whips around us, making the tall trees in the woods behind the buildings at the city limits creak as they sway.

Colt runs a check for any on site security before he gives us the all clear. We gather at the back of one of the cars, decked out in the same gear we used to apprehend the frat boy from campus.

"Surveillance only," I remind everyone in a muted commanding tone. "No moves until we know who to take out at the knees."

Jude and Colton grant me twin vicious smiles before Colt unpacks his drones. They're small and almost undetectable from how silently they fly. Once he's set up to operate them, he pops open a small case with sets of earbuds. We each grab a pair to keep in contact on the private radio frequency while we look around.

"Take these too." Colt offers a set of tactical binoculars from the supplies and tech he brought with him to Levi. "I know you like to pretend you're like the Dark Knight and shit, but Batman still needed gadgets to see at night. No one naturally has night vision."

Levi rolls his eyes, but accepts the binoculars.

"This looks like even less security than they kept back in Colorado," Fox says. "Either they feel comfortable out here or they think they have protection."

"Then we all need to stay alert," I say.

Before we split up, Colt's drones take to the air. I nod to Jude and Colton, then head to one side of the warehouse with Levi.

A fence separates the wide parking lot from the jagged edge of the cliffs, but it's not completely closed off. The windows on the building are smudged and dusty. One of the lights is on inside toward the back.

The place seems deserted and out of use otherwise. Perhaps by design so anyone who might happen to come out here would think nothing of a nondescript run down building at the edge of the city and move along.

"Uh oh." Colt's voice is a mumble in my earbud.

My gaze shoots around, but I don't see anything amiss on this side of the property. "What?"

"I'm by their dumpsters. I found a broken pair of glasses that look like the same ones Hannigan had on in the photos I pulled when I did the initial search on him. He was here."

I exchange a tense look with Levi.

Plunging my hand into my pocket, I grip Charlotte's locket. The shape of the heart bites into my palm, making it ache from how hard I clutch it. Shadows cloud my mind, putting me right back to the day I found my sister's dead body. Taking a jagged breath, I force it all back behind the numbness and anger that fight for dominance every day. Always one or the other. I've only felt flashes of something more when I'm distracted by Rowan's presence.

"You good?" Levi asks.

Instead of answering him, I address Colton. "Any other signs of him?

Can you tell if anyone's inside? They could be keeping him here."

It's what we would do if we found someone like Ethan infiltrating our businesses to expose the information he found. If they decided he wasn't worth keeping alive, well...they picked a prime location. The high cliffs and expansive woods both make it easy to dump a body.

"Give me five to find an entry point. I'm working on the fly here."

"I could go around front and provide a distraction if anyone's home," Jude offers.

"No. I don't want to tip them off if they've been watching us without making us aware of them," I say.

We wait while Colton takes his drones around the building. Unease ties my stomach in knots. I can't kick the bad feeling.

"No dice on entry, but I got close enough to the windows for a visual." His sigh makes my shoulders tighten. "If he was here, he's gone now. There's some evidence of someone being held in a room on this side. Metal rings are cemented to the wall and a lump that might be a mattress. I doubt the dude left his cracked glasses here on purpose."

"Right." Exhaling, I glare at the building.

Fuck. I'm going to have to tell Rowan about this. If I do...

The thought of her face crumbling sends a lance of pain into my heart. I shake my head. Not yet. First I'll do what I said I would—find him. I won't give her false hope and stand by while she walks the same dark path I traveled in grief.

Silent and watchful, Levi touches my arm and nods in the direction of the entrance. We slip into the shadows to remain hidden when there's movement. A group of people spill into the night from the warehouse. We're too far off to hear their discussion clearly, but their satisfied laughter carries on the wind.

Levi uses the binoculars to get a better vantage point. He stiffens at my side. It never bodes well when he's taken aback.

I eye him warily. "What is it?"

"Take a closer look at who they're meeting with." He hands over the tactical binoculars from Colt's toy box. "This is bigger than we think, not just seedy criminals looking to put down easy roots."

I peer through the binoculars and my spine goes rigid after a minute of focusing on the group of men. Swearing under my breath, I rack my brain for what this means.

The two men in expensive wool pea coats are friends of my father's and Levi's uncle. They're known throughout the city as high-profile business men. They shake hands with the other people who came out of the building. One of them is the man who shot our informant at the docks.

This network Ethan Hannigan was investigating for his story must have uncovered more than he bargained for if he saw something—or someone—he shouldn't have.

"I guess Stalenko Corp was looking for new investors to make up for the losses their operation suffered." Gritting my teeth, I pass the binoculars back. An idea begins to take shape. "This changes things. Let's use the upcoming founders gala to see what else we can learn from up close."

If some of the wealthiest men in Thorne Point are funding a drug ring, I want to know why. More importantly, I want to know what Stalenko is providing in exchange for this deal.

CHAPTER SEVENTEEN
ROWAN

In the last few days I haven't had any other nightmares about Ethan. I hated the one that plagued me before, but my dreams have been the opposite since the night Wren and his friends brought me further into their underworld. When I close my eyes, my head is full of Wren's rough touch, deep voice, and sensual kisses dominating me in my fantasies.

I'm so hot and bothered every time I wake up from a sexy dream of Wren, my folds are slick when I slip my fingers into my underwear to relieve the ache of wanting him again. He's kept away, but he answers my texts. This morning I had the lust-fueled idea to send him a photo of myself languid and twisted in my sheets post-orgasm. I've never done anything like that before, but he seems to make me more impulsive and wild.

Wren didn't take the opportunity to play sensual photo tag. The smug bastard only sent a single heart-stopping response: *let those thoughts of me tide you over until I get my hands on you, then I'll wreck you so good your fingers and toys won't be enough to bring you the same pleasure, kitten.*

Even without a photo, I could picture the expression on his face, hear the gravel in his tone, and it left me breathless with my pulse thrumming in my clit.

My cheeks flush as I dart my eyes around to look for my perpetual shadows, hoping my dirty thoughts aren't written all over my face. For once it seems like they're not stalking me around campus today. Or if they are, they're doing so discreetly. Neither Colton or Levi were in my morning lecture and I found myself disappointed—plus missing the amazing coffee they bring. I was forced to settle for suffering through vending machine coffee until I hit up a coffee cart when the professor allowed a fifteen minute break.

It's odd to go from having their constant company to nothing. I was growing used to their presence. Levi's surliness has become a comforting steadfast silence and Colton's outrageous joking is one of the few things to make me smile. I actually miss them—something I never thought possible when I first met the Crowned Crows in their smoky nightclub. My suspicion tweaks at their absence, but I put it from my mind as I head for the student union to grab lunch.

Isla's new dance classes mean we can't grab food at the same time. Without Colton and Levi here, I expect to eat alone today if they don't plan on showing their faces. It's the first time in the last two weeks I've been by myself for most of the day, left alone to my thoughts.

I take out the note I've been carrying around with me and smooth my thumb over the creased paper. The most I've figured out about the address on South Cove Road is the dock for a holding company. Googling it, another story from the midwest pulled up from last year about the DEA busting a pharmaceutical company for illegal drug distribution. I purse my lips to the side. My spring semester was hectic last year, but I remember Ethan FaceTiming me a few times with the Rocky Mountains in the background.

Tonight. I don't have work, so I'll go down to the shipyard to see this through Ethan's eyes.

While I'm tucking the note back into my bra, a figure in my peripheral vision makes the hair on the back of my neck stand on end. At first I assume it's Levi doing that creepy silent stalking thing, but when I turn for a better look, it's not him.

The man is barrel-chested and older than the college students milling around campus. Sunglasses hide his eyes, but his mouth is pulled into a permanent frown. He casually hovers several feet behind me, checking a map kiosk to play it off like he's not following me. I'd buy it, except when I move on, he follows once I'm about to pass through the wrought iron gates that connect this section of campus to the central part.

Narrowing my eyes, I pretend I don't notice to test if he's really tracking my movements. I fake a stop at a restroom in the student center and pass him waiting at a bulletin board outside the bookstore in the atrium before I leave.

What he wants with me remains a mystery. I don't know him. The only answer is he might know Ethan, but the possibility winds my stomach in knots. Something is off about this.

Keeping my cool, I act like I have no idea he's there while my heartbeat thumps erratically. I angle my phone as if the bright sun is making it hard to see the screen. In reality, I'm discreetly taking some photos for Colton. I don't know if it'll be enough to identify him, but if anyone can do it, it's Colton.

Another idea pops in my head. If I have the Crows in my corner, maybe that's enough to scare this guy into backing the hell off.

I scroll through the limited numbers on my phone, press dial, and sit on a stone bench. The stalker slows to a stop close enough to listen to my call.

"Missed me?" Wren's tone is amused and sultry when he answers.

I bite my lip, my body responding with a shiver. "You wish, King Crow." He chuckles knowingly. Glancing over my shoulder, I speak louder. "I was thinking of what to wear to the Crow's Nest. Colton said there are theme nights. Are we talking like a toga party, or should I shop for some spandex and glow sticks?"

Wren smothers a muffled groan on the phone while the man following me stiffens. This time he looks right at me and my heart lurches. His lip curls, but he backs away. Shit. What would he have done to me if I didn't show my hand?

The man's strides are agitated. He shoves a student out of the way when they don't move from his path. I watch his retreat until he's gone.

"Rowan?" Wren's tone turns demanding. "You there?"

"Yeah." I clear my throat. "I thought I saw someone I knew. I've gotta go, or I'll miss my window to get something to eat before my next class."

"I'd rather be eating you right now," he rumbles.

A strained laugh escapes me. "So come and catch me again, big guy. You're the one who's been too busy. Keep it up and I'll see if one of your boys will give me what I need."

This time his dangerous growl is possessive and dark. "Don't even think about it. I told you, you're mine."

"Prove it before I forget," I tease.

"I intend to." Wren pauses. "Enjoy your lunch."

I hang up and hurry to the student union. Evading stalkers cuts into my window to eat. Once I reach the crowded cafeteria, I pull up short.

Wren sits at my usual table attracting a lot of stares. His muscular arms are crossed over his broad chest, stretching the black t-shirt. Those icy blue eyes lock on me and my stomach dips in excitement.

Was he sitting here waiting for me when we were on the phone?

Swallowing, I put my bag down at the table and survey him. He's dressed down instead of the tailored suits he favors. It doesn't make him appear any less imposing. I match his stance, standing before him with folded arms.

"What's the special occasion that the King Crow would deign to walk amongst the rest of us peasants?"

Wren reaches out to grab me by the wrist with a wry curve of his mouth. "Cute."

Tugging me closer, his other hand threads into my hair, using the leverage to draw me into a deep kiss that leaves me dizzy. It's over too soon. His gaze takes in my expression and turns arrogant, proud of his effect on me.

I slip free from his grasp to rifle through my bag for my wallet, ignoring the heat tingling my cheeks. "What was that for?"

"So everyone here knows you're mine." He comes with me to order food. "Now they know not to touch you."

My brows flatten. I might find it hot when he says it, but part of me has to fight him anyway. "What if I want them to?"

It's a totally unfounded hypothetical. I don't make many friends outside of Isla, I'm not a big flirt, and I barely go out to party.

The air in my lungs puffs out of me when I'm pulled back against his hard chest. His lips graze my ear. "Try it and see how many severed hands I leave at your doorstep."

"Jesus," I push out hoarsely. Inexplicably, his promise of violence born of jealousy sends a thrill through me. "You're like a deranged oversized cat."

His chest vibrates with his laughter. "Anything to make you scream."

There's no stopping my shudder and he makes a pleased sound, sliding his big palm across my stomach. After I put in my order at the Mediterranean bistro, he stops me from opening my wallet. Before I can blink, he hands over a black credit card to pay for my meal.

"You do have manners," I say in mock wonder as he carries my tray to the table. "That was almost boyfriend-y. Are we going steady or something?"

"You're mine," he grunts, taking a seat and tugging me into his lap. "Nothing else to discuss."

"Dude."

I toss a grape at him, but it bounces off with little consequence. All I get for my protest is his arm tightening around me and a piece of warm pita bread dipped in hummus offered against my lips.

"Eat," he commands in a low voice.

I part my lips and take a bite. His thumb lingers at the corner of my mouth, gaze intent.

"You're tempting me to make good on what I promised you right now." The sultry words are a soft, warm puff against my neck. His nose grazes my pulse point. "Here on this table while everyone watches me take you apart. I don't think I could wait to get you alone."

My mouth opens and closes, battling the confused arousal spiraling through me. Maybe it's just Wren—the dark thing about this man that attracts me to him, making me want whatever depraved thing he comes up with.

I rake my teeth over my lip. "I don't think I'd like that."

His lips brush my throat in a light kiss. "I'd make you like it, baby. No matter what I do to you, you'd be begging for it all."

Well, shit.

Desperate for a subject change, I take out the folded note from my bra. "Since I don't plan to get arrested for public indecency today, I want to show you this."

Wren's teeth scrape a sensitive spot on my throat. He grumbles, but sits back and takes Ethan's note.

"I found it at the apartment I share with my brother when I was cleaning,"

I explain. "He wrote it like he was in a rush. Something had him on edge in the last week or so before he said he was leaving to follow a story."

His eyebrows furrow. "You're sure it's his handwriting?"

"Definitely. I looked it up. It's an address at the shipping docks."

"I'm aware."

The lack of surprise makes me straighten. "Do you know something about this? Why didn't you tell me if you found out something about it?"

"Because that's not how this works." His gaze flicks up to me through his lashes. "We're not private detectives. I'll tell you if I think you need to know, otherwise I'll continue to operate as I see fit."

"So I'll just find out for myself," I say mutinously. "I plan to check it out tonight anyway."

Wren's body goes rigid beneath me. "You will not go near this address." Leaning into me, his fist thumps on the table with finality. "We'll be handling everything. You're not to go off half-cocked on your own. I mean it, so don't do something stupid if I tell you not to."

"You don't get to decide that for me." Annoyed, I push off his lap. I don't spare a moment to be surprised that he lets me go, too wrapped up in my indignation at his ultimatums. "When you agreed to help me, I didn't think it meant you'd shut me out like I'm some fragile little thing. That's not me. All I want is to find my brother, and if you're going to keep being a dick about it, then I don't think I want your help anymore."

A muscle in his jaw jumps when he clenches it. "There's no backing out of a deal with us."

I open my mouth to challenge the statement, but he's on his feet in a swift movement, grasping my chin to angle my head before his mouth crashes over mine. I claw at his t-shirt as his tongue pushes past my lips.

This time his kiss is controlling, forcing me to submit to his will. When

I attempt to pull away, he holds me in place with a feral noise and kisses me harder. As mad as he makes me, this thing between us pulls me under with the strength of a tidal wave. I kiss him back, biting his lip.

Wren ends the kiss before I'm ready, leaving me to sway against him, head clouded. He offers a pretentious grin that makes my blood boil, burning away the desire he stirred.

"Behave, kitten. Or I'll find a pretty cage to hold you in. You'll only get to come out when I want you to."

At his sinister warning, I close my eyes for a moment as my stomach tightens with wicked desire despite how irritated I am. Centering myself, I let my head clear. He can believe he won this round, but I'm not giving up so easily because of his sinfully good kisses. Seething, I snatch my brother's note off the table and dump what's left of my lunch in his lap when he sits down again.

"What the fuck, Rowan?" he shouts.

"That's for being the biggest asshole in the world," I snap. "You deserved it. I'm going to be late for my next class. Don't follow me."

Wren glares at me, still foreboding even with hummus smeared across his jeans. I leave him like that, ignoring the gaping stares and whispers of questioning if I have a death wish for taking on Wren Thorne.

* * *

I do it anyway, because *fuck him*.

If he expects me to sit by and do nothing to help find my brother, he doesn't know me at all. He can kiss the hell out of me all he wants, but that controlling prick still doesn't decide where I go and what I do. Armed with pepper spray and a cat-shaped metal self-defense key chain since I'm alone at night, I intend to get some answers.

The address brings me to an industrial shipyard by the coastline. I park down the block at the lot that leads to the lookout point with a lighthouse on a rocky jetty to get a better idea of what kind of security I'll need to sneak past to get to the location on Ethan's note. The moon is out tonight, cutting through the eerie mist clinging to the rocky Maine seaside to light my path.

Waves splash against the rocks at the lighthouse. It provides a perfect vantage point. The docks themselves are brightly lit, but some of the shipyard is shadowed around the warehouse buildings. I use my phone camera to zoom in. A tall chain link fence encloses everything, but the entrance only has a boom gate that lifts its long pole arm to allow late shift workers to drive onto the lot. Bingo, that's my in.

If I was worried this place was heavily guarded, I had nothing to stress over. The gate guard is easy to slip by while he's distracted talking to someone with a clipboard. Keeping to the shadows, I sneak around, counting the warehouses until I reach the one Ethan wrote down. SynCom is painted on the metal siding beneath a single lamp.

It's much like every other warehouse and dock here, surrounded by stacked shipping containers and crates awaiting intake or their ride on a ship. I creep closer to one column of crates and shine light from my phone screen on the side. A crease forms between my brows.

Medical-grade manufacturing supplies? When I searched for the company, weren't they connected to a drug bust?

Two men storm out of the warehouse and I duck behind the crate to remain out of sight. Their argument carries, their voices thickly accented.

"How can we still trust them? They consider themselves kings, but only look out for themselves." The taller man slashes his arm in an agitated move. "Look what they allowed to happen to our operation in Colorado."

"There was no avoiding that," the second man says. "Come now, Sergei. They provide us what we need to rebuild our supply chain here."

"You only say that because of their money." The taller guy spits on the ground. "We do their dirty work."

"It's necessary when there's a rat to be weeded out."

The tall man grunts an affirmative. "His evidence is destroyed like they instructed."

"As long as the partnership is beneficial, their investment is good. You want to sit at their table, you play by their rules."

"Pompous Americans and their keys." The first man swears in another language—Russian, maybe? My mind snags on the mention of keys.

They move further away toward a row of shipping containers. I come out of my crouch to follow them.

A hand covers my mouth and I freeze, a scream working up my throat. I'm lifted off my feet, but my frantic kicking does nothing to throw off the strong guy who has me in his arms. He keeps mine pinned with a sure grip so I can't get to my pepper spray or stab him with my pointy cat ears keychain.

Shit, shit, shit.

Great idea. Isn't this exactly why Wren warned me not to do something stupid? I struggle harder as I'm carried further away, not planning to end the night kidnapped.

"Shh," a familiar muffled voice whispers. "It's only us."

Forcing my pounding heart to calm down, I seek out the source of the voice in the shadows and find Jude's bright golden eyes peering back at me. He has a baseball cap and a half face mask on to obscure his features. Twisting, Levi allows me to see him from the corner of my eye. He doesn't take his hand off my mouth.

Levi keeps me trapped in his arms. I wriggle to get free, but it's no use.

Jude pulls his mask off, tucking it into a pocket, acting like this is a casual night out. When we're away from the shipyard, Levi removes his hand.

"Let me down! How the hell did you know I'd be here tonight?"

Jude tilts his head, peering at me through his dark lashes. "Followed you. Wren sent us. He suspected you wouldn't listen to him."

"Damn it," I hiss.

"Aww, cheer up, sweetheart." Jude chucks me under the chin and waggles his thick eyebrows, nodding to Levi over my shoulder. "We brought the bikes. You must've really buttered this guy up for him to let you ride one."

I hold out for a moment, savoring the sullenness and fighting the prickle of excitement. Losing the battle, I sigh. "Really?"

"You still don't get to drive," Levi says brusquely as he finally puts me back on my feet. "You ride bitch with Jude. I don't take passengers on my bike. And this?" He grabs my metal self-defense keychain. "Does nothing if you're not alert. I told you to be more aware of your surroundings."

Glaring, I rip it away from him. "I would've been fine. You have superhuman skills for sneaking up on people."

"Let's not keep him waiting," Jude says ominously as Levi leads me by the arm through the shadows.

A pit tightens in my stomach that isn't entirely born of dread. Part of me broke Wren's rules and disobeyed because I like the thrill I get when he exerts control over me, subconsciously goading him to seek a repeat of catharsis I experienced before. Heat shoots through me and my breathing grows short.

"What about my car?" I ask when we reach the secluded spot the bikes are parked.

"It's fine." Jude gets on one and hands me a helmet. "We'll take care of it."

We speed away from the docks. The ride is exhilarating, but my thoughts are stuck on what I heard those men talking about. I grip Jude's leather jacket tighter when we reach the winding incline that leads up to the Crow's Nest.

Wren says nothing when we enter the main room. Unlike earlier at the TPU campus, he's in a suit, seated on one of the couches, a lit cigar perched between his teeth. Power is the first word that comes to mind when I lay eyes on him.

Levi and Jude flank me. I can't help feeling like it's on purpose to make sure I don't run. Wren's eyes drag over me, much like the first night we met in the decrepit ballroom upstairs. When I jut my chin, his mouth curves in a slow feral grin.

Taking a long puff of his cigar, he pushes the bitter smoke out through his nose while watching me. It has no business being so sexy, but heat throbs between my legs.

My heart skips a beat when he rises from the couch and takes my wrist, leading me away from the main room. I pull to test his hold, but his fingers tighten. He takes me through the underground level, down long hallways. I had no idea this much was down here. After a few minutes, he stops in front of a door, unlocking it.

It's a bedroom. Wren tugs me inside and my stomach bottoms out.

The room has a large bed with dark gray sheets taking up the majority of the space. One of Wren's suit jackets is draped over a chair by an ornate carved wooden desk against the wall. Another door is ajar, leading to a bathroom.

"You sleep here?" My words come out hoarse and shocked. "Sorry, I just—I was picturing like an apartment at a glitzy high rise downtown, or something more mansion-like than a sparse dungeon bedroom beneath your crumbling hotel."

"I have both of those," Wren murmurs. "This will do for tonight. Remember what I told you earlier about my impatience?"

He slips a hand in his pocket and takes out something on a long chain. A necklace, I realize. He smooths a thumb over the polished metal heart with a deep frown. The cigar dangles from his other hand, forgotten.

"I told you not to go there alone," he rasps. "It was reckless."

He keeps his voice deceptively light, but his anger blankets the room. Curling my hands into fists, I stand my ground.

"I'm not sorry." I slide my lips together. "If I didn't go, I wouldn't be able to tell you what I found out. These two guys came out of the warehouse arguing about the people paying them. They mentioned evidence being destroyed and doing the dirty work of the people paying them. Could they have been who Ethan was doing a story on? They could've taken him if they discovered him."

Whether he's interested to hear what I have to say or not, he turns his back on me, setting the cigar in an ashtray and the necklace on the desk. His fingers linger on it, shoulders tensing for a moment. My gaze falls to the necklace. It's important to him.

Wren turns to face me again at last. "You broke my rules, Rowan."

With methodic movements, he removes his expensive watch and leaves it on the nightstand, then unbuttons his cuffs and rolls up the sleeves of his shirt, revealing his strong forearms.

I swallow at the weight of his stare as he prowls toward me.

Wren stops in front of me. Grasping my chin, he lifts it so I meet his cunning gaze. "You're begging for that punishment I promised, my curious little kitten."

CHAPTER EIGHTEEN
WREN

Not only do I plan to punish Rowan for her brash defiance, I want to tame her once and for all. She won't disobey me again.

I had a hunch she'd go, so I sent Jude and Levi. But the thought of her in the hands of the same people that might have killed her brother—the thought of her in danger at all is unacceptable. It makes my chest itch with a sharp sensation.

"You wouldn't," she sasses. "I thought you were joking around."

Her tone eggs me on, but heat flickers in her eyes. Naughty little brat.

I arch a brow. "When have I ever joked with you?"

Rowan licks her lips, darting her gaze to the door. She takes in the lack of a door handle and shoots me a confused glance.

"Nifty trick of Colt's. It comes in handy when we don't want to be disturbed." I tilt my head, watching her. "There's a hidden fingerprint scanner embedded into the door. If yours isn't programmed, you don't get access."

Her eyes go round. "You can't keep me here. I have classes, a job—"

"I told you if you didn't behave I'd find a pretty cage for you." I sit down on the bed and give my thigh a commanding pat. "Come here."

Her lashes flutter, but she doesn't move. Good. I like her fight, it makes my cock hard. If she gave in too easily, I wouldn't be so obsessed with her.

"So stubborn. It'll only prolong the inevitable, kitten." I put steel in my tone. "Get your ass over here now."

This time she only resists a few moments before she crosses the room, chest heaving beautifully. If I stripped off her jeans and stroked her pussy, I know I'd find her panties soaked. Reaching out, I circle my fingers around her arm and pull her between my knees.

"You think if you act like a brat and do whatever you want, there won't be consequences?" There's a dangerous airiness to my tone.

"Seeing as how you're not the fucking boss of me, yeah." She folds her arms, but it does nothing to hide the way her hardened nipples strain against the thin fitted top beneath her leather jacket. "Sounds about right."

I give her a predatory grin at her back talk. She brings out something in me that's been dormant for too long.

"Is that so?" Without warning, I yank her face down across my lap and land a quick smack against her ass. She yelps, mostly in surprise rather than pain, squirming. "How about now? Are you ready to behave?"

"Fuck you," she snarls.

"Wrong answer."

Rowan cries out when my hand comes down on her ass again with slightly more force. The jeans muffle the effect I want. With a deft move, I reach beneath her to pop the button, ripping them down far enough to trap her legs and expose her pert ass to me. I hook my fingers under her thong, pulling it taut between her cheeks to enjoy the decadent view, running my fingers back and forth along the material before I let go. The fabric snaps against her crease with a satisfying *crack*.

"Jesus! I hate you," she swears, fisting the sheets for leverage. "So fucking much."

"Keep telling yourself that lie, my sweet kitten," I croon, stroking her ass. "We both know your pussy is wet for me right now. Shall I find out now, or after your punishment?"

One of her hands flies at me, catching me across the chin. I grunt, snatching her wrist and twisting it behind her back easily.

"That won't do. If you can't sit still and take the punishment I promised like a good girl, I'll have to tie you up."

"Goddamnit, Wren!" Rowan bucks and gets her frustration out with a fierce yell.

"Scream all you want, baby." Grinning savagely, I lean down to speak against the back of her neck. "The walls are soundproof."

Her indignant shouts are music to my ears as I maneuver her onto the bed and take off her jacket and camisole, revealing the mouthwatering sight of her tits. I hold her wrists in one hand while taking my belt off with one swift tug. She kicks and I get a knee over her thighs to pin her to the bed. I make a loop for one wrist, feeding the end of the belt through the buckle to make the second restraint and pull tight enough to restrict her.

"What a gorgeous sight you are all tied up for me, baby," I murmur.

She bares her teeth. "You're an asshole."

Flexing my grip on her wrists, I palm one of her breasts.

"You have such great tits." I tease the pebbled nipple, pinching it when her lips part on a gasp. "I should pierce these to give myself something to yank on when you're naughty."

"You—fucking shit," Rowan hisses, a clash of arousal and wariness clouding her eyes.

Interesting.

A menacing laugh rolls out of me as I sit back down and drag her back into my lap for more.

The next time my palm collides with her ass I feel the tingling warmth and the room fills with the crisp sound of skin clapping on skin. Another hoarse cry leaves her, ending on an aroused moan. She arches her back and wriggles, likely attempting to seek relief from my torment and find somewhere to rub against on my lap for friction.

My cock strains in my pants. Part of me wants to pin her to the bed and fuck her senseless. But the monstrous side of me wants to keep pushing her until she's a beautiful broken mess.

"See, kitten." I smooth my hand over the pink flush blooming on her cheek. "Told you I could make you like anything. Bad girls don't get to come, though."

"No," Rowan says breathlessly.

"Afraid so." I click my tongue in disappointment. "A real shame. You're so pretty when you come undone for me."

Her panting grows ragged as she struggles, but I offer no respite from my hold. After a couple of minutes, she flops bonelessly, tiring herself out. I pat her ass, enjoying her hiss of surprise.

"I'm not doing this just because you didn't listen." My fingers delve between her cheeks and I smirk when I find her slick from desire, even wetter than when I devoured her pussy. She enjoys some pain with her pleasure. "You put yourself in danger."

"I had it under control," Rowan mumbles into the sheets. "Brought pepper spray and something to stab anyone who tried anything with me."

A snort jerks my head. "How'd that work out for you?"

Instead of answering, she turns her head away and grinds on my fingers. I indulge her for a moment, slipping into the side of her panties to glide through her folds. She sucks in a sharp gasp as I tease her. When I pull away to suck my fingers clean, she curses under her breath. I swat her ass and chuckle at her little shriek.

"I told you. Bad girls don't get to come."

I give her one more smack. Another urge overtakes me and I welcome it, leaning down to bite her ass cheek. Her body trembles, thighs pressing together.

"Oh god!" Rowan pants. "Just let me—"

"No."

I want to see her come, but not yet.

She gets another spank for her insolence. It tears a choked noise from her as I sooth her flushed skin. When the fight bleeds out of her at last, I stroke her back. Body relaxed, she sprawls across my lap, finally pliant for me. I take the time to explore, brushing my touch over her skin, earning faint hums of pleasure from her.

I get lost in the moment, longer than I ever would with someone else. Each shiver and tremble my caresses earn stokes an ember glowing in my chest. I need more. Want her in every way imaginable.

"You look so goddamn gorgeous like this," I rasp, tracing the length of her spine to the curve of her ass.

Rowan's backside is warm to the touch when I pick her up and deposit her on her back, peeling her thong off and tossing it aside. She closes her eyes and writhes for a moment at the initial sensation of the cool sheets against her tormented flesh. The corner of my mouth lifts. She left her arms overhead where I put them. When I step back, she moans in protest.

Another low chuckle rolls through me. "Spread those legs and let me see how fucking wet you are."

At my demand, her eyes fly open, the green almost swallowed by her blown pupils. I swipe my thumb over my lip and press a palm to my straining cock, watching her intently. After a few shallow breaths, she swallows and does as I say, opening her legs.

Fuck. Her folds are glistening. Glorious body naked and splayed for me. She's perfection. She's *mine*.

With effort, I drag my feral gaze up to meet her eyes. "Your pussy is begging to get fucked. Begging me to wreck you."

Her gaze doesn't waver as I strip out of my shirt. She drinks my body in, tongue darts out to wet her lips as she stares at my tattoos. Instead of fear or shying away from the damaged monster before her, the only thing alight in her eyes is desire.

It stirs an unfamiliar and elusive yearning in my chest when she looks at me like that. The shock of it almost startles me out of the moment. I've never felt anything like that around someone.

Emotions have evaded me after Charlotte—I only care for my best friends. Otherwise I'm nothing but anger and emptiness. To have Rowan inspire more than lust messes with my head.

Shaking myself out of it, I remove my pants, not caring where they end up for once, and throw a condom on the sheets.

"Tell me," I order. "Tell me how much you need my cock right now."

Heat pulses in my groin when she rolls her lips between her teeth and spreads her legs wider. Wicked, tempting little devil. A deep rumble leaves me as I prowl back to the bed.

"You have to use your words."

An unspoken challenge blazes in her eyes. One I'll answer until she's screaming her need. I close my mouth around one of her nipples and torture it with my tongue. Satisfaction shoots through me at her gasp. When she's whimpering my name, I move to the other, pinching the first one.

"Say it, Rowan," I growl against her tits. "Or I'll leave you here and make sure you can't get yourself off. Break for me, baby."

She remains quiet and I go back to ravaging her nipples. A beat later, she shatters.

"Please."

It's a single, wobbling surrender.

And it's beautiful.

Bracing over her with one hand, I smooth hair back from her face. "Please, what?"

"I...I want..." She sucks in air through her clenched teeth, distracted when I dip my fingers between her thighs to rub her clit. "*Nngh*, I need to feel your cock. Fuck me, Wren."

Leaning down further, I lick the tears staining her cheeks. "Are you still going to be a brat?"

She arches against me, raking her teeth over her lip when my barbell piercing teases her sensitive nipple. "Probably. It's a character flaw."

A surprised huff of amusement punches out of me at her honesty. I can't help myself. I have to taste those lips. With a rough sound, I cover her mouth with mine in a hungry kiss. She melts into it, her fierceness resurfacing. I could kiss her for hours, but I tear away, needing to be inside her right now.

"Come on," she urges as I roll the condom on.

"Do I need to teach you a lesson on patience, too?" I chide, nipping her thigh with my teeth before burying my face in her sweet cunt.

"Ah! Fuck yes!" Rowan cries, legs closing on my face.

I groan into her folds as I suck on her clit. She whimpers out a litany of pleading for more when I sink a finger into her pussy. It doesn't take long before she comes with a sob, clenching on my finger. As she shakes, I lift up and press my cock into her inch by torturous inch. Once she adjusts to it, I pull back and sink back in. Her cries of pleasure grow louder on the first thrust.

"That's it." I reach up to grasp her bound wrists against the bed, fucking her with hard snaps of my hips. My lips graze her throat and I bite down, groaning again at the way her pussy tightens around me. Being inside her is better than I imagined. "Shit, the way you take it. I could get addicted to you."

"Such a romantic diabolical asshole," she snarks, wrapping her legs around my hips.

"That goddamn mouth. You drive me fucking crazy." I punctuate each gritted word with a powerful thrust. I'm not stopping until the outline of my cock is permanently embedded inside her.

"The feeling's mutual," she bites out. "Fuck, harder. Make me come again."

Fisting a hand in her hair, I part my lips to remind her who is in control here, but the words evade me before I can get them out. I'm too caught up in driving my dick into her. More than that, I have to make her come again. I want to take her apart so thoroughly she's ruined for anyone else because this girl is mine.

We're not done yet and I'm already thinking of next time. I could fuck her all night, for days, until we're both wrung out and still not have my fill of her.

I push a hand between us to stroke her clit while bending to kiss her. I swallow her moans and bring her closer to the edge with each touch as we fuck. When she comes, her body bows against mine. I tense as the pleasure crests and crashes over me. We ride out our orgasms in a tangled embrace, my fingers in her hair and my cock buried deep inside her while she shivers.

Blood rushes in my ears, the aftershocks taking a while to fade. We stay like that for long minutes, panting raggedly. When I can think straight, I pull out and discard the condom. The confusing tender feeling from before returns when I meet her eyes. She hasn't moved and a pretty soft smile plays on her lips.

A faint sound slips out of Rowan when I remove the belt and rubs her wrists. They're pink, but no lasting damage was made by my rough treatment. She sways drowsily, blinking as if her delicate eyelashes are weighted while I tug her closer in bed. I lock my arms around her, my chest pressed against her back.

Rowan stretches, releasing a yawn and my hand automatically finds one of her tits, massaging it as I kiss a line up her neck. Another delicious little noise escapes her. It makes me want to flip her onto her belly and drive my cock in her tight pussy again.

The possessiveness I feel for her doesn't fade, even with her tucked into my embrace. I've never been this guy in bed. I fuck women and send them on their way. It's a transaction, nothing more. The thought of sending Rowan home is one that my whole body revolts against. She's right where I want her.

Only dangerous part is, it's not just here. I want her with me everywhere. It's a different sort of possessive urge to know she's mine whether I need to devour her or brush my lips over her temple—to not only rule her body, but her heart.

Can I trust her when she refuses to follow my rules? It doesn't matter anymore. Keeping her safe is what's important, and if she insists on following her impulses then I need to bring her in further.

"That was great sex, but don't think it will work to distract me," Rowan murmurs with a sated exhale. "We're totally talking about what I saw tonight later."

"Fight me all you want, kitten," I mutter in her ear in a somber tone. "But don't be an idiot. You could've gotten yourself killed going off alone. The people you saw at the docks are dangerous."

"Like you?"

I hold her closer, stomach tensing. "Like me and worse. Don't pull that again."

Rowan huffs. "Fine, King Crow. Have it your way."

My lips twitch, the corner of my mouth hitching up. I graze my fingers over her skin, mapping a path down between her breasts, across her stomach, and over her hip. The gala at the Thorne estate will be short notice for her, but a thrill of anticipation tugs at me.

"How do you feel about formal wear?"

"Fancy isn't really my style unless it comes in plaid flannel or leather." She turns her head to peer at me from the corner of her eye. "For what?"

A chuckle rumbles in my chest. "I quite like the idea of you in leather." I reward her soft laugh with a kiss beneath her ear, then grow serious. "There's a party at my family's estate. You're coming."

"Am I now?"

"Yes. If I can't keep you out of this, then understand you're in my world now, Rowan. That means you play by my rules. From now on, if you get the urge to go somewhere dangerous, it's with one of us for your protection. Understand?"

She shuffles to her back to face me, worrying her lip with her teeth. "So you won't tell me I can't do something anymore?"

My nostrils flare with the breath I force out. Bracing over her on my forearm, I shift a lock of auburn hair from her face. "I'll still tell you not to do it. The difference is, you won't go alone."

"Okay."

I smirk. "Good. Now, about this party..." I thumb her lower lip. "This time I'm going to dress you, since you'll need to look the part. This is a different world than when I took you to dine with the dean of a rival college."

Rowan's eyes hood. Watching how turned on she gets from all the wicked thoughts that run through my head when it comes to her is the sweetest sin.

For the first time ever, I willingly break one of my biggest rules. I fall asleep with someone else in my bed. And it doesn't feel wrong. It feels like something clicks into place that's been smashed to pieces.

CHAPTER NINETEEN
ROWAN

Wren might have called this a party, but I don't think it's an accurate description when we pull up to his family's estate. The place is huge, even from a distance, and older than the Crow's Nest Hotel. We drive through an arched iron gate onto a long path that leads to a circular drive with a gothic fountain that reminds me of the hedge maze at the hotel.

Stretch limos and luxury brand cars fill the driveway. Valets rush to greet them.

I fiddle with the black gem bracelet on my wrist, carefully tracing the gold beads separating the stones. It matches the gown and shoes he bought for me—all designer. Even a small purse to complete the ensemble.

"What did you say this party was for again?"

Wren's fingers brush the back of my neck. The gesture is comforting, grounding me. "The founders gala. It's held in honor of all the families descended from the founders of Thorne Point every fall." His tone shifts from cool disdain to amusement when he glances at me. "You're going to unclasp that by accident if you keep playing with it."

Something shifted between us after the other night. The sex was incredible, but it was the way he held me after that stuck in my heart. He clutched me so close as we slept, it was as if he feared ever letting me go.

"I can't help it." My face flushes and I lay my hands across my lap. "This is the nicest *everything* I've ever worn."

Not to mention far outside of my price range. He insisted, not listening to any of my feeble protests. Truthfully, despite being a comfort queen who lives in my Vans and a worn denim jacket, I feel beautiful in the backless black dress. It stirred a warmth in my heart because if I had to pick something fancy, the choices he made suit me.

Knowing he picked every piece of my outfit out, I imagined his hands on my body when I put it on. The intimacy of the little fantasy still lingers.

Isla insisted I get ready with her for tonight. Her stylist pinned my hair into an elegant twist before Wren picked me up from Senator Vonn's estate in his sleek Aston Martin.

"I can't decide if I like you more in it, or if I'm dying to get you out of it." Wren's smoky tone curls around me as he traces the shell of my ear with his thumb.

I suppress a shiver of excitement and peer at him through my lashes. "Later."

It comes out husky, but I don't care. The wolfish smile he gives me means he knows exactly where my mind goes.

The tenderness from being spanked faded by the following morning and I might have been seeking a way to repeat it. The roughness of sex with him was alluring. I've never been with someone who understands what I need before I consider it. Heat spreads over me in a rush just thinking of the other night. Maybe I was in danger of becoming addicted to him, too.

Wren pulls up when the line of cars moves and tosses his keys to the young valet. He circles the car before I can get my door open, then he's there, helping me out and tucking my hand in his arm as if he's a refined gentleman and not the brutal man who thrives on chaotic violence.

"Don't let your guard down tonight," he murmurs in my ear as we enter.

I dart my gaze up to meet his. "Why?"

He casts a veiled look around, his cool eyes hardening. "They can dress up all they want, but most of them are vipers waiting to strike. Remember what I told you. One of us with you at all times."

I nod, a flutter tickling my stomach.

The inside of the estate is even more ornate with dark carved wood accents. A grand staircase leads up to a hall that splits in two wings. Thick curtains hang from the tall windows and antique art pieces that must have cost a fortune are everywhere. It's hard to believe Wren grew up like this when he's so rough around the edges. He can wrap himself in an expensive designer tuxedo, but it doesn't hide the power in his body, the brutal animal waiting to be unleashed.

It doesn't make him any less handsome. He stole my breath when he arrived to pick me up, his suit tailored to perfection to accentuate the strong lines of his broad frame. With his blond hair slicked back as usual and his signature cunning smirk, I admit, I may have gone a little weak in the knees.

We sidestep the crowd of mingling guests as he leads me into a room with masculine touches and plush leather club chairs. The rest of the Crows are inside, each decked out in their tuxes.

"You all clean up nicely," I say.

Colton beams and thumbs his suspenders, doing a little spin to show off.

"Right?" Facing me again, his grin widens. "We ain't got nothing on you, girl. Nah. If I may say so myself, *damn*."

Wren rumbles, sliding an arm around my waist. "We all clear?"

"Yeah. We know," Jude says.

Their cryptic words are lost on me. I squint, peering between them all. "What are you up to?"

"Madness," Colton teases, waggling his brows.

Jude smirks and nudges him toward the door. "A little chaos never hurt anyone."

"A lot will, though." Levi follows, hands tucked in his pockets. If I had to guess, I'd say he has at least two knives hidden on him.

I'm left with Wren. He pins me beneath his gaze, a smirk playing in the corner of his mouth.

"What?" The question comes out as a whisper in the quiet room.

He tucks a loose curl behind my ear. "Still thinking about getting you out of this."

"You'll have to settle for a kiss." I gesture at myself. "I promised Isla not to mess any of it up since it took so long."

The sound of his wicked laugh is deep and gravelly, winding around me as he grasps my chin and kisses me like he'd eat me whole if he could. He brushes his fingertips down my exposed spine. The crisp scent of his aftershave envelops me. Between that and his demanding kiss, I'm dizzy by the time he pulls away.

His focus locks on my mouth as he swipes his thumb beneath my lip to fix my lipstick. My chest tightens and my heart flutters.

"Come on. Time for us to twirl through the circus."

As out of my element as I am at this party, I'll get through it. We enter a ballroom with high ceilings that have intricate crown molding. Compared to other parts of the estate, this room is the most brightly lit and lively, while the rest I've seen so far has a pervading sadness hanging in the air. The lavish room is full of important looking people enjoying live music from musicians and hors d'oeuvres.

Several couples are on the dance floor. Isla and Colton are one of them. She waves at me enthusiastically, blowing a kiss before Colton dips her with flair. I laugh at their antics. Levi watches raptly from the side of the room, dark eyes narrowed.

Wren stiffens and grumbles something when he spots a man that looks strikingly similar across the room, deep in discussion with a group of men.

"Your father?" I guess.

"Yes," he growls. "Let's try to avoid him at all costs."

A pang hits me in the chest and I cover the flash of sorrow by surveying the room. "You don't get along with him?"

"Never have."

Wren accepts a champagne flute from a server and offers another to me. Other than his father, I don't see anyone else who bears his resemblance. He doesn't point anyone else out, either.

"Is it just you and him?" At the questioning furrow of his brows, I elaborate. "Your family. Are you an only child?"

Pain flickers across his features. My mind jumps to the necklace he keeps close. I've seen him rubbing it when he's deep in thought. Maybe it belonged to his mother?

As soon as the thought pops into my head, my eyes widen and I grip my champagne glass tighter.

"I'm sorry, I didn't mean to say anything. I didn't know. I—" My throat closes, but push out the words. They taste like bitter ash. "My dad died, too. The summer before I started at the university."

Wren clears his throat. "My sister. I...had a younger sister."

He doesn't have to say more. My chest aches for him. The thought of Ethan being gone is something that makes me buckle when it invades my worries.

"I'm sorry," I whisper, placing a hand on his arm in sympathy.

"Yeah." The single word is jagged and laced with anguish. "My mother is—" He scans the room and sighs forcefully. "Unwell. She most likely has already retired for the evening."

Feeling awkward, I search for a way to change the subject when Jude takes me by surprise. He's glaring at a girl in a stylish red satin dress like he can't stand the sight of her. I've never seen him so angry.

"Who is that? The one Jude can't stop scowling at?"

Wren looks in the direction I motion and shakes his head. "Pippa Bassett. Pain in our asses detective for Thorne Point's finest." At my arched eyebrow, he hitches a shoulder. "The law and us don't particularly go together. But more than that, she went to high school with us at Thorne Point Academy. Her parents are well-respected in the community. They're not socialites like Colton's parents, the DuPonts, or old money like my family and Levi's. But enough to garner an invite to these things."

He waves a hand dismissively like it's the norm. I guess it is. I've been in this city so long that the atmosphere of wealth throughout Thorne Point is starting to feel normal to me compared to the small Maryland beach town I grew up in.

"So what do we do?" I tip my head in the direction of Colton and Isla. "Dance? Mingle? Is there a schedule of events?"

"Mostly stand around bored out of our skulls. The guys and I used to sneak out to the gardens with stolen bottles of alcohol to drink and smoke. We got Colton's foster brother so wasted he puked in my mother's prize winning rosebushes and they didn't bloom that year." His shoulders shake with the force of his laugh. He points to a young couple across the room. "That's him. Fox and his fiancé Maisy from Colorado. They're with Colton's parents. Come on, I'll introduce you."

He guides me over to them and offers a charming smile for Mrs. DuPont. She gasps in delight and places her hand in his.

"Mrs. DuPont." Wren kisses her knuckles.

While he's occupied, I overhear Fox making plans with his gorgeous fiancé.

"I promise, we'll do this, and then I'll take you to the cove tonight," he murmurs to her, kissing her temple.

"A mini adventure is exactly what we need," she says.

"Wren, I've told you to call me Delia," Mrs. DuPont chides.

"Of course." He puts his hand on my lower back. "This is Rowan."

"A pleasure," she says.

My mouth curves politely. "It's nice to meet you."

"I admit, I'm a little surprised. You never bring dates." She gives me an assessing once over. "Now just where did you snap this beauty up, Wren?"

"The college." He flashes me a look that ignites my blood. "Now that I've found her, I'm unwilling to let her go."

My cheeks heat. "I have some classes with Colton."

"How wonderful," she says.

"Delia," her husband cuts in.

"Right, right. Well, enjoy yourselves. We have people to catch up with."

They leave us with Fox and Maisy.

"I'll be back in a minute." Wren's focus is on a man with graying sideburns lurking by himself at the edge of the ballroom. "Stay here. Fox? Keep an eye out."

"Yeah." His brooding gaze sweeps the room and he puts a protective arm around Maisy.

My brows pinch. "What's with the bodyguard act? Are the canapés going to jump us?"

"If they do, I've got your back," Maisy jokes, flexing her arm.

I laugh. "You never know around these guys. They're always so intense."

"You get used to it." She shrugs. Her laid-back nature is a welcome breath of fresh air.

Isla and Colton join us when their dance ends and he wastes no time ruffling Fox's hair out of place with a mischievous chuckle.

"Colt," Fox grits out.

"I like it like that," Isla says. "Very dashing and edgy."

Maisy gives Fox a secretive smile full of love and helps him pat his tousled brown hair into place. "You don't need the extra help for that."

Wren returns a few minutes later, frowning. As if pulled to me by a magnet, his arm finds its way around my waist and his lips brush my temple. My stomach dips.

"Anything good?" Colton asks.

"Not yet," he answers.

"Back to it then." Colton offers his hand to Maisy. "Milady, might I interest you in a dance?"

Maisy plays along, batting her lashes. "Good sir, you enchant me." She rises on her toes to kiss Fox on the cheek. "Love you."

Fox's vigilant expression turns soft and tender. "I'll be watching, daisy."

They take to the dance floor, spinning in wide arcs around the edges and weaving between other couples. I tilt my head, intrigued. Their dance takes them close to the richest men in the room without looking like they're eavesdropping.

As the night goes on, my curiosity snags on the way Wren, Levi, Colton, and Jude all scan the room with precise focus. They seem more on edge than me even though this is their world. Each conversation they're pulled into with various businessmen and politicians carries an air of veiled interrogation.

Before long, I suspect they're doing more than making appearances. They're working the room, perhaps looking for the secrets they covet. It's impressive to watch them at it.

Colton and Jude are more talkative than Levi and Wren when they make their rounds. Jude told me this wasn't his scene, but he fits in like a glove, knowing all the right things to say and moves to make. He charms everyone he speaks to. There's one point where I swear I see him bump into someone and slip something to Colton as he passed the group, but when I watch for it I can't catch it again.

Isla manages to steal me away from Wren's side, a willful force to be reckoned with, even for the King Crow himself. His gaze bores into me and I hide a smile in my champagne glass as we hook arms and skirt around the stuffier guests.

"Um, hot," Isla says decisively. "That tailoring is fire. They knew what they were doing. Please tell me his dick is as huge as it looks from the hint his pants give."

I choke on laughter at the scandalized gasp an older couple makes when we pass them. Whatever is written on my face is answer enough.

Isla grins and kisses her fingertips. "Knew it. You getting laid is chef kiss. Now we need to find me someone who isn't boring like everyone else here. I'm so tired of these uptight society boys my dad forces me to endure for publicity. I want someone wild who isn't afraid to toss me around."

"Saw you dancing with Colton earlier. Is there something there?"

She scoffs. "No. He's cute, and fun to flirt with, but not really my type."

"Levi was watching pretty closely." I lift my brows when she gapes at me. "You said you wanted wild."

"Not that wild. I think he hates me anyway. What about the one with the sexy smile?"

"Jude?" I nod across the room where he's standing closer than is polite to the beautiful girl Wren said was named Pippa. "I think he's busy."

"I remember a rumor about them being a thing when they were in high school. The whole academy was talking about it. Very Romeo and Juliet." Isla sighs dramatically. "I guess it's another night of riding the vibe train."

Over her shoulder, a man's distinct profile catches my eye and makes my skin tingle with awareness. I lose him for a minute amongst the guests and almost have myself convinced it was my mind playing tricks when I spot him leaving the ballroom. It's him—the guy who followed me on campus.

I know Wren said not to go anywhere by myself, but if I go get one of them I risk not knowing where the guy went. I need to follow him now.

"I'll be right back. I have to use the restroom."

"Don't worry, you're not missing anything."

After handing my champagne flute to Isla, I slip through the crowded room to scope him out. Determination spurs me on. I exit the ballroom into a quiet hall, different from the one we used earlier to get to the party from the entrance. The man is near the end, ducking into a room and leaving one of the double doors ajar. This is my chance.

Before I'm close enough to peek in the room, someone grabs me from behind and my heartbeat stutters in a rush of fear.

CHAPTER TWENTY
WREN

Rowan's surprised gasp is stifled when I kiss her. The dress I bought for her is driving me insane, leaving her back exposed to tempt me all night. My mouth waters with the primal urge to push her into a dark alcove and leave a trail of biting kisses to mark her as mine. More than once it's split my attention from the task of finding out who has invested in Stalenko Corp. Even utilizing the best secrets we've held on to as a way to ply the information we need, most of the people we've spoken to have remained tight-lipped.

I allow myself to get lost in the taste of her perfect mouth to soothe the frustration of the night. Christ, we need to leave soon so I can get her out of this gown and into my bed. She relaxes into my body, kissing me back for a few moments, then pushes at my chest insistently to end it.

"Behave," I murmur against the corner of her mouth. "What did I tell you about going off on your own? That curious streak of yours makes you a naughty little kitten."

"I was until I saw that guy." She glances over her shoulder. "There wasn't time and I wanted to know why he was here."

The playful air of flirting I was enjoying vanishes. "What guy?"

Before she answers, the door to my father's study opens and he steps out, followed by a bulky man who seems out of place amongst the gala's high society guest list. Tensing and drawing Rowan closer, I narrow my eyes. The man is about the same build as the man who shot our informant at the docks. His attention lingers on Rowan in a way I don't like at all.

"Hugo," Dad says in a scrutinizing tone. "I was waiting for you to greet me half the night."

I grit my teeth and curl my fingers around Rowan's wrist. "Dad. I was occupied with making the rounds." My attention veers to the man still staring at Rowan. "I'm sure you understand."

"All the same, it's important for the family to appear unified. Especially at events like this. You know how our peers in the community have shark-toothed smiles." He turns to the guy. "We'll reconvene at my offices downtown to continue this discussion."

"My company only wishes to ensure the preliminary measures are met," the man replies in a heavy Russian accent. "You understand securing investments."

"Certainly." Dad flicks a calculating gaze to Rowan before his eyes shift to me. "Hugo, perhaps it would be good for you to come by the offices as well this week. I'll have one of the secretaries forward details of my schedule. It'll be an opportune way for you to get a sense of the way things work and prepare you to step into the role awaiting you."

My nostrils flare at his presumption that I'll work for him. That's never happening.

"If you'll excuse us, we'll be returning to the main festivities."

I don't wait for my father's answer before I lead Rowan back to the ballroom, not slowing until we're on the dance floor so I can keep her in my arms until my heart stops drumming fiercely. It's the only way to protect how off balance I feel without losing face in front of every powerful player in the city poised to act if they smell blood in the water. It's the only useful lesson my father ever taught me—never show weakness.

She touches my neck. "That was tense."

My jaw works and I calm myself by stroking the exposed skin at her back. Unable to help myself, my fingers dip beneath the fine material of the dress to have more of her. "I said earlier my father and I don't exactly see eye to eye."

"Like insisting on calling you a name you clearly don't like?" Her wry tone draws a cynical scoff from me.

"Among other things." My hold on her imperceptibly tightens as we dance, driven by a strange emotion clawing at me. "Tell me about the man you saw. The one who came out of the study with my father?"

Her lips twist and her lashes brush against her cheeks. I tip her chin up so she's unable to hide another secret from me and she relents.

"Yes. I recognized him."

"Where did you see him before?" The calmer beat of my heart picks up again. "Tell me."

Sighing, she focuses on straightening my bowtie as she speaks. "The other day on campus. When you were waiting for me at the student union." She pauses, biting her lip. A low, insistent growl from me drives her on. "He followed me."

The arm I have around her waist becomes an iron band when I crush her against me. Every cell in my body turns to an icy rage. First someone comes for the informant, and now they follow Rowan in broad daylight? Something bigger is at work here and I will find out who the fuck is behind it.

"Followed you?" I bite out.

"It was creepy as hell. At first I wasn't sure, but he was waiting for me in the atrium outside of the bookstore when I pretended to stop there. Once I was sure, I called you and it spooked him off."

We're nearly at a standstill now, barely moving after drifting to the edge of the dance floor. My fist clenches around the draped fabric at the base of her spine. "Why didn't you tell me sooner? I'll kill him."

She leers at me, eyes hooding. "I meant to. You distracted me with your attitude at lunch. I was a little busy after that. Pretty sure you remember how that turned out."

"My stubborn girl. You should have told me. What if he was still following you that night? Christ, it's good I put Levi on your tail."

I cup her face, threading my fingers into her styled hair. Resisting the need to pull it loose and kiss her is next to impossible. I settle for pressing my lips to hers with poorly restrained fierceness.

"I did get some photos of him on my phone. It's kind of blurry, but I didn't delete it. I was planning to give it to Colton to check out."

"Good."

"When I saw him tonight, I had to follow him. I didn't realize he was going to meet with your dad. Why would someone want to watch me, though? I don't get it. I'm just a college student."

Because we're pressed together under the guise of dancing, she's able to pick up on the slight change in my demeanor. My chest expands strangely at the thought she's learning to read me.

"Someone has either taken notice of you when we're around, or..." I don't want to tell her the more plausible reason. My tone turns foreboding. "Or it has to do with your brother. Either way, they consider you an easy target."

Rowan's throat works on a swallow, eyes shimmering.

Having one of us or someone we trust on her at all times isn't enough anymore. I have to do more, keep her closer in order to protect her.

If they're sending people to follow her because Ethan got himself tangled in a Russian mafia's business, I can't be careless.

Rowan won't like it. I expect when she finds out what I'm planning, she'll fight me tooth and nail. I'm not waiting for her permission. It's for her own safety, so she'll have to accept that I'll do whatever is necessary.

Without needing to speak, I alert the guys of trouble by meeting each of their gazes. We're attuned to each other to recognize the subtle things our expressions mean. It's the result of the deep bond we share. They converge on us as I direct Rowan away from the dancing to the row of glass paned double doors that lead to the terrace.

"We might have a problem." Jude throws a glance over his shoulder at Pippa, clenching his teeth at the smirk she shoots back. "She's way too smug tonight. I think she's either got evidence on the Leviathan cases or she's planning something big to come after us."

"Worry about it later, we have a bigger problem." A muscle jumps in my jaw. I'll need to spend time in the training room tonight or spar with Levi to dispel the anger. "They targeted Rowan and followed her on campus."

The three of them respond the same as I did, proving how quickly she's wormed her way past the impenetrable walls we shield ourselves with, even the most formidable of them—mine. The instinct that she belongs amongst monsters was right before.

"Shit, seriously?" Colt's lip curls. "No way in hell are we letting anyone mess with you, Ro. We've got your back."

"Thanks," she says. "I have photos I took on the sly."

Levi nods, approval flaring in his dark eyes. "Smart. Good job."

"Text it to me, babe. I'll start a search stat." Colton has his phone out. For him, this is his protective mode.

A commotion behind me cuts our tense conversation short. The murmurs from the guests become scandalized whispers that grate on my crumbling patience.

"Wren," Jude says grimly.

Someone yelps. It's followed by shattering glass and a tray crashing to the floor. The music stops and the room falls silent except for the hushed gossip.

Damn it. I don't want to turn. Don't want to face what I know I'll find.

My eyes find Rowan's and my heart only shudders harder, old wounds scraped raw. I expect pity, but instead there's understanding in her gaze. In that moment it pushes me to break another rule—makes me want to give her my trust. It's something I haven't granted anyone outside my circle in years.

Rowan squeezes my hand. Somehow it's that small gesture that gives me enough strength to turn around.

The sight sears my throat. My mother is in her nightgown, eyes glassy from whatever she's baked out of her mind on, stumbling around. Her hair is unkempt, knotted on one side from laying in bed. People stare, forgetting propriety when there's a train wreck playing out before them.

If she knew what she was doing she'd hate herself, hate anyone who allowed her to leave her room like this. The woman she was before she lost her daughter to suicide was always put together. She was the height of a society woman, the bar others strived to reach.

Dad chooses to ignore her instead of getting her the help she needs. Now she's broken beyond repair. Maybe worse than I am.

Mom sways on her feet and spots me. "I heard there was a party. I love parties."

My throat clicks on a thick swallow as I stride across the parquet floor to her side. Up close, my nose wrinkles at the strength of her sour breath. Her satin nightgown is stained from stale sweat and something that might have been red pasta sauce. An invisible force carves out my chest when I grasp her elbow to guide her away, knowing how much she'd despise anyone seeing her in this state.

"Come on, Mom," I say hoarsely.

She draws a shaking breath, leaning into me. She feels so fucking frail. Pressing her face into my chest, I feel her chin wobble as she chokes on her whispered words. "Charlotte loved parties."

My heart clenches. Fuck.

A violent sob rocks my mother's body. She breaks down in the kind of bone-deep tears that overtake her when the clarity hits—when she remembers that Charlotte is gone. It's moments like this I hate my sister for what she did. For leaving us to deal with the fallout. And then I hate myself more.

As I cradle her greasy blonde hair, my gaze collides with Dad's across the room. He's annoyed, speaking with jerky movements to a maid who pales and nods before hurrying over to collect the heartbroken woman in my arms.

"I'm sorry, sir." The maid speaks so softly it's difficult to hear her over Mom's wailing cries. "I was preparing a bath and she slipped out."

"Get her to bed," I order. She encourages Mom away from me with gentleness. I grab the maid's arm before she goes. "If this ever happens again, you're fired. You won't work again in this city."

Her face drains of color. "Yes, sir. Come along, Mrs. Thorne."

Once the maid and my mother exit the room, the stifling atmosphere hangs in the air. I make sure to pass a withering glower around the room. Several people avert their gazes in the face of my ire. The last person I glare at is my father, who laughs with the man he met with in his study like nothing happened. Ruthless fucking bastard.

The constant simmering anger is close to exploding. Its claws are sunken deep within me, threatening the imminent loss of control. A hand slipping into mine pulls me back from the edge I teeter on, cutting off my jagged breathing.

"Are you okay?" Rowan asks quietly.

Something shifts again between us. Sympathy is evident in her expression and she threads her fingers with mine, caressing the back of my hand with her thumb. Her touch grounds me, allowing my head to clear enough to think straight.

The guys stand behind her, Fox and Maisy hovering nearby. I don't answer her question. The reality is that I'll never be fine. Before my sister died, I wasn't a good person. Charlotte's death, the revenge I got by killing her demented predator, the blood soaking my hands—it all chipped away at any remaining shred of humanity I had. It left me with an empty heart that has just enough capacity to care for the few people I consider family.

I know I'm a monster. I'm not capable of the kind of love she deserves. The question is, can Rowan live with that? If not, we're doomed to go up in flames once we find her brother and shatter her world. But I've made her mine and I'm never letting her go, villainous enough to damn her to the misery of despising me now that we've brought her into our inner circle. At least I'll understand the pain she faces if her brother is dead.

"Let's get out of here. I think we've seen enough," I grit out.

We've done all the talking we can. Jude and Colt took care of the rest by running a con to gain access to the phones of the wealthiest players in the room so Colt could bug them.

Rowan finds her friend to say goodnight while everyone else prepares to go. I don't leave her side for a second, too alert for potential threats to stand letting her out of my sight.

On our way through the entrance hall, Dad and Levi's Uncle stop us.

"Boys," Baron Astor says.

"We've made enough of an appearance for the founders foundation." Levi's lips thin. "We're heading out."

His uncle frowns. Unlike Levi's late father who Levi resembled closely, his uncle is a portly man with a thick beard. He's the brother of Levi's mother, but Levi's father was his business partner. The two of them haven't seen eye to eye since Levi was a kid. The experience he went through was enough of a nightmare to never trust his uncle again.

"A word before you go," Dad says.

My arm tightens around Rowan's waist for a beat, but I allow Colton to escort her out with an unspoken understanding passing between the four of us, needing her far away from my father if he's connected to this mess. Jude, Fox, and Maisy go with them, leaving Levi and I behind. She looks at me over her shoulder with a worried pinch creasing her brows.

"Go. I'll be right behind you."

Colt gives me an imperceptible nod and throws an arm over Rowan's shoulder. My body tenses, but I know he's protecting her. I trust him.

He speaks loudly on the way to the door, shooting finger guns at the butler. "Anyone in the mood for ice cream? I could totally go for ice cream. Rowan?"

"Sounds good." She glances at me once more and I dip my head in encouragement. "You're buying."

I set my jaw and face my father and Levi's uncle. "Make it quick. What else do you want?"

"So much impatience in your generation," Baron says airily.

"They'll learn." Dad fiddles with his gilded signet ring. "Everyone does."

Baron has a matching one. Most of the high society men of Thorne Point do.

"Indeed."

"Well?" I prompt.

"I keep trying to convey the importance of your responsibilities. The commoner company you're keeping falls under that," Dad says.

Rowan.

I'll never let anyone touch her, least of all him. If I'm a monster with my own skewed moral compass and agenda, he's an evil devil without a heart.

My fists ball and I sneer. "You seem to be keeping commoner company as well."

"You can't play games forever, Wren. Eventually your place in this world needs to be secured." Dad's gaze bores into me. "*Carpe regnum.*"

I stare at him. I've always hated the Latin motto my grandfather repeated to me over and over. *Seize the kingdom.*

CHAPTER TWENTY-ONE
ROWAN

"If you insist on being in my classes, you should pitch in so I pass," I tell Colton and Levi after my Monday morning lecture finishes. Isla waits for us at the end of the hall. "Seriously, if my grades drop there's no way I can afford tuition. And you assholes never let me pay attention. I'm trying to finish my degree and graduate."

Colton waggles his brows, tilting his head to give me a charming smolder. It shows off the crow tattoo on his neck. "What do I get in return?"

"I won't pay you to do my coursework."

"Nah, I don't need the dough. Unless you're offering head, then—" Levi smacks him and he holds up his hands before I throw the punch I'm aiming. "Hey! Kidding, jesus. Let's do a movie night. Hang out with us and I'll write your Ethics paper."

I grin. He's figured out my least favorite class on my schedule. "If I can get Wren to stop breathing down my neck, deal."

After the gala, I spent the weekend in his bed at the Crow's Nest, most of it sweaty and naked. He didn't want me to go to classes, but finally relented when I sucked his dick in the shower this morning while presenting my argument. I was almost late because he caged me in after he came and went down on me until he was hard again, then I was lifted into his strong arms and fucked within an inch of my life against the wall.

In the brief moments we came up for air, I told the guys what I saw when the creepy man followed me on campus and what I overheard the night I went to the docks.

"Good luck with that," Levi says.

"Good luck with what?" Isla asks when she joins us.

Levi returns to being a silent jerk around her. I roll my eyes.

"Colton wants a movie night, but Wren's been monopolizing my time all weekend," I explain.

"Oh, fun. Love a good movie binge," Isla says.

"They don't believe I'll be able to get away, but look—" I spread my hands. "—I'm here without him. Also, he's not in charge of what I want to do."

Levi snorts, tonguing his lip ring. Isla sticks her tongue out at him. He blinks at her, momentarily frozen. I cover a smile with my hand.

"The big guy's just looking out. It means he likes you when he's all intense like that," Colton says. "Some kind of primal mating ritual dance to mark his territory. At least, that's my working theory. He doesn't really date."

My heart stutters and I bite my lip. I'll admit, part of me likes how he's been all over me. Before when he wanted to control me it pissed me off because it came off like he was better than me and that was the reason he expected me to kneel for him like everyone else does.

"Most men say it with flowers," Isla says.

"We're not most guys, baby," Colton shoots back. "We carve it in blood or not at all."

"That's for damn sure," I mumble.

Levi hears me and his lips twitch. "Flowers are bullshit anyway. They die."

"It's the gesture that counts," Isla insists. "As long as it comes from the heart."

"What heart?" Colton's chuckle is light and playful, but tinged with something caustic as he knocks on his chest. "Nobody's home."

"That's because you're all eight different shades of psycho," I say.

"Bet." Colton winks at me. He checks his phone. "Lev and I have to cut the personal escort service short today, ladies." Under his breath, he adds, "Which is it, Wren? Watch her or not? Can't do both."

They're supposed to walk Isla and me to the library. Wren made them swear they'd be with me as he went over my schedule this morning.

It was an odd sight with his hair freshly showered, a half-eaten bowl of cereal forgotten at his elbow while he scrolled through the schedule on my phone and mapped out who would be with me while he took care of other matters he refused to elaborate on when I pried.

"We're almost to the library. It's fine," I say. "Nothing's gonna happen to me in the five hundred feet it'll take to cross the lawn from here."

Colton claps his hands once as we reach an intersection in the path. "Okay, Fox knows you're coming. He's inside now. You go straight there, got it?"

Once we part ways with the guys, Isla heaves a sigh, looping her arm into mine. We steer toward the lawn in front of the library.

"What's up?" I bump her with my hip.

"Well, my dad has been so weird lately. I don't know, he's having all these late night meetings that stress him out. He's been so tied up in it he hasn't said anything to me about changing my schedule around to have more dance classes and dropping Econ even though I'll need it as a prereq for the law school he wants me in after undergrad."

"It's not an election year."

"No, that's why it's odd. And there's something up with my driver. They had a meeting and in the last few days he's been staring at me when I'm not looking."

"Ew, creeper. Want me to ask the guys if they can find out anything about him?"

"Maybe. It's just wigging me out and—"

At my sharp inhale, she cuts off. I squeeze her arm and freeze. The guy from the gala—the same one who followed me before—stands beneath the shaded stone arches outside the library entrance.

"Oh my god. It's him again. Quick, come here."

We duck behind a bush and watch him check his watch before he strides off at a clipped pace.

"He's not here to follow you this time," Isla says. "He's headed for Withermore Hall."

I purse my lips. "Let's find out why he's here."

What I love about Isla is that she doesn't balk or cower away from anything. She might dress in a delicate feminine style with her fashionable blouses and heels, but beneath that she's a brave fighter. When I told her over the weekend about what happened at the gala and the first time he stalked me, she was ready to send a minimum of three bodyguards from her family's private security detail. She shares my determination to find out what this creep is doing on campus.

Wren might kill me for this, but there's no time to waste. If I did tell him, he'd only forbid me from finding out more information. Tough shit. I'm not a sit back and wait for a man kind of girl.

Keeping our distance so we aren't caught, we follow him. The students filtering in and out of rooms in Withermore provide cover while we track the guy. He stops by a stone bust of one of Thorne Point's founders. Isla's nails dig into my arm as she drags me behind a display case. Getting a good angle with my phone, I record a video of the scene.

My jaw drops open when a secret door opens to admit the man. Isla and I exchange a shocked look.

"That was medieval as fuck," she whispers.

"I didn't know the college had any hidden rooms or passages."

"Me either. Who else do you think is in there?"

I bite my lip, thoughts churning. "No clue. But I want to see it."

We wait a few minutes until the hall empties before inspecting the wall. Isla runs her fingers over the bust, mouth pulled to the side. I take photos of the wall from a few steps back and close up. Molded wood paneling runs the length of it and my pulse spikes when I get a closer look at the symbol engraved in it—a set of crossed keys.

Once again I wonder what the hell Ethan was working on. The need to know everything burns in me.

"Does it say who it is on the bust?"

"No. These old dudes all look the same to me, so I'm not sure who it is." Isla waves a hand. "It just says some stuffy Latin about keys to the kingdom."

"You know Latin?"

She shrugs. "Dad made me learn."

I take another photo of the statue and the plaque. Placing a palm to the secret door, I think about how I can't escape keys lately.

"We'll have to come back later to figure out how to get in," Isla says.

The words have barely left her mouth when we both freeze at muffled voices on the other side of the wall. She grabs my hand and we run for it.

We make it to the library late. Fox gives us a stern look, but lets it go when Isla primly tells him she had to powder her nose and change her tampon.

What we found doesn't leave my head and I'm left with more questions than ever about the history of this school and how it connects to my Russian stalker and my brother.

* * *

After spending a couple of hours at the library without being able to focus, I arrive back at my apartment building, fingers twitching with the need to sink into research mode. I didn't want to do it with Fox watching so closely in case he tipped Wren off before I could piece things together for myself.

Levi followed me home in his SUV. Mom called when I parked and I feel awful about it, but I tune her out, only half-listening to her chat about how her Paint and Sip night went and her plans for the week. Phone pressed to my ear, I wave to him on my way into the building.

"Mhm," I interject at intervals to make it seem like I'm less of an asshole.

If she knew the truth—that I killed my dad, her beloved husband—she'd never talk to me again. I swallow against the guilt eating at me as I jab the elevator button. The ride to my floor is short. When the doors open Mom's voice fades into white noise and I gape down the hall.

Wren and the landlord stand in front of my apartment talking. What the hell?

"Mom? I have to go."

"Okay, sweetheart. Have a good day. I love you."

"Yeah." Hanging up, I hurry down the hall. "What's going on?"

"I'll make copies," the landlord says. "Congratulations, miss."

Another wave of confusion washes over me.

"Thank you." Wren shakes the landlord's hand and eyes me after he walks off. The door is unlocked and I shoot an accusatory look over my shoulder as I enter. He follows me inside. "You're coming with me."

"Uh, okay," I drawl. "What does that have to do with my landlord? Why did he let you in?"

Wren stands in the middle of the cramped living room, hands in his pockets while I bustle around the chaotic mess. "To move your things out. He believed the story I fed him that we're newlyweds. As I said, you're coming with me."

I jerk to a halt, bag dropping off my shoulder into the overstuffed armchair. "*What?*"

"You heard me."

"Wren, what the hell is going on? What are you talking about?"

Forcing out a tense exhale, he goes to the kitchenette and grabs my favorite coffee mug from the drying rack. A strange flutter moves through my chest. It fades to disbelief again when it sinks in that he's serious.

"Wait, no. I live here. This is my apartment. The lease is long-term. I have rent and utilities and—"

Wren waves a hand. "All paid off. Pack whatever you need. Except the perishables. I've seen the sad state of your fridge. I have a premium grocery delivery. The quality far exceeds the cheap bullshit you've subsisted on. Coffee isn't a food group, little kitten."

A hot flare of indignation licks at the inside of my chest. After an emotional day, this is not what I want to deal with. He's pissing me off again.

"Is this because I didn't meet up with Fox when I was supposed to? I'm sorry, alright?"

"You what?" He turns his glare to the open doorway, where the rest of his stooges have appeared, lurking with boxes.

Even Levi. Goddamn traitors. A heads up would've been great, but friends or not, their loyalty lies with their bastard king first. It's what's inked into the scroll around the crow tattoo on Wren's back—*loyalty above all else*. I traced those words yesterday in bed and today I want to drive a knife into them.

None of them meet my eye as they enter, passing the crooked unit number without comment.

Wren pinches the bridge of his nose. "We'll discuss it after you pack. This was already in motion. Your apartment is terrible anyway."

I suck in a breath so fast and sharp it hurts my throat. This was the matter he was taking care of and the reason why he didn't shadow me himself on campus?

Stomping across the small, cluttered space, I get in his face to shout. "Shithole or not, it's mine! And Ethan's. You can't just uproot me because you feel like it. This is the place I share with him, asshole."

Wren's jaw works and he hands off my mug in a white-knuckled grip to Levi when he edges closer with a box. He drags a hand through his blond hair roughly, some of it falling in his face without product to slick it back. Eyes flashing with something similar to what I saw the night of the gala when his mother broke down, he takes me by the shoulders and clears his throat. It's the only crack in his cold veneer. A glimpse of the man I spent the weekend with instead of the controlling brute who acts the way he sees fit.

The landlord knocks on the doorframe, interrupting whatever Wren was about to say. He squeezes my shoulders, then retrieves paperwork from the landlord and hands it to me.

"Now it isn't." His voice is devoid of emotion while I skim the updated lease agreement.

Panic wells up in a rush. I clench the papers to the point of wrinkling while Colton, Levi, and Jude move around the space I shared with my brother piling our things into boxes. My breaths come too quickly, chest rising and falling. Wren turns his back on me and goes to the window where I love to write curled up in my chair.

Something snaps inside me when Jude picks up Ethan's thinking rock and tosses it like a baseball. I fly across the room, latching onto his wrist. My voice cracks on a frantic yell. "No! Don't touch that. Don't touch anything!"

"Easy." Jude keeps his tone even and puts the rock in my hand, curling my fingers around it. He shoots a hard look of disapproval at Wren. "I'm sorry. We'll give you a minute. Guys."

Colton hugs me on his way out. "Just listen to what the big guy has to say, Ro. There's a good reason."

I cradle the rock and sniffle. Everything in the apartment is exactly the same as when he left. I was too afraid to move his things because it felt like acknowledging how long he's been gone. It's irrational, but the last few months have felt like if I moved anything it meant he wasn't coming back. His stuff has gathered dust as my clutter grew around it, as if I was living around the memory of him.

The possibility I refuse to acknowledge rears in the back of my mind, but I won't entertain the idea that he's beyond my reach.

With everything going on from the mysterious man stalking me to being pulled further into the Crows' orbit, I've allowed myself to get distracted from finding Ethan. Shame explodes in my stomach. How could I do that?

Guilt pokes at me like a hot iron. If I leave, it makes my irrational thought go from a possibility to a reality.

Wren hovers in my peripheral vision, his broad frame imposing. Gulping back the lump in my throat, I lay down Ethan's thinking rock next to his chipped mug on the coffee table.

"Why are you doing this?" I demand without looking at him.

He walks up behind me, chest brushing my back. "Because I do whatever needs to be done. If you still want our help—and trust me, you need it—this is what it looks like. It's for your own good."

A brittle noise tears out of me. "You don't get to decide that for me."

"It's already done." Taking my hand, he puts something small in it.

Curiosity wins out over stubbornness and I examine the object. It's a small lens—a hidden camera. A chill runs over my body.

"Whole place was bugged." Wren's voice is rough and angry. "I found this in your bedroom. You're not staying here a minute longer, Rowan."

I scrub at my face, turning around. He holds out his hand and I shove the lens back at him, skin crawling at the violation of being listened to and watched without my knowledge. What makes me so special? I'm no one.

A sickening thought races through my head and I grab him. "Is my mom safe?"

I'm the reason my dad ended up on life support and died. My brother is missing—maybe gone forever, though I'm not ready to touch that possibility. I can't lose her, too. She's all I have left in the world.

Sliding his fingers in my hair, he sighs. "Yes. I sent someone down to Maryland to keep an eye on her while you were in class this morning. She'll be protected."

I sink my teeth into my lip, eyes bouncing between his. It's not an apology for what he's doing. If anything, it seems like further justification for himself.

Logic cuts through the storm of emotions. The apartment was violated without Ethan or I knowing about it. The guy who I've seen on campus twice now is bad news. I'm not safe here by myself. It's undeniable.

"I saw him on campus again today. He wasn't there for me this time, so Isla and I followed him."

Wren stiffens and takes my phone when I pull up the video I recorded.

"Why do you insist on being so goddamn reckless? You look at dangerous situations and dive in with no thought for potential consequences."

"I had to," I argue. "And I'd consider you a dangerous situation, yet I still ride your dick. Get your head out of your hyper-masculine ass for two minutes and watch the video."

An aggravated breath gusts out of him and he starts the recording. Ten seconds in, his brows draw together, then fly up when the stalker activates the secret door.

"See?" Wren pins me with a flat look at my smugness. I press on tiptoe to show him the photos. "Did you know about this secret room?"

"No."

A knock at the door interrupts us. Colton leans in from the hall. "All good?"

I survey the apartment, seeing every memory I've had with Ethan since I moved here three years ago. Heart in my throat, I pick up Ethan's chipped lucky mug. My vision is misty, but I nod.

"Does that mean I can pack up your underwear drawer?" he jokes as he saunters back in. A feral noise from Wren and my bitten off *fuck you* stop him in his tracks. Hands up placatingly, he offers me a lopsided apologetic smile. "Put me to work, babe. We're here to help, so show us what you want packed up and what should go in storage."

"Storage?" It's embarrassing how fast my throat thickens with another lump. "You'll store it for me?"

"Of course," Jude says. "Home means something and we're ripping you out of yours."

I offer a wobbly smile and he returns it with an understanding look.

The four of them follow me around the small apartment, collecting whatever I point at and put it in boxes. It's slow going work when I'm stalled by my emotions. For as controlling as Wren was when I arrived, he allows me to take my time. At one point I almost laugh because it occurs to me that some of them probably have staff for packing, but no one would suspect they weren't used to doing it themselves.

Little by little the apartment empties of any signs of mine and Ethan's life here. Even though I know it makes sense to leave, a nagging feeling clawing at my gut won't let me escape the thought that without the apartment the way he left it, Ethan won't ever return to the home we shared again.

CHAPTER TWENTY-TWO
ROWAN

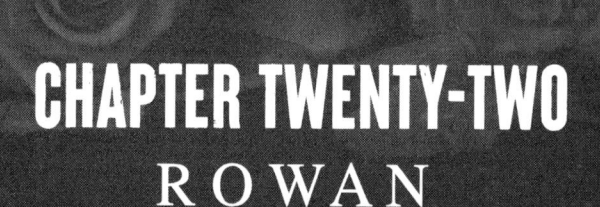

The penthouse is exactly what I pictured someone as arrogant as Wren Thorne living in when I first met him. It's a lifeless and uninviting space, dominated by expensive dark furniture better suited to a modern art museum than somewhere to live and a strange sense of claustrophobia despite the open floor plan. Compared to this, I preferred Wren's sparse room at their lair beneath the Crow's Nest Hotel. Somehow it felt like it had more warmth in it than this penthouse.

I stand before the rain-speckled floor-to-ceiling windows staring out at downtown Thorne Point. Fog curls around the buildings, matching my mood. The oversized cuffs of Ethan's long sleeve university t-shirt are stretched out the more I twist the worn material around my fingers. It skims my bare thighs and I feel Wren's piercing gaze more than once while he moves around the kitchen area.

"You really want coffee this late?" It's the third time he's asked while brewing it.

"Yes."

"You should eat something instead." Coming over to hand me a steaming mug, he brushes his lips over my temple. "You'll make yourself sick."

I shake my head. Colton picked up a stack of pizzas when they finished packing up my apartment, but the thought of food turns my stomach. Wren's fingers thread through my hair as I sip coffee. I pull a face, smacking my lips. Even my favorite drink tastes like bitter emptiness.

"Why do you live here?"

Wren's sigh fans warmth over the side of my face. "I told you before, I have a few properties."

"Wouldn't we be better off beneath the hotel?"

"Colt and Levi are doing security upgrades because of everything going on. For now, this is where you'll stay."

There's something off in his tone. I haven't known him long, and he's the king of secrets, but I'm learning to read his moods. This feels like he's putting distance between us. There's something he's not telling me. After taking me from my home, he owes it to me to be truthful.

If he refuses to tell me, I'll find out what it is. I'll steal a secret from the man who takes them as payment from everyone else.

Wren stands at my side until I finish the coffee. He plucks the mug from me and sets it aside on a table with an ugly, twisted gargoyle statue.

"Come on, kitten. Time for you to get some rest."

He lifts me into his arms, cradling me close to his chest. I feel so much smaller than I am next to his massive frame engulfing me. In the bedroom, he sets me down on cool luxurious sheets. He peels them back for me, but instead of getting under I sit up on my knees.

"Are you going to find my brother?"

Wren's expression is an unreadable mask, partially shadowed in darkness. My resolve to discover what he's keeping from me strengthens.

After a moment, he answers. "Yes. We have an agreement. I won't go back on it."

Relieved, I lay down, only to shoot back up when he backs away.

"Where are you going?"

"Sleep, Rowan. You'll be safe here. I'll be back as soon as I can."

Eyes widening, I trip out of the bed, untangling myself from the messed up sheets to follow him through the penthouse. "Wait—you're seriously leaving?"

"No rest for the wicked."

I pull up short, watching him set the security system. The claustrophobic feeling intensifies, the large walls shrinking around me. I don't want to be here alone.

"Look, I'm not used to explaining my actions." Wren glances at me with a frown. "This is the safest place for you right now. Believe that. Colton and Levi will attend your classes and bring your assignments for the rest of the week."

My jaw drops and I grab at his arm. "What the fuck, you can't keep me locked up here!"

With a stern expression, he corrals me out of the elevator. "Until I know I can protect you, I can."

The doors close in my face. I stab the button to call the elevator back, but the digital input prompting for a key code mocks me. White-hot fury races through me and I slam my palm against the door.

I can't believe he's trapping me here after forcing me to leave my apartment. It's a reminder of the rumors I first heard before I got to know him—a reminder of the cruelty he's capable of.

* * *

A strangled protest pulls me from sleep, heart racing, gasping harshly. Sweaty and disoriented, I forget where I am for a minute until my pulse steadies and I remember. Wren's penthouse.

Grumbling, I scrub my tearstained face and flop back against the tangled sheets. Flashes of the nightmare cling to me, drowning me in the inescapable shame that's plagued me for years.

A rainy night like tonight.

The rumble of thunder.

Arguing with Dad about sneaking out and getting caught.

His hands, always his hands on the wheel. Weathered and wrinkled from a lifetime of hard work.

Blinding headlights and the dream-like feel of floating in midair as the world tumbles in an endless swirl that leaves me dizzy.

Worst of all, the blare of a horn that becomes the haunting beep of life support machines.

All of it weighs down on my chest, making it difficult to breathe. The nightmare never changes. It was worse when he was still kept alive in a vegetative state, plaguing me nightly. Fresh tears burn a path from the corners of my eyes.

* * *

When I wake from a nightmare again the following night, my harsh pants cut off when I realize a strong embrace cinches tighter around me. Wren.

He murmurs to me in low tones until my heartbeat stops thundering, stroking damp hair away from my sweaty forehead.

"You're here," I whisper.

"Sleep." His lips brush my shoulder.

My throat is thick and scratchy. It's hard to swallow.

"I have nightmares sometimes."

"I'm here now. You need rest. Just sleep."

The sheets didn't smell like him before. Not the first night, when I was completely alone. They do now.

My lashes flutter as he holds me. Before I know it, the horrible images fade away and I fall asleep once more.

Every night after is like that. I'm alone when I fall into bed, but if I'm pulled from sleep in the middle of the night, he's there. By morning, he's gone.

* * *

All week Wren has come and gone, remaining cryptic and short with me, unless we're in his bed and he's keeping bad dreams at bay. Until tonight.

The elevator ding makes my heart race, promising the small hope of freedom. At first I ran to it, driven to madness by being left alone with my thoughts and the guilt that tortures me when I don't have anything to shut it out.

At least he left me with my laptop. After the nightmare woke me I couldn't sleep the first night, so I got up to write. I wrote a book in the span of four days, funneling every feeling I was experiencing into a dark tale that I didn't know I was capable of.

There's a folder on my computer with half-started ideas, but I've never finished anything until now. The accomplishment threw me more off balance—journalism is the major I've hacked away at because I want to be like Ethan and he encouraged me to pursue it. I'm not a fiction author.

My hurried steps skid to a halt in the entrance hall. Wren is covered in blood, his eyes overtaken by cruelness. The brutality of who he is in the fight ring bleeds into every measured breath he takes. His gaze captures mine. It makes my heart stutter when the cruelness doesn't fade entirely, but blends with possessiveness.

"Is that your blood?" I whisper.

"No." The word is a feral growl.

Heat throbs between my legs. I don't understand why his darkness and violence calls to me, but I've stopped attempting to analyze why I'm wet at the sight of him drenched in enough blood that I'm sure someone is dead.

I'm not afraid.

I'm not revolted.

All I see when I look at him is someone I can't walk away from. In a short time we've become locked together, every sinister layer of his world dragging me deeper into its depths.

Wren passes me and I follow all the way to the bathroom, fixated on the ripple and flex of his powerful muscles as he strips out of the ruined clothes. Dizzy, I swallow at his sculpted body. Blood soaked through what he was wearing, coating his skin.

Steam fills the room when he starts the shower. His eyes flick to me for a beat before he steps into the large open design. Water sluices over his dirty skin and he scrapes his fingers through his hair, ducking beneath the spray. The water runs red, some of it splashing on my feet from how close I stand to watch.

"What did you do?" I ask.

Wren turns to face me, expression unyielding. His cock hardens under my gaze and my breathing grows heavy.

"I fixed it."

My heart pounds hard. If he fixed it, that means the man who followed me is gone. I'm not naïve enough to think it means everything is over—someone still went through the trouble of bugging the apartment—but the ardent way he studies me pierces into my chest and doesn't let me go.

One of his hands clamps around the back of my neck and drags me into the shower. I close my eyes against the water and a moan escapes me when he kisses me, mouth hard and unrelenting as he devours me. Our movements become possessed with need. He peels off my drenched camisole while I push off my sleep shorts, the soaking wet clothes plopping on the floor forgotten while he hooks a hand beneath my thigh and lifts. My legs wrap around his waist and he braces my back against the wall, captivated by the sight of his cock sinking into my pussy.

My entire body aches with arousal, even with his cock filling, stretching my body to fit him. A wicked hunger fills me and I need him to sate it.

We fuck with the blood of another man still running off his body. It's messed up and heady. Tinged with a forbidden air that crackles with the frantic rhythm he sets. He buries his face in my neck and bites down hard enough that it rips scream from me.

"Don't stop," I beg.

Gritting his teeth, he grips my ass with bruising force and picks up the pace of his thrusts. The pleasure becomes too much. My nails dig into his shoulders when I fall apart. With a hoarse noise, he pulls out, right there with me as his come smears the back of my thigh and my ass.

My body is wrung out. He doesn't let me down on my trembling legs, keeping me in his embrace. I can feel the steady drum of his heart against my breasts pressed to his chest. We don't move until we're no longer panting and the water runs clear, free of the blood on his hands.

Wren is a killer, but so am I. The dark shards of our souls fit together.

CHAPTER TWENTY-THREE
ROWAN

By the following night, I've stewed long enough in the opulent penthouse. I never want to see these walls or that hideous gargoyle statue near the windows again.

Levi confirmed I was free to go when he arrived with detailed lecture notes and my assignments for the day. Wren put me through a week of hell and even after the intense passion that happened between us last night, I want some retribution for treating me like I'm fragile.

I'm not Wren's motherfucking princess to lock up in a tower and I'll make sure he never forgets it.

It's Friday and for the first time ever, the Crow's Nest nightclub is where I plan to be. When I texted Isla she FaceTimed me immediately to scream her head off in excitement before she arrived.

She helps me dress up, armed with the perfect little black dress and heels with thin velvet ankle straps. I might not dress up often, but the confidence is undeniable as I check myself in the mirror. The short hemline kisses my thighs just below my ass and the low-cut neckline highlights my cleavage.

"Jesus, you knockout," Isla praises from behind me.

"Yeah?"

"Definitely." She fans herself. "You rock the grunge chick look, but all the fire emojis for you in this, babe."

Before we go, I spare myself one last look, fluffing my hair. The corner of my mouth curls up in satisfaction.

"Let's do this."

The ride from downtown out to the cliffside at the coast is charged, Levi gripping the wheel of his SUV while Isla chatters and flips radio stations. More than once his brooding gaze studies her in the rearview mirror. I smirk, turning out the window. Those two are complete opposites.

Much like the first night I came here desperate for help and answers, the hypnotic music, smoky atmosphere, and flashing lights fill the decayed ballroom of the Crow's Nest Hotel. The room is packed with people dancing and drinking. It's an alluring kind of chaos.

"Go get him. I'll be over there." Isla kisses my cheek and points to the bar. She grabs Levi by one of his hoodie strings. "I'm borrowing you."

They make an amusing picture as she drags him after her. I'm surprised he went willingly, but glad someone will guard her. No one will try anything while a Crowned Crow is with her.

I spot Colton on the dance floor with Fox and Maisy, the three of them laughing.

Weaving through the crowd, I make my way to the raised platform at the back. Wren is alone on his vintage throne when I reach it, lost in his thoughts. He's not as put together tonight. Instead of a full tailored suit he wears only a buttoned shirt with the sleeves rolled up and black slacks. Our eyes lock. This time I don't pause at the base to plead my case, climbing the dais until I walk into the space between his spread knees.

Tilting my head coyly, I clasp my arms behind my back and wait while he takes me in. His gaze smolders. The only other time he's seen me dressed up is the night of the gala. Slowly, he leans forward, wrapping his arms around my legs. One hand caresses my calf while the other creeps up the back of my thigh, teasing beneath the hem of the tight dress.

Wren pulls me down for a kiss. I indulge him for a minute, then push back out of his reach.

"Don't touch."

His cool, cunning eyes flash at the direct challenge. "I told you what would happen if you played games with me, little kitten."

I lift a brow, retreating a step. His smirk is lethal as he unfolds himself from his wingback chair, following me through the hazy ballroom. People part for us, some gaping. Rumor has it the King Crow never comes off the dais.

No matter which direction I go, he's close behind. Tracking me. Hunting me.

I pick a spot to dance and he stands there, hands in his pockets, watching with a hooded leer. I move to the music, dancing for him, tempting him to touch me. The tip of his tongue swipes over his lip in a slow arc. My nipples harden and an ache throbs between my legs. Not yet.

This is a revenge seduction.

The tension between us pricks at my skin like tiny shocks of electricity, heightening the anticipation of what we both know is coming. This is war—whoever breaks first loses.

"Do you know what this place is?" Wren asks without taking his eyes off the sway of my hips.

I shake my head.

"It was once the finest hotel in New England at the height of its time." He shifts closer, the space almost nonexistent between us. I can feel the heat of him at my back, his breath fanning over my neck when I pull my hair to one side. "When it closed, it fell into disrepair. It was condemned, scheduled to be sold and demolished. I saw something else, though. So I bought it."

"A crumbling, creepy old estate perfect for scaring the hell out of people while you hang out in the grime?"

"An escape," he rasps against my ear. "A dark fantasy come to life."

It rings true. I didn't see it before the first time I came here, or when I avoided this place, but now, with his hands hovering over my hips, the beat of the music vibrating through me, and every part of me begging for him to give in and touch me, I understand.

Shit, I might be the one to crack. My imagination runs wild with lust as I think of the possibilities, the kind of debauchery we could give our bodies over to in this atmosphere. It's sensual and spellbinding.

Before my resolve shatters, I whirl around, narrowing my eyes. "If you want me, you have to make a deal."

He matches his expression to mine. "You know the price if you want me to do something. A secret or a favor. Give up something that hurts."

"I already did, King Crow," I reply in a steely tone. "A week in your penthouse as your captive."

"For your protection," he grits out.

Something tightens in my chest at his conviction to take care of me.

Filled with determination, I straighten my spine. "I'm not your delicate toy. Never lock me away again or I'll steal one of Levi's knives and stab you in your sleep."

A muscle jumps in his jaw and fire blazes in his eyes. He doesn't answer, but he breaks first, taking my hand to lead me to a shadowy corner of the club blocked behind the remains of a half wall. It's chillier at the edge of the room away from the people dancing, but Wren's body heat seeps through the back of my dress when he tugs me against him. I tip my head back on his shoulder and close my eyes at the hard length of him digging into my ass.

"Enough games," he growls before biting my ear. "This is what you do to me."

I hiss, clenching my thighs together. He pries them open with a chiding noise and runs his fingers up my inner thigh, dangerously close to my aching pussy. Another inch and he'll find out I'm not wearing underwear.

"I want you to writhe for me, you goddamn cocktease." His chest rumbles with devious humor when he reaches higher and finds me wet and bare. He glides his touch through my slickness and rubs my clit at a torturous pace. "My naughty little kitten."

"Make me come."

"Filthy girl."

Wren stops touching me and my needy protest is silenced by his fingertips prodding my lips. I open and feel the satisfied curve of his mouth against my cheek as he strokes my tongue, the taste of myself hot and illicit as he makes me suck his fingers clean.

"You want to come in front of a room full of people that have no idea I'm taking you apart in the shadows? They won't be able to see if I make you get on your knees and fuck your face, or if I peel this sexy little dress up and fuck you right here while they're none the wiser—well, unless you scream loud enough." At my strangled cry, he presses a gravelly chuckle into my neck. Sagging into him, my eyelashes flutter and my stomach dips. "Fuck, why are you so perfect?"

Taking his wet fingers from my mouth he growls and presses two of them into my pussy. I arch, gasping, forgetting where we are for a moment while he pumps in and out in the exact way to light me up and bring me to the brink.

"Oh god," I choke.

"Like that, baby?"

My lips part as my orgasm builds. I rock against his hand, grinding my clit to the pulsing beat of the music.

"Not yet," he rumbles abruptly, pulling free. He shushes my whimper at being denied pleasure when I was so close and licks the taste of me from his fingertips. "You're going to come with my cock buried inside you."

The clink of his belt is almost inaudible and he tugs at the dress roughly until my ass is exposed. Tingles rush over my skin in excitement at how wrong this is. A condom wrapper drops to the ground and I reach back to hold onto him for balance as his cock teases my folds. It's madness, but I can't stop how much I want him right now.

Wren whispers dirty encouragement in my ear while his touch roams everywhere, forcing the dress higher. The red lights flash, adding to the immoral atmosphere. We're shrouded by foggy smoke and hidden in the shadows behind the half wall while we fuck. Only he and I know that anyone might look over and see us.

"You're so fucking wet." He fists my hair, angling my head to brush his lips over the side of my face. "Every time I pull out your pussy soaks me when I sink back into it. Feel it? You love this, dirty girl. It's how I know you're fucking *mine*."

I feel full with each thrust, biting my lip to stifle my moans as he buries his cock in my pussy, obscured in a dark corner of his crowded estate hotel-turned-nightclub while people get lost in the revelry of partying.

He grabs my jaw. "Don't you dare hold back. Give me every goddamn sound."

The order is punctuated by his cock driving into me sharply. I reach blindly, nails clawing at any part of him I grab onto as I moan. My heartbeat thrums and my skin flushes with scorching fire.

"Look at them, Rowan. Watch." My eyes open, struggling to focus when he's pounding the spot that makes me see stars with brutal precision. As he speaks, he shoves a hand down the neckline of the dress and pinches my nipple. "See how they're wild with abandon? They give themselves over to it completely. I love the power of control, and here I get to control all of their surrender because I gave them this place."

He groans when I clench around him as I look at the drunken dancers basking in the hedonism the nightclub offers. He rewards me by circling his fingers on my clit. In my head, I imagine the people looking at us fucking in the shadows and pleasure ripples through me.

"Yes. Let go for me," Wren commands, holding my throat.

The pressure he squeezes with isn't enough to cut off my air completely, but it sends another erotic thrill to my core. He slams into me and it sends me over the edge in a wave of ecstasy.

"Oh god," I whimper, sagging against him.

Grunting, he supports my weight while I tremble from my orgasm. He holds my hips in a bruising, white-knuckled grip and with another low groan, his cock throbs inside me. Panting he drops his forehead against my hair, flattening his palm over my stomach. He allows himself a moment while I'm still delirious from coming so hard. I'm vaguely aware of him pulling out, fixing my dress so I'm covered, and the condom dropping to the dusty ground.

It's only with him I get this euphoric release where I don't have to hide from the darkness swirling in me. His own darkness is right there to catch me.

Wren presses me into the wall, caging me between his arms. He captures my lips in a sultry kiss that leaves me breathless when he puts enough space between us to hold my gaze. He grasps my jaw and tilts my head up, speaking fiercely.

"There is nothing fragile about you. It's in your eyes." He kisses me once more, swallowing my startled exhale. "Don't ever fucking forget it."

CHAPTER TWENTY-FOUR
WREN

Eliminating the immediate threat doesn't mean more aren't on the horizon. It's become a growing concern, an impossible instinct to ignore. But I also know locking Rowan up was only a temporary solution. My little fighter won't stand for that again. The primal side of me wants to do it anyway to control her safety.

The threat she served up last night made up my mind. She needs to learn to protect herself.

Her taut ass captivates me in a tight pair of jeans on the way up the wooded path from where we parked. No one but me, my family, and my best friends know my grandmother bought more land than she knew what to do with. The shooting range I had built lies at the top of the hill. Further south is the only part of the property I allow people on—the Crow's Nest. Not far off is my real house that I use when I'm not crashing at the Nest or using the penthouse for business purposes and appearances.

The temptation to bring her to it and show her my sanctuary is strong.

Slipping a hand in my jacket pocket, I run my thumb over Charlotte's locket and consider how Rowan continues to sneak past my defenses. She's more than business, more than an enticing fuck, more than the intriguing woman who holds my attention. Somehow she's become important to me—a rare occurrence when I trust few people in this world.

She strays from the path to explore and I follow, twigs crunching under my boots. "Keep moving, kitten."

Rowan tightens her ponytail after I tug on it and picks her way back to the path. "When you said dress in warm layers, I gotta admit, I didn't think it meant hiking the cliffside. I've never looked at you and thought *outdoorsy type*."

A smirk curves my mouth. "You'd be correct. This isn't a random public stretch of wooded cliffside, though. It's my property."

She darts a look over her shoulder, pausing from taking a photo of the Maine coastline painted in autumn colors with her phone. "Of course it is. I don't even know why I'm surprised. You ooze money. Did you inherit it or something?"

"Or something." The day I bought my great-grandmother's sprawling estate is a point of pride. My father and grandfather only saw a barren failure they wanted to liquidate while I saw possibility. Between Colton's cryptocurrency investments, our income stream, and aggressive financial strategies, we built the foundations of our own legacy, allowing me to purchase it. "And we're not out here for a hike."

Rowan's expression turns mischievous and she cants her hip to lean against a tree. "I'm into it, but don't strip me naked. It's too cold and I'm not a fan of bugs crawling all over me when I'm clothed, let alone with my tits hanging out. Like, if my choice was middle of the woods sex or car sex—both uncomfortable and inconvenient—I'd rather ride your dick in your cramped Aston Martin just so I could laugh about how you even fit your giant-sized everything in there."

"As enticing as that sounds…"

I close the distance between us, prowling until I reach her. Bracing an arm against the bark above her head, I encircle her throat with my fingers. Her pulse jumps and her lips part, a pink tinge coloring her cheeks.

"Either you learn to protect yourself or I make you a permanent fixture in my penthouse. I promised you a pretty cage once, didn't I?" My mouth crashes over hers and she curls her fingers in my jacket. I speak against her lips. "If you're going to stab me when I piss you off, you might as well learn how to do it with lethal accuracy."

The sound of Rowan's laugh unfurls an unfamiliar feeling in my chest. Her gorgeous eyes gleam with feistiness. She's beautiful like this, so full of life. I brush my thumb underneath her jaw and steal one more kiss.

Admittedly, it turned me on when she threatened to stab me. My stubborn girl. Her fire is the thing I'm drawn to most. I thought it was a passing infatuation, but I've only grown to like her more, evident in every rule I've broken to bring her in closer instead of keeping her away. That bold courage is how I know she can hold her own and belongs in my world at my side.

In the distance I hear the muted echo of car doors slamming closed. Everyone else has arrived.

We reach the shooting range first. It's a fully functioning private facility that covers a wide array of practice options, and includes a lounge and kitchen. Rowan takes in the large facility with wide eyes as I show her the outdoor areas before taking her inside to the weapon storage room.

"This is legit." She squints at me, poking my chest. "What do you need an arsenal like this for?"

"Always be prepared for anything." I size her up and take a Glock from the wall. "This should do."

I walk her through the basic parts of the gun and make her repeat them back to me three times before I deem her ready to learn to use it.

Once she's equipped, we return to the outdoor range and find the guys and Maisy waiting there for us. It makes me pause for a moment when I realize it's only ever been the guys out here. Fox and Penn have come here, but not Penn's girl Serena. Maisy and Rowan are the outsiders we've let in.

Things are shifting around. Not only in me, but for all of us, change as present in the air as the leaves turning orange.

"Ready to add another level of sexy to your hotness factor?" Colt teases. "I'm sure the big guy hasn't told you, but his favorite movie franchise is Lara Croft, which, yeah." He rakes his teeth over his lip. "I'm about that, too."

Jude snickers and elbows Colt. Rolling my eyes, I lead the way.

"Is that for knife throwing?" Rowan points to the area Levi spends most of his time.

"Yeah. I'll show it to you later." Levi flicks his tongue against his lip ring, casting a longing look at his favorite spot to train. "First, you learn to use that."

"You guys expect us to learn everything in one day?" Maisy scrunches her nose. "I'm really more about peace and love."

Fox tucks her against his side. "Knowing how to defend yourself makes a difference. You only have to use the skills to stay safe."

"I know," she murmurs.

The two of them share a private moment when her features become closed off. Colt mentioned before that she was targeted as collateral by the same bratva syndicate we're up against now.

We reach the clearing for the range. Jude and Colton grow serious. Levi's focus is always laser sharp when he's here, and Fox never fails to follow in his mentor's footsteps. They each spread out and take a position for target practice. Rowan remains with me.

She watches Levi's precision as he hits an entire magazine of headshot bullseyes in a row. "Damn, are you all secretly marksmen?"

"We've trained in a lot of areas. Mostly fighting. Lev's the one who's essentially an unregistered lethal weapon." Checking the clip, I load her gun and hand it back to her. "Your turn. Unload it, then reload it and aim like I showed you."

Her tongue sticks out from the corner of her mouth and her face pinches in concentration as she finds the release, examines the clip for the magazine of bullets, and clicks it back into the gun. Taking position, she aims.

"Good. Lower your shoulders."

I walk her through the next steps. Nodding along, she fires at the target. It's not perfect, but she hit it. Not bad for her first try when she's never shot anything before. I offer a correction and let her try again, allowing her to figure most things out for herself. It's important for her to get used to it so her body builds the instinct and muscle memory.

"This isn't as weird as I thought."

"Shooting at the blank outline of a person is easy. The harder part is looking them in the eye and pulling the trigger. You have to be able to do it though. It could mean your life or theirs."

A lie for her benefit. I lost the empathetic part of my humanity long ago. Maybe I didn't have it to begin with. I have no trouble pulling the trigger on someone I decide to shoot. I'm not haunted by the lives I take. They deserved what they got.

Watching her learn, I'm struck by the urge to kill the guy who stalked her all over again. I took my time, painting the room we use for interrogation at the Nest red, but it wasn't enough. I should've brought her his bloody heart.

For her, I'd readily kill anyone who tried to harm her.

"You've been quiet for a few minutes." Rowan angles her head to peek at me. "Watching my ass and thinking of Lara Croft fantasies?"

My lips twitch. "You do look good with a weapon in your hands."

"I thought I'd hate it, but I kind of feel like a badass bitch." She aims carefully and squeezes the trigger. She emits a delighted yelp when her bullet hits inside the target outline for a chest shot. "I finally hit it right!"

"Well done." A warm ember expands in my chest.

As much as I love control, this is better. It fills my head with dangerous thoughts of a future I never thought to wish for, but with her...I want it.

Levi comes over when he runs out of ammo, generally bored by guns. He stands as a sentry, arms crossed, assessing everything around him. After several minutes, he speaks in low tones.

"You seem better since meeting her."

I cast a sidelong glance in his direction. He isn't the emotional type to use his words—none of us are, really—but for those he considers family, he takes notice. He doesn't elaborate, but I know he means the worry he harbored for me in the last few months. I'm still a brutal, cruel monster, but with Rowan around I'm less empty, latching on to a new sense of purpose.

"Come on," Levi says to her while he signals Fox and Maisy. "I'll show you a move to disarm anyone who comes at you close range with a gun."

It speaks volumes that he takes an interest in training her the same as he's trained the rest of us. Colton and Jude finish up, goading each other and exchanging money for the bet they challenge each other with on who can hit the best shots.

"Come on, you might have beat me on accuracy this time, but you have to admit how masterful that last shot was," Colt argues. "I gave him a smiley face in his chest cavity."

"Creative, but it doesn't beat hitting the kill zones. You play with your food too much." Jude's grin is wide. "Let's go again. I'll win your money all day."

I follow Levi, Fox, and the girls to another open field. Fox volunteers to help Levi show them the basic movements, pulling the gun on Levi several times. Each demonstration ends with Levi's fast reflexes disarming him by grabbing his wrist and turning the gun around on Fox by the barrel. Maisy whistles, impressed.

"This depends on a few factors." Levi nods to Fox to go again while he explains. "Timing, positioning, and how recently the gun was shot. The barrel might be hot. Come try."

He has Fox come at Rowan and stands behind her, talking her through the steps he showed them. She tries a few times, then Maisy takes a turn. Colt and Jude eventually make their way over to watch the lesson. Jude chuckles and Colt claps when Rowan gets it right. A burst of pride fills me.

"The girl is ready for a special fight night." Colton snaps his fingers. "Maybe I can program a premium livestream. It'll be dope."

"I heard that," Rowan calls.

Colt sticks his pierced tongue out.

"The privilege of that fight is reserved for me and me alone," I rumble.

Jude smirks and shakes his head. "Gotta say, I'm enjoying this side of you." I arch a brow and he scratches the tip of his nose. "Usually it's the eager chicks at the Nest. Someone you can use and throw away. But this girl makes you different. You treat her like one of us."

A flash of somberness crosses his face. It's the look he gets when he's thinking about the past, before Pippa screwed him over and turned her back on him. When he was in love with her and she was his world.

I mull his words over. It's impossible to hide how I am around her in front of the guys who know me best, who understand how my mind works.

The girls huddle together during a break, whispering. My attention shifts between their plotting and Levi, waiting for what they're planning. He calls them to come at him together and my head jerks with a snort. They tag team him, but underestimated just how much of his life he's spent honing his body to fight. It's an unfair match for two inexperienced people to take him on.

Maisy jumps on his back and Rowan goes for his legs while he has one of her arms incapacitated. Satisfaction fills me when my clever girl unbalances him by breaking the foundation of his stance. It's not easy to best him. The three of them topple to the ground in a heap, the girls cracking up and high fiving.

Fox huffs, smile soft.

"Nice." Their laughter cuts off abruptly, exchanged with yelps when Levi pulls a counter maneuver that ends up with both girls tied up by their own hoodie sleeves.

"Dude! Not cool." Maisy squirms, but even her flexibility from yoga doesn't help her out.

Rowan bumps their shoulders together. "We'll get him back later." She shoots him a cunning look. "I know his weakness."

"I have no weaknesses." He gets to his feet, dusting his hands as he continues his lecture. "Next time don't make your attacks so obvious. We'll work on projection and masking your intent another time. Back to work."

Once Levi's satisfied they have it down, he waves me over and hands me the unloaded gun. Rowan shakes out her hands and locks eyes with me. The corner of my mouth lifts.

"Come at me, big guy. I'm ready."

"That's what you think, kitten."

I circle her, keeping her guessing when I'll make my move. She bares her teeth playfully and swipes at me. When I think she's dropped her guard, I move.

She played me. Her fingers latch around my wrist and the gun swings to point at me. Triumphant, she bounces on her toes. With a ferocious sound, I pull another trick to overpower her, kicking out her balance. We go down in a tangle of limbs, rolling until I land on top of her.

"Well that's just cheating the exercise. Let me even the score if you're going to play dirty." Rowan locks her legs around my waist and grinds against me.

"Fuck," I grit out. "Brat. I'll punish you for that later."

She wraps her arms around my neck to whisper against my jaw. "I'll probably like it."

Somewhere behind us, my brothers heckle us. One of them wolf-whistles.

It would be too damn easy to haul her ass over my shoulder and hike down the hill to my place, lay her out and devour her body. The desire to let her all the way inside my walls flares in me as I meet her dancing gaze.

My heart gives an odd little clench. It aches in my chest.

Would allowing her to know me fully be a mistake that puts me at a disadvantage? Countless broken rules or not, I'm still unsure if it's a risk I'm willing to take.

CHAPTER TWENTY-FIVE
WREN

*C*ARPE REGNUM.

The parting words my father said the night of the gala still linger. It's been just over a week. This is the kind of instinctive suspicion I won't leave alone. If there's a stone to overturn for information we can use, we'll grind every rock to dust.

Beneath the Crow's Nest, I pace the main room while we work with what we've been gathering. Using what we know about people's secrets, we've applied pressure to discover how many of the city's businesses had stakes in SynCom, Stalenko Corp's shell company. Most shares were sold in the last year, so this has been going on under our noses.

We know from Rowan's solo expedition to the docks that the Stalenko underlings aren't all happy they need to rely on the investors. Levi and I questioned the guy who killed our informant and stalked Rowan, but we didn't get anything useful out of him. Not that I gave him long to answer before the rage won out.

My gaze flickers to the laughter coming from the open door of the gym more than once. Maisy and Rowan are doing yoga. Since the shooting range yesterday, the knot of tension Rowan carried with her from the moment we met has eased slightly.

The broken pair of glasses that I've hidden from her will bring that tense worry back and I'm reluctant to do that. I've kept her brother's glasses to protect her from the pain of reality and loss that awaits her.

I refocus on the speed of Colton's fingers moving over his keyboard. "What did cell phone mining get us? Anything new we can use?"

"My loyal subjects are still working on hacking financial reports to dig up concrete proof, but Harrington's camera roll is filled with a juicy affair, Ludman is embezzling, and Roucher has a secret second family. Scandalous." Colt uses his tongue to toy with the stick of the lollipop he's playing with instead of finishing and waggles his brows. "No direct mentions of *carpe regnum*, but the message logs did have some weird conversations. I've been separating those ones out while sifting through the data in the last week. Look."

Jude and I step closer to the screen while Levi remains leaning against the wall with his arms crossed. Each message is cryptic to hide the real meaning, but two in particular catch my eye.

It's top priority to take care of the rat infestation. The key to our success is at stake.

Our rodent problem has been responding well to Mr. King's wisdom. Testing bait to see if anything in the historic castle brings more friends out to be dealt with.

Jude ruffles his dark hair. "Rat infestation. Hannigan?"

"An investigative journalist stumbling into something they don't want found out? Yeah," I say. "Stalenko Corp's mafia ties are only rumored, but if it became public who was funding their operation here, the investors' status or business holdings could fall apart. They might be using Stalenko as their criminal lap dogs for a cut, but when it comes down to it, they'll protect themselves first. If it were us and he had information on what we do, we'd hold him, find out what he knew, destroy his evidence, and make sure he didn't talk, too."

"These dates don't bode well," Levi says.

He's right. These messages date back over a month. According to Rowan, her brother has been missing for three months by now. The last message is from the night before the founders gala.

"Any way to trace the locations of the sender?" I prompt.

"Some originated downtown, but I ran the numbers and they're using burner phones." Colt glares at his screen, clacking his tongue ring against the lollipop. "No mention of rats since the last text, though."

The chance Ethan is alive is slim.

I set my jaw and deal with the information in front of me. "They baited to see if anyone else is a threat. The royal mentions could mean locations, but where?"

"I have some possible ideas, but I don't know." Colt brings up a map of the city with several areas highlighted. "A couple of parks, a building on Old King's Road downtown, a church. There's a building on campus that sort of looks like a castle."

Scanning the map, my frown deepens. No pattern emerges. What are we missing that has allowed all of this to unfold beneath our radar?

It draws mine and Fox's attention like a beacon when the girls come out of the gym with towels draped around their necks. They halt at the other side of the couches.

"Well, there goes my zen." Maisy sidles over to Fox, slipping her hand in his back pocket. "The mood is pretty heavy in here, boys. What have I said about holding in the negative energy?"

"Did you find something new?" Before I'm able to stop or shield Rowan, she's at Colt's side, scanning his screen.

"We think these are coded, but they could mean places your brother was kept," I explain gruffly.

She clenches the towel in her grip. "Where? Let's go right now and find him."

"We don't know," Jude says. "These are some of the most well-respected people in the city. Tracking them to their meetings hasn't gotten us anywhere we didn't already know about and rule out."

Eyeing the dates on the messages, her shoulders slump. It twists my gut to see her defeated. I move to stand behind her, pulling her into my body. At this point, it would be better if we never found Ethan. Seeing his dead body might break her and if I can keep that from happening, I will.

"Wait." Rowan points to the upper screen. "Make that one bigger."

Colton clicks on it and it fills another monitor. He studies her with his brows drawn down. "What do you see?"

"A piece of the puzzle I haven't given you yet." Handing over her phone, she shows him the recording she played for me almost a week ago on the day I moved her out of the apartment. Distractions piled up in the days following, leaving me so preoccupied by protecting her that I'd almost forgotten about this. "Isla and I found this on Monday when we spotted this guy on campus again right after you left. What if this is what they're referring to?"

"Oh shit." Colt replays the short clip, then sends it to the computer to start again. "This is in the same hall as your Ethics class?"

"Yeah. Isla said the statue doesn't have a name, but a Latin phrase about keys to the kingdom. This talks about a castle and a king. The night I snuck around the warehouse, I overheard them talking about keys."

I stiffen. Keys to the kingdom. *Seize the kingdom.* It's too similar to my grandfather's motto.

"You didn't tell me this part."

"It was an emotionally draining day and I was mad at you after." Rowan sinks an elbow into my gut and I grunt. "I've been trying to research the keys symbol, but I haven't gotten far. We need to find a way inside."

"I'll pull the full history of the campus' schematics to look for it. If there's one secret room, there could be more." Colt types as he speaks, pausing only to swivel to address us. "How would you feel about adding a secret sliding library shelf to the Nest?"

"Is that really important right now?" Rowan asks in a strained tone.

"Focus," Levi says.

"Right, right. Sorry, babe." Colton taps his temple. "My brain tends to bounce around. I fire on all cylinders sometimes."

With another sequence of keystrokes, Rowan's photos of the wall fill another monitor.

"Foxy, how do you feel about a field trip? Bring Penn," Colton says.

Fox grumbles about the nickname and swats at his foster brother.

"If there are others, this might be how they differentiate locations on the down low." Jude strokes his chin in thought. "You said this statue had a plaque with the kingdom phrase?"

"Right." Turning to me, Rowan licks her lips. "Do you think someone is holding Ethan in a hidden room since you haven't been able to find any trace of him?"

An invisible iron band winds around my chest. The hunt hasn't been entirely fruitless, but I can't tell her about the glasses hidden in a safe in my room.

"Possibly."

The answer tastes foul.

"He has to be," she whispers to herself.

Rowan's small voice is filled with so much determination and faith that her brother is still alive that it stabs into my gut.

Fuck. Fucking *fuck*.

The truth is going to destroy her. And there isn't shit I can do about it to protect her from the earth-shattering pain.

CHAPTER TWENTY-SIX
ROWAN

For the third time in Wren and Levi's weight training session, my eyes drift from researching the history of Thorne Point University on my laptop to watch sweat roll down Wren's hard body, mouth watering at the flex of his biceps while he bench presses twice my weight. The cotton workout shorts dip low on his hips, giving me the perfect view of the carved muscles there. Why did I think it was a good idea for my productivity to sit in here?

Uhhhh...

I give myself a mental shake from drooling at his glistening abs. Jesus. *Jesus.* A fantasy of straddling him on the bench and licking them fills my head.

After pestering Colton and threatening him with becoming an irritating barnacle if he didn't give in—*"Don't threaten me with a good time, babe."*—he agreed to let me help, providing my research task. Their plan is to gather as much information as we can to find out how to enter the room

I saw. An uneasy pit twists my stomach with the worry we're wasting time when we could be doing, searching in person. Wren's kept close watch and won't let me go to campus alone. He's figured out what I might try to pull on my own without them backing me up.

So far between the two of us we've guessed the location of two other rooms. Later tonight Fox is sweeping the campus to give us something more concrete to go on.

"Break for a circuit, then do another set," Levi directs.

Wren emits a low groan and accepts the towel offered to him. Levi has worked him hard and I've enjoyed the show. Setting the weights on the bar, Wren sits up and swipes the towel over his sweaty skin.

He catches me watching from my spot on the mats on the floor and smirks. "Busy over there?"

"Yes." Cheeks hot, I return to my research.

"No sex in the gym," Levi deadpans.

My mouth drops open. "We weren't—"

"Eye fucking counts. And you've been doing enough of it for the last twenty minutes."

Levi dodges the rolled up towel I lob at him with a laugh. The guys continue their workout in the corner of the room while I click on another PDF from the campus library's digital archive. The crest was established when the college was founded. Originally it admitted men only, much like most of the more elitist schools around the country.

I chew on my lip as I skim the information, noting down anything I think could be a connection to the triggers we're looking for to access the hidden room. It still boggles my mind that the company Ethan has been researching is connected to this secret. He stumbled into this looking for corruption and got more than he bargained for.

The lack of information I'm able to find bugs me. I wish more than anything I could just call Ethan and ask what he does when he hits a research wall.

After Wren completes another set of weight lifting, the guys finish up. I pack up my laptop and follow them from the room.

"How much of the city's history do we know?" I ask.

Wren hitches a shoulder. "I'm from a founding family. *The* founding family of the men who started this town. My name is on every damn business or historic building in town. But I've never heard of hidden rooms or passages, or any other secrets of the city that mine or any of the other founding families could keep buried."

The bitterness in his tone makes me blink. He's never seemed to hate the money he has, so I'm left wondering if there's another reason he draws a line in the sand between himself and his family.

* * *

Something about watching the fight nights makes adrenaline race through me. It's the best kind of foreplay. My tits have been tingling, nipples tight, and my skin flushed for half the night. Every time I met Wren's eyes I've been eager to get him alone. Levi was the main fighter, but Wren took on a cocky challenger from the crowd. The guy hit on me and Wren knew it, letting his jealousy loose in the ring.

Knowing what seeing him fight does to me, he made sure I was watching before he laid out the frat boy after toying with him.

I needed tonight to forget, to shut my brain off from everything, otherwise I'll continue to drive myself insane needing to act.

Jude and Colton are drunk, leaning heavily on each other when we arrive at their lair. Levi disappears into the gym and seconds later, angry music blasts from the speaker system. The other two trip over nothing and end up in a collapsed heap on the couch. Colton nuzzles into Jude's shoulder.

"I'm hungry," Jude slurs.

"You jus' crushed my entire bag o'fries."

"Leftovers," he announces, making an attempt to move that goes nowhere.

"No," Colton moans, clamping his arms around his friend's waist. "Comfy."

They're both snoring less than a minute later. Wren goes to the kitchen and places two water bottles on the table before turning to pin me with a hooded leer.

We've been dancing around the electric heat simmering between us all night in an unspoken game of who snaps first. Instead of pressing against him like I want to, I keep one of the couches between us, flashing him a daring look.

The corner of his mouth hitches up. He moves and I dodge.

"Why do you prolong the inevitable?" he rumbles.

My breathing turns shallow, nipples hard from the way he stalks me around the room. I bite my lip.

"I love making you work for it."

The chase is on again. This time I dart down the hall. A muted shriek escapes me when his big arms lock around my waist and haul me against his chest.

"Now you're all mine," he growls in my ear.

His voice is sinful and full of gravel. My clit throbs.

Wren spins me and bends to put me over his shoulder, slapping my ass when I squirm. I run my hands over the firm muscles in his back as he weaves through the halls until we reach his room. Inside, he drops me to my feet and nudges me.

My back hits the wall and then he's on me, the taste of alcohol on his tongue and the masculine scent of his musky sweat making me dizzy with want.

"Wren," I gasp against his lips. "I need you. Right now."

"I know what you need, kitten." He cups my pussy through my cut off shorts, grinding the heel of his palm into my aching clit. "*Mine.*"

"Yes."

Scrabbling for the hem of his Henley, I rip it up, exposing his abs and the barbell in his nipple that drives me crazy. He fists my hair and trails biting kisses down my neck. I arch into him and clench my thighs.

"Please," I push out.

His teeth scrape my collarbone and he grabs my ass, lifting me again without stopping his attack on my neck. A moan bubbles out of me before I hit the bed. I struggle out of my leather jacket and shirt while he yanks my shorts and ripped tights off. Stepping back, he loses the rest of his clothes while leering at me. I spread my legs in invitation.

A rumble of approval vibrates in his throat. He joins me on the bed, grabbing the sides of my thong as leverage to grind his cock against me.

"Fuck!" My nails dig into his shoulders and I rock into the pressure. "I could come like this."

He pulls harder on the sides of my underwear. "I'm going to fuck you through the mattress tonight, little kitten."

Heat races over my skin. I hook my ankles behind him and reach up to twist the sheets while delicious pressure builds in my core. His movements light me up each time his erection teases me.

"Been wet for me all night, baby? These panties are so soaked I can smell how much you need me to fuck you right now."

"Oh god." I squeeze his hips with my legs as an orgasm ripples over me.

I sink my teeth into my lip and ride the wave.

"Time to get rid of these."

Wren adjusts his grip and tears the lace. Air stutters out of me at the way his heated gaze drinks in my pussy. He brushes his knuckles over my folds, rewarding me with a firmer touch when I spread my legs wide again. Leaning over, he nips my hip. The sharp sting makes me cry out, but it's forgotten when he moves to take a nipple in his mouth.

"Tonight I have you bare," he rasps against my flushed skin. "Nothing between us."

My stomach dips and I nod, burying my fingers in his hair as he returns to tormenting my nipples with tongue and teeth. Adjusting the angle of my hips and lifting my knees, he glides his cock over my slick folds until I'm squirming. Flashing me a savage grin, he enters me in one thrust that makes me scream.

"Fucking stunning." He covers my body with his and moves. Pulling almost all the way out, he thrusts deep and hard with a rough groan. "You feel so good wrapped around my cock, baby."

The fullness of him inside me is exquisite. Each snap of his hips elicits a spark of liquid fire that builds into an inferno. Another orgasm is imminent.

Wren's attention fixates on the bounce of my tits. My eyes rove over him with equal admiration for the strength of his broad shoulders, the sharp line of his jaw, the alluring dominance in his eyes.

The ringing of his phone on the nightstand startles me. A short laugh slips out and I relax back into the sea of pleasure. I expect him to ignore it, but he surprises me by leaning over to grab the phone without breaking his pace.

He presses the phone to his ear and answers. "Yeah."

I gape at him while he drives his cock into me. Brows furrowing, he looks away while listening, then glances down at me.

"No, now's good, Penn. Tell me." The smooth, business-like command in his tone makes my pussy clench and he smirks.

He doesn't stop fucking me. Not a lazy pace, but the same forceful rhythm that has me trembling. It makes me wetter. The only indication he's affected by my reaction is the darkening desire in his eyes.

Wren listens to Penn, absently playing with my clit in a way that makes me gasp. His gaze drops to the sight of his cock sliding in and out of me and he gathers some of my wetness to continue teasing my clit, alternating between rubbing it and pinching it when I least expect it. My panting could give me away and I clamp my lips together.

I've never been so turned on in my life from him taking me apart with precise control while carrying out business as if his cock isn't buried inside me.

"Colt and Levi took care of security. You and Fox sweep the buildings and report back."

When he angles his hips and the pleasure intensifies, I begin to whine. Flicking his cool gaze to me, he holds my throat and squeezes to cut off my desperate noises. His piercing eyes burn into mine while he continues to speak on the phone.

"Check it against the blueprints he sent."

Finally, he hangs up and tosses the phone aside. Neither of us pay attention to where it lands.

Wren's lips capture mine in a ravenous kiss and he swallows my cries as he brings me over the edge. I've never come so hard, my entire body riding the explosion of ecstasy. Tensing above me, he closes his eyes and fills me when he comes.

"That was..." I have no words for it.

"I always know what you need."

The smooth tone and his words wrap around me in a blanket of contentment. At first Wren was a mystery I needed to unravel, then a challenge of authority that excited me, but now...he's beginning to feel like something else. Something more.

CHAPTER TWENTY-SEVEN
ROWAN

In the morning, I wake to Wren sitting at the desk across the room. The locket is out, but today he doesn't cradle it like the world is ending. It rests next to his expensive watch by his elbow, a comforting presence instead of a lifeline.

Drifting lazily between peaceful sleep and consciousness, I watch him typing on his phone, periodically sipping from a steaming mug of coffee. The aroma is heavenly, drawing a faint envious moan from me.

"There's coffee brewed for you, caffeine demon. This one's mine."

He glances up, drinking me in. I slide my thighs together beneath the sheets. He must have cleaned me up after I fell asleep in his arms. Warmth expands in my chest.

"I'll never tire of waking up to the sight of you in my bed."

Another flutter moves through me. Thoughts from last night return. We aren't just drawn to each other, but it's the way we are around each other that's grown how I feel about him. When he takes control, I've allowed my walls to come down and be vulnerable. At first his control was something I fought, but now it's different, carrying a weight of importance I don't want to resist.

"Can I explore the hotel today?" I ask.

He considers me over the rim of his mug. When we met, he was impossible to read, but subtle emotions flicker over his features as he comes to a decision.

"It's safe here, so yes. Don't stray too far, my curious kitten."

Grinning, I stretch and get out of bed. Something else has changed since spending time at the Nest—I find it a lot less creepy. It almost feels like it could be a home. Insane, considering the decrepit state of the place upstairs, but somehow there's connection here.

Half-dressed, he drags me over by his grip on my open oversized flannel shirt and gives me a coffee-flavored kiss. I lick his lips and hum at the crisp scent of aftershave.

"Mine," he rumbles.

"Me or the coffee?" I tease, reaching for his mug to steal a sip.

He smacks my ass and grips it. "Both. Better get dressed fast, or I'm dragging you back to bed."

For a moment, I'm frozen between my curiosity and climbing into his lap. I rake my teeth over my lip at his amused huff. The chance to discover more of the hotel wins out. I finish dressing, slipping into my Vans and swiping my phone.

Wren follows me to the main area. Colton is still sprawled on the couch, ass up and snoring, but Jude is awake, eating a chipotle-scented shredded chicken stew from a reused butter container. He lifts two fingers in greeting. I stop to pour a mug of coffee. At the tug on my braid, I angle my head back against Wren's chest and accept another kiss.

"If you wander out there for too long, I'll come to catch you again."

A shiver moves down my spine. "Like the hedge maze?"

"And this time I won't stop," he promises in a low rasp.

Cheeks prickling with heat, I take my coffee and set off to look around. In the chilled light of day, I admit there's a somber beauty to the overgrowth of vines creeping through broken windows, faded dusty paintings, and peeling wallpaper from a bygone era.

Without any students partying, the ballroom is an expansive room that was exquisite once. Sunlight streams in, creating dancing pools of dust motes. The ocean air gusts in on the breeze and a pair of gulls call to each other in the distance. Closing my eyes, I imagine it in its prime one hundred years ago.

Leaving my empty mug in the ballroom, I move down arched stone hallways and poke in unlocked rooms to sate my need for knowledge. A few creaks and the scurry of small animals make my heart race, but the eeriness no longer makes me uneasy. As I search the place, I try to view it through Wren's eyes to understand what he sees.

The back of the building overlooking the sea has a beautiful solarium. A dome of glass extends high and the vines have made this their home, nature happily reclaiming the old greenhouse. I skim leaves as I pass, soaking in the peaceful stillness.

I move outside and descend the wide terrace steps. A weed-choked path takes me to the cliff's edge.

This is the first time in days—weeks—things have slowed down enough to have a moment to myself.

In a way, getting caught up with the Crows has been a blessing in disguise. It's kept my thoughts at bay, but up here on the cliff the things I've attempted to ignore creep back in. The only other time I've been alone with my thoughts was when Wren locked me in the penthouse. I channeled it into feverish creativity, writing that book so I didn't have to face what I'm feeling directly.

I hug my waist. The wind whips flyaway hairs from my braid.

I came to Thorne Point to follow my brother. To be like him. But it was also an escape from what I couldn't deal with. My past. Guilt.

If I became like Ethan, I didn't have to be myself.

And it's harder to lie to myself without him here.

Am I strong and independent as I've always told myself, or do I choose to isolate myself from most people because of what I went through out of fear of opening my heart? Other than my brother, I wanted to be alone. I didn't let Mom in—couldn't even look her in the eye. I distanced from the friends I did have and other than Isla and the Crows, I've never let anyone in.

Without Ethan around, it casts the things I do in sharp relief. My single-minded stubbornness, the insatiable impulsiveness, the need to act alone. Asking for help has become a foreign concept. If I don't ask for it, no one has to see how much I struggle.

Before the Crows, my brother was the one person I trusted in and relied on. The only person I clung to.

I don't know if it's the growing trepidation to find him or gradually giving in to Wren's control that's peeled the curtain of my denial back, but I see it now. See how much the traumatic experiences of my past shaped me to the point of extreme independence, never wanting anyone to do things for me. Acting on my own before anyone could tell me not to.

Maybe in a way it's to make myself relive my biggest mistake—disobeying Dad and damning him to his death.

I push away hard from the truth of how damaged I am, digging my grip into my shirt. It's my fault.

Ethan has always been my benchmark. Since we were little kids, all I wanted was to mimic everything he did. After the accident with Dad, that need only grew. Without him, I'm floundering to keep it together.

Again, the dark shadows of my mind prod me with the question of life without my brother.

I *miss* him. His terrible jokes, his crooked smile, the way he'd ruffle my hair when I was in a mood.

The argument we had before he left sits heavy on my shoulders. I shouldn't have told him the truth. Trembling, I close my eyes and breathe. Icy fear swallows my heart.

I don't know how long I stay like that before crunching footsteps and the telltale scent of crisp aftershave pull me from my thoughts. When Wren reaches me, he grasps my chin and draws me into a deep kiss that soothes the pain.

The corner of my mouth curls. "Come to catch me?"

"Before you find trouble, yes."

He stands behind me and I lean into him. We watch birds swoop to the ocean for fish and listen to the waves crashing against the jagged rocks below. I slip a hand into his, finding the locket held in his grip. He tenses, then gradually relaxes when I lock our fingers together to cradle the locket between our palms. I've never seen him let anyone else touch it and it stirs my heart.

"This is a nice spot to think."

"It is," he agrees.

We walk the edge of the cliffs. The familiar view has me pursing my lips to the side.

"Are we near the shooting range? The coastline looks the same."

He glances at me. "Yes. I had it built on this property."

"How far is it?"

"About half a mile."

My brows lift. "Big place. Is it all woods other than the range and the Nest?"

Wren licks his lips, cutting his gaze out to the ocean. His fingers flex around the locket tucked between our joined hands.

"A couple other buildings. But yes, mostly it's woods."

"You prefer it here to the penthouse." I watch his handsome features for a reaction and catch the tightening around his eyes. I'm right. "And you like this better than your family's estate."

"I hate it there." His voice turns gruff. "It's nothing but a mausoleum to me."

A sharp ache cracks through my chest. I nod in understanding. I couldn't wait to get away from home when I left for college.

Wren stops walking and studies me for a moment. "It's only been my brothers by my side for years. I haven't let anyone in for a long time. I can't give myself over easily."

The thought of his stony mask chipping away little by little in my presence flits across my mind. I listen to what he wants to tell me, too cautious to break the tenuous mood.

"This place is left as it is because it reminds me that all things wither and die."

"Not entirely," I murmur. He regards me with interest. "There are plenty of plants thriving happily. Death is…" I search for how to phrase the feeling that filled me as I explored. "An ending, but it's also a beginning for something else. Whatever is lost finds a way to go on."

My vision mists and Ethan and Dad's voices fill my head, their laughter living on in my memory. A lump forms in my throat and I swallow it back. Wren's eyes bore into mine and he tucks a flyaway hair behind my ear.

"The Crow's Nest Hotel was a business established by my great-grandmother. She was my grandfather's mother on my dad's side. Years of family history and tradition of a founding family bloodline held a life she had no interest in." His lips twitch and warmth infuses his words. "She was a stubborn woman from what I understand, much like you."

"That's amazing that she started a business."

"After the hotel closed, it sat for years. My grandfather Hugo never cared for it. The guys and I used to come here when we were younger and snuck in. It was our spot."

I smirk, picturing them as teens banding their boy's club together. "Is this why you're called the Crows?"

"A coincidence. Crows are intelligent. They can remember faces, recognizing who to trust and who wronged them. They resonated with us."

"They're also an omen according to superstitious wives' tales. Do you consider yourselves as four for wealth, or do Fox and the guy you talked to last night count if you want to send the message sickness and death are coming?"

The slow smile he gives me is cunning and sinister.

"How did you turn this place into a nightclub?"

"I bought it. The deed had been in my family, but my father and grandfather put it up for sale intending to cash in on it. I convinced them to sell it to me."

"You had to buy the deed off your own family?" I can't hide the surprise in my tone.

"It was the first thing I'd built for myself."

"That must have made them proud."

Wren goes quiet, rubbing the locket with a complicated expression.

"Sorry. You don't have to tell me."

"It's not that. You made me think of something else." The distance in his eyes pulls at my heartstrings. Dropping my hand, he turns away, then angles his head back to speak. "I want to know if you've thought about what we might find when we search the hidden rooms."

I freeze. "What do you mean?"

I don't want him to say it. His jaw works.

"Rowan, your brother might not be there. He might not be anywhere we can reach anymore."

Denial springs to my tongue, but I bite it back. It's what I've been thinking, isn't it? The nightmares, the heinous whisper in the back of my mind. I ball my fists.

"Ethan has to be alive."

Wren whirls on me, grabbing my arms. "And if he's not?"

"He *has* to be," I repeat on a growl.

If my brother is dead, I'll never be able to make things right between us for what I did.

After the admission tumbled from my lips, Ethan went still. He'd been in a weird mood for several days, but he'd never looked at me like that before. Like he couldn't stand the sight of me.

"You made him drive out in a deadly storm despite the state of emergency warnings to come get you after he told you not to go?"

I flinched at his tone. All I could do was nod. He knew I'd been in the car, but he never knew what really happened that night.

"We...had a huge fight the night before he left," I start. The wind steals my words, whipping them off the cliff's edge to drown the truth in the sea. "I kept something from him for a long time, but I couldn't any longer."

The memory of that night slams into me hard.

I wanted to take my confession back, but it was out there. The awful, selfish way I acted out in the open.

"Does Mom know?" he asked in a voice that scared me.

I shook my head. "You can't tell her. I just—I had to get it off my chest. I've kept it a secret for so long. It was a mistake."

He had no sympathy for the tears streaming down my face.

"Siblings fight. It's normal," Wren says distantly, as if my story makes him remember something else. "It can't be helped."

"This is different. He was so angry. I'd never seen him like that, not with me." I swallow past the ache in my throat. "I just want to make things right with him."

Ethan always looked at me with kindness and sympathy. He was my rock, but once I confessed, he suddenly looked at me like I was a stranger.

"You're such a fucking brat, Rowan. I can't believe you lied about this for so long." His features contorted, stealing away the fun-loving brother I'd always looked up to. *"I'll never forgive you for this!"*

Releasing a horrible yell, he threw his fist through the wall, leaving a hole. Panic overtook me. Ethan had never shouted at me once in my life. "I hate this. I hate myself. I hate you! I wish I'd died in the accident instead of Dad!"

"Good," he spat. "Because I'm never talking to you again. When I get back, you'd better be gone. Find somewhere else to live, because you're not welcome here anymore."

Days after he was gone I patched up the hole. It was supposed to be a surprise and an apology for when he returned. A desperate hope that he didn't mean what he said, because I didn't mean what I told him either.

Wren waits for me to continue, but I'm lost in my head. He clears his throat, tucking his hands in his pockets. The stoic set of his jaw reminds me of how closed off he was when I came to the Crow's Nest, contrasting how much he's opened up around me.

"You lied to me that first night." His inescapable gaze traps me. "You thought you got away with it, but I've collected enough secrets over the years to know when someone hides something from me."

At first, my instinct is to play it off and stick to my story—that I have no secrets worth his time. But I'm tired of running from this.

"So what if I did? I couldn't...not this."

"I broke my rules by allowing you to keep it. We don't do that for anyone—even family pays the price we demand. It's why Fox is here. He owed us for the help we offered him." Wren dips his head, studying me closely. "I'm giving you the choice to tell me now."

My throat closes and my breathing turns shallow. I want to give him this because he asked instead of stealing it from me. By his own word he doesn't offer this, but he did for me. Out of everyone in the world, he might be the only person that would understand and accept me for what I've done.

It's time to come clean and confess my darkest secret.

CHAPTER TWENTY-EIGHT
WREN

I<small>F</small> there's any chance of trusting Rowan, I need to know. That's how things work, my brothers and I know every corner of darkness in our hearts and minds. The fact I offered her the choice, the out to keep the secret, is huge. I wait with bated breath as she visibly weighs her options.

"This secret could tear my family apart." Rowan's features crumple. "I've never told my mom. Not after what she went through losing Dad. It already broke things between me and Ethan."

I shift to watch the ocean, allowing her to take her story at her own pace. The only reason I broached the subject of her brother is because I don't want to keep what I know from her anymore. Holding it back is taking a toll on me. It was for her benefit that I hid what I believe is true, but I need to prepare to protect her from the unavoidable pain awaiting her. It makes it harder that things were rough, leaving lingering guilt that won't resolve.

Rowan's voice grows distant as she recounts, the anguish of an old wound coming open seeping into her tone. "I was fourteen and so damn rebellious. I've always looked up to my brother, but when he left for college I was kind of floundering. We were so close growing up, but at times we reached those in between stages where we couldn't stand each other."

My lips twitch as similar memories of going through the same thing with Charlotte cross my mind. She was my light, but I squandered the time I had with her when I thought I was too cool to hang around my little sister.

"My friends were going to a party. It's a small enough town that it's noticeable who does and doesn't go to these things." Her voice cracks. "Dad told me I wasn't allowed to go, but I was stubborn. So I snuck out."

Fondness expands in my chest for the picture she paints, even while she's sad. I rub the locket in my hand with my thumb.

Releasing a shaky exhale, she goes on. "He must have checked for me, because he found out I wasn't home and came to get me. God, it was so embarrassing." She rubs her face with her plaid oversized sleeve. "We had a blowout fight right on the beach. It started to rain and I got drenched because I wasn't ready to leave. Dad and everyone else went under the porch or retreated inside. He threatened to call Ethan to tell me to get my ass in the car, and I hated disappointing him."

An unsettling chill creeps into my veins. She told me her father died. I have a sinking feeling I know where this story goes next.

"The storm was crazy. High speed winds and rain pelted the car. No one was supposed to be on the road, the state shut everything down in preparation." Rowan's tone takes on an eerie detached quality. "The news warned that a hurricane could veer toward our small beach town. Dad was too busy yelling at me on the ride home and I was too headstrong not to argue back. The headlights came out of nowhere when I was shoving at my dad. I don't remember what I was saying, only that I pushed him. It's weird to feel the weightlessness when a car flips. It stole my breath and I banged my head on the window."

Unable to feign interest in the ocean, I turn to her and take her by the shoulders, wishing I could pull the weight of her misery onto mine.

"He—" She hiccups out another uneven breath, closing her eyes. "He tried to put his arm over me so I wouldn't get hurt. Even though I was being such a bitch. Even though my mistake caused the accident, he still tried to do it. The angle...his seatbelt couldn't keep his upper body protected. He had severe brain damage. I got out with barely a scratch and he was broken beyond repair. There wasn't anything the doctors could do for him. Mom chose to keep him on life support. We decided to turn it off the summer before my freshman year at Thorne Point."

A leaden weight settles in my stomach. I caress her cheek with my knuckles. My understanding of her grows. Even before she told me, I recognized the pieces of her that fit with the razor-sharp shards of myself.

Rowan stares at me with years of guilt clear on her face. "I'm the reason my dad died. That's my secret. I killed my own father."

There's no way I can break her more, not right now. The glasses will remain in my safe. But when the truth about Ethan comes out, I dread how much I'll crush her from another loss I can't defend her from.

"I'm no stranger to death." I pull her into my arms and stroke her back. "You know there's far more blood on my hands."

The blood of the man who posed a threat to Rowan, the blood of my sister's predator, the blood of enemies I've made.

"I'm a terrible person," she says in an empty tone.

I squeeze her. "You're not, Rowan. You're the farthest from it. Between the two of us, I'm the gruesome monster."

She rests her head on my chest and I offer her my own darkness. I'm at a point where my feelings for her outweigh my lack of trust in others, but the fortress around my heart is almost cracked open for her. I want to let her in as an addition to the few people I consider family, the few I truly have the capacity to care for.

"My sister was everything to me. She was sweet and smart. She outshone me, and I was happy for her achievements." My hold on Rowan becomes the support I need instead of something I offer to her. Sensing the change, she burrows deeper into my arms. "She committed suicide."

"Wren," Rowan whispers. "I'm so sorry."

Her sympathy washes over the brittle ache of the past. "It destroyed my family. We weren't the greatest family to begin with, but we all loved Charlotte. You've seen what it did to my mother. My father shut us out. And I... I became single-minded in hunting down the sick fuck who drove her to it. Her teacher."

Thinking of Coleman ignites the all-consuming fury that controlled me, pulled me from the emptiness that numbed me otherwise until she came along.

"I wanted justice. It was my focus for years."

"I would want that, too," Rowan murmurs. Drawing back, she traces what's visible of the rose tattoos winding around my arms beneath the pushed up sleeves of my sweater. She pauses on the white roses spattered in blood. "These are for her?"

"Yes."

For a moment, her attention drifts to the other arm covered in black roses swallowed by flames, the stark representation of myself.

"And the locket you always take out when you're thinking. That's hers too."

I squeeze the necklace tighter before showing it to her. "Last piece of her I have."

"That's not true." Rowan places a palm over my chest where my heartbeat drums. "She's in here. They live on with our memories. You'll always carry her with you."

"Considering how blackened the damn thing is, I hope not," I snark. "For my sister's sake."

Rowan's mouth quirks. "Maybe they're the pieces of light that pierce through the shadows."

"You don't have a dark heart, little kitten." I press my lips to her forehead. "You're not guilty of anything. None of it was your fault, not the accident, not what happened after. You were just a kid."

Wrenching back to peer at me, her throat works. Unlike the burden she carried before, she loses some of the tension weighing her down. "You're the only other person I've told about this after it destroyed my relationship with Ethan."

"He would forgive you." I cup her face and draw her near.

The relief she exudes is palpable. She clasps my wrist. I'm struck by how important she's become to me. How much I would give to keep her happy.

"Remember what I told you. There is nothing fragile about you."

When our lips touch, the kiss is emotionally charged from both our confessions. I hold her close when she breaks down from the emotional turmoil she's kept locked inside, ready to take on every one of her demons to stop her tears.

I'm still a cold bastard who wants nothing more than to control the world around me, but Rowan has rule over a softer part of my heart. A fitting throne for my queen.

CHAPTER TWENTY-NINE
WREN

The tension in the car is oppressive. Jude's body is like a statue as he weaves through downtown traffic, jaw clenched and brows furrowed. I glance at him and frown, equally unhappy that we have to play this card.

"I didn't want to use this," Jude says.

"I know." I rub my temple, gaze sliding to Rowan in the backseat. "We have to do something."

Jude exhales forcefully through his nose. He'll have to suck it the hell up. Pippa isn't one of us anymore, so she doesn't deserve our loyalty. She's already proven that she doesn't give a shit about us. He needs to accept it most out of all of us.

The Thorne Point Police Department looms in the middle of the street we turn down. Jude's grip tightens on the wheel the closer we get to the red brick building.

"If the cops didn't care about Ethan missing before, why are we going to the station?" Rowan asks.

"We're buying what they know," I say.

She's silent for a beat. "They know?"

"They'll know something," Jude cuts in. "Always fucking do."

"So they could've helped find my brother sooner?"

Rowan swallows and grips her seatbelt, meeting my eyes when I turn to face her. If they'd helped her—and they wouldn't have, not without the right bribe—she never would've become mine. I reel in the urge to climb back there and stake a claim on her again so she knows it.

"Thorne Point's *finest*," I spit, "are an unhelpful bunch of greedy bastards and lowlifes. Whatever help they could have offered would have come with a price tag you couldn't afford or worthless assistance."

"More or less than the price you demanded?"

Her expression pinches and her eyes shimmer. My heart squeezes, the damn thing impossible to control now that it's woken up to beat for her. I get out once we're parked and go to her door to help her out, pulling her close to murmur against her ear.

"They wouldn't have helped you." Swallowing, I push out husky words I rarely offer. "Trust me."

Rowan nods, taking my hand. "Sorry. I know, and I do—" My misbehaving heart leaps into my throat and I squeeze her hand. "—it's just hard when I don't know what I could do to help find him."

It's lucky Jude knows the schedule of the department's front desk. The sweet old woman doesn't stand a chance against his charms.

"Rosemary," Jude greets warmly, leaning an elbow on the desk.

"Jude." Rosemary lights up, adjusting her Coke bottle glasses. "What a lovely surprise."

Reaching into his pocket, he puts down a coin wrapped in protective plastic on the counter and slides it across. The quirk of his crooked smile is practiced to perfection and smooth as fuck. "Found you something."

"The 1870 Liberty silver dollar I've been on the hunt for? Oh, Jude, this will complete my collection!"

If possible, Rosemary becomes livelier. Rowan peeks at me curiously and I shrug. Before Rosemary can snatch up the coin, Jude drags it back with a charming smirk that makes a dimple appear.

"Ah, ah. Rosie, you know I can't just give it up." He leans closer to flirt our way in. "What kind of favor will this buy me?"

Rosemary flushes, her mouth open in a tiny, wrinkled *O*. She blinks owlishly and peers around.

"What kind of favor?"

"For you? The Rosie special." Jude holds his fingers close together and squints. "Just a tiny one."

Her rapt gaze drops to the coin he rolls through his fingers in a showy dance of skill. She watches it go back and forth twice before she flashes another look around at the few other people in the lobby area.

Jude tosses the coin and snatches it from the air. "Let us back there. I found something for one of Detective Bassett's ongoing cases, but she made me swear to keep it on the down-low. You know how she gets." He winks. "We're just doing what she asked. So, for the price of this baby, will you waive procedure for us?"

Rosemary takes less than thirty seconds to decide and is the chipper owner of some useless collectible coin. Jude's smile drops once we pass the barrier to get past the civilian section.

"You really aren't above bribing old ladies?" Rowan whispers.

He shrugs. "I do what I have to, sweetheart."

"Was the coin even authentic?"

"That would be telling."

I know him. While he has no qualms screwing over most people to run a successful con, he probably did hunt down the real deal for Rosemary.

Pippa is filling out paperwork at her desk in the open floor plan space when we slip in. It's a slow afternoon for the force, most officers milling around with half-eaten sandwiches and chatting like gossipy hens. Pippa is the only one hard at work.

The second she glances up, her features contort and her gray eyes darken with fury. Jude offers her a severe smile.

"What the hell are you doing here?" Pippa is pissed, her dark curly ponytail whipping back and forth as she glares from us to her colleagues laughing in an office with the door ajar.

I pick up a framed photo from her desk and keep my tone light. "Is that any way to greet your old friends?"

"You called us, remember?" Jude plants his hands on the desk, bracketing her elbows before she sits up and covers case files labeled *Leviathan*. "That's what your call log will say."

"You son of a—"

"Save it, pipsqueak." Her mouth clicks shut at the old nickname. Jude toys with the other items on her desk, choosing the pen she was using to twist between his fingers. "We need to talk."

Seething, she explodes from her seat. "If you think I'm going to have anything to do with you—"

"I suggest we find a nice private room." This time the threat is clear. I tip my chin toward the other officers having their boys club lunch while Pippa works through hers. "Wouldn't want to tarnish that gold star you've been shining since you joined the force, detective."

"Please," Rowan adds, shooting me and Jude a sharp look. "I really need your help to find my brother."

Pippa's freckled cheeks blossom with color, but she swallows back her retort. "Fine. Come with me." She leads us to an empty office and checks her watch. "You have twenty minutes until Bill comes back from lunch. I'll give you five. Make it quick."

For all the smooth work he did to get us this meeting, Jude hesitates. It's a testament to how much this girl once owned him body and soul that betraying her cuts him deep. She did it to him first. In my eyes, she deserves his retribution.

"Tit for tat, brother," I mutter.

Jude grunts. "Do you remember that night?"

Doing this with an audience must kill him. I commend his resolve to do what it takes. We've all seen him torture himself going over what happened and what he could've done differently to keep his ass out of juvie. It's all Pippa's fault.

She sucks in a breath and closes the door. "How could I ever forget the worst night of my life?"

"You and me both, baby girl." Jude's mouth curves without any trace of humor.

"Don't," she hisses. Stricken, she casts a hateful look at me and Rowan. "Stop playing games."

Jude dips his head and crosses the room to tower over her, face hidden from view by the sweep of his hair. She's horrified by whatever expression twists his features.

"You know you were there," he starts in an emotionless tone. Pippa flinches. "I know you were there. We all do."

"You don't know anything," Pippa bites out.

"Oh, but baby, I do. I have proof." Jude makes sure she's watching as he slips a flash drive from his pocket, waving it before doing a sleight of hand trick to make it seem like it vanished.

Pippa's face drains of color. "No."

"Yes."

"You've been holding out all these years to fucking blackmail me, asshole?" Her breathing speeds up and her fists ball.

Jude sucks on his teeth. "Been holding out for a lot of things. Now, if you don't play nice, this could mean the end of this career you've worked so hard for. They'll find out what you're complicit in, and then what?"

She clenches her teeth. "I won't let you."

"Good," I cut in, popping away from my slouch against the wall. "Then you understand what's at stake if you don't give us what we want."

"I fucking hate you," Pippa fumes.

"Likewise. These are the details of a call that came in at 2 a.m. yesterday." I show her the notes Colt copied to my phone once he went through his recordings of 911 calls and caught this one about a noise complaint coming from the campus. "We need the report details."

Pippa's eyebrows furrow. "That… Okay, ignoring the fact you are even privy to information like that, this is nothing. I checked it out but no one could corroborate. My supervisor told me to write it off. I have the report."

"Give it to us," Jude says.

"And if I don't? No matter how small the matter, it's still a police report. I can't just give you that shit without putting my job in jeopardy."

"Your job is already in jeopardy," Jude says cruelly.

Pippa clamps her mouth shut, mulling over his warning. After a minute, she makes the right choice. "Wait in the hall. I don't want anyone to see."

She leaves and Jude stares after her, his face painted in regret and the pain of losing her.

"Are you okay?" Rowan asks.

Jude clears his throat. "Yep. Let's go. I hate the stench of pigs."

We move to the hallway. It's not long before Pippa speed-walks by without acknowledging us, slipping a nondescript folder in Jude's outstretched hand for the pass off out of the line of sight from the camera with me blocking the exchange. Rowan's eyes widen and I wink at her.

"Spy shit," she murmurs on our way past Rosemary.

"Just business," I say.

We wait until we're in the car before reading the report. Jude hands it to me and I skim its contents.

"Noise complaint was called in by a freshman who stayed too late at the library. Heard it on her way back to the dorms. She describes it as a struggle that ended in a scream."

"Let me see that." Rowan takes the paperwork, eyes flying over it. "This says she was near Withermore Hall at the time. The secret room." She covers her mouth with her hand. "Oh my god, he might have been there."

I stiffen. "We don't know that for sure."

"It's written right here in the report."

"It could be anyone." I work my jaw. "But...I hope it was your brother."

"Let's get this to Colt." Jude starts the car and pulls out into downtown traffic.

I leave Jude to his brooding over the past. Each time I glance back, Rowan is staring out the window with unfocused eyes, on edge but hopeful since we read the report. Her hope turns my insides to stone.

As the city buildings whip by and thin out on the way to the Nest, my thoughts churn coldly over what this means for her and her brother. If it was Ethan screaming that caused the noise complaint, then he was alive—*was*. Now more than ever I believe we're too late, allowing the distraction of Stalenko Corp to keep us from finding what I thought was a body.

But it was necessary when Rowan was the one at risk. If the choice was to save Ethan Hannigan or his sister, I choose her every time. Even if she returns to hating me for it.

Once again, I'm conflicted by whether to tell her what's in my safe or not. I already questioned if I should tell her before, no longer comfortable lying to her, even if it might protect her heart. It's a first for me to take someone's feelings into consideration before I act.

Would it be cruel to leave her to her hope or a mercy to kill it?

The thought doesn't leave me alone as we arrive at the Nest. Jude handles passing off the report to Colt while I take Rowan's arm and tow her with me to my room.

"What about—"

"I have to show you something important," I confess.

I tested the topic on the cliffs yesterday. Hearing how she views herself, her part in Ethan's disappearance, firms my grim determination to lay the truth out.

She sits on the edge of the bed while I kneel to access the safe inside one of the drawers at my desk. The cracked plastic frames lay where I left them when we discovered them.

"About three weeks ago, we found these by a dumpster at a warehouse on the north side of the city." Turning them over in my hands, I sigh and hand them to her, watching recognition dawn on her face. "I think your brother is dead."

"W-what?" Rowan's voice is barely above a whisper. "You—you had these this whole time?"

I grimace. "Yes."

"You've kept them from me?" She cradles the glasses as tears well in her beautiful eyes. "They're Ethan's."

"I know."

"How did you find them?" She demands, jumping up from the bed to rush me. Her voice cracks as she thumps my chest with her fists and it slices my insides to ribbons. "Tell me right now, Wren."

I catch her wrists. "When you first came to us, we already thought it was futile. The men who sent the guy to follow you also killed the best informant who works for us. That's how we ended up at the warehouse. I thought these made it a clear-cut answer when we found them busted up. It paints a vivid enough picture."

The tears stop and my fierce girl pins me with the fire blazing in her eyes. "Why didn't you give them to me then?"

"You..."

I trail off. Being at a loss for words isn't common for me. I find it unsettling to not know how to wield my most powerful tool against someone.

"Tell. Me."

Even as we argue, I can't stop the reaction I have to her effect on me, heat and anticipation pulling into my groin.

"I thought it was for the best to keep you in the dark."

Her gaze hardens and her throat convulses with a swallow. "You should have given them to me as soon as you found them. All this time I've—"

She breaks off with a choked noise.

"I did what I had to. If we went back, I'd make the same choice if it meant you didn't have to face this horror."

Pushing out of my grasp, she goes to the desk to lay down the broken glasses. Beside them is Charlotte's locket, left behind for once instead of carried with me. I never forget it, but today it slipped my mind before we left.

My heart stops when she grabs it and whirls to face me. I lift a hand automatically, stupidly attached to a goddamn useless hunk of precious metal. It's only a locket, but it's the last piece I have of my sister, much like her brother's cracked glasses.

"Listen, you cold, unfeeling bastard—"

I move across the room, caging her against the wall. Snatching her wrists again, I pin them to the wall and grind my dick into her stomach.

"Tell me, is this unfeeling?"

The problem is I feel too damn much for Rowan—more than I've felt for any lover, more than I feel for my mother and sister, more than I feel for my own fucking brothers. She's captured my heart irrevocably.

Caught off guard, she stares at me, unconsciously returning the pressure with a swivel of her hips. A feral groan leaves me and I crush my body against hers. We've walked this path too many times and our bodies have become attuned to the arousal dancing in our veins.

"I'm trying to protect you," I rumble. "Everything has been to protect you. I've fucking killed for you and I'd do it a million times over. I know how it feels to have your world ripped apart, so forgive me from wanting to shield you from that pain."

She shudders, emitting a tormented gasp. When I pry the locket from her death grip, she drops her forehead to my chest while I return the necklace to safety on the desk beside us.

"You took the choice from me."

"Because I didn't want to see you hurting."

"He has to be alive," she says in a voice so small and brittle it sinks razor sharp claws in my gut. "I need to make it right."

Understanding empathy lances through me. Enough guilt rests on her, but resolving the fight she had is the last hope she clings to.

Cupping her jaw, I make her meet my eyes. "Your brother was caught up with dangerous people. You know that. I know it. They followed you, definitely intent on killing you. Either to cover their tracks, or make sure he never sent you any of the information he collected on them. It's probably too late for him."

"You don't know that," she accuses. "You don't fucking know, that 911 caller—"

"Rowan." Inhaling, I bring my forehead to rest against hers. Emotion tinges my words without restraint. "Just think, baby. I know how people like this work because I work like this. He might be gone, but it's not too late for you and I'm trying to fucking keep it that way. You're important to me and I'll do anything to ensure you're safe."

Laying my heart on the line feels monumental. It's a risk I've never taken before, but it feels right to give it to her.

I intend to step back, but she grabs onto my shirt and kisses me angrily. Sifting my fingers in her hair, I let her. The taste of her fear is plain, telling me how frightened she is that I'm right. *I understand*, I say with the stroke of my tongue. I know the need to shut off intimately—I give into that darkness and violent thirst when I crave the escape she's begging for.

Pulling back, I stare at Rowan. Her glare bounces between my eyes and my mouth. When she goes for another kiss, I shift my head back, lifting my brows in a question she needs to answer first.

Releasing a furious growl, she shoves me away. I back up and she plants her hands on my chest, pushing until my knees hit the bed behind me. With another shove, I allow her to knock me down. She rips out of her flannel, discarding it before she climbs over me, capturing my mouth again.

I squeeze her hips and let her take control for once. She needs this and I'll give her anything she needs.

Our bodies do the talking. Rowan gives me her fears to swallow whole with each ferocious kiss, each rough touch. I'll take every burden from her she wants to be free of.

We strip, pausing only to trade biting kisses that leave her lips swollen. She straddles me and sinks down, bracing her hands on my chest for balance as she sets a wicked pace. I close my eyes and curse at the heat of her clenching my cock. Her head tips back and her mouth parts on a ragged cry.

Grabbing her around the waist, I flip our position and pin her to the bed. Each snap of my hips makes her beg for more. I fuck her with a savage brutality I've never used with her, and she gives it right back to me, clawing her anger into my skin until she draws blood while I drive into her without stopping.

Rowan has asked for my monster before and I'll give him to her again, shrouding her in the pitch darkness of my soul so she can hide from everything she believes taints hers.

CHAPTER THIRTY
ROWAN

Thorne Point University has one of the most beautiful college campuses I've ever seen. At night, it's the opposite. Terrifyingly haunting, the ominous air pervades the grounds.

I match the guys, dressed in black clothes and a hat pulled down to hide my face. They move in a fluid synchronicity that speaks to years of doing stuff like we're doing now—sneaking around, breaking in.

After Wren's confession last night I snapped. I needed the release of wildness or I would go insane. Reliving the accident converged with the angry last words my brother said to me to create a storm threatening to devastate me if I didn't find some way to express the anger and pain.

Wren followed me in that dive off the edge without question. He makes me face hard truths with his cruel calculative nature, but he never leaves me alone, not since the penthouse.

When we were finished, the tears came. He held me until I cried myself to sleep. And even then, he never left my side.

At first I was pissed at him, but when I think of how much it would have crushed me to know about the glasses before everything else that's happened, part of me is glad he kept them from me. Maybe he understands me better than I understand myself.

I don't know if I'm ready to believe the logical side of my brain that turns over the possibility we're too late to save my brother, or if I'd rather remain optimistic. For my sake, Wren has acted as if this is a rescue mission, referring to Ethan as alive.

Tonight will give me the answer once we get inside the hidden room. My stomach is a mess of anxious knots.

"Feeling very horror movie pansy right now," I mutter to Colton. "Like I can only hack it during the day. This place is creepy as fuck at night."

He winks, eyes crinkling at the corners. A smile is hidden behind his half-mask. "I love it at night. It's my goal in life to meet a ghost on campus."

"A legit one?"

"Yup."

"Quiet down," Wren orders.

We reach Withermore Hall and I shake my hands out. It seems like a lifetime ago I was existing as a normal college senior. I'm not sure I could go back when this is over. The thought is worrying, but I push it away to focus on the plan.

"Ready?" Colton nudges me.

I nod and follow their lead. Jude picks the lock with practiced ease. When we passed the security booth, Levi pulled some kind of martial arts sleeper move to knock out the guard. The gadget Colton carries is meant to scramble anything on the WiFi and cellular networks.

It occurs to me that they all trust me to show me the full extent of their gray morality. They don't abide by any laws but their own.

Inside the dark building, we locate the hall with the bust. Colton counts the wood panels to the one we need and marks it while Levi locates the trigger we found—one of the keys carved into the lacquered wood can be pressed. The craftsmanship is masterful, almost invisible to someone who wouldn't know what to look for. Fox admitted he missed it the first time when he and Penn came to check this out.

I hold my breath as the wall gives way, granting us access to a darker hallway.

"Moment of truth," Jude murmurs.

Every inch of me is wound tight, ears strained for any sound, eyes wide as we step into the unknown. I jump when Wren's big hand clamps the back of my neck. He traces his thumb on my skin with soothing pressure.

"Easy, kitten. I'm right here. You're with us."

"I don't know if you noticed, but I'm not as criminally inclined as you are."

"Aren't you?" he teases. "Penchant for trespassing and snooping around. You fit right in."

The short hallway is musty, but the room at the end is brightly lit. A long cherry wood table takes up most of the room surrounded by matching high-back chairs. The room itself is austere, not much more than stone walls. At the other end of the room, there's a different wooden chair, one rough hewn with alarming restraints for arms and legs.

What the hell did we stumble into?

"Um," I say.

"I see it." Wren passes me, holding out an arm to silently tell me to stay where I am while they spread out to search the room.

Levi and Wren check out the chair while Jude runs his fingers along the wall seeking other triggers that might lead off from this room and Colton records everything with a drone. He told me in the car he planned to create a digital 3D map of what we found to overlay with the blueprints of the college.

I survey the long table. "This looks like something to have a conference at."

Someone grunts in acknowledgement of my observation. Each seat has the crossed keys carved into them. Beneath them are the words *clavis ad regnum*. Keys to the kingdom, just like the plaque on the statue outside. I snap a photo.

Levi kneels down and touches the floor. "Blood."

My heart stops and I spin to him. "No."

Wren darts an uncharacteristically somber look from the floor to me. Levi moves back when I stumble over, pulse rushing in my ears.

It's not a lot of blood, but it turns my stomach. The stain is a dark brown, spattered in a line away from the chair. Like someone was hit across the mouth, maybe.

I can feel the way the guys exchange glances, silently communicating with each other while I struggle to hold it together. The blood doesn't have to be Ethan's, but my mind already makes the decision, imagining him strapped to a chair while men seated at the table watch him fight for his life.

Focusing on anything else going on around me is impossible.

"There's nothing else here." Jude's words cut through the fog my mind is caught in.

I'm frozen in the center of the room by the wooden chair and the dried blood staining the floor. There's no other concrete sign of Ethan. I thought there would be something, anything to give us answers. It's another dead end.

Defeat chokes me as I cover my face. Wren's arms circle me and I lean into his comforting rich scent as I battle the fatal crack in what's left of my hope.

"He's not here," I say hoarsely.

Wren holds me tight, lips pressed to the top of my head. His words from before sink in, shaking me to the core with a likelihood I can't deny anymore.

"I'm sorry, Rowan."

Colton, Levi, and Jude echo Wren's sentiment. I can't stop trembling in his arms. The adrenaline that kept me going tonight drains. All that's left is an unrelenting ache.

Ethan might be beyond my reach. I'll never be able to hear his laugh, or have him edit what I've written, or be able to right things between us.

CHAPTER THIRTY-ONE
ROWAN

Without Wren's strong arms around me, his murmurs in my ear keeping me going, I might have stayed in the hidden room.

What we discovered left us unable to move forward for a few days until Colton finishes his 3D map rendering. I skipped midterms. Emails from three of my professors sit unopened in my inbox. A missed text from Mom asks if I'm feeling better—my feeble excuse the last couple of weeks to get out of our weekly dinner calls. If I talk to her, she'll know how wrong things are and I can't lie to her anymore about Ethan traveling for work.

Apprehension plagues me. The ominous sense of knowing what must be coming hangs in the air.

Wren stands before the partially fogged mirror in the bathroom connected to his room at the Nest taking care of the blond scruff shadowing his jaw. He's shirtless, sweatpants hanging low on his hips. Heat pulses between my legs as he drags the old fashioned razor over his skin, shivering at each audible scrape.

It ignites a tingling ember in my chest that he allows me to see him so unkempt. Despite the feeling of running from the inevitable, being with him keeps me from spiraling.

Rising from the bed, I go lean in the doorway to watch him shave, eating up the steady concentration, the ripple of his broad shoulders, the methodical way he rinses the blade after each pass beneath the warm water running in the sink. It's erotic, the tantalizing show tightening my nipples to hard pebbles that poke through the t-shirt I stole from him to wear.

I just want to feel good and forget, like when he helped me before.

Slipping behind him, I take my time tracing random patterns on his skin, running my fingertips over his shoulders. He stills, angling his head back to peer at me, then resumes shaving.

His powerful body is a work of art. While he's occupied, I take my time exploring the expanse of his skin.

The tension builds in each short breath I take, each brush of my breasts against his hard body, each inch of his skin I lavish with attention. My lips press to his back, tongue sneaking out to taste him. I hum in pleasure, enjoying the way his abs contract beneath my hands.

"You know I have a straight razor pressed to my throat, right? You're playing with fire."

"So play me back." I bite his shoulder to entice him to fall into oblivion together. "Live dangerously with me."

"Kitten," he rumbles as my touch delves into his waistband to stroke him. "Fuck, you drive me crazy."

The razor clatters into the sink. It's my only warning before he grabs me and spins to lift me on the counter. He barges into the space between my spread legs and pulls me in for a scraping, messy kiss. I trace the contrasting rose tattoos on his arms from memory. Shaving cream smears on our cheeks and a laugh bubbles out of me. He swallows it, along with the gasp I make when he glides his fingers over my bare folds.

"Always so ready for me," he rasps against my lips.

"Yes," I breathe. "I need you."

"I like the way that sounds on your perfect lips." He grasps my jaw in one hand, watching the arousal dance across my face as he sinks a finger in my pussy, hooking it right where I need. I gasp. "That right there. Heaven on earth, baby."

Pulling his finger free, he licks it before kissing me. I can taste myself as his tongue pushes into my mouth. He lifts the hem of the t-shirt to expose me and lowers the waistband of his sweatpants far enough for his hard cock to bob free.

"Spit," he demands, clamping the back of my neck and directing me to bend.

I follow his order, working my saliva and letting it fall to his cock. He groans, slathering it over himself. My lips part when his cock nudges my entrance and I tip my head back.

His mouth grazes the column of my throat and with a sharp thrust, he enters me. It chases away the terrifying thoughts looming in every corner of my mind.

"Feels so good." I wrap my arms around his neck, smearing what's left of the shaving cream.

"This what you needed?" Wren speaks into my neck, the remaining stubble creating a delicious burn where he nuzzles.

"Yes. Always."

"Mm, damn right. I like the sound of that. You're mine and you're not going anywhere."

"Yours," I echo on a moan.

Wren fucks me like he wants the world with me. He drives his cock into my pussy like he's trying to put a baby in me despite my birth control. Holds me like he never intends to let me go.

Overwhelmed tears prick my eyes. I don't want to let Wren go either. Not ever.

Our arms lock around each other and he captures my mouth for a searing kiss while he circles my clit with his sure fingers, knowing exactly how to play my body to bring me the most pleasure.

"With me, baby," he urges.

A cry tears out of my throat as I feel the throb of his come filling me, tipping into my own oblivion.

Our feverish promises ring in my ears. *Always.*

It's only two days later my world falls apart in the worst way imaginable.

* * *

The call comes when we're all laughing in the main lounge. The afternoon has been enjoyable, a rare one amidst the revolving door of bad news. The seven of us are hanging out with beer and pizza. It's a much-needed moment so I don't go insane from worrying and wondering.

"Oh, come on." Maisy looks to me for support. "He totally likes her."

"He definitely feels something." I waggle my eyebrows and take a sip of beer. "I think it changes from hate to something else depending on the day. Didn't know you could love anyone but the guys and your creeper knife collection, buddy."

Levi's lips twitch and he rests his elbows on his knees, dangling the neck of his beer bottle from his fingers. Maisy perches on Fox's lap at the opposite end of the couch. Wren and I are on the other with Jude, both of them enjoying their cigars. Colton sprawls on the floor making his way through another slice.

Contentment fills me with a warm glow. Even with everything in the air right now, I feel like I've found a place for myself amongst this strange family of friends. I can ignore everything else wrong in my life if I can just keep this.

"Who are we talking about again?" Jude questions. "And why are we gossiping about it?"

"Don't," Levi says when I open my mouth.

Smirking, I mime zipping my lips.

"A secret?" Jude perks up. "One fifty."

"Three hundos," Colton chimes in, waving his wallet.

"Fuck you all," Levi grumbles.

I turn to Wren. "What's happening?"

He holds up a thick roll of cash. "Betting who will be the first to ferret out his secret."

"You're betting that much?"

"I have an advantage I intend to press." Wren's arm over my shoulders draws me closer.

"Which is?"

"You."

I huff out a laugh. "Nah. Good luck with that. I'm a fortress."

"We'll see about that, kitten. I'm very persuasive."

A bolt of excitement makes me grin in challenge. I lean into his side.

Not long after, Wren exhales smoke through his nose and jostles me as he fishes his ringing phone from his pocket. "Yeah?" The lazy smile drops from his face and he sits up, putting out his cigar. "When? Fuck. Okay, we're coming."

"What is it?"

The expression he gives me makes my stomach clench and I scramble from the couch to follow everyone. "I'm coming with you."

He freezes, shoulders rigid. "That was Penn. A body washed up by the docks. It could be your brother."

Everything crashes into me at once—dread, fear, denial.

"I'm coming."

The words are firm but my insides are a riot of anxiety. This feels important. The shoe drop I've been waiting for. I have to go with them.

He's silent for a long beat. "Alright. That's your decision. I won't keep you from this, but don't leave my side."

"Fine."

In a tense parade, we leave the party atmosphere behind. The ride over is hell on my nerves. Once I recognize where we're headed, I dig my nails into my hands.

When we arrive at the shipyard, Penn meets us by the gate and the Crows walk in like they own the place. Penn leads us to a spot in the shadows of a large ship docked. The area is deserted except for the conspicuous lump covered by a tarp. My pulse drums in my veins at the sight of it, my mind trying to process there's a body underneath.

"Took care of security already," Penn says. "They think I'm doing an OSHA inspection. Caught them before they saw."

"How was it found?" Wren asks.

"A homeless guy spotted it and fished the body out. He took the shoes, but that's it. It spooked him when I got here. If I wasn't swinging by on my rounds to check up on their operation, things might have been different."

Wren looks in the direction of the SynCom warehouse I cased when I found the address in the apartment. "No other activity?"

"It's dead over there on Sundays." At the heavy silence, Penn clears his throat and ruffles his disheveled hair. "Uh, sorry."

"Sloppy," Levi mutters.

Wren grunts in agreement. "Tide must have swept back in after..." He pauses, glancing at me. "After they disposed of the remains."

"Dumping the body. You can say it." Is that my voice? It sounds strangely clinical and detached.

Wren brushes a hand over my back. "Are you sure you want to be here for this? This isn't easy for anyone. I'll take you home."

My chest constricts. "I'm not going anywhere."

We're too far away to see any details under the tarp. Nausea churns my stomach, the threat of throwing up hovering at the edges of my senses.

It's not Ethan. I repeat it over and over to myself.

Maisy takes my hand. My palms are clammy, fingers stiff.

"Anything on him?" Jude asks.

"Just a phone. Water damage might have wrecked it." Penn passes it to Colton.

"I'll see if I can put it through rehab," Colton says.

"Is this the guy?" Penn asks.

Fox holds out an arm to bar Maisy and I from following. She squeezes my hand as he, Penn, and Levi stride over and remove the tarp.

"Shit. It's him," Fox confirms. He covers his mouth with the back of his hand and puts the tarp partially back over the body. "Stay back, Maise. You don't need to see this."

Icy dread spreads over my nerve endings.

Cursing, Wren shifts to block me with his massive body, but the need to move takes over. Letting go of Maisy's hand, I shove past Wren and Colton.

"Rowan—fuck—just wait!"

Wren's words don't reach me. He grasps at my jacket, but I wrench free. Weird things become my only focus, time moving slow and fast all at once. The scrape of my shoes on the pavement is too loud in my own ears and the piercing call of seagulls makes me flinch. My eyes grow so wide they hurt, but I can't look away.

"No." It's a single, broken whisper. "No, no, no, *no!*"

A horrid rattling scream rips my throat raw, the full-body rejection of what's before my eyes exploding with nowhere to go but out in an unintelligible cry. My hands shake as I clutch the sides of my face. It's difficult to draw a full breath.

Ethan's green coat is what I see first. I'd recognize it anywhere. Knees buckling, I stagger another step. I need to see. I force myself to overcome the fear flooding my system to close the distance.

"No," I moan, the denial hiccuping out of me.

"Ro..." Colton trails behind me, reaching out to touch my shoulder.

"Let her go," Wren says solemnly. "It's her right."

"She shouldn't have to see this," Colton snaps. "It's fucked up."

"She can do anything she wants right now. I'm not stopping her anymore. If she wants to see, she sees."

Vision blurry from tears, I stumble the final few steps to the lumpy form Penn, Levi, and Fox kneel beside. I barely register Levi's gruff words of sympathy. I blink and the tears roll down my cheeks. My knees give out and slam hard against the pavement when I collapse. Stinging pain radiates, but I ignore it. I ignore everything around me except what's in front of me.

This is wrong. All wrong.

Worse than the accident with Dad.

The smell makes me gag. It's rotten, soaked in death. There are...pieces missing where there shouldn't be. My mind revolts and I block out what I can't handle.

There's no way to deny it's Ethan's jacket. A frayed patch he won at the boardwalk in our hometown is sewn into the shoulder to cover up a hole. The hood strings are knotted three times because he thinks it's the only way to keep himself from losing them. Each distinctly *Ethan* thing pricks a fresh fatal stab wound in my chest.

"Show me." My voice wobbles, so raw it's unrecognizable.

Levi exhales, flexing the fist perched on his bent knee. "You don't need to see the rest. It won't help."

"Please."

His stern gaze burns into the side of my face. I can't rip my eyes from the patch on my brother's jacket.

My brother is dead.

Washed up with the tide, hauled in by a stranger. So close to me finding him, but I'm too late, too fucking late.

The truth clangs in my head. In my soul, ripping me to pieces.

Levi places a hand on my shoulder and moves the rest of the tarp out of the way. An anguished noise of horror leaves me and I clap a hand over my mouth.

Wordlessly, I shake my head. The sight is unbearable. Without the jacket, I might not be able to identify him. Instinct begs me to close my eyes, to shy away from the truth, but I make myself look so I know what was done to my brother.

Ethan's features are there, underneath the gruesome bloating. My heart aches so much it feels as if it will never beat right again. I hunch over. The chill spreading through me seeps deep into my bones, dragging me down.

Wren's shoes appear beside me and he reaches down to caress my head. I fall against his leg, clutching at his jeans for support as silent sobs rack my body.

"I'm sorry," he says. "I'm so sorry it ended like this."

The last things Ethan and I said to each other haunt the edges of my thoughts.

"Jude, can you—?"

"Got it covered." There's a short pause, then, "Sorry, Rowan."

Behind us, Colton speaks rapid-fire on the phone and Jude takes point, giving orders. Wren stays with me the whole time while I'm lost in unimaginable sorrow.

Fuck, what will I tell Mom? After all the lies I fed her. This will kill her all over again.

With a trembling hand I slowly reach to stroke Ethan's hair. Wren crouches to my level and clasps my wrist.

He keeps his tone firm, but speaks to me with an understanding tenderness. "I know all you want is to give him a hug, but his body might not be able to withstand it in this state. I also can't let you leave any fresh evidence of yourself post-mortem."

Right. I know that. The true crime documentaries I like talk about the effects of water on deterioration and decomposition. Bile rises in my throat and I bury my face in Wren's neck. I can't even hug Ethan goodbye.

"I'll never get to tell him I fixed the hole in the wall," I choke.

Wren cups the back of my neck, squeezing supportively. "He knew because he knew how you are, my brave girl. Never doubt it."

I twist my fingers helplessly in his shirt. "Everyone leaves and it's my fault."

"I'll never leave you." He kisses the top of my head as fiercely as the tone of his words. "I swear."

The activity around me blurs in and out while I allow the ice in my bones to drag me deeper. Instead of following the urges to act, do, move I give in and succumb to the empty sanctuary in my mind.

"Rowan." Wren's voice is firm as he grabs my hand and tugs me with him, startling me out of my catatonic daze. "We have to go *now*. The police are coming."

"The guy must have called it in after he left," Penn says.

The wail of sirens sound in the distance.

Frozen and numb, I only stumble, my attention locked on the horrible sight of my brother's body. I should still be screaming and crying, but there's nothing left except this intense, cold emptiness carving out a cavernous hole in my chest.

Wren curses and tosses something to Jude before sweeping me up in his arms. He carries me away, but I crane my neck to see. The sirens get closer as we move further from Ethan.

My world collapses in darkness.

CHAPTER THIRTY-TWO
WREN

Guilt bears down on me as I watch Rowan drift through the shock in the following days. I failed and it eats me up inside. All I wanted was to shield her from this grief.

No one should have to see someone they love meet a gruesome end like Ethan's, his body bloated, his sagging skin a sickening shade of gray, and pieces of him missing where marine life fed on his remains.

If I could have kept her from seeing anything like that, I would have. But she'd only hate me for hiding something else from her. She needed closure after what she'd been through searching for him.

I'm primed with the urge to rip the damn world apart to destroy anyone who hurts her, but we don't have a definite on who dumped Ethan's body yet. It's possible his disposal was purposefully sloppy to cast blame on Stalenko Corp if he was meant to be found, but then why put the investment in their operation at risk? Insurance, perhaps. A threatening reminder of the puppet master in control—the one who holds power over a mafia organization to use as their lackeys.

The questions plague me, but I put them all aside to take care of Rowan. She needs me. I failed her in finding her brother, but I'll never fail her again.

Trapped in mourning, she spends most of the time in my bed. When she's not sleeping, I coax her to eat, help her wash up, and hold her when she wakes from her nightmares.

Her mother has called a few times. Rowan's left me to handle it. I let the calls go to voicemail and listen to the woman's soothing voice assuring Rowan that they'll get through this, and that if Rowan wants to come home or wants her to come up to Maine, she's ready to book a flight.

When I'm clearing a plate away, I find a crumpled letter from the college on the floor. It's a warning about her grant status if she doesn't bring up her GPA. I hand it off to Colt to pull his strings and reverse. If she wants to return to her studies and complete her degree, I'll make damn sure she's able to do it.

We tell Fox he's free to go. In our eyes, he fulfilled the favor owed and he deserves a happy life. Whatever threat awaits us when Colt finishes his work, we won't involve Fox further to drag him into the storm I feel brewing. Before they left yesterday, Maisy stopped by my room to say a heartfelt goodbye to Rowan, telling her the door to their bungalow in California was always open if she decided she needed a change of pace. The idea of her leaving doesn't sit well with me, but I said nothing while Rowan mustered up a thank you and accepted a hug.

It's getting late when I lay down next to my girl and guide her into my arms. She's awake, as she's been most of the day, peering at me in a way that wrenches my heart. Her despair chokes the room. I tangle my fingers in her hair and kiss her forehead.

"Are you hungry?"

Rowan shakes her head.

"You barely let me feed you today."

"I don't want anything," she whispers, burrowing closer. "Just this."

After stroking her back, I break the silence. "What are you feeling?"

Not *how are you*, not *you're going to be okay*. No one has time for that bullshit when they're mourning a traumatizing loss. It all becomes empty platitudes that do fuck all. I'm asking her to let me in.

Rowan takes a long stretch to answer. When she does, my arms tighten around her.

"Murderous." She gives me a dead-eyed look I'm all too familiar with when I look in the mirror. Her words drip with venomous loathing. "I want to make the people that did it hurt."

She's succumbing to the same terrible beast that dragged me under and ruled me after I lost my sister. I understand anger is the easiest emotion to latch on to. Sometimes it's the only reason to get out of bed.

I smooth her hair back and brush my thumb over her cheek. "If that's what you want, I'll help you. I'll pull the trigger for you." Bringing her closer, I ghost my lips over hers, breathing my words between almost-kisses. "But there's something you should know about revenge. It doesn't take away the pain."

Even after I took Coleman's life for preying on my sister, the ache of her loss is as sharp as ever.

"I don't care," Rowan growls.

If this is the path she chooses, I'll be with her every step of the way.

"As long as you're aware it's not a cure to what you're feeling. There's one other thing you need to know."

"What?"

Grasping her jaw, I tilt her face to meet my commanding stare.

"Whatever you want to do, we'll do it together. You won't go off to seek revenge on your own."

She jerks to escape my hold, but I squeeze, keeping her in place. I wait expectantly.

"You'll stay like this all night if that's what it takes."

She bares her teeth and wicked delight fills me. My vicious little kitten.

"Tell me, Rowan."

She skates her eyes away, only to grumble when I shift her head where I want it. There's no getting out of this ultimatum. She can have as much chaotic destruction as she wants, as long as I'm there to keep her safe.

"Say it."

Rowan licks her lips. "Fine."

"Good girl." My mouth quirks.

Once I release her, she rolls over to give me her back. It's much like she's been for days, but a spark ignites in my chest with hope that she's coming out of the shock. She's not ready to give up yet. My fighter is still in there.

Colt pokes his head in, takes one look at Rowan, and his shoulders sag. At my questioning stare, he nods to tell me to come with him. I rub Rowan's back and she curls into a tighter ball.

"I'll be back."

Dropping a kiss on her head before leaving, I follow Colt to the main room. He jerks his thumb at the security feed.

"So, we've got company."

"How long has she been there?"

"Twenty minutes," Levi mutters from the couch. "Won't shut up. I begged him to turn off the audio."

I return my attention back to the monitor where Rowan's friend Isla Vonn waves her arms by the entrance for the nightclub, spitting mad and red in the face from her tirade.

"Turn the audio on," I order.

Within seconds her fierce tone fills the room. "—swear I will kick this door down with my Valentinos and livestream the whole thing. Let me in to see my friend! She needs me!"

Levi gets up and stomps away, grumbling about target practice.

Pinching the bridge of my nose, I head for the exit. "I'll handle it."

Stopping to retrieve what I'll need from the trunk of my car, I circle around from the terrace to the public entrance for the students who flock to our nightclub. She's still kicking up a storm, using a designer handbag as a weapon to threaten the camera. Fearsome little thing.

"Can I help you? You're trespassing."

"Jesus fucking christ!" Isla startles when she senses me looming behind her, slapping a hand over her chest.

I lift a brow, waiting for her to get a hold of herself. Her nostrils flare and she gets in my face, unafraid of me or my reputation. Well, tries to. She's about a foot shorter than me.

"Listen, you giant, I don't care who you are or what secrets it costs me, you're going to let me in there to see Rowan. I need to hug the shit out of her like fifty times minimum."

Cocking my head, I study her without giving anything away. "I see that political science degree is working wonders in your favor. Hasn't anyone told you not to lay your cards on the table during negotiations? Promising any amount of secrets to one of us is a dangerous game, Miss Vonn."

"I don't care." Isla stamps her foot. "You'd better not be locking her up again. That's right," she adds at the flash of surprise that slips out through my mask. "I know all about that."

"I didn't plan to keep her friends from her. I'll need to blindfold you to let you in, though."

Isla sets her jaw, not backing down. Impressed, I fish the black cotton bag from my pocket. Her eyes widen, but she lets me slip it over her head before leading her to another access point to get to the underground level.

I lean close before we go in. "And don't think we won't strip as many secrets as we please from you before we let you leave."

Isla's grumble is muffled by the hood obscuring her head.

Family may be hard for me, but no one should doubt that the people I care for are my world. I loved my sister, but after she died the only true family I had left were my brothers.

Now that includes Rowan.

Protecting all of them is what matters most to me.

CHAPTER THIRTY-THREE
ROWAN

I EXIST in a hazy fog that makes me question if anything is real for a long time. Maybe I died on the spot when I saw Ethan like that. Everything is a blur, melding together in a way I can't pick any details apart. The only thing I remain aware of is Wren's rich scent, my one anchor keeping me tethered from imploding completely.

On some level, a growing part of me knew the truth in what Wren tried to get me to see long before we found my brother. It still doesn't make it any easier to deal with the fact he's gone. That I'll never see him or hear his voice again. Much like when we lost Dad, there's a sick sense of relief and finality that comes in knowing Ethan's dead.

Days or hours after we arrived back at the Nest—I'm not sure how long had passed—I became lucid enough to frantically check my voicemails. One. I have one message from him. Listening to it stirs a new wave of tears every time I hear his carefree laugh because I screened his call to keep writing. Colton saved it for me so I won't lose it if it's accidentally deleted.

Missing him is like cutting out a piece of me I won't ever get back. He was always the one I looked up to, wanted to emulate. Now I feel like I need to do everything myself without his guidance.

As the sadness grows, so does my anger. It pushes me out of the fog, its hold stronger each time.

The mood swings come out of nowhere. One minute I'm smiling at a memory, then I'm lashing out. Mourning has no rules or logic, it just is.

Intrusive thoughts and an urge for unstoppable violence rise up and wind around me. They whisper sweet, monstrous promises if I give in.

No matter what Wren said about revenge, the hatred poisons me like a drug. The first hit was all it took to spread through me and take hold. In the darkest moments, it's beckoning vows to bring relief I desperately want.

I must be messed up, because the allure is strong. Now I have Wren's word he won't hold me back. I'm already capable of killing, but can I do this?

It seemed like the answer should be no. It's wrong. But he made me promise to let him help me. The possibilities make me dizzy when I know cruel brutality is what he's skilled at.

Shifting around on the freshly laundered sheets of our bed, I seek him out. He's still not back. He's made sure not to leave me for long, so it doesn't alarm me as much as it did in the first days.

Once a day he gives me a bath, carefully washing me. He tells me stories of growing up with his sister, what Colton and Levi were like when they were younger, how Jude pulled a con on him to steal his money when they first met in high school.

He appears in the doorway, eyes roving over me as if he's checking to make sure I haven't hurt myself in his absence.

"Where did you go?" I ask.

"An unexpected visitor is here. I escorted her to a room where you two can talk."

"Cryptic." I squint. "Do I have to get up?"

He crosses the room to tip my chin up. "Only if it's what you want."

I mull it over for a moment. Yes, I decide. I do want to get up. As soon as I welcome the change, a jittery energy tingles beneath my skin, like it was building up all this time. He takes me through the maze of hallways to a room far away from the central main room.

The second I see Isla, an overwhelming flood of emotions drowns me. Everything I've been blocking out comes back in a rush and I drag in a pained gasp.

"Oh, babe," she whispers, enveloping me in a hug when I rush her. "I'm so sorry. I'm here for you."

"He's...he's..." I can't get the words out.

"I know. I saw the news after your mom called me."

I flinch. "She called you?"

A new guilt takes root and grows alongside the one I've lived with for so long. I couldn't take her calls. Wren dealt with the voicemails she left when I panicked and threw my phone at him. Was that yesterday? The day before? Time has been weird.

"It's okay," Isla soothes. "I know you don't go home to see her a lot during breaks. She was only worried about you, but she also said she was used to your independence. The police haven't released Ethan yet, so she's holding off on funeral arrangements until they do. I told her you would call when you were ready and she understood."

I close my eyes and promise myself I'll call her soon. We have a lot to talk about. I can't keep lying to her—not about any of it.

The room finally registers and I glance around to find Wren leaning by the door, bulging arms folded over his chest. My brows flatten. The distraction is enough to pull me further out of the fog making my brain sluggish.

"Did you kidnap her?"

A faint smile twitches his lips. "No. I reserve that for you and you alone. She showed up ready to kick the door in."

"He did blindfold me though," Isla says.

I glare at Wren and he shrugs unrepentantly. "Nest rules."

"How long have I been out of it?" I ask, unsure if I want to know the answer.

"About a week," he answers.

I see it in the dark circles smudged beneath his eyes and the tired slump in his shoulders. He's run himself ragged to be everything I needed. I bite my lip at the affection blooming in me. To know I could fall apart and he'd catch me means so much to me.

"Before you ask, we haven't found anything new or useful." A flash of savagery twists his handsome features. "If we did, I wouldn't be here right now."

I close my mouth, swallowing back the slew of questions ready to spill out. The need to be proactive itches beneath my skin, restless from disuse by ignoring the world for days.

Isla takes me by the shoulders. "What do you need? You name it and I'll make it happen."

Wren emits a low, possessive grumble across the room. A smile ghosts across my lips.

"Coffee." It's the only thing I could stomach right now.

"Of course that's what you want." Isla's fond expression is tinged with sadness.

"I'd rather see you eat something more substantial," Wren says.

"I'd really prefer coffee." In addition to coffee, I could use some room to breathe so I can sort out my thoughts. "From that place across town—the little shop by campus? They should still be open."

Wren's mouth thins into a line. "Is that so." It's more of a statement than a question. He doesn't want to leave me alone. I nod and he stalks across the room, offering a wad of dark fabric to Isla. "Miss Vonn?"

"Do I even want to know what that's for?"

Isla winks. "Coffee and those little bistro sandwiches you like. Coming right up! We'll be back in twenty."

"I'll be back. You'll be dropped off at the senator's estate," Wren corrects. Isla pouts. Rolling his eyes, he concedes another inch. "You can come here tomorrow."

"Look at you, making more friends," I say.

He rumbles his response against my lips, stealing a swift kiss. "Don't push yourself too hard while I'm gone. I mean it. I will find out if you don't listen."

"I won't." Claiming one more kiss, I whisper, "Thank you."

I don't say it, but I mean it to encompass everything. He presses his forehead into mine until Isla clears her throat.

"Ya girl is still blindfolded here. Not a cute look. I'll only stand it for so long because I love Rowan."

Wren marches her from the room, stirring a momentary worry, but I trust he's not going to hurt her. I follow into the main room. After days mostly trapped in the hazy confines of my mind, it feels like a long time since I was last in this room. A pang hits me in the chest. The last time was right before…

Shoving back the thought, I hover behind Colton, watching him work. He glances back and grins, lifting a closed hand over his orange and black chair for a fist bump I return.

"I'm glad you're here." He points to one of the screens on the wall. "Watch the bets and let me know if Queen_Q calls, would you? Today is the day I beat her, I feel it."

I scan the online poker match. "What are you doing?"

"Multitasking like a pro, babe." He types at lightning speed on his wireless keyboard, head swiveling from one screen to the next. "The rendering is almost complete, but I have to program the app so we can do a live run with it. Also have my minions helping me scrub through surveillance footage to see what we pick up."

One of the screens further down catches my eye. It's a livestream of local news on low volume.

The reporter stands by the gate to the shipyard and the scroller beneath reads *BODY DISCOVERED AT THORNE POINT SHIPPING DOCKS.*

I flick my gaze to Colton. He hasn't noticed, too absorbed in the computer code he's frowning at. Swallowing, I listen to the report.

"The tragic story of Ethan Hannigan, a twenty-six year old Thorne Point resident, draws to an end today when police closed the case."

I can't stop the harsh recoil at those words. To the reporter, it's another story, another day, but to me it's my brother's life. If his case is closed, do the police know something Wren doesn't?

"His body was discovered last week by a homeless gentleman who came forward when asked by police to cooperate with their investigation."

Photos of two police officers display on the screen and I bite down on my tongue to smother my sharp inhale. Those are the cops who wouldn't take my missing persons report no matter how many times I tried. Everything burns—my eyes, my throat, my whole damn body.

A memory of a different news report surfaces, mixing with the one on the screen, recounting the tragic story of the car accident I caused. Reliving my past mistakes while grieving Ethan bowls me over with a sense of having no control.

"The medical examiner ruled the death a suicide by overdose when the autopsy revealed a deadly level of a synthetic opioid in Mr. Hannigan's system. With that, the police have been able to close the case. Our thoughts and prayers go out to Mr. Hannigan's family. Back over to you for the weather, Terry."

I'm shaking as the report ends and the news moves on. *Back over to you.* Just like that.

The murderous ember that flickered to life in the tumultuous last few days sparks with new energy, growing into an inferno that won't be stopped. It swallows me, fueled by so much fury and an inescapable need to do something.

They're lying. Ethan never did hard drugs. He would never kill himself.

They took him. Tormented him for god knows how long. *Killed* him. And now they're covering up his murder with this lie.

Fists curled into tight balls, I give in to the anger consuming me.

* * *

It's cold at the shipyard tonight. The wind nips at my cheeks with a stinging chill that leaves my skin raw. I grit my teeth against the rising surge of rage. Unable to wait for anyone to help, I broke my promise to Wren. He's going to be furious when he finds out after he made me agree not to go alone.

But I needed to act. I need to get revenge for my brother.

The ire of Wren and his Crows is something I'll need to face later. If I make it out of this.

I gave myself enough time to change into dark clothes and search the desk, taking Wren's silver lighter and a gun before I hopped in my car and sped away from the Crow's Nest. After sneaking into the shipyard, a plan formed on the fly through the haze shutting everything else out.

It's insane. Dangerous enough to get people killed. Exactly what I'm going for with my intent to destroy everything by burning it to the fucking ground.

The onsite gas station has medium size propane tanks lined up. A viral video I saw once popped into my head when I spot them. When surrounded in flames, pressure builds up enough to cause them to explode.

Perfect.

I steal them one by one, keeping to the shadows as I place a few around the perimeter of the warehouse, hidden amongst the crates. The last thing I take from the gas station is a canister of gas to spill over anything flammable before I light this bitch up.

Crouched in the exact spot as the night I came to investigate the SynCom warehouse, I scan the labels on the crates. From my search before, I know these assholes were connected to a drug bust. The rat they spoke of that night, information destroyed—they were talking about Ethan. They did this to him and I'm making them pay.

They're here, strolling around, smoking cigarettes and laughing. They have no idea what I'm about to do. Each bark makes me seethe. My brother won't ever laugh again.

The rest of the shipyard is empty for the night, but these men keep a close eye on their section. They must store their drugs here before shipping it out to poison the world for their profit.

These are bad people who deserve this.

I hate them with every fibre of my being.

Like a vengeful angel of death, I tuck my heart away and set my jaw. I avoid the men on guard as I spill gasoline, creating a death trap for when I ignite the lighter. It's lucky the wind is coming off the ocean tonight, masking the strong scent.

I start the fire at the back of the warehouse. Kneeling cautiously, I hold the flame close and gasp as the fumes flare up. It spreads faster than I expect.

I scuffle back, hypnotized by the hungry fire licking anything in its path. Within mere minutes it eats through the gasoline-soaked crates and wreaks destruction anywhere it touches.

I imagine the fire is me, burning everything important.

For Ethan.

A wicked satisfaction fills me watching the flames engulfing the warehouse. Shouts of alarm ring out in the night. The heat warms my raw cheeks.

I've never danced with my darkness as much as I do in this moment. Instead of running away from it, I embrace it.

A loud bang startles me, followed by more shouting.

"There!" someone yells in a thick, angry accent.

Another bang buzzes by, closer this time, lodging into a wooden crate not far from my head. Every hair on my body stands on end and fear floods my system.

Gunshots.

That didn't factor into the plan. Heart racing, I scramble for cover as another shot rings out overhead.

"Fuck! This is bad."

The plan blowing up in my face level bad.

An explosion follows the next shot and yelled curses have me poking my head up. I watch in horror as two propane tanks shoot sky high in the opposite direction I meant them to go. Instead of crashing into the warehouse windows, one takes out one of the shooters with a violent blow to the head that turns my stomach. The other crashes into the nearby crates, blocking my exit with towering flames that engulf the narrow path I was supposed to leave through.

The warehouse is surrounded by fire...and so am I.

CHAPTER THIRTY-FOUR
ROWAN

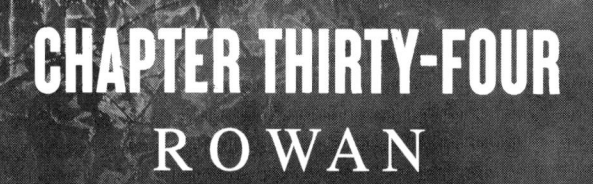

This was a terrible idea. Clarity hits me like shattering glass, ripping me from the hold of insanity. Frantic and in survival mode, I search for a way out. The other shooter is distracted by his buddy's death, but with a snarl he starts firing in the direction he last saw me.

"Shit!" I duck and crawl as fast as I can.

When I find another tall crate, I stand, leaning heavily against it while my heaving gasps end in coughs on the acrid smoke rising from the blaze. I take out the gun I brought, but I can't see where the guy went when I aim.

A shot comes from a different direction and I veer away on instinct, only to duck with a scream when another propane tank explodes in my path. This one does its job, taking out the window and a good chunk of the metal siding to leave a gaping hole. Pulse pounding, I force my feet to move, squeezing the trigger to return fire. Someone bellows in pain, but more bullets keep coming my way. The men are converging on me.

As I weave through the crates and navigate the dangerous fire, I know I fucked up big time. Wren made me promise for a reason. I should have waited for him instead of doing what I always do—isolate myself so no one sees me struggling. He wasn't stopping me, only demanding that I let him help.

My goddamn independence got the best of me and giving the urge power over me might cost me my life.

Reckless, Rowan. Completely fucking reckless and it might get you killed. In my head it sounds like Wren.

Is that what I wanted by chasing impulsiveness to the point of destruction?

No. I'm not dying. I don't want to leave Wren like this.

I pull up short, blocked by more fire. Panic pricks at my awareness, mixing with the out of control adrenaline.

"Fucking get that little bitch!"

I stay low, squeezing through crates that have yet to catch fire. There are more voices than the first two who noticed me. They're pissed and out for blood. A stack of flaming empty crates crashes over me when it can't stand on its own anymore. I narrowly escape, but cry out as a burning piece of wood catches my shoulder.

"There she is!"

Heavy footsteps head in my direction and I run, forced to leave the gun I dropped. They chase me, giving me no choice but to do another stupid thing. It's my only option. Every other route is blocked by fire or people who want to kill me for what I've done.

Heart in my throat, I run into the burning warehouse.

It's not as loud inside, the flames busy eating through the wood crates awaiting shipment and sorting outside. Black smoke billows out through the broken windows and coats the top of the rafters. I duck low as I move, desperate for a clean breath of air.

Someone is screaming in pain and calling for help. I don't answer his pleas.

There are two other exits to this place. I saw them when I set the trap. Fuck, I didn't think I'd have to use them to get out of this mess myself.

It was cold out there, but inside it's sweltering, both from the flames surrounding me and the radiating heat from my shoulder. I think I was burned. Grimacing, I hurry for the first door.

"Ah, fuck!" I yank my hand back from the handle, shaking it out from the pain of how hot it was.

Glaring at the door, I don't waste time backing away over broken glass to try the other way. Outside it seems like they've given up on finding me. Maybe they believe chasing me in here was enough. Unless they're focused on putting out the fire to save their product before coming to gun me down.

The man who was crying before has stopped. My stomach lurches, but I push myself to keep moving.

"Damn it."

Dread fills me as I reach the other wall past an office. The exit is blocked by a tower of crates. Smoke seeps in through the cracks between them. I'm not getting out that way either.

Spinning around, I keep a feeble grasp on myself before hysteria condemns me to death. Flames lick up the interior of the metal siding from the window the propane tank exploded through. I don't have long to figure something out.

I'll make a run for it. It's the only choice I have.

Rapid gunfire sounds again from the way I came in to escape. It halts me in my tracks. Tears sting my eyes and a coughing fit chokes me, sending me to my knees.

It's no fucking use. I'm trapped in here. I'm going to die because of my selfish, vengeful brashness. I've always prided myself on not being helpless, but this is my own fault. If I'd listened to Wren, this wouldn't be happening.

Bitter ash coats my throat, but I don't know if it's the real deal or from the fear and regret cloying at me.

A terrified sob tears free when something breaks down in the rafters holding up the roof.

I don't want to die. Not like this.

Regrets fly through my head one after another, each one more heartbreaking. I wish I'd told Mom everything, wish I hadn't ignored her the last few months. Sniffling, I'm unable to withhold a pained whimper as I picture hugging her, Ethan, Isla, every one of the Crows—

Wren.

"I'm sorry."

The ache in my chest steals what little breath I have left. I'll never see him again. I want to keep fighting to get back to him. He's my rock, my wicked protector. For him, I need to try. I can't give up yet. I need him.

Pushing to my feet, I smear soot and tears from my cheeks, looking around in desperation.

Plan, plan, need a new plan.

Everything is loud, wood and metal groaning and hissing. I start moving again, searching for a weak point in the walls or rolling bay doors. Sweat runs down my neck and my eyes burn from the fumes coming off the flames. Everything is too hot. I feel as if I'm being cooked alive.

Probably because I am.

Something cracks ominously and my gaze flies up.

A scream rips my throat raw as another part of the roof caves in.

I'm sorry, Wren.

I lo—

CHAPTER THIRTY-FIVE
WREN

It's a good thing my goddamn hunches are always right. I had a feeling Rowan would defy me and choose recklessness anyway, because that's what my curious, vengeful little kitten does.

She wasn't there when I got back from taking Isla home, fresh coffee brewed the way she likes it and a bag of sandwiches in hand. Colton said she came out for a minute, but said she needed to lay down. He was confused until we both heard the replay of the news livestream. He swore, but I didn't wait around, barking orders to search for her. I could ring his neck for his carelessness, but there wasn't time—I needed to get to where I knew she was headed.

The shipyard.

I curse that defiant streak I'm so addicted to in her when it could spell her death. I will not lose her.

Everything is in chaos when I arrive. No sirens yet, so either no one's noticed, or it hasn't been long enough.

I don't spare a minute, throwing myself into the fray of flames and smoke billowing into the clear starry sky. Half the Stalenko Corp men scurrying around are hosing down their product, but it's too late. Everything is charred, melted, singed to a goddamn crisp, the awful fumes stinking up the sea air.

Later I'll have time to be impressed at Rowan's ingenuity and latent skill for arson. After I make sure she's safe, then ensure she never disobeys an order like this again. I have to find her.

"Rowan!"

My yell draws the wrong attention. Growling, I aim my gun and squeeze the trigger with zero regard for these pissants in my way. Nothing will stand between me and my fierce girl.

Two men go down with my bullets in their skulls. Another clutches his neck to stop the spray of blood, eyes bulged as he falls to his knees before me.

"Where is she?" The demand is a feral snarl.

He spits at my feet. "You're too late. Your little bitch should be dead by now."

"Oh, my friend." My humorless grin is savage and promises pain. "That was the wrong thing to say."

Ripping his hand from the graze wound on his neck, I wrap my fingers around his throat and jam my gun to his groin. I don't have time for anything more elaborate.

"No—*No!*"

"Too late." I pull the trigger twice for good measure.

The man's shrieks of agony bring little satisfaction. Releasing him with a shove, I search for Rowan. She's not outside. My gaze shifts to the warehouse. It doesn't look like it has long before it collapses.

A wall of flames encircles the whole damn thing. I have no choice but to grit my teeth and run into the fire. A flash of searing pain makes me grunt as I do my best to shield my face. Keep moving, I have to keep moving.

If I stand still, then I'm dead. If I'm dead, she's dead and that is not fucking happening.

Once I'm on the other side, I find the way into the building.

The sound of her scream, so full of fear and anguish, tells me where to go. It guts me, but I'm almost there.

The fucking roof caves in on one side and I duck with a grunt, not stopping until I find her. Around the next row of crates, she's there and my heart splinters.

"Rowan!" I bark, grabbing her. She cries out in pain and I let go of the singed fabric at her shoulder. "Shit. Look at me."

Blinking, she focuses on me and her eyes go round. "You're here."

She sounds as if she can't believe it.

"Of course I am." My hands pass over her quickly, checking for other injuries. "We have to get the hell out of here."

"I'm sorry." She hugs me, squeezing heartbreakingly tight. "I just wanted—"

"I know. Later." After I get her to safety. "Now, are you going to let me help you?" Her head bobs against my chest. "Good. Don't do anything but what I tell you to, understand?"

I don't wait for her to agree. We're both lucky the flames haven't moved to devour the whole building yet. It gives me enough time to release the clip and check how many bullets are in my magazine before reloading my gun.

There's something in the way she watches that twists my insides. She made a mistake acting alone, but now that I'm here we can face this problem together.

I hand a smaller gun holstered at my ankle to her. "We're doing this together. I'll protect you. You have my back?"

Her eyes shine as she accepts it. "Yes."

She doesn't have to do anything—I could get us out of this alone, but I give up some control to her. She needs this. Now she doesn't have to do it by herself.

The burned skin on my arm and the back of my neck throbs as we go back the way I came in. I keep her close behind me, shielding her from danger. The hole I made in the wall of fire is minimal, the flames seeking to close us back in. We have to be fast.

Turning to her, I clasp the side of her jaw. "Almost home free, baby. This part is hard. It's the only exit point and it might hurt. Once we're past this, then we're out of the fire, but we're probably running right into a gunfight with these guys."

Rowan's overwhelmed gaze shifts from the fire at my back to me. Pursing her mouth in determination, she nods.

"Brave girl." I kiss her. "Don't stop and don't let go. Keep your head down, fire at anyone who wants to kill us, and stay close behind me."

Facing the flames once more, I take her hand and we run. Sweat beads at my temples and my lungs burn. For her, I can't stop. Not until I get her out. She yelps as the heat surrounds us. The white-hot blaze presses in on all sides. It agitates the burns I got coming in, but it's over in moments once we're outside.

"Left!" Rowan squeezes my hand.

A man charges us and I give myself over to the ever present need to dominate the situation. Everything empties from my mind except for cold calculation. Two shots to the chest and head put the guy on his back.

Rowan looks at me in awe, not judging the monster but embracing him.

A brutal spark of pleasure flares to life.

My precision is deadly as I take down anyone in our path to escape. She fires off a few shots at the guys who come around the warehouse from behind. We leave the fire and devastation in our wake until we reach the car.

She pauses, taking in the broken boom gate and the busted headlight on the SUV. "Did you drive through that?"

"A gate wasn't keeping me from saving your ass from this little suicide mission." I open the passenger door and lift her inside.

"Suicide." She bites her lip and nods, turning her face to her lap. "I thought I was going to die. It was stupid. And you still came for me?"

I pull Rowan into a fast, demanding kiss. My fingers clench in her hair to keep her near, the thought of any inch separating us unbearable. She leans into me as if she feels the same after what she went through tonight.

"Because a king always comes for his queen. Even the reckless ones."

CHAPTER THIRTY-SIX
WREN

We drive to the only place where I can guarantee her safety—the house I really live in. The white and gray stone two-story cottage is tucked away on a private path that connects to the Crow's Nest property. Another path leads up to the shooting range. The porch light flickers on when I lead Rowan to the door.

She stares at the Adirondack chairs Jude and I smoke cigars from. "Where are we?"

I wait for the twist of distrust, but the tension never comes. I trust her wholeheartedly. A huff of surprise jerks my head.

"This is my house—my real one," I say when she parts her lips to sate her endless curiosity. "Remember when we went to the shooting range?"

"Yeah."

"And that tree you pointed out with the gnarled knot?"

Another slow nod. "The one that looked like a wrinkled ballsac."

The corner of my mouth quirks up. "If you'd followed in that direction you'd reach this house in less than five minutes."

Unlocking the door, I bustle her inside, flicking on lights as we go. The burns on my neck and arm tug annoyingly, demanding my attention now that we're out of danger. I also need to check her more thoroughly to ensure she wasn't hurt.

In the kitchen, I sit her down and grab a first aid kit from a cabinet. I grimace as I shrug out of my jacket, scowling at the superficial burn irritating the back of my wrist.

"This is..." Rowan hesitates, peering around. "Nice. Really cozy. And the total opposite of what I'd picture for someone like you."

I'm not aware I'm holding my breath until she finishes. Warmth stirs in me at knowing she likes it here.

"Don't let that hideous penthouse or the empty room at the Nest fool you, kitten. I'm a man of comfort. I appreciate the solitude out here."

A smile tugs at her lips and she takes the antiseptic wipe from me to gently clean my burned arm. The gesture winds around my heart.

"I told you not to go on your own," I say sternly.

"I know." She bows her head over her task, angling my arm to coat it with ointment. "I'm sorry. I was totally out of my head with anger." After bandaging my injury, she focuses on my hand, fitting her splayed palm against mine. "You were right. It was reckless suicide. I just—I couldn't stand the thought of what they did to him. I should have let you help me instead of trying to do it all on my own."

I soften when her voice breaks, the admission costing her. Tucking her hair back, I murmur, "If you wanted to burn the world down, I would have done it for you. All you had to do was ask."

She snorts and rests her head against mine. "That's romantic, but kinda fucked up, King Crow."

"I'm serious. I'd do anything for you." I lift her from her seat and set her on the wood table so I can stand between her legs and have her mouth at kissing level. The need to keep her in my arms is potent. "Now let me take care of you."

"Yessir," she sasses in a husky tone.

I take her face in both hands and kiss her deeply, restoring every empty hole in my chest with the feeling of being with her. I could have lost her tonight. If I had, it might have destroyed me worse than anything has in my life. It's so unthinkable that my grip tightens on her, not letting up until she emits a faint sound.

Not only do I want to protect her, she's done the impossible by worming her way into my heart—a dead, unfeeling carcass that hasn't beat for any woman in my life after my sister died and my mother drank herself into the bottom of a pill bottle.

I take my time examining her, running my fingers all over her body. Her eyelids droop and she murmurs where it hurts, tempting me with directions to touch her where it'll make her sigh in pleasure. She squirms when I stop palming her breast to peel back the singed flannel fabric at her shoulder.

"That's not where I said," she hisses, grabbing on to me to weather the pain.

"I have to clean and bandage this. Stay still."

Rowan grumbles under her breath, but sits through the process. Her shoulder is burned, but not much worse than mine. The large bruise is likely to hurt worse judging by the way it makes her gasp uncomfortably when I prod around her skin.

"Consider the pain right now your punishment."

"Not going to spank me for being a brat?" she pushes out through her teeth.

I smirk. "Not while you're injured. After that? Absolutely. The lesson didn't stick last time."

Heat flares in her eyes. After I bandage her up, I caress her soot-smudged cheek. She turns into it, lips brushing my palm. I pack up the kit and get her some water to wash down painkillers with.

"The things we do for them don't help," I say.

Her brows pinch. "What do you mean?"

"My sister. I never told you the full story." Familiar heaviness weighs me down, yet it's not as potent as usual. Rowan threads her fingers with mine. "She was so young. You remind me of her, the spirit she had." My brief smile fades and my tone hardens with hatred. "She had this teacher at the junior academy, Coleman. He was a sick fuck that preyed on her. His manipulation and grooming tore her apart."

Rowan gasps and wraps her arm around me, tucking our joined hands between us.

The locket sits in my pocket, but I leave it there rather than disentangle from her comforting embrace.

"Losing Charlotte was devastating. I lost my way for a long time, driven only by the goal of seeking revenge. It took me two years of searching after Coleman fled town."

"What did you do?"

"Made him hurt for every pain he caused my sister." Her arm tightens around me. "I tore him apart piece by piece until he begged for mercy that wasn't coming." I pause, sweeping my palms down her back. She presses closer. "You're not afraid of me."

"No," Rowan murmurs. "You make me feel safe."

A rumble rolls through me and I tuck her head against my shoulder.

"My point to all this is that even though I sought revenge, it didn't bring her back. I still miss her."

"I'd do it again." When I tense, she hurries to continue. "I meant with your help. For Ethan. I know it wouldn't bring him back, but the people who killed him are bad."

I nod in understanding. "Coleman deserved to die."

The moment is interrupted by the growl of her stomach. She covers it with a hand.

"I never got to give you the sandwiches and coffee I went out for."

"Is there food here?"

I hum, moving around the kitchen to throw together a quick meal, grabbing bread, some fruit from the refrigerator, and cheese. I break off a hunk of fine aged cheddar to feed to her. She groans in appreciation for the flavor. In minutes, she polishes off half the meal. It's the first time her appetite has returned in days.

This place has always been my sanctuary. With Rowan in it, it feels more complete.

"I've taken many choices from you, but I'm going to leave one in your hands this time."

She lifts her head and gives me a crooked smile. "What's that?"

"I want you to stay with me. Here, at my real home. Not just for your protection, but..." I trace the curve of her jaw. "You invaded my heart. No one has ever done that. I want you to stay here because I always protect what I love."

She releases a shaky breath. "Wren."

"Be my queen, Rowan."

CHAPTER THIRTY-SEVEN
ROWAN

Hearing Wren's ardent words touches a deep part of my soul. Tender warmth courses through me, winding around me like a hug.

I see what I was afraid of before, how much I've isolated myself with my excuse of independence to soften the blow that I couldn't handle letting people in. But around him, he allows me to be vulnerable and still knows I'm strong.

When I needed him, he came, then still allowed me to fight with him by his side.

"You have my heart," I murmur. "You can't get rid of me."

"Wouldn't dream of it." Smiling, he draws me close for another kiss. "Good choice, because if you said no, I might have taken drastic measures."

A laugh bubbles out of me. "Psycho."

The word is laced with affection.

"As much as I want to remind you who you belong to, I have to call the guys and let them know you're safe. Go look around, I know you're dying to by the way you keep peeking everywhere."

Wren steps back and I hop down from the table to explore. The cozy vibe continues throughout the house. Amidst the inviting rooms, I find little touches of Wren that make me bite my lip around a smile. I end up in the living room looking at a framed photo of Wren and a girl who must be his sister.

While I listen to his deep murmuring tone in the other room, I pull out my phone and take a fortifying breath. There's no more putting this conversation off and I want to hear Mom's voice. I press the call button and pace the living room.

"Rowan? Is everything okay?"

Her voice is groggy and on edge. Crap, I didn't think about how alarming a late night call after days of silence would be.

"Sorry, I know it's late. I just, um, wanted to say hi. I miss you and I wanted to hear your voice. See how you were holding up."

"That's okay, sweetheart. You can always call me, anytime of day." It sounds like she's sitting up in bed, murmuring to the dog. "It's good to hear your voice, too. I love you so much."

A lump forms in my throat. "I love you, too. I'm sorry I didn't say something sooner about Ethan. He was m-missing." I clear my throat. "I was scared. I didn't think—"

The line goes silent for a moment except for an audible sniffle when I break off. I squeeze my eyes shut.

"I know, my darling. I know." Mom's exhale is full of the same grief I drowned in for the last week. "One day at a time, okay? We choose happiness. We choose to think of the good memories."

Mom is so strong when she doesn't have to be. No one would blame her for breaking. She's lost her husband and her son.

The confession I should have told her years ago spills from me.

"Mom... I never knew how to tell you this." She doesn't interrupt, listening with the patience of a saint. I bite back a curse again for keeping her in the dark. "The night of the accident. I snuck out and when Dad found out, he came to get me. We were arguing. It—It was all my fault. I'm sorry."

The last part comes out as a hoarse whisper. Fear that she'll hate me suffocates me.

"Rowan," she says softly. "Sweetheart, I know. Your father called me before he went to pick you up. Nothing is your fault. It was an accident."

She had been away for the weekend. It was the reason I thought I could get away with sneaking out.

My throat closes, making it hard to push out a response. "But you never said anything."

"I didn't want you to carry any guilt for something out of your control. I'm sorry you felt like you had to put yourself in that position for so long."

Her absolving words wash over me. "I love you."

It's all I can muster up in my stunned state.

"I love you, too. Thank you for feeling like you could tell me now. You can tell me anything."

I nod, though she won't see it.

"Do you want to come home?"

"I—" My throat closes. The thought of leaving Thorne Point and returning to a place I've run from for so long, even knowing I had nothing to fear twists my stomach. "No, I'd like to stay here for now. Are you mad?"

"Of course not." There's nothing but love in her tone. "We all process grief differently. I won't push you into something that makes you uncomfortable."

We have a lot to talk about, but it's late. "I'll talk to you tomorrow."

"Okay. Get some rest, sweetheart."

"You too."

"Goodnight. Teddy says so, too."

A wet laugh leaves me. "Night."

I hang up and swipe beneath my eyes. Wren leans against the doorframe. I don't remember hearing him come in here. Popping off the wall, he closes the distance between us, tugging me into his embrace.

"She knew. The whole time, she knew," I say.

Wren strokes my hair until I stop trembling. "Come on. Let's go to bed."

* * *

Wren keeps me to himself for two days before we return to the Nest. His friends blow up both our phones, but we're too lost in each other to notice. When I walk into the lounge, Colton practically tackles me with his hug.

"Never ever *ever* again." His words are muffled into my shirt on the non-bruised side.

"You're crushing me. I thought you guys thrived on chaos," I tease.

"Um, yeah. When we're causing it. When you're doing shit like that?" He leans away, shaking his head. "Thought I was gonna suffer from a heart attack. I'm too young to go out like that, babe."

Colton passes me off to Jude, who also hugs me, being mindful of my healing shoulder. "Gave us a real scare, firecracker. You might be crazier than all of us."

He steps back and, to my surprise, Levi joins the hug fest, locking his arms around me. It's a good hug, considering he's so standoffish. I smirk at him and he flicks his gaze away, ruffling his hair.

Wren watches with his hands braced on the back of the couch. He's my home, which makes each of these guys like my family. I never would have imagined I could find friendship with the most feared guys on campus.

"Sorry for going rogue, guys."

Wren snorts, prowling closer to wind an arm around my waist from behind. "Suicidal is a step further than rogue."

"Well, I'm still sorry I made you all worry." My cheeks heat and I duck my head. I haven't had this many friends in a long time. "Um, thanks for looking for me."

"Duh," Colton says. "Come on, I want to show you what I found. I was able to take apart your brother's phone. Luckily those idiots didn't smash it to pieces and just banged it up a little. Probably figured the water damage would take care of it."

My mouth drops open. "Did you get it to connect?"

"Yeah. Come see."

Colton clasps my wrist and pulls me to his wall of computer screens. Hope bounces around my insides like a spring loaded ball. I look back to Wren. They all follow, each of us eager to see what information might be salvaged.

"Ethan always kept his stuff digital." Saying his name makes my throat ache, but I push it out in a hush. "He liked to be mobile. Backed up. He always thought journals could get stolen."

"Smart cookie." Colton fiddles with the delicate looking tools connected to the phone's inner workings. "Let's see what we've got."

We all hold our breath while he works. It seems to take forever for its home screen to boot using one of Colton's monitors as a display. Wren's hand finds mine to keep me from digging my nails into my palm. He soothes his thumb over my knuckles.

"I got it to connect this morning, but I wanted to wait until you were with us to look around," Colton says.

"Let's do it." I put a hand on the back of Colton's chair. "Try his email first."

He navigates into the email app. Before he can search through anything, an unsent email draft pops up, like Ethan was in the middle of it before he was taken. My throat goes dry. It's addressed to me. Sadness pangs sharply. Even in trouble that would lead to his death, he was reaching out to me.

The subject line reads *sorry*. Then the body is another single word—*danger*.

Wren guides me to lean against him. I shut my eyes and breathe.

"There's an attachment," Jude says.

"Hang on." Colton hums. "Partial file. I'll need to work on it to see if it's corrupted. Let me see if it'll preview the contents from a backdoor."

He clicks around, sending the file to a different screen. When he opens the preview window, it shows the beginning. Only a few words are legible before the rest of the text devolves into an array of symbols.

"It's still gibberish," Levi says.

"I see that."

Colton mutters as he types. A few symbols reveal words. Network. Elite. Key.

There isn't much to go on, but a name jumps out that makes us all freeze.

Astor.

"Well, fuck." Blowing out a breath, Colton falls back in his chair, holding his head.

Jude leans over as if being closer will change anything. "What is going on?"

"It has to be my uncle," Levi growls. "Because I don't know what the hell this is."

"Whatever it is, they're one step ahead of us time and again," Wren says darkly. "I'm sick of it."

"Keys," I murmur. They stop bickering to look at me. "It all keeps coming back to keys."

They return their stares to the screen, each of them going quiet and contemplative. They don't like not being in control. It threatens the power they've built their thrones on. A predator is only a predator as long as it's the biggest shark in the ocean. Once a killer whale comes along, it's game over.

I know it's not Ethan's fault he got mixed up in this. He was doing what he did best—dig up corruption to find his story.

His murder is connected to something bigger at work in this city.

I entered this dark underground world as my last hope to find my brother. Going back to my life before Wren and the Crowned Crows isn't an option. I'm part of this now.

CHAPTER THIRTY-EIGHT
WREN

It feels good to be at a fight night. The burns Rowan and I got the night of the fire have mostly healed. I could get in the ring, but it's Levi's turn tonight. He needs it after we found Ethan Hannigan's file with his last name in it. The deranged look in his eyes grew worse in the last week, his demons wrapping their claws around his throat.

The crowd gasps and goads Levi on above the remorseless sounds of his fists colliding with his opponent's jaw. I catch Jude's eye across the room on the other side of the ring and he nods.

Neither of us will let Levi kill someone in the ring tonight. We might all have blood-stained hands, but tonight isn't a fight to the death.

My shrewd gaze moves around the room, cataloguing every face in attendance. If Baron Astor is involved in what we discovered, who else might be?

It could be any of the elite businessmen, socialites, or politicians filling the warehouse tonight.

The shipyard is only a few blocks from this location. When we sent Penn by to cover Rowan's arson tracks and check things out in the aftermath, he said it was deserted, the burned shell of the warehouse gutted and already wiped of any traces of the cause for the fire. I doubt things could be so easy. Those that made it out could have taken their grievances to their investors.

This isn't over, but we'll be ready.

People in this city can call us whatever they like—a twisted brotherhood, a fearsome gang, Thorne Point's own heartless silver-spooned mafia. It doesn't matter what the Crowned Crows are. What's important is knowing we wield the secrets of this city like merciless swords. No one should forget that ending up on the wrong side of our wrath will result in us wreaking havoc for the enemies we make.

For someone to threaten us knowing that, we'll make them regret it.

This game of cat and mouse is over. It's time to remind this city who reigns in the darkness.

Me and my brothers haven't spent years building our legacy for someone to threaten it without consequence. We won't fall without a fight.

Slender arms slip around my waist and familiar fingers smooth over the buttons of my vest. Full armor seemed appropriate tonight. I capture her fingers.

"You have your evil thinking face on. I could see it from across the room."

"It's not evil, kitten." I turn to smirk at Rowan. "It's strategy. There is no good and bad, only those who come out on top of it all because they have no qualms doing what's necessary."

She hums, squinting at me in mock skepticism. "Sounds a lot like getting your hands dirty to win."

"If they're already dirty, what's a little more?" My voice dips as I drag my fingers down her spine, smirk stretching into a wolfish grin when she shivers. "Dirty is always better."

She laughs and I eat up the sound before it dies off. She can smile and still be shattered by grief inside.

The shock of her brother's death is still fresh. It will take her time to come to terms with it. She's thrown herself into the question of who has been toying with us as her way to cope with his loss. My girl is a brave fighter at heart and I wouldn't want any queen but her by my side.

I take her hand and we watch Levi unleash hell on his opponent.

Someone bumps into me, but when I turn to look there's no one there. Suspicious, I keep searching.

"There's something sticking out of your pocket," Rowan says.

"What?" No way would someone have the skill to slip something on me without me noticing. Jude's shown me all the tricks he uses.

Sure enough, there's a crisp square envelope in my suit pocket. I slip it out and flip it over. There's nothing written on it. Before I can open it, something else catches my eye that makes my blood pressure spike.

Like goddamn clockwork, Pippa arrives to kick up a fuss. There's no fresh-faced academy graduate with her this time. She's alone.

"She was at the founders gala," Rowan says.

"So were most of the people here tonight. Like the Crow's Nest, they come for the escape and to feel like they've walked on the dark side." I narrow my eyes as Pippa stops in front of me. My greeting drips with venom. "Detective Bassett, as always. I'm curious, are you aware of the definition of insanity?"

"Thorne," Pippa sneers.

"Don't you get bored of this song and dance? It's so trite." I look her cheap suit up and down. "It was beneath you once."

Ignoring my comment, she turns to the ring, her gaze snagging on Jude first. "What are tonight's odds?"

"We wouldn't touch your money if it promised to save us from poverty."

Rowan covers a laugh, sliding her hand into mine and squeezing. The memory of the first night we met hits me. I told her I didn't need her money either.

"Doesn't matter," Pippa says. "I just wanted to know what this will cost you."

"Ah, yes. I do enjoy the part where I call Warner. You must enjoy being choked every time he yanks your leash back."

Pippa's self-assured smirk puts me on edge. Usually she's clawing at any feeble chance of beating us. She's never won.

"I'm going to remember the look on your face for a long time," she says conversationally while unclipping a radio from her belt. "Initiate."

My brows flatten as a horde of officers pour through the doors, weaving between the crowds. A pair of them head for us. I swing my scowl on Pippa. Her eyes gleam with confidence in her success tonight.

"You will regret this," I tell her. "Before, we granted you leniency because you were one of us. Tonight, you've killed that mercy."

"Big words for a criminal," Pippa says.

Rowan shoots me a terror-stricken look, dragging me down to whisper in my ear. "Are they going to arrest me for arson?"

"No," I say vehemently. "I'll never let anything happen to you."

Her fear is unfounded when the officers breeze by us to drag Levi from the ring. Pippa pushes me aside to oversee. Colt appears at my side.

"The fuck is going on?"

"Pippa. No matter what happens, keep her safe," I order.

"Got it."

Rowan grabs at me, the people around us jostling as they move to watch.

I clamp a hand on the back of her neck and kiss her hard and quick.

"Trust me. We'll be fine."

"I do," she breathes.

I stalk after the pain in my ass miniature detective, Colt and Rowan following in my wake. This vendetta of hers is getting old. We don't have time to play around with her and the law when we have bigger problems looming.

Unlike other times when Pippa has attempted to raid our fight nights, this time the presence of her and her team of uniformed officers causes chaos to erupt. Some press close to watch, but when the officers turn their attention on them, they move as one in retreat. The patrons who came to see violence and bloodshed scramble to hide their faces and leave. If they're caught and implicated, it could spell their ruin.

They shove and bump into me as I fight against the mass exodus to get to the ring. I step in front of Rowan, reaching back to keep her from being trampled. Colt trips a few people until we're given a wide berth to cross the room.

I freeze when Sergeant Warner steps in our path just before we reach the ring. That's not how this plays out. He's never come here. When Pippa tests the limits she's allowed, we call him to rein her back in.

"Why are you here?" Colton barks.

His grim expression gives nothing away. "Cooperate."

With that single cryptic word, he turns his back on us to stand with Pippa. Colt and I exchange a look.

Sweat drips down Levi's tattooed body, making the Crow tattoo glisten under the lights. He bares his teeth, more wild than stable at the moment. They should have let him finish his fight.

Pippa motions to one of her officers. It takes two of them to wrestle his hands behind his back and slap handcuffs on him.

Jude grabs her arm. "What the hell are you doing?"

She ignores him.

"Levi Astor, you are under arrest," Pippa announces above the clamor, eyes flashing with triumph and hatred for the four of us.

This can't be fucking happening.

Levi clenches his jaw, remaining silent.

"You don't have shit, Pip," Jude growls in her face, wrenching her arm. "You're grasping at straws if you think this will stick."

"Step back, or I'll arrest you, too. Assaulting an officer is a felony. They'll lock you back up for it. That would break your grandmother's heart, wouldn't it?"

Seething, Jude releases her with a vicious snarl.

I turn a glare on Warner. He's cuffing the other fighter and reading him his rights. The deal we've had with him for years is clearly over.

Jude, Colton, Levi, and Rowan look to me.

Fuck.

The thick card in my hand crinkles and I drop my furious gaze to it. I freeze, going cold all over. No...

Fury rolls off me in waves as I tear into the envelope and take out the black card. An address with a date and time are printed in stark white on the back. On the other side...gold crossed keys. My eyes fly up to meet Rowan's.

There's only one other thing printed on the card.

Clavis ad regnum.

CLAVIS AD REGNUM

THANK YOU + WHAT'S NEXT

Thank you for reading Crowned Crows of Thorne Point! If you enjoyed it, please leave a review on your favorite retailer or book community! Your support means so much to me!

Need more Crowned Crows series right now? Have theories about which characters will feature next? Want exclusive previews of the next book? Join other readers in Veronica Eden's Reader Garden on Facebook!
Reader group: bit.ly/veronicafbgroup

Are you a newsletter subscriber? By subscribing, you can download a special bonus deleted scene for the Crowned Crows world.
Sign up to download it here: veronicaedenauthor.com/bonus-content

ACKNOWLEDGEMENTS

Readers, I'm endlessly grateful for you! Thanks for reading this book. It means the world to me that you supported my work. I wouldn't be here at all without you! I love all of the comments and messages you send! I hope you enjoyed your read! I'm really excited to bring you more characters to love!

Thanks to my husband for being you! He doesn't read these, but he's my biggest supporter. He keeps me fed and watered while I'm in the writer cave, and doesn't complain when I fling myself out of bed at odd hours with an idea to frantically scribble down.

At times this book tried its best to break me. Thank you to Sarah, Becca, Ramzi, Sara, Kat, Jade, Mia, Bre, Heather, Katie, and Kandace for keeping me arguably sane and on track until the end! With every book I write my little tribe grows and I'm so thankful to have each of you as friends to lean on and share my book creation process with!

To my lovely PA Heather, thank you for taking things off my plate and allowing me to disappear into the writing cave without having to worry. And for letting me infodump at you, because that's my love language hahaha! You rock and I'm so glad to have you on my team!

To my beta queens Jade, Katie, Mia, Bre, Kandace and Rachel, y'all I could never put books out there without you! Thank you for reading my raw, sometimes messy words, and helping me see the forest instead of the tree. Thank you for offering your time, attention to detail, and consideration of the characters and storyline in my books!

Bre, you've been with me since the beginning and got to see these guys spring from my head and we're finally here!

Mia, your love of your husband Wren kept me going through this book, thank you for your encouragement and for always making me smile!

To my street team and reader group, y'all are the best babes around! Huge thanks to my street team for being the best hype girls! To see you guys get as excited as I do seriously makes my day. I'm endlessly grateful you love my characters and words! Thank you for your help in sharing my books and for your support of my work!

Thank you to Ashlee of Ashes & Vellichor for the amazing book trailer for this series! I love the way you can look at something (or in this case, barely anything) and get it so perfectly, and I've been in awe of what you've come up with to bring my books to life!

To Shauna and Wildfire Marketing Solutions, thank you so much for all your hard work and being so awesome! I appreciate everything that you do!

To the bloggers and bookstagrammers, thank you for being the most wonderful community! Your creativity and beautiful edits are something I come back to visit again and again to brighten my day. Thank you for trying out my books. You guys are incredible and blow me away with your passion for romance!

ABOUT THE AUTHOR

ROMANCE WITH DARING EDGE

Veronica Eden is an international bestselling author of romances with spitfire heroines, irresistible heroes, and edgy twists.

She loves exploring complicated feelings, magical worlds, epic adventures, and the bond of characters that embrace us against the world. She has always been drawn to gruff bad boys, clever villains, and the twisty-turns of morally gray decisions. She is a sucker for a deliciously devilish antihero, and sometimes rolls on the dark side to let the villain get the girl. When not writing, she can be found soaking up sunshine at the beach, snuggling in a pile with her untamed pack of animals (her husband, dog and cats), and surrounding herself with as many plants as she can get her hands on.

* * *

CONTACT + FOLLOW

Email: veronicaedenauthor@gmail.com
Website: veronicaedenauthor.com
FB Reader Group: bit.ly/veronicafbgroup
Amazon: amazon.com/author/veronicaeden

ALSO BY VERONICA EDEN

Sign up for the mailing list to get first access and ARC opportunities! Follow Veronica on BookBub for new release alerts!

DARK ROMANCE

Sinners and Saints Series

Wicked Saint

Tempting Devil

Ruthless Bishop

Savage Wilder

Crowned Crows Series

Crowned Crows of Thorne Point

Standalone

Unmasked Heart

REVERSE HAREM ROMANCE

Bound by Bounty Series

(coming soon)

Standalone

More Than Bargained

CONTEMPORARY ROMANCE

Standalone

Jingle Wars

Printed in Great Britain
by Amazon